Boxing Stories

The Works of Robert E. Howard

Boxing Stories

Robert E. Howard

Edited and
with an introduction by
Chris Gruber

University of Nebraska Press
Lincoln

© 2005 by REH Properties, Inc.
Introduction © 2005 by the Board of Regents
of the University of Nebraska
All rights reserved. Manufactured in the United
States of America
Set in Fred Smeijers' Quadraat by Bob Reitz.
Designed by Richard Eckersley.
Printed and bound by Edwards Brothers, Inc.

Library of Congress Cataloging-in-Publication Data
Howard, Robert Ervin, 1906–1936
Boxing stories / Robert E. Howard;
edited and with an introduction by Chris Gruber.
p.   cm. – (The works of Robert E. Howard)
ISBN 0-8032-2423-0 (cl.: alk. paper) –
ISBN 0-8032-7352-5 (pbk.: alk. paper)
1. Boxing stories.   2. Boxers (Sports) – Fiction.
I. Gruber, Chris.   II. Title.
PS3515.O842A6   2005c
813'.54 – dc22
2004027779

CONTENTS

Introduction

Those familiar with the pulp magazine *Weird Tales* will undoubtedly recall
the impact Robert E. Howard made in the realm of weird fiction and fantasy during the 1920s and '30s. Conan, Kull, Solomon Kane, Bran Mak
Morn . . . Howard is best remembered for creating some of the most en-
duringly popular and famously brutal fantastic heroes in literature. But
while his legacy may be forever entwined with scarlet-soaked fantasy, he
was also a fan, participant, and chronicler of a *modern-day* blood sport:
boxing. Unlike his *Weird Tales* work, it was a love of the squared ring that
inspired Howard to write the stories contained in this collection.

The sport of boxing had claimed Robert E. Howard early on as one of
its own. At the turn of the century iconic figures like John L. Sullivan, Jim
Jeffries, and Bob Fitzsimmons were the newly crowned gods of boxing's
golden era – and hence became the legends of Howard's boyhood. As he
grew older Howard acquainted himself with the ring heroes of his own day,
fighters like Jack Dempsey, Jess Willard, and Jack Johnson. At that time
the prominence given to great champions like Dempsey bordered on hero
worship, so it's no surprise that a young Bob Howard became a huge fan
of the sport.

As an adult, Howard developed into more than just a fan of boxing:
he *lived* for the sport. His surviving papers show that Howard was an astute scholar of prize-fighting, spending many hours scrutinizing fight re-
ports, taking precise notes on each boxer's ring tendencies, and recording
height, weight, and ring records. He would sometimes travel clear across
Texas – hitchhiking if he had to – just to catch a fight card live. Some
of Howard's letters contain laments at having missed even minor local
contests. All of this suggests a love for the sport that bordered very near
to devotion.

The most interesting thing about Howard's love of boxing is how he
turned all of the statistics, lore, and ring science into practice. That's right:

he did what most fans of boxing only dream about, he actually boxed. Pouring as much energy into learning how to box as he had into studying it, Howard went about hardening his own body through a rigorous regimen of weight training. He also began to box regularly with friends and oil-field workers at the Cross Plains icehouse, where he was able to act out savage battles that would later fire his fictional imagination.

Undoubtedly these experiences gave him an intimate knowledge of physical conflict that later served his writing well. Jack London, Damon Runyon, Ring Lardner, Ernest Hemingway, Joyce Carol Oates, and Nat Fleischer are among the great American authors who have set savage tales of the ring to paper. Howard has to be seen as a notable member of that group: the years between 1929 and 1934 saw Howard publish dozens of popular boxing stories in several sports magazines. This brief period of Howard's all-too-short literary career introduced fight fans to such memorable characters as Sailor Steve Costigan, Kid Allison, and Iron Mike Brennon. His boxing yarns are a unique blend of humor and brutality that are told with the kind of hard-fisted, singing vitality only Robert E. Howard can muster.

Yet despite Howard's success in the genre, today the average boxing aficionado knows very little about his personal connection with boxing or the stories that relate directly to it. That his boxing stories have lain dormant for so long is a shame, because these stories contain some of Howard's best writing. Howard's style was perfect for writing boxing tales. The fighters he read and wrote about were ultimately defined as much by their pain as their successes. Much of Bob Howard's own life had revolved around confrontation, both real and imagined. The barbaric and violent collision of man and will, tensely contested in a dark pit of physical exertion and seething emotion, truly are the hallmarks of Howard's fiction.

Howard's boxing stories flow with realistic descriptions of ring warfare. In sheer ferocity they stand tall against his better-known tales of Conan and Kull. Even in the more comedic Steve Costigan stories, where the violent tall tale is stretched beyond reality, the action sequences still follow the form and science of boxing, with a nod of respect to both the real sport and its red-handed devotees. Howard – ever the astute scion of the ring – carries the reader on a narrative wave that is as breathtakingly vivid as it is harsh and unyielding in its honest portrayal of combat.

The contents of this collection are all fine examples of the Howardian boxing tale. Together, they represent an excellent starting point for the reader interested in learning about this long-ignored aspect of Howard's career. Opening the volume is Howard's poem "The Ring." Though it was never published during his lifetime, it demonstrates the vigorous style and action sequences that would come to define his boxing stories.

Much of Robert E. Howard's fiction has been described as dark, but his tales of Sailor Steve Costigan and his white bulldog, Mike, reveal a humorous and sometimes touching side. At first glance, they may even seem incongruous with Howard's literary legacy. But don't be fooled by the slapstick nature of the stories: the themes of love, responsibility, sacrifice, and honor churn just beneath the surface of the rugged, burlesque humor. Real-life issues near and dear to Howard's heart – death, honor, pride, a man's love for his dog – all resonate fiercely in these stories, providing a substantive element of drama.

"The Pit of the Serpent" was the first Sailor Steve Costigan tale to be published, appearing in the prize-fight pulp *Fight Stories* in July 1929. It was this story that put together many of the elements that would later make the series so memorable. Exotic ports of call, dastardly villains, and Howard's brilliant blue-collar humor all conspire to delight readers and leave them wanting more. It was a fantastic way to start a series.

Howard himself was quite pleased with the story, as this excerpt from a June 1929 letter to his friend Tevis Clyde Smith demonstrates:

> My story "The Pit of the Serpent" came out in *Fight Stories* this month. Get a copy and read it. It will give you a good idea of how to write sport stories. The style and form are not much, but the mechanics are perfect. Writing is a lot like architecture. The whole structure has to suit – each piece has to be in place. A master of the game, like Kipling, for instance, or Jack London, always places the pieces right. A dub like me stumbles onto the right combination once in every five hundred stories he writes. But as I say, the architecture of this story is more nearly perfection than any other I ever wrote, regardless of the general merits of the story.

With the second story in the series, "The Bull Dog Breed," Howard introduces the final missing piece to the Costigan formula: his beloved white bulldog, Mike. As a lifelong dog lover myself, this story is one of my personal favorites due to the emotional way in which Howard portrays the bond between man and dog. This story, even more than "The Pit of the Serpent," really sets the tone for the rest of the series, as it is here that we learn the type of no-quit character Costigan is.

In "The Champion of the Forecastle" Costigan may not be champion of the world, but he covets the title of his ship the *Sea Girl* just as much. Here we begin to see the fleshing out of the Costigan universe, as Howard introduces members of the crew of Costigan's ship. Their humorous and distinct personalities add yet another layer of real life to the series. Just like Conan's Hyborian Age, we see an ever-widening, consistent universe begin to appear, with intertwining characters and histories that carry on from tale to tale.

If someone were to ask me what story best defines Sailor Steve Costigan, "Waterfront Law" would be my choice. It has all the elements that make the Costigan stories so humorous and exciting: excellent fight scenes, deceitful crooks, and an all-too-easily duped Costigan. By this time the series was really taking off. In September 1930 Howard wrote to Tevis Clyde Smith: "Since seeing you I sold 'Waterfront Law' to Fiction House. Yeah, a Steve Costigan; a new and original plot: Steve engages in a bloody battle to get some money which a crooked woman gyps him out of. They offered me $70.00. I've got to figure some way of making these stories longer. They've been too short lately."

Enter "Texas Fists." This story leaves behind the dreamy, exotic locales of the previous tales and brings Costigan back to his – and Howard's – home state of Texas. We learn something of Costigan's history in this story, and the dialogue is truly hilarious. Those readers familiar with another Howard character, Breckinridge Elkins, will no doubt see his genesis in this raucous, over-the-top western yarn.

"The Fightin'est Pair" is not only my favorite Costigan story, it's my favorite *Howard* story, regardless of character and genre. Anyone who has felt that special bond with a dog cannot help but share Costigan's every emotion. The anguish Steve describes when Mike is stolen and sent to the fighting pits develops into some of the rawest, truest emotions Howard ever wrote. As a dog-trainer and advocate of pit bull rescue, I can vouch for the fact that Howard knew exactly what he was writing about in this story. The way he describes the sounds and sights of a dog fight, and the ways in which seasoned dog owners control their animals, all ring terribly, frighteningly true to anyone with experience with such dogs. For so many reasons, "The Fightin'est Pair" stands apart as one of the best stories I have ever read. The fact that it will never win any literary awards or be as popular as Conan doesn't change my opinion one bit.

"Vikings of the Gloves" tosses us right back into the thick of Howard's particular brand of brutal slapstick. It's a hilarious tale that provides a laugh a minute. The goofy innocence of Costigan really shines through in this story, and his victory speech is priceless.

The next two Costigan stories presented here have had a strange history. By 1932, the Great Depression had knocked the starch out of all of Howard's boxing markets, leaving him with nowhere to sell his Costigan stories. Howard suddenly saw an opportunity, however, with the appearance of a magazine called *Oriental Stories* (later renamed *Magic Carpet Magazine*), which was edited by Howard's main literary benefactor, *Weird Tales* editor Farnsworth Wright. Howard promptly sent Wright four Costigan stories, which were quickly bought.

But there was a problem: Howard also had stories of historical fiction appearing in the same magazine. Indeed, Wright intended to print one of the Costigan stories, "Alleys of Darkness," in the very same issue that also featured Howard's "Shadow of the Vulture." It being poor form for the same author to appear twice in the same issue, Wright asked Howard to use a pseudonym for his Costigan tale. Howard chose the pseudonym Patrick Ervin, and also changed the name of Steve Costigan to "Dennis Dorgan" in order to further disguise the fact that the story was his. Anticipating having to do this for future issues of *Magic Carpet*, Howard also went through some of his other Costigan typescripts, changing the name Costigan to Dorgan and slapping the name "Patrick Ervin" over his own name.

But the possibility of selling lots of Costigans using the Dorgan cognomen never materialized. *Magic Carpet* folded soon after printing "Alleys of Darkness," and the unused Dorgan stories were returned to Howard, who put them aside and never used the name "Dennis Dorgan" again. A year later, when a new boxing market presented itself in the form of *Jack Dempsey's Fight Magazine*, Howard wrote and submitted only Costigan stories.

It's obvious that Dorgan – never a real character to begin with – died completely when the failure of *Magic Carpet* eliminated the need for Howard to use a pseudonym for these stories. Unfortunately, at the time of Howard's death he had not gone back and changed his Dennis Dorgan typescripts back into Steve Costigans, even though his letters show that he never considered Dorgan as anything more than a flimsy, temporary disguise for Costigan.

Fast-forward decades later, to the Howard boom of the 1970s. Most of Howard's unpublished manuscripts were being dug up and printed in some form or another. A company called FAX put out a book called *The Incredible Adventures of Dennis Dorgan*, unwittingly using the bastardized Dorgan versions Howard had left behind rather than publishing them as Costigans as Howard originally intended. And so, ever since the release of that publication, readers have assumed that Dorgan is a separate character, and that Howard had actually rewritten parts of the Costigan stories in order to make distinctly separate Dorgan tales. But the truth is that the stories are in every way Costigans, with the only changes being "Steve Costigan" to "Dennis Dorgan," "Mike" the bulldog to "Spike" the bulldog, and the *Sea Girl* to the *Python*. Nothing else was changed by Howard, not even the names of Costigan's shipmates!

Thankfully, after loads of research conducted by various Howard scholars, it is finally possible to bring these wayward Dorgan stories back into the Costigan canon where they belong. So here in this book, for the first time ever, I present to you two of the best "Dorgan" stories, each restored to its original Costigan roots: "Cultured Cauliflowers" and "A New Game for Costigan."

The first story, "Cultured Cauliflowers," was inspired by a letter sent to Howard by his *Fight Stories* editor, Jack Byrne. In May 1931 Howard wrote to Tevis Clyde Smith:

> I got a long letter from Byrne which said in part:
> "My idea of a Steve Costigan yarn is one in which Steve is recovering from an overdose of belladonna that some tricky opponent has put in his eyes before the bout. He is wearing glasses and has a scholastic, weak-kneed appearance. They get him to box an exhibition bout for society with the east coast champ refereeing. And the heat of battle, plus

Steve's near-sightedness causes him to sock the champ by mistake . . . the champ comes back at Steve . . . Mike, the bulldog, leaps into the ring, tearing the champs pants off in front of the society queens. And then in the things that follow you have Steve in his normal sphere, doing the things we like to see him doing."

Howard took this idea and ran with it, and the hysterical "Cultured Cauliflowers" is the result. The other story, "A New Game for Costigan," shows Steve trying to turn over a new leaf and become "civilized," a goal that – of course – is always a losing proposition for Howard's characters. Together, these "de-Dorganized" tales help to broaden the Costigan universe, introducing new plots and twists that Howard always intended to be a part of the series – but which have been missing for far too long. Hopefully someday the entire Costigan canon will be published in one complete volume, with all of the Dorgan stories reverted back to their pure-text Costigan versions.

Rounding out the Costigan selections for this volume is "Hard-Fisted Sentiment." Here Howard explores Costigan's relationship with his salty, colorful captain, known only as the Old Man. The tale examines the depths of loyalty and responsibility Costigan feels towards both his ship and his captain. Additionally, this is a story that allows Howard to flaunt his wealth of combat knowledge, as Costigan faces off against several fighters whose styles are all different. The situation Howard paints here was well ahead of its time, especially when one considers Howard wrote this tale decades before Chuck Palahniuk's *Fight Club* entered our popular vernacular.

Leaving the Costigan stories behind, we move on to Howard's more serious and dramatic boxing efforts. The poem "When You Were a Set-up and I Was a Ham" is a parody of a poem Howard was fond of called "Evolution (When You Were a Tadpole and I Was a Fish)." It serves as a fitting bridge between the bawdy and humorous Sailor Steve Costigan yarns and the more dramatic and somber tone of the rest of this book.

Most critics agree that the portrayal of unyielding and stubborn heroes is where Howard truly shines. Unlike Conan or most of his other literary creations, Howard's boxers rarely ascend to the throne of greatness. Indeed, only one fighter in Howard's imaginary stable of boxers ever actually gains the coveted championship belt. That character is featured in

Howard's first published boxing story, "The Spirit of Tom Molyneaux." This tale appeared in the pulp *Ghost Stories* in April 1929 and was a curious marriage of ghost and sport story. It featured Ace Jessel, an African-American boxer with lots of talent and a heart of gold. In its touching portrayal of a black heavyweight champion, this story shows a little-known side of Howard – his often sympathetic treatment of characters of various races.

The next story, "Crowd-Horror," was the only tale Howard managed to land in the venerable and respected pulp *Argosy All-Story Weekly*, a market Howard attempted to crack for years. Seven decades after its first publication the story still entertains, with a unique twist that anyone familiar with stage fright will appreciate.

In a February 1930 letter to Tevis Clyde Smith, Howard had more fight story sales to report: "Fiction House – *Fight Stories* – took another Steve Costigan story for $100. Also they finally located "Iron Men" and accepted it for $200. This is by far the best fight story I ever wrote. In many ways the best story of any kind I ever wrote. I guess my destiny is tied up with the Costigan family. I've never sold *Fight Stories* a story that didn't deal with them. The central figure of 'Iron Men' isn't a Costigan, but both Steve and his brother Iron Mike figure in the story."

Calling this "the best story of any kind I ever wrote" is high praise from Howard. While such a claim is certainly debatable, the reader cannot deny the importance the story held for Howard. "Iron Men" is an emotional story steeped in the aura of the Great Depression. In its own way it recalls many of the great fight movies, pictures like *The Champ* (1931), *Body and Soul* (1947), *Requiem for a Heavyweight* (1962), and *Rocky* (1976). One imagines that if filmed, it could well achieve a classic status rivaling the aforementioned movies.

Unfortunately, when the story was finally published in *Fight Stories*, it was in a heavily edited form. Howard complained in an April 1930 letter to Tevis Clyde Smith that "Fight Stories was kind enough to give me the cover design this month but they changed the title and the chapter headings and made quite a number of changes throughout the story which seemed not only needless to me, but in some places entirely distorted the original meaning. I think some of the changes must surely have been mistakes in printing."

We now know that this bastardized version, published under the revised title "The Iron Man," was missing a whopping *ten thousand words*! And all of the story's subsequent appearances over the years have also used this chopped version. As with the Dorgan tales, research by Howard scholars has finally allowed us to rectify this. For the first time ever, this book reprints "Iron Men" using Howard's original typescript, eliminating all of the edits that Howard disapproved of, and restoring the missing ten thousand words of text. More than any other Howard story, "Iron Men" captures the primitive and brutal fighter that Howard most admired. This Howard character staple, dubbed by Howard the "iron man," was the epitome of unrelenting will and determination, and as such proved to be the perfect vehicle for Howard's dark and brutal ring heroes. No collection of Howard's best boxing yarns would be complete without this story, and so it is an honor to finally present the definitive version to Howard fans everywhere.

"Kid Galahad" was a tale originally written for *Sport Story*, a pulp whose editors had been begging Howard for a series similar in nature to the Costigan series running at *Fight Stories*, their main competition at the time. This tale introduces the distinctive Kid Allison, light-heavyweight contender and popular character in his own right. It is a delightful retelling of the life and deeds of Galahad, but with a uniquely Howardian twist, gritty atmosphere, and some reserved humor that mirrors the ambiance of the 1930s.

"Fists of the Desert" and "They Always Come Back" make use of the same dramatic and bloody themes that mark their predecessor, "Iron Men." In fact, Jack Maloney, the highly skilled heavyweight who falls to the brutish attack of Iron Mike Brennon in "Iron Men," is the focus of "They Always Come Back." By having characters drift from story to story, their fates and histories intertwining, Howard seems to have been creating a realistic, richly populated boxing universe. A thorough analysis of all Howard's boxing stories reveals a continuity of names, places, and events that helps to create the illusion of a real world. The details and attributes that he painstakingly recorded in his private notes served as a template for creating the detailed characters that inhabit these stories. Such attention to even the most minor detail helps lend a feeling of legitimacy and cohesiveness to the canon. One begins to see the whole as more than just a collection of short stories and novellas. Together they begin to take on the feeling of a large, consistent body of work.

To wrap up this book, I have chosen one of Howard's first published boxing items. In 1928 one of the greats of boxing's golden age, George "Kid" Lavigne, died. As a tribute to the memory of this fallen great, Howard penned a poem entitled "Kid Lavigne is Dead" and sent it to *Ring Magazine*, the premier boxing magazine in the world. They accepted it and printed it in June 1928. I feel that the poem – just as it did so many decades ago – still serves as a fitting close to both a life and this book.

When taken in total, these stories represent an excellent sampling of Howard's boxing yarns. But, notably, they remain just that – a sampling. Robert E. Howard wrote a very large number of boxing stories, most of which are first-rate narratives worth the effort of hunting down. So consider this book just a small preview, a quick peek, into the universe of Howard's fistic imagination. And if these stories fire your emotions and stir your blood, I urge you to seek out the rest of Howard's boxing stories. You won't be disappointed.

After decades of neglect, this significant aspect of Howard's literary output is finally moving past preliminary bouts and is closing in on the championship status it so richly deserves. Howard's obsession with the sweet science was fueled by a genuine reverence for the sport, one that I myself share. Like Howard, I have studied boxing for years, both as a fan and scholar. Also like Howard, I have done my fair share of amateur boxing. I even have a white pit bull that is a spitting image of Steve Costigan's bulldog Mike (my own dog, appropriately enough, is named Kull). Speaking as a passionate fan of both boxing in general and Howard's fight stories in particular, it is a true privilege to have edited this collection of Howard's best boxing tales. So slip into your trunks, mosey on down the aisle, and climb into the ring to meet up with the eternal heavyweight champion of prose, Robert E. Howard.

Ding-Ding!

Boxing Stories owes many thanks to Leo Grin and Rusty Burke for all their help and guidance, and to my lovely wife, Yoshiko, without whose patience I could not have answered the bell.

Boxing Stories

In the Ring

Over the place the lights go out,
Except for the cluster above the ring;
The crowd begins to thunder and shout;
At the tap of the gong I whirl and spring.
And I hear the snarl of my chargin' foe,
The Cobra Kid from Old Mexico.

And the ropes ain't there, and the crowd ain't there;
It's me and him, in the ring lights' glare;
Like cavemen foes in an age of stone,
On the ridge of the silent world, alone.

He ducks my lead as he surges in
And his left hook crashes against my chin,
And he shuts my eye with a roundhouse slam
That feels like the bunt of a batterin' ram.

The lights are swimmin' and so is the ring;
Blind I fall in clinch and cling;
The referee grunts as he tears us apart,
And I ram a left in under the heart.

As he batters me across the ring –
Jab and uppercut, hook and swing –
A torrent of smashes that never slack –
I feel the ropes against my back.

Hard to the head he cannonades
And I hit the mat on my shoulder-blades.

In the Ring

My brain's full of fog, my mouth's full of brine,
But I hear the referee countin', "Nine!"

And up I reel, though my legs won't work
And the ring lights swim in a crimson murk.
The Cobra rushes, set for the spill,
Wild and wide open, blind for the kill.

And desperate, reelin', I shoot my right
The last blind blow of a losin' fight.
And my right connects and his head goes back,
Till it looks, begod, like his neck would crack.

New strength surges through every vein
And the panther wakes in my punch drunk brain.
His knees, they buckle, his white lips part
As I blast my right in under the heart.

His jaw falls slack, his eyes, they blink,
As deep in his belly my left I sink;
Then every ounce of my beef goes in
To the right I heave to his saggin' chin.

The leather bursts and the hand gives way,
But it's the end of a perfect day.
He hasn't stirred at the count of ten,
The referee lifts my hand and then
I hear the yells of the crowd again.

The Pit of the Serpent

The minute I stepped ashore from the *Sea Girl*, merchantman, I had a hunch that there would be trouble. This hunch was caused by seeing some of the crew of the *Dauntless*. The men on the *Dauntless* have disliked the *Sea Girl*'s crew ever since our skipper took their captain to a cleaning on the wharfs of Zanzibar – them being narrow-minded that way. They claimed that the old man had a knuckle-duster on his right, which is ridiculous and a dirty lie. He had it on his left.

Seeing these roughnecks in Manila, I had no illusions about them, but I was not looking for no trouble. I am heavyweight champion of the *Sea Girl*, and before you make any wisecracks about the non-importance of that title, I want you to come down to the forecastle and look over Mushy Hansen and One-Round Grannigan and Flat-Face O'Toole and Swede Hjonning and the rest of the man-killers that make up the *Sea Girl*'s crew. But for all that, no one can never accuse me of being quarrelsome, and so instead of following my natural instinct and knocking seven or eight of these bezarks for a row, just to be ornery, I avoided them and went to the nearest American bar.

After a while I found myself in a dance hall, and while it is kind of hazy just how I got there, I assure you I had not no great amount of liquor under my belt – some beer, a few whiskeys, a little brandy, and maybe a slug of wine for a chaser like. No, I was the perfect chevalier in all my actions, as was proven when I found myself dancing with the prettiest girl I have yet to see in Manila or elsewhere. She had red lips and black hair, and oh, what a face!

"Say, miss," said I, the soul of politeness, "where have you been all my life?"

"Oooh, la!" said she, with a silvery ripple of laughter. "You Americans say such theengs. Oooh, so huge and strong you are, Señor!"

I let her feel of my biceps, and she give squeals of surprise and pleasure, clapping her little white hands just like a child what has found a new pretty.

"Oooh! You could just snatch little me oop and walk away weeth me, couldn't you, Señor?"

"You needn't not be afraid," said I, kindly. "I am the soul of politeness around frails, and never pull no rough stuff. I have never soaked a woman in my life, not even that dame in Suez that throwed a knife at me. Baby, has anybody ever give you a hint about what knockouts your eyes is?"

"Ah, go 'long," said she, coyly – "Ouch!"

"Did somebody step on your foot?" I ask, looking about for somebody to crown.

"Yes – let's sit theese one out, señor. Where did you learn to dance?"

"It comes natural, I reckon," I admitted modestly. "I never knew I could till now. This is the first time I ever tried."

From the foregoing you will see that I am carrying an a quiet conversation, not starting nothing with nobody. It is not my fault, what happened.

Me and this girl, whose name is Raquel La Costa, her being Spanish that way, are sitting peacefully at a table and I am just beginning to get started good telling her how her eyes are like dark pools of night (pretty hot, that one; I got it offa Mushy Hansen, who is all poetical like), when I notice her looking over my shoulder at somebody. This irritates me slightly, but I ignore it, and having forgotten what I was saying, my mind being slightly hazy for some reason, I continue:

"Listen, cutey – hey, who are you winkin' at? Oh, somethin' in your eye, you say? All right, as I was sayin, we got a feller named Hansen on board the *Sea Girl* what writes po'try. Listen to this:

Oh, the road to glory lay
Over Old Manila Bay,
Where the Irish whipped the Spanish
on a sultry summer day.

At this moment some bezark came barging up to our table and, ignoring me, leaned over and leered engagingly at my girl.

"Let's shake a hoof, baby," said this skate, whom I recognized instantly as Bat Slade, champion box fighter of the *Dauntless*.

Miss La Costa said nothing, and I arose and shoved Slade back from the table.

"The lady is engaged at present, stupid," says I, poking my jaw out. "If you got any business, you better 'tend to it."

"Don't get gay with me, Costigan," says he, nastily. "Since when is dames choosin' gorillas instead of humans?"

By this time quite a crowd had formed, and I restrained my natural indignation and said, "Listen, bird, take that map outa my line uh vision before I bust it."

Bat is a handsome galoot who has a way with the dames, and I knew if he danced one dance with my girl he would figure out some way to do me dirt. I did not see any more of the *Dauntless* men; on the other hand, I was the only one of the *Sea Girl*'s crew in the joint.

"Suppose we let the lady choose between us," said Bat. Can you beat that for nerve? Him butting in that way and then giving himself equal rights with me. That was too much. With a bellow, I started my left from the hip, but somehow he wasn't there – the shifty crook! I miss by a yard, and he slams me with a left to the nose that knocks me over a chair.

My brain instantly cleared, and I realized that I had been slightly lit. I arose with an irritated roar, but before hostilities could be renewed, Miss La Costa slipped between us.

"Zut," said she, tapping us with her fan. "Zut! What is theese? Am I a common girl to be so insult' by two great tramps who make fight over me in public? Bah! Eef you wanta fight, go out in ze woods or some place where no one make scandal, and wham each other all you want. May ze best man win! I will not be fight over in public, no sir!"

And with that she turned her back and walked away. At the same time, up came an oily-looking fellow, rubbing his hands together. I mistrust a bird what goes around rubbing his hands together like he was in a state of perpetual self-satisfaction.

"Now, now, boys," said this bezark, "le's do this right! You boys wanta fight. Tut! Tut! Too bad, too bad! But if you gotta fight, le's do it right, that's what I say! Let fellers live together in peace and enmity if they can, but if they gotta fight, let it be did right!"

"Gi' me leeway – and I'll do this blankety-blank right," says I, fairly shaking with rage. It always irritates me to be hit on the nose without a return and in front of ladies.

"Oh, will you?" said Bat, putting up his mitts. "Let's see you get goin', you – "

"Now, now, boys," said the oily bird, "le's do this right! Costigan, will you and Slade fight for me in my club?"

"Anywheres!" I roar. "Bare-knuckles, gloves, or marlin-spikes!"

"Fine," says the oily bird, rubbing his hands worse than ever. "Ah, fine! Ah – um – ah, Costigan, will you fight Slade in the pit of the serpent?"

Now, I should have noticed that he didn't ask Slade if he'd fight, and I saw Slade grin quietly, but I was too crazy with rage to think straight.

"I'll fight him in the pit of Hades with the devil for a referee!" I roared. "Bring on your fight club – ring, deck, or whatever! Let's get goin' "

"That's the way to talk!" says the oily bird. "Come on."

He turned around and started for the exit, and me and Slade and a few more followed him. Had I of thought, I would have seen right off that this was all working too smooth to have happened impromptu, as it were. But I was still seething with rage and in no shape to think properly.

Howthesomever, I did give a few thoughts as to the chances I had against Slade. As for size, I had the advantage. I'm six feet, and Slade is two inches shorter; I am also a few pounds heavier but not enough to make much difference, us being heavyweights that way. But Slade, I knew, was the shiftiest, trickiest leather-slinger in the whole merchant marine. I had never met him for the simple reason that no matchmaker in any port would stage a bout between a *Sea Girl* man and a *Dauntless* tramp, since that night in Singapore when the bout between Slade and One-Round Granni-gan started a free-for-all that plumb wrecked the Wharfside A.C. Slade knocked Grannigan out that night, and Grannigan was then champion slugger aboard the *Sea Girl*. Later, I beat Grannigan.

As for dope, you couldn't tell much, as usual. I'd won a decision over Boatswain Hagney, the champion of the British Asiatic naval fleet, who'd knocked Slade out in Hong Kong, but on the other hand, Slade had knocked out Mike Leary of the *Blue Whale*, who'd given me a terrible beating at Bombay.

These cogitations was interrupted at that minute by the oily bird. We had come out of the joint and was standing on the curb. Several autos was parked there, and the crowd piled into them. The oily bird motioned me to get in one, and I done so.

Next, we was speeding through the streets, where the lights was beginning to glow, and I asked no questions, even when we left the business section behind and then went right on through the suburbs and out on a road which didn't appear to be used very much. I said nothing, however.

At last we stopped at a large building some distance outside the city, which looked more like an ex-palace than anything else. All the crowd alighted, and I done likewise, though I was completely mystified. There was no other houses near, trees grew dense on all sides, the house itself was dark and gloomy looking. All together I did not like the looks of things but would not let on, with Bat Slade gazing at me in his supercilious way. Anyway, I thought, they are not intending to assassinate me because Slade ain't that crooked, though he would stop at nothing else.

We went up the walk, lined on each side by tropical trees, and into the house. There the oily bird struck a light and we went down in the basement. This was a large, roomy affair, with a concrete floor, and in the center was a pit about seven feet deep, and about ten by eight in dimensions. I did not pay no great attention to it at that time, but I did later, I want to tell you.

"Say," I says, "I'm in no mood for foolishness. What you bring me away out here for? Where's your arena?"

"This here's it," said the oily bird.

"Huh! Where's the ring? Where do we fight?"

"Down in there," says the oily bird, pointing at the pit.

"What!" I yell, "What are you tryin' to hand me?"

"Aw, pipe down," interrupted Bat Slade. "Didn't you agree to fight me in the serpent pit? Stop grouchin' and get your duds off."

"All right," I says, plumb burned up by this deal. "I don't know what you're tryin' to put over, but lemme get that handsome map in front of my right and that's all I want!"

"Grahhh!" snarled Slade, and started toward the other end of the pit. He had a couple of yeggs with him as handlers. Shows his caliber, how he always knows some thug; no matter how crooked the crowd may be, he's never without acquaintances. I looked around and recognized a pickpocket I used to know in Cuba, and asked him to handle me. He said he would, though, he added, they wasn't much a handler could do under the circumstances.

"What kind of a deal have I got into?" I asked him as I stripped. "What kind of a joint is this?"

"This house used to be owned by a crazy Spaniard with more mazuma than brains," said the dip, helping me undress. "He yearned for bull fightin' and the like, and he thought up a brand new one. He rigged up this pit and had his servants go out and bring in all kinds of snakes. He'd put two snakes in the pit and let 'em fight till they killed each other."

"What! I got to fight in a snake den?"

"Aw, don't worry. They ain't been no snakes in there for years. The Spaniard got killed, and the old place went to ruin. They held cock fights here and a few years ago the fellow that's stagin' this bout got the idea of buyin' the house and stagin' grudge fights."

"How's he make any money? I didn't see nobody buyin' tickets, and they ain't more'n thirty or forty here."

"Aw, he didn't have no time to work it up. He'll make his money bettin'. He never picks a loser! And he always referees himself. He knows your ship sails tomorrow, and he didn't have no time for ballyhooin'. This fight club is just for a select few who is too sated or to vicious to enjoy a ordinary legitimate prize-fight. They ain't but a few in the know – all this is illegal, of course – just a few sports which don't mind payin' for their pleasure. The night Slade fought Sailor Handler they was forty-five men here, each payin' a hundred and twenty-five dollars for admission. Figure it out for yourself."

"Has Slade fought here before?" I ask, beginning to see a light.

"Sure. He's the champion of the pit. Only last month he knocked out Sailor Handler in nine rounds."

Jerusha! And only a few months ago me and the Sailor – who stood six-four and weighed two-twenty – had done everything but knife each other in a twenty-round draw.

"Ho! So that's the way it is," said I. "Slade deliberately come and started trouble with me, knowin' I wouldn't get a square deal here, him bein' the favorite and – "

"No," said the dip, "I don't think so. He just fell for that Spanish frail. Had they been any malice aforethought, word would have circulated among

8

the wealthy sports of the town. As it is, the fellow that owns the joint is throwin' the party free of charge. He didn't have time to work it up. Figure it out – he ain't losing nothin'. Here's two tough sailors wanting to fight a grudge fight – willin' to fight for nothin'. It costs him nothin' to stage the riot. It's a great boost for his club, and he'll win plenty on bets."

The confidence with which the dip said that last gave me cold shivers.

"And who will he bet on?" I asked.

"Slade, of course. Ain't he the pit champion?"

The while I was considering this cheering piece of information, Bat Slade yelled at me from the other end of the pit.

"Hey, you blankey-dash-dot-blank, ain't you ready yet?"

He was in his socks, shoes, and underpants, and no gloves on his hands.

"Where's the gloves?" I asked. "Ain't we goin' to tape our hands?"

"They ain't no gloves," said Slade, with a satisfied grin. "This little riot is goin' to be a bare-knuckle affair. Don't you know the rules of the pit?"

"You see, Costigan," says the oily bird, kinda nervous, "in the fights we put on here, the fighters don't wear no gloves – regular he-man grudge stuff, see?"

"Aw, get goin'!" the crowd began to bellow, having paid nothing to get in and wanting their money's worth. "Lessee some action! What do you think this is? Start somethin'!"

"Shut up!" I ordered, cowing them with one menacing look. "What kind of a deal am I getting here, anyhow?"

"Didn't you agree to fight Slade in the serpent pit?"

"Yes, but – "

"Tryin' to back out," said Slade nastily, as usual. "That's like you *Sea Girl* tramps, you – "

"Blank, exclamation point, and asterisk!" I roared, tearing off my undershirt and bounding into the pit. "Get down in here you blank-blank semicolon, and I'll make you look like the last rose of summer, you – "

Slade hopped down into the pit at the other end, and the crowd began to fight for places at the edge. It was a cinch that some of them was not going to get to see all of it. The sides of the pit were hard and rough, and the floor was the same way, like you'd expect a pit in a concrete floor to be. Of course they was no stools or anything.

"Now then," says the oily bird, "this is a finish fight between Steve

Costigan of the *Sea Girl*, weight one-eighty-eight, and Battling Slade, one-seventy-nine, of the *Dauntless*, bare-knuckle champion of the Philippine Islands, in as far as he's proved it in this here pit. They will fight three-minute rounds, one minute rest, no limit to the number of rounds. There will be no decision. They will fight till one of 'em goes out. Referee, me.

"The rules is, nothing barred except hittin' below the belt – in the way of punches, I mean. Break when I say so, and hit on the breakaway if you wanta. Seconds will kindly refrain from hittin' the other man with the water bucket. Ready?"

"A hundred I lay you like a rug," says Slade.

"I see you and raise you a hundred," I snarl.

The crowd began to yell and curse, the timekeeper hit a piece of iron with a six-shooter stock, and the riot was on.

Now, understand, this was a very different fight from any I ever engaged in. It combined the viciousness of a rough-and-tumble with that of a legitimate ring bout. No room for any footwork, concrete to land on if you went down, the uncertain flare of the lights which was hung on the ceiling over us, and the feeling of being crowded for space, to say nothing of thinking about all the snakes which had fought there. Ugh! And me hating snakes that way.

I had figured that I'd have the advantage, being heavier and stronger. Slade couldn't use his shifty footwork to keep out of my way. I'd pin him in a corner and smash him like a cat does a rat. But the bout hadn't been on two seconds before I saw I was all wrong. Slade was just an overgrown Young Griffo. His footwork was second to his ducking and slipping. He had fought in the pit before, and had found that kind of fighting just suited to his peculiar style. He shifted on his feet just enough to keep weaving, while he let my punches go under his arms, around his neck, over his head or across his shoulder.

At the sound of the gong I'd stepped forward, crouching, with both hands going in the only way I knew.

Slade took my left on his shoulder, my right on his elbow, and blip-blip! his left landed twice to my face. Now I want to tell you that a blow from a bare fist is much different than a blow from a glove, and while less stunning, is more of a punisher in its way. Still, I was used to being hit with bare knuckles, and I kept boring in. I swung a left to the ribs that made Slade grunt, and missed a right in the same direction.

This was the beginning of a cruel, bruising fight with no favor. I felt like a wild animal, when I had time to feel anything but Slade's left, battling down there in the pit, with a ring of yelling, distorted faces leering down at us. The oily bird, referee, leaned over the edge at the risk of falling on top of us, and when we clinched he would yell, "Break, you blank-blanks!" and prod us with a cane. He would dance around the edge of the pit trying to keep in prodding distance, and cussing when the crowd got in his way, which was all the time. There was no room in the pit for him; wasn't scarcely enough room for us.

Following that left I landed, Slade tied me up in a clinch, stamped on my instep, thumbed me in the eye, and swished a right to my chin on the breakaway. Slightly infuriated at this treatment, I curled my lip back and sank a left to the wrist in his midriff. He showed no signs at all of liking this, and retaliated with a left to the body and a right to the side of the head. Then he settled down to work.

He ducked a right and came in close, pounding my waistline with short jolts. When, in desperation, I clinched, he shot a right uppercut between my arms that set me back on my heels. And while I was off balance he threw all his weight against me and scraped me against the wall, which procedure removed a large area of hide from my shoulder. With a roar, I tore loose and threw him the full length of the pit, but, charging after him, he side-stepped somehow and I crashed against the pit wall, head-first. Wham! I was on the floor, with seventeen million stars flashing before me, and the oily bird was counting as fast as he could, "Onetwothreefourfive–"

I bounded up again, not hurt but slightly dizzy. Wham, wham, wham! Bat came slugging in to finish me. I swished loose a right that was labeled TNT, but he ducked.

"Look out, Bat! That bird's dangerous!" yelled the oily bird in fright.

"So am I!" snarled Bat, cutting my lip with a straight left and weaving away from my right counter. He whipped a right to the wind that made me grunt, flashed two lefts to my already battered face, and somehow missed with a venomous right. All the time, get me, I was swinging fast and heavy, but it was like hitting at a ghost. Bat had maneuvered me into a corner, where I couldn't get set or defend myself. When I drew back for a punch, my elbow hit the wall. Finally I wrapped both arms around my jaw and plunged forward, breaking through Slade's barrage by sheer weight. As we came together, I threw my arms about him and together we crashed to the floor.

Slade, being the quicker that way, was the first up, and hit me with a roundhouse left to the side of the head while I was still on one knee.

"Foul!" yells some of the crowd.

"Shut up!" bellowed the oily bird. "I'm refereein' this bout!"

As I found my feet, Slade was right on me and we traded rights. Just then the gong sounded. I went back to my end of the pit and sat down on the floor, leaning my back against the wall. The dip peered over the edge.

"Anything I can do?" said he.

"Yeah," said I, "knock the daylights out of the blank-blank that's pretendin' to referee this bout."

Meanwhile the aforesaid blank-blank shoved his snoot over the other end of the pit, and shouted anxiously, "Slade, you reckon you can take him in a couple more rounds?"

"Sure," said Bat. "Double your bets; triple 'em. I'll lay him in the next round."

"You'd better!" admonished this fair-minded referee.

"How can he get anybody to bet with him?" I asked.

"Oh," says the dip, handing me down a sponge to wipe off the blood, "some fellers will bet on anything. For instance, I just laid ten smackers on you, myself."

"That I'll win?"

"Naw; that you'll last five rounds."

At this moment the gong sounded and I rushed for the other end of the pit, with the worthy intention of effacing Slade from the face of the earth. But, as usual, I underestimated the force of my rush and the length of the pit. There didn't seem to be room enough for Slade to get out of my way, but he solved this problem by dropping on his knees, and allowing me to fall over him, which I did.

"Foul!" yelled the dip. "He went down without bein' hit!"

"Foul my eye!" squawked the oily bird. "A blind man could tell he slipped, accidental."

We arose at the same time, me none the better for my fiasco. Slade took my left over his shoulder and hooked a left to the body. He followed this with a straight right to the mouth and a left hook to the side of the head. I clinched and clubbed him with my right to the ribs until the referee prodded us apart.

Again Slade managed to get me into a corner. You see, he was used to the dimensions whereas I, accustomed to a regular ring, kept forgetting about the size of the blasted pit. It seemed like with every movement I bumped my hip or shoulder or scraped my arms against the rough cement of the walls. To date, Slade hadn't a mark to show he'd been in a fight, except for the bruise on his ribs. What with his thumbing and his straight lefts, both my eyes were in a fair way to close, my lips were cut, and I was bunged up generally, but was not otherwise badly hurt.

I fought my way out of the corner, and the gong found us slugging toe to toe in the center of the pit, where I had the pleasure of staggering Bat with a left to the temple. Not an awful lot of action in that round; mostly clinching.

The third started like whirlwind. At the tap of the gong Slade bounded from his end and was in mine before I could get up. He slammed me with a left and right that shook me clean to my toes, and ducked my left. He also ducked a couple of rights, and then rammed a left to my wind which bent me double. No doubt – this baby could hit!

I came up with a left swing to the head, and in a wild mix-up took four right and left hooks to land my right to the ribs. Slade grunted and tried to back-heel me, failing which he lowered his head and butted me in the belly, kicked me on the shin, and would have did more, likely, only I halted the proceedings temporarily by swinging an overhand right to the back of his neck which took the steam out of him for a minute.

We clinched, and I never saw a critter short of a octopus which could appear to have so many arms when clinching. He always managed to not only tie me up and render me helpless for the time being, but to stamp on my insteps, thumb me in the eye and pound on the back of my neck with the edge of his hand. Add to this the fact that he frequently shoved me against the wall, and you can get a idea what kind of a bezark I was fighting. My superior weight and bulk did not have no advantage. What was needed was skill and speed, and the fact that Bat was somewhat smaller than me was an advantage to him.

Still, I was managing to hand out some punishment. Near the end of that round Bat had a beautiful black eye and some more bruises on his ribs. Then it happened. I had plunged after him, swinging; he sidestepped out of the corner, and the next instant was left-jabbing me to death while I floundered along the wall trying to get set for a smash.

I swished a right to his body, and while I didn't think it landed solid, he staggered and dropped his hands slightly. I straightened out of my defensive crouch and cocked my right, and, simultaneous, I realized I had been took. Slade had tricked me. The minute I raised my chin in this careless manner, he beat me to the punch with a right that smashed my head back against the wall, laying open the scalp. Dazed and only partly conscious of what was going on I rebounded right into Slade, ramming my jaw flush into his left. Zam! At the same instant I hooked a trip-hammer right under his heart, and we hit the floor together.

Zowie! I could hear the yelling and cursing as if from a great distance, and the lights on the ceiling high above seemed dancing in a thick fog. All I knew was that I had to get back on my feet as quick as I could.

"One – two – three – four," the oily bird was counting over both of us, "five – Bat, you blank-blank, get up! – Six seven – Bat, blast it, get your feet under you! – eight – Juan, hit that gong! What kind of a timekeeper are you?"

"The round ain't over yet!" yelled the dip, seeing I had begun to get my legs under me.

"Who's refereein' this?" roared the oily bird, jerking out a .45. "Juan, hit that gong! – Nine!"

Juan hit the gong and Bat's seconds hopped down into the pit and dragged him to his end, where they started working over him. I crawled back to mine. Splash! The dip emptied a bucket of water over me. That freshened me up a lot.

"How you comin'?" he asked.

"Great!" said I, still dizzy. "I'll lay this bird like a rug in the next round! For honor and the love of a dame! 'Oh, the road to glory lay – ' "

"I've seen 'em knocked even more cuckoo," said the dip, tearing off a cud of tobacco.

The fourth! Slade came up weakened, but with fire in his eye. I was all right, but my legs wouldn't work like they should. Slade was in far better condition. Seeing this, or probably feeling that he was weakening, he threw caution to the winds and rushed in to slug with me.

The crowd went crazy. Left-right-left-right! I was taking four to one, but mine carried the most steam. It couldn't last long at this rate.

The oily bird was yelling advice and dashing about the pit's edge like a lunatic. We went into a clinch, and he leaned over to prod us apart as usual. He leaned far over, and I don't know if he slipped or somebody shoved him. Anyway, he crashed down on top of us just as we broke and started slugging. He fell between us, stopped somebody's right with his chin, and flopped, face down – through for the night!

By mutual consent, Bat and me suspended hostilities, grabbed the fallen referee by his neck and the slack of his pants, and hove him up into the crowd. Then, without a word, we began again. The end was in sight.

Bat suddenly broke and backed away. I followed, swinging with both hands. Now I saw the wall was at his back. Ha! He couldn't duck now! I shot my right straight for his face. He dropped to his knees. Wham! My fist just cleared the top of his skull and crashed against the concrete wall.

I heard the bones shatter and a dark tide of agony surged up my arm, which dropped helpless at my side. Slade was up and springing for me, but the torture I was in made me forget all about him. I was nauseated, done up – out on my feet, if you get what I mean. He swung his left with everything he had – my foot slipped in some blood on the floor – his left landed high on the side of my skull instead of my jaw. I went down, but I heard him squawk and looked up to see him dancing and wringing his left hand.

The knockdown had cleared my brain somewhat. My hand was numb and not hurting so much, and I realized that Bat had broke his left hand on my skull like many a man has did. Fair enough! I came surging up, and Bat, with the light of desperation in his eyes, rushed in wide open, staking everything on one right swing.

I stepped inside it, sank my left to the wrist in his midriff, and brought the same hand up to his jaw. He staggered, his arms fell, and I swung my left flush to the button with everything I had behind it. Bat hit the floor.

About eight men shoved their snoots over the edge and started counting, the oily bird being still out. They wasn't all counting together, so somehow I managed to prop myself up against the wall, not wanting to make no mistake, until the last man had said "ten!" Then everything began to whirl, and I flopped down on top of Slade and went out like a candle.

Let's pass over the immediate events. I don't remember much about them anyhow. I slept until the middle of the next afternoon, and I know that the only thing that dragged me out of the bed where the dip had dumped me was the knowledge that the *Sea Girl* sailed that night and that Raquel La Costa probably would be waiting for the victor – me.

Outside the joint where I first met her, who should I come upon but Bat Slade!

"Huh!" says I, giving him the once over. "Are you able to be out?"

"You ain't no beauty yourself," he retorted.

I admit it. My right was in a sling, both eyes was black, and I was generally cut and bruised. Still, Slade had no right to give himself airs. His left was all bandaged, he too had a black eye, and moreover his features was about as battered as mine. I hope it hurt him as much to move as it did me. But he had the edge on me in one way – he hadn't rubbed as much hide off against the walls.

"Where's that two hundred we bet?" I snarled.

"Heh, heh!" sneered he. "Try and get it! They told me I wasn't counted out officially. The referee didn't count me out. You didn't whip me."

"Let the money go, you dirty yellow crook," I snarled, "but I whipped you, and I can prove it by thirty men. What you doin' here, anyway?"

"I come to see my girl."

"Your girl? What was we fightin' about last night?"

"Just because you had the sap's luck to knock me stiff don't mean Raquel chooses you," he answered savagely. "This time, she names the man she likes, see? And when she does, I want you to get out!"

"All right," I snarled. "I whipped you fair and can prove it. Come in here; she'll get a chance to choose between us, and if she don't pick the best man, why, I can whip you all over again. Come on, you – "

Saying no more, we kicked the door open and went on in. We swept the interior with a eagle glance, and then sighted Raquel sitting at a table, leaning on her elbows and gazing soulfully into the eyes of a handsome bird in the uniform of a Spanish naval officer.

We barged across the room and come to a halt at her table. She glanced up in some surprise, but she could not have been blamed had she failed to recognize us.

"Raquel," said I, "we went forth and fought for your fair just like you said. As might be expected, I won. Still, this incomprehensible bezark thinks that you might still have some lurkin' fondness for him, and he requires to hear from your own rosy lips that you love another – meanin' me, of course. Say the word and I toss him out. My ship sails tonight, and I got a lot to say to you."

"Santa Maria!" said Raquel. "What ees theese? What kind of a bizness is theese, you two tramps coming looking like theese and talking gibberish? Am I to blame eef two great tramps go pound each other's maps, ha? What ees that to me?"

"But you said" – I began, completely at sea, "you said, go fight and the best man – "

"I say, may the best man win! Bah! Did I geeve any promise? What do I care about Yankee tramps what make the fist-fight? Bah! Go home and beefsteak the eye. You insult me, talking to me in public with the punch' nose and bung' up face."

"Then you don't love either of us?" said Bat.

"Me love two gorillas? Bah! Here is my man – Don Jose y Balsa Santa Maria Gonzales."

She then gave a screech, for at that moment Bat and me hit Don Jose y Balsa Santa Maria Gonzales simultaneous, him with the right and me with the left. And then, turning our backs on the dumbfounded Raquel, we linked arms and, stepping over the fallen lover, strode haughtily to the door and vanished from her life.

"And that," said I, as we leaned upon the bar to which we had made our mutual and unspoken agreement, "ends our romance, and the glory road leads only to disappointment and hokum."

"Women," said Bat gloomily, "are the bunk."

"Listen," said I, remembering something. "How about that two hundred you owe me?"

"What for?"

"For knockin' you cold."

"Steve," said Bat, laying his hand on my shoulder in brotherly fashion, "you know I been intendin' to pay you that all along. After all, Steve, we are seamen together, and we have just been did dirt by a woman of another race. We are both American sailors, even if you are a harp, and we got to stand by each other. Let bygones by bygones, says I. The fortune of war, you know. We fought a fair, clean fight, and you was lucky enough to win. Let's have one more drink and then part in peace an' amity."

"You ain't holdin' no grudge account of me layin' you out?" I asked, suspiciously.

"Steve," said Bat, waxing oratorical, "all men is brothers, and the fact that you was lucky enough to crown me don't alter my admiration and affection. Tomorrow we will be sailin' the high seas, many miles apart. Let our thoughts of each other be gentle and fraternal. Let us forgit old feuds and old differences. Let this be the dawn of a new age of brotherly affection and square dealin'."

"And how about my two-hundred?"

"Steve, you know I am always broke at the end of my shore leave. I give you my word I'll pay you them two hundred smackers. Ain't the word of a comrade enough? Now le's drink to our future friendship and the amicable relations of the crews of our respective ships. Steve, here's my hand! Let this here shake be a symbol of our friendship. May no women ever come between us again! Good-bye, Steve! Good luck! Good luck!"

And so saying, we shook and turned away. That is, I turned and then whirled back as quick as I could – just in time to duck the right swing he'd started the minute my back was turned, and to knock him cold with a bottle I snatched off the bar.

The Bull Dog Breed

"And so," concluded the Old Man, "this big bully ducked the seltzer bottle and the next thing I knowed I knowed nothin'. I come to with the general idea that the *Sea-Girl* was sinkin' with all hands and I was drownin' – but it was only some chump pourin' water all over me to bring me to. Oh, yeah, the big French cluck I had the row with was nobody much, I learned – just only merely nobody but Tiger Valois, the heavyweight champion of the French navy – "

Me and the crew winked at each other. Until the captain decided to unburden to Penrhyn, the first mate, in our hearing, we'd wondered about the black eye he'd sported following his night ashore in Manila. He'd been in an unusual bad temper ever since, which means he'd been acting like a sore-tailed hyena. The Old Man was a Welshman, and he hated a Frenchman like he hated a snake. He now turned on me.

"If you was any part of a man, you big mick ham," he said bitterly, "you wouldn't stand around and let a blankety-blank French so-on and so-forth lay out your captain. Oh, yeah, I know you wasn't there, then, but if you'll fight him – "

"Aragh!" I said with sarcasm, "leavin' out the fact that I'd stand a great chance of gettin' matched with Valois – why not pick me somethin' easy, like Dempsey? Do you realize you're askin' me, a ordinary ham-an'-egger, to climb the original and only Tiger Valois that's whipped everything in European and the Asian waters and looks like a sure bet for the world's title?"

"Gerahh!" snarled the Old Man. "Me that's boasted in every port of the Seven Seas that I shipped the toughest crew since the days of Harry Morgan – " He turned his back in disgust and immediately fell over my white bulldog, Mike, who was taking a snooze by the hatch. The Old Man give a howl as he come up and booted the innocent pup most severe. Mike instantly attached hisself to the Old Man's leg, from which I at last succeeded in prying him with a loss of some meat and the pants leg.

The captain danced hither and yon about the deck on one foot while he expressed his feelings at some length and the crew stopped work to listen and admire.

"And get me right, Steve Costigan," he wound up, "the *Sea-Girl* is too small for me and that double-dash dog. He goes ashore at the next port. Do you hear me?"

"Then I go ashore with him," I answered with dignity. "It was not Mike what caused you to get a black eye, and if you had not been so taken up in abusin' me you would not have fell over him.

"Mike is a Dublin gentleman, and no Welsh water rat can boot him and get away with it. If you want to banish your best A.B. mariner, it's up to you. Till we make port you keep your boots off of Mike, or I will personally kick you loose from your spine. If that's mutiny, make the most of it – and, Mister First Mate, I see you easin' toward that belayin' pin on the rail, and I call to your mind what I done to the last man that hit me with a belayin' pin."

There was a coolness between me and the Old Man thereafter. The old nut was pretty rough and rugged, but good at heart, and likely he was ashamed of himself, but he was too stubborn to admit it, besides still being sore at me and Mike. Well, he paid me off without a word at Hong Kong, and I went down the gangplank with Mike at my heels, feeling kind of queer and empty, though I wouldn't show it for nothing, and acted like I was glad to get off the old tub. But since I growed up, the *Sea-Girl*'s been the only home I knowed, and though I've left her from time to time to prowl around loose or to make a fight tour, I've always come back to her.

Now I knowed I couldn't come back, and it hit me hard. The *Sea-Girl* is the only thing I'm champion of, and as I went ashore I heard the sound of Mushy Hansen and Bill O'Brien trying to decide which should succeed to my place of honor.

Well, maybe some will say I should of sent Mike ashore and stayed on, but to my mind, a man that won't stand by his dog is lower down than one which won't stand by his fellow man.

Some years ago I'd picked Mike up wandering around the wharfs of Dublin and fighting everything he met on four legs and not averse to tackling two-legged critters. I named him Mike after a brother of mine, Iron

Mike Costigan, rather well known in them higher fight circles where I've never gotten to.

Well, I wandered around the dives and presently fell in with Tom Roche, a lean, fighting engineer that I once knocked out in Liverpool. We meandered around, drinking here and there, though not very much, and presently found ourselves in a dump a little different from the general run. A French joint, kinda more highbrow, if you get me. A lot of swell-looking fellows was in there drinking, and the bartenders and waiters, all French, scowled at Mike, but said nothing. I was unburdening my woes to Tom, when I noticed a tall, elegant young man with a dress suit, cane, and gloves stroll by our table. He seemed well known in the dump, because birds all around was jumping up from their tables and waving their glasses and yelling at him in French. He smiled back in a superior manner and flourished his cane in a way which irritated me. This galoot rubbed me the wrong way right from the start, see?

Well, Mike was snoozing close to my chair as usual, and, like any other fighter, Mike was never very particular where he chose to snooze. This big bimbo could have stepped over him or around him, but he stopped and prodded Mike with his cane. Mike opened one eye, looked up and lifted his lip in a polite manner, just like he was saying': "We don't want no trouble; go 'long and leave me alone."

Then this French dipthong drawed back his patent leather shoe and kicked Mike hard in the ribs. I was out of my chair in a second, seeing red, but Mike was quicker. He shot up off the floor, not for the Frenchman's leg, but for his throat. But the Frenchman, quick as a flash, crashed his heavy cane down across Mike's head, and the bulldog hit the floor and laid still. The next minute the Frenchman hit the floor, and believe me he laid still! My right-hander to the jaw put him down, and the crack his head got against the corner of the bar kept him there.

I bent over Mike, but he was already coming around, in spite of the fact that a loaded cane had been broken over his head. It took a blow like that to put Mike out, even for a few seconds. The instant he got his bearings, his eyes went red and he started out to find what hit him and tear it up. I grabbed him, and for a minute it was all I could do to hold him. Then the red faded out of his eyes and he wagged his stump of a tail and licked my nose. But I knowed the first good chance he had at the Frenchman he'd rip out his throat or die trying. The only way you can lick a bulldog is to kill him.

Being taken up with Mike I hadn't had much time to notice what was going on. But a gang of French sailors had tried to rush me and had stopped at the sight of a gun in Tom Roche's hand. A real fighting man was Tom, and a bad egg to fool with.

By this time the Frenchman had woke up; he was standing with a handkerchief at his mouth, which latter was trickling blood, and honest to Jupiter I never saw such a pair of eyes on a human! His face was dead white, and those black, burning eyes blazed out at me – say, fellows! – they carried more than hate and a desire to muss me up! They was mutilation and sudden death! Once I seen a famous duelist in Heidelberg who'd killed ten men in sword fights – he had just such eyes as this fellow.

A gang of Frenchies was around him all whooping and yelling and jabbering at once, and I couldn't understand a word none of them said. Now one come prancing up to Tom Roche and shook his fist in Tom's face and pointed at me and yelled, and pretty soon Tom turned around to me and said: "Steve, this yam is challengin' you to a duel – what about?"

I thought of the German duelist and said to myself: "I bet this bird was born with a fencin' sword in one hand and a duelin' pistol in the other." I opened my mouth to say "Nothin' doing' – " when Tom pipes: "You're the challenged party – the choice of weapons is up to you."

At that I hove a sigh of relief and a broad smile flitted across my homely but honest countenance. "Tell him I'll fight him," I said, "with five-ounce boxin' gloves."

Of course I figured this bird never saw a boxing glove. Now, maybe you think I was doing him dirty, pulling a fast one like that – but what about him? All I was figuring on was mussing him up a little, counting on him not knowing a left hook from a neutral corner – takin' a mean advantage, maybe, but he was counting on killing me, and I'd never had a sword in my hand, and couldn't hit the side of a barn with a gun.

Well, Tom told them what I said and the cackling and gibbering bust out all over again, and to my astonishment I saw a cold, deadly smile waft itself across the sinister, handsome face of my tête-à-tête.

"They ask who you are," said Tom. "I told 'em Steve Costigan, of America. This bird says his name is Francois, which he opines is enough for *you.* He says that he'll fight you right away at the exclusive Napoleon Club, which it seems has a ring account of it occasionally sponsoring prize-fights."

As we wended our way toward the aforesaid club, I thought deeply. It seemed very possible that this Francois, whoever he was, knew something of the manly art. Likely, I thought, a rich club man who took up boxing for a hobby. Well, I reckoned he hadn't heard of me, because no amateur, however rich, would think he had a chance against Steve Costigan, known in all ports as the toughest sailor in the Asian waters – if I do say so myself – and champion of – what I mean – ex-champion of the *Sea-Girl*, the toughest of all the trading vessels.

A kind of pang went through me just then at the thought that my days with the old tub was ended, and I wondered what sort of a dub would take my place at mess and sleep in my bunk, and how the forecastle gang would haze him, and how all the crew would miss me – I wondered if Bill O'Brien had licked Mushy Hansen or if the Dane had won, and who called hisself champion of the craft now –

Well, I felt low in spirits, and Mike knowed it, because he snuggled up closer to me in the rickshaw that was carrying us to the Napoleon Club and licked my hand. I pulled his ears and felt better. Anyway, Mike wouldn't never desert me.

Pretty ritzy affair this club. Footmen or butlers or something in uniform at the doors, and they didn't want to let Mike in. But they did – oh, yeah, they did.

In the dressing room they give me, which was the swellest of its sort I ever seen and looked more like a girl's boodwar than a fighter's dressing room, I said to Tom: "This big ham must have lots of dough – notice what a hand they all give him? Reckon I'll get a square deal? Who's goin' to referee? If it's a Frenchman, how'm I gonna follow the count?"

"Well, gee whiz!" Tom said, "you ain't expectin' him to count over you, are you?"

"No," I said. "But I'd like to keep count of what he tolls off over the other fellow."

"Well," said Tom, helping me into the green trunks they'd give me, "don't worry none. I understand Francois can speak English, so I'll specify that the referee shall converse entirely in that language."

"Then why didn't this Francois ham talk English to me?" I wanted to know.

"He didn't talk to you in anything," Tom reminded me. "He's a swell and thinks you're beneath his notice – except only to knock your head off."

"H'mm," said I thoughtfully, gently touching the slight cut which Francois' cane had made on Mike's incredibly hard head. A slight red mist, I will admit, waved in front of my eyes.

When I climbed into the ring I noticed several things: mainly the room was small and elegantly furnished; second, there was only a small crowd there, mostly French, with a scattering of English and one Chink in English clothes. There was high hats, frock-tailed coats, and gold-knobbed canes everywhere, and I noted with some surprise that they was also a sprinkling of French sailors.

I sat in my corner, and Mike took his stand just outside, like he always does when I fight, standing on his hind legs with his head and forepaws resting on the edge of the canvas, and looking under the ropes. On the street, if a man soaks me he's likely to have Mike at his throat, but the old dog knows how to act in the ring. He won't interfere, though sometimes when I'm on the canvas or bleeding bad his eyes get red and he rumbles away down deep in his throat.

Tom was massaging my muscles light-like and I was scratching Mike's ears when into the ring comes Francois the Mysterious. Qui! Qui! I noted now how much of a man he was, and Tom whispers to me to pull in my chin a couple of feet and stop looking so goofy. When Francois threw off his silk embroidered bathrobe I saw I was in for a rough session, even if this bird was only an amateur. He was one of these fellows that look like a fighting man, even if they've never seen a glove before.

A good six one and a half he stood, or an inch and a half taller than me. A powerful neck sloped into broad, flexible shoulders, a limber steel body tapered to a girlishly slender waist. His legs was slim, strong and shapely, with narrow feet that looked speedy and sure; his arms was long, thick, but perfectly molded. Oh, I tell you, this Francois looked more like a champion than any man I'd seen since I saw Dempsey last.

And the face – his sleek black hair was combed straight back and lay smooth on his head, adding to his sinister good looks. From under narrow black brows them eyes burned at me, and now they wasn't a duelist's eyes – they was tiger eyes. And when he gripped the ropes and dipped a couple of times, flexing his muscles, them muscles rippled under his satiny skin most beautiful, and he looked just like a big cat sharpening his claws on a tree.

"Looks fast, Steve," Tom Roche said, looking serious. "May know somethin'; you better crowd him from the gong and keep rushin' – "

"How else did I ever fight?" I asked.

A sleek-looking Frenchman with a sheik mustache got in the ring and, waving his hands to the crowd, which was still jabbering for Francois, he bust into a gush of French.

"What's he mean?" I asked Tom, and Tom said, "Aw, he's just sayin' what everybody knows – that this ain't a regular prize-fight, but an affair of honor between you and – uh – that Francois fellow there."

Tom called him and talked to him in French, and he turned around and called an Englishman out of the crowd. Tom asked me was it all right with me for the Englishman to referee, and I tells him yes, and they asked Francois and he nodded in a supercilious manner. So the referee asked me what I weighed and I told him, and he hollered: "This bout is to be at catch weights, Marquis of Queensberry rules. Three-minutes rounds, one minute rest; to a finish, if it takes all night. In this corner, Monsieur Francois, weight 205 pounds; in this corner, Steve Costigan of America, weight 190 pounds. Are you ready, gentlemen?"

'Stead of standing outside the ring, English style, the referee stayed in with us, American fashion. The gong sounded and I was out of my corner. All I seen was that cold, sneering, handsome face, and all I wanted to do was to spoil it. And I very nearly done it the first charge. I came in like a house afire and walloped Francois with an overhand right hook to the chin – more by sheer luck than anything, and it landed high. But it shook him to his toes, and the sneering smile faded.

Too quick for the eye to follow, his straight left beat my left hook, and it packed the jarring kick that marks a puncher. The next minute, when I missed with both hands and got that left in my pan again, I knowed I was up against a master boxer, too.

I saw in a second I couldn't match him for speed and skill. He was like a cat; each move he made was a blur of speed, and when he hit he hit quick and hard. He was a brainy fighter – he thought out each move while traveling at high speed, and he was never at a loss what to do next.

Well, my only chance was to keep on top of him, and I kept crowding him, hitting fast and heavy. He wouldn't stand up to me, but back-pedaled all around the ring. Still, I got the idea that he wasn't afraid of me, but was retreating with a purpose of his own. But I never stop to figure out why the other bird does something.

He kept reaching me with that straight left, until finally I dived under it and sank my right deep into his midriff. It shook him – it should of brought him down. But he clinched and tied me up so I couldn't hit or do nothing. As the referee broke us Francois scraped his glove laces across my eyes. With an appropriate remark, I threw my right at his head with everything I had, but he drifted out of the way, and I fell into the ropes from the force of my own swing. The crowd howled with laughter, and then the gong sounded.

"This baby's tough," said Tom, back in my corner, as he rubbed my belly muscles, "but keep crowdin' him, get inside that left, if you can. And watch the right."

I reached back to scratch Mike's nose and said. "You watch this round."

Well, I reckon it was worth watching. Francois changed his tactics, and as I come in he met me with a left to the nose that started the claret and filled my eyes full of water and stars. While I was thinking about that he opened a cut under my left eye with a venomous right-hander and then stuck the same hand into my midriff. I woke up and bent him double with a savage left hook to the liver, crashing him with an overhand right behind the ear before he could straighten. He shook his head, snarled a French cuss word and drifted back behind that straight left where I couldn't reach him.

I went into him like a whirlwind, lamming head on full into that left jab again and again, trying to get to him, but always my swings were short. Them jabs wasn't hurting me yet, because it takes a lot of them to weaken a man. But it was like running into a floating brick wall, if you get what I mean. Then he started crossing his right – and oh, baby, what a right he had! Blip! Blim! Blam!

His rally was so unexpected and he hit so quick that he took me clean off my guard and caught me wide open. That right was lightning! In a second I was groggy, and Francois beat me back across the ring with both hands going too fast for me to block more than about a fourth of the blows. He was wild for the kill now and hitting wide open.

Then the ropes was at my back and I caught a flashing glimpse of him, crouching like a big tiger in front of me, wide open and starting his right. In that flash of a second I shot my right from the hip, beat his punch and landed solid to the button. Francois went down like he'd been hit with a pile driver – the referee leaped forward – the gong sounded!

As I went to my corner the crowd was clean ory-eyed and not responsible; and I saw Francois stagger up, glassy-eyed, and walk to his stool with one arm thrown over the shoulder of his handler.

But he come out fresh as ever for the third round. He'd found out that I could hit as hard as he could and that I was dangerous when groggy, like most sluggers. He was wild with rage, his smile was gone, his face dead white again, his eyes was like black fires – but he was cautious. He side-stepped my rush, hooking me viciously on the ear as I shot past him, and ducking when I slewed around and hooked my right. He backed away, shooting that left to my face. It went that way the whole round; him keeping the right reserved and marking me up with left jabs while I worked for his body and usually missed or was blocked. Just before the gong he rallied, staggered me with a flashing right hook to the head and took a crushing left hook to the ribs in return.

The fourth round come and he was more aggressive. He began to trade punches with me again. He'd shoot a straight left to my face, then hook the same hand to my body. Or he'd feint the left for my face and drop it to my ribs. Them hooks to the body didn't hurt much, because I was hard as a rock there, but a continual rain of them wouldn't do me no good, and them jabs to the face was beginning to irritate me. I was already pretty well marked up.

He shot his blows so quick I usually couldn't block or duck, so every time he'd make a motion with the left I'd throw my right for his head haphazard. After rocking his head back several times this way he quit feinting so much and began to devote most of his time to body blows.

Now I found out this about him: he had more claws than sand, as the saying goes. I mean he had everything, including a lot of stuff I didn't, but he didn't like to take it. In a mix-up he always landed three blows to my one, and he hit about as hard as I did, but he was always the one to back away.

Well, come the seventh round. I'd taken plenty. My left eye was closing fast and I had a nasty gash over the other one. My ribs was beginning to feel the body punishment he was handing out when in close, and my right ear was rapidly assuming the shape of a cabbage. Outside of some ugly welts on his torso, my dancing partner had only one mark on him – the small cut on his chin where I'd landed with my bare fist earlier in the evening.

But I was not beginning to weaken, for I'm used to punishment; in fact I eat it up, if I do say so. I crowded Francois into a corner before I let go. I wrapped my arms around my neck, worked in close and then unwound with a looping left to head.

Francois countered with a sickening right under the heart and I was wild with another left. Francois stepped inside my right swing, dug his heel into my instep, gouged me in the eye with his thumb, and, holding with his left, battered away at my ribs with his right. The referee showed no inclination to interfere with this pastime, so, with a hearty oath, I wrenched my right loose and nearly tore off Francois' head with a torrid uppercut.

His sneer changed to a snarl and he began pistoning me in the face again with his left. Maddened, I crashed into him headlong and smashed my right under his heart – I felt his ribs bend, he went white and sick and clinched before I could follow up my advantage. I felt the drag of his body as his knees buckled, but he held on while I raged and swore, the referee would not break us, and when I tore loose, my charming playmate was almost good as ever.

He proved this by shooting a left to my sore eye, dropping the same hand to my aching ribs and bringing up a right to the jaw that stretched me flat on my back for the first time that night. Just like that! Biff – bim – bam! Like a cat hitting – and I was on the canvas.

Tom Roche yelled for me to take a count, but I never stay on the canvas longer than I have to. I bounced up at "Four!" my ears still ringing and a trifle dizzy, but otherwise OK

Francois thought otherwise, rushed rashly in and stopped a left hook which hung him gracefully over the ropes. The gong!

The beginning of the eighth I come at Francois like we'd just started, took his right between my eyes to hook my left to his body – he broke away, spearing me with his left – I followed swinging – missed a right – *crack!*

He musta let go his right with all he had for the first time that night, and he had a clear shot to my jaw. The next thing I knowed, I was writhing around on the canvas feeling like my jaw was tore clean off and the referee was saying: " – seven – "

Somehow I got to my knees. It looked like the referee was ten miles away in a mist, but in the mist I could see Francois' face, smiling again, and I reeled up at "nine" and went for that face. *Crack! Crack!* I don't know what punch put me down again but there I was. I beat the count by a hair's breadth and swayed forward, following my only instinct and that was to walk into him!

Francois might have finished me there, but he wasn't taking any chances for he knowed I was dangerous to the last drop. He speared me a couple of times with the left, and when he shot his right, I ducked it and took it high on my forehead and clinched, shaking my head to clear it. The referee broke us away and Francois lashed into one, cautious but deadly, hammering me back across the ring with me crouching and covering up the best I could.

On the ropes I unwound with a venomous looping right, but he was watching for that and ducked and countered with a terrible left to my jaw, following it with a blasting right to the side of the head. Another left hook threw me back into the ropes and there I caught the top rope with both hands to keep from falling. I was swaying and ducking but his gloves were falling on my ears and temples with a steady thunder which was growing dimmer and dimmer – then the gong sounded.

I let go of the ropes to go to my corner and when I let go I pitched to my knees. Everything was a red mist and the crowd was yelling about a million miles away. I heard Francois' scornful laugh, then Tom Roche was dragging me to my corner.

"By golly," he said, working on my cut-up eyes, "you're sure a glutton for punishment; Joe Grim had nothin' on you.

"But you better lemme throw in the towel, Steve. This Frenchman's goin' to kill you – "

"He'll have to, to beat me," I snarled. "I'll take it standin'."

"But, Steve," Tom protested, mopping blood and squeezing lemon juice into my mouth, "this Frenchman is – "

But I wasn't listening. Mike knowed I was getting the worst of it and he'd shoved his nose into my right glove, growling low down in his throat. And I was thinking about something.

One time I was laid up with a broken leg in a little fishing village away up on the Alaskan coast, and looking through a window, not able to help him, I saw Mike fight a big gray devil of a sled dog – more wolf than dog. A big gray killer. They looked funny together – Mike short and thick, bow-legged and squat, and the wolf dog tall and lean, rangy and cruel.

Well, while I lay there and raved and tried to get off my bunk with four men holding me down, that blasted wolf-dog cut poor old Mike to ribbons. He was like lightning – like Francois. He fought with the slash and get away – like Francois. He was all steel and whale-bone – like Francois.

Poor old Mike had kept walking into him, plunging and missing as the wolf-dog leaped aside – and every time he leaped he slashed Mike with his long sharp teeth till Mike was bloody and looking terrible. How long they fought I don't know. But Mike never give up; he never whimpered; he never took a single back step; he kept walking in on the dog.

As last he landed – crashed through the wolf-dog's defense and clamped his jaws like a steel vise and tore out the wolf-dog's throat. Then Mike slumped down and they brought him into my bunk more dead than alive. But we fixed him up and finally he got well, though he'll carry the scars as long as he lives.

And I thought, as Tom Roche rubbed my belly and mopped the blood off my smashed face, and Mike rubbed his cold, wet nose in my glove, that me and Mike was both of the same breed, and the only fighting quality we had was a everlasting persistence. You got to kill a bulldog to lick him. Persistence! How'd I ever won a fight? How'd Mike ever won a fight? By walking in on our men and never giving up, no matter how bad we was hurt! Always outclassed in everything except guts and grip! Somehow the fool Irish tears burned my eyes and it wasn't the pain of the collodion Tom was rubbing into my cuts and it wasn't self-pity – it was – I don't know what it was! My grandfather used to say the Irish cried at Benburb when they were licking the socks off the English.

Then the gong sounded and I was out in the ring again playing the old bulldog game with Francois – walking into him and walking into him and taking everything he handed me without flinching.

I don't remember much about that round. Francois' left was a red-hot lance in my face and his right was a hammer that battered in my ribs and crashed against my dizzy head. Toward the last my legs felt dead and my arms were like lead. I don't know how many times I went down and got up and beat the count, but I remember once in a clinch, half-sobbing through my pulped lips: "You gotta kill me to stop me, you big hash!" And I saw a strange haggard look flash into his eyes as we broke. I lashed out wild and by luck connected under his heart. Then the red fog stole back over everything and then I was back on my stool and Tom was holding me to keep me from falling off.

"What round's this comin' up?" I mumbled.

"The tenth," he said. "For th' luvva Pete, Steve, quit!"

I felt around blind for Mike and felt his cold nose on my wrist.

"Not while I can see, stand, or feel," I said, deliriously. "It's bulldog and wolf – and Mike tore his throat out in the end – and I'll rip this wolf apart sooner or later."

Back in the center of the ring with my chest all crimson with my own blood, and Francois' gloves soggy and splashing blood and water at every blow, I suddenly realized that his punches were losing some of their kick. I'd been knocked down I don't know how many times, but I now knew he was hitting me his best and I still kept my feet. My legs wouldn't work right, but my shoulders were still strong. Francois played for my eyes and closed them both tight shut, but while he was doing it I landed three times under the heart, and each time, he wilted a little.

"What round's comin' up?" I groped for Mike because I couldn't see.

"The eleventh – this is murder," said Tom. "I know you're one of these birds which fights twenty rounds after they've been knocked cold, but I want to tell you that this Frenchman is – "

"Lance my eyelid with your pocketknife," I broke in, for I had found Mike. "I gotta see."

Tom grumbled, but I felt a sharp pain and the pressure eased up in my right eye and I could see dim-like.

Then the gong sounded, but I couldn't get up; my legs was dead and stiff.

"Help me up, Tom Roche, you big bog-trotter," I snarled. "If you throw in that towel I'll brain you with the water bottle!"

With a shake of his head he helped me up and shoved me in the ring. I got my bearings and went forward with a funny, stiff, mechanical step, toward Francois – who got up slow, with a look on his face like he'd rather be somewhere else. Well, he'd cut me to pieces, knocked me down time and again, and here I was coming back for more. The bulldog instinct is hard to fight – it ain't just exactly courage, and it ain't exactly blood lust – it's – well, it's the bulldog breed.

Now I was facing Francois and I noticed he had a black eye and a deep gash under his cheekbone, though I didn't remember putting them there. He also had welts a-plenty on his body. I'd been handing out punishment as well as taking it, I saw.

Now his eyes blazed with a desperate light and he rushed in, hitting as hard as ever for a few seconds. The blows rained so fast I couldn't think and yet I knowed I must be clean batty – punch drunk – because it seemed like I could hear familiar voices yelling my name – the voices of the crew of the *Sea-Girl*, who'd never yell for me again.

I was on the canvas and this time I felt that it was to stay; dim and far away I saw Francois and somehow I could tell his legs was trembling and he was shaking like he had a chill. But I couldn't reach him now. I tried to get my legs under me, but they wouldn't work. I slumped back on the canvas, crying with rage and weakness.

Then through the noise I heard one deep, mellow sound like an old Irish bell, almost. Mike's bark! He wasn't a barking dog; only on special occasions did he give tongue. This time he only barked once. I looked at him and he seemed to be swimming in a fog. If a dog ever had his soul in his eyes, he had; plain as speech them eyes said: "Steve, old kid, get up and hit one more blow for the glory of the breed!"

I tell you, the average man has got to be fighting for somebody else besides hisself. It's fighting for a flag, a nation, a woman, a kid, or a dog that makes a man win. And I got up – I dunno how! But the look in Mike's eyes dragged me off the canvas just as the referee opened his mouth to say "Ten!" But before he could say it –

In the midst I saw Francois' face, white and desperate. The pace had told. Them blows I'd landed from time to time under the heart had sapped his strength – he'd punched hisself out on me – but more'n anything else, the knowledge that he was up against the old bulldog breed licked him.

I drove my right smash into his face and his head went back like it was on hinges and the blood spattered. He swung his right to my head and it was so weak I laughed, blowing out a haze of blood. I rammed my left to his ribs and as he bent forward I crashed my right to his jaw. He dropped, and crouching there on the canvas, half supporting himself on his hands, he was counted out. I reeled across the ring and collapsed with my arms around Mike, who was whining deep in his throat and trying to lick my face off.

The first thing I felt on coming to was a cold, wet nose burrowing into my right hand, which seemed numb. Then somebody grabbed that hand and nearly shook it off and I heard a voice say: "Hey, you old shellback, you want to break a unconscious man's arm?"

I knowed I was dreaming then, because it was Bill O'Brien's voice, who was bound to be miles away at sea by this time. Then Tom Roche said: "I think he's comin' to. Hey, Steve, can you open your eyes?"

I took my fingers and pried the swollen lids apart and the first thing I saw, or wanted to see, was Mike. His stump tail was going like anything and he opened his mouth and let his tongue loll out, grinning as natural as could be. I pulled his ears and looked around and there was Tom Roche – and Bill O'Brien and Mushy Hansen, Olaf Larsen, Penrhyn, the first mate, Red O'Donnell, the second – and the Old Man!

"Steve!" yelled this last, jumping up and down and shaking my hand like he wanted to take it off, "you're a wonder! A blightin' marvel!"

"Well," said I, dazed, "why all the love fest – "

"The fact is," bust in Bill O'Brien, "just as we're about to weigh anchor, up blows a lad with the news that you're fightin' in the Napoleon Club with – "

" – and as soon as I heard who you was fightin' with I stopped everything and we all blowed down there," said the Old Man. "But the fool kid Roche had sent for us loafed on the way – "

" – and we hadda lay some Frenchies before we could get in," said Hansen.

"So we saw only the last three rounds," continued the Old Man. "But, boy, they was worth the money – he had you outclassed every way except guts – you was licked to a frazzle, but he couldn't make you realize it – and I laid a bet or two – "

And blow me, if the Old Man didn't stuff a wad of bills in my sore hand.

"Halfa what I won," he beamed. "And furthermore, the *Sea-Girl* ain't sailin' till you're plumb able and fit."

"But what about Mike?" My head was swimming by this time.

"A bloomin' bow-legged angel," said the Old Man, pinching Mike's ear lovingly. "The both of you kin have my upper teeth! I owe you a lot, Steve. You've done a lot for me, but I never felt so in debt to you as I do now. When I see that big French ham, the one man in the world I would of give my right arm to see licked – "

"Hey!" I suddenly seen the light, and I went weak and limp. "You mean that was – "

"You whipped Tiger Valois, heavyweight champion of the French fleet, Steve," said Tom. "You ought to have known how he wears dude clothes and struts amongst the swells when on shore leave. He wouldn't tell you who he was for fear you wouldn't fight him; and I was afraid I'd discourage you if I told you at first and later you wouldn't give me a chance."

"I might as well tell you," I said to the Old Man, "that I didn't know this bird was the fellow that beat you up in Manila. I fought him because he kicked Mike."

"Blow the reason!" said the Old Man, raring back and beaming like a jubilant crocodile. "You licked him – that's enough. Now we'll have a bottle opened and drink to Yankee ships and Yankee sailors – especially Steve Costigan."

"Before you do," I said, "drink to the boy who stands for everything them aforesaid ships and sailors stands for – Mike of Dublin, an honest gentleman and born mascot of all fightin' men!"

The Champion of the Forecastle

I don't have to have a man tell me he craves war. I can tell it by the set of his jaw, the glare in his eyes. So, when Sven Larson raised his huge frame on his bunk and accused me of swiping his tobaccer, I knowed very well what his idee was. But I didn't want to fight Sven. Havin' licked the big cheese three or four times already, I seen no need in mauling him any more. So somewhat to the surprise of the rest of the crew, I said:

"Sven, that's purty crude. You didn't need to think up no lie to pick a fight with me. I know you crave to be champion of the *Sea Girl*, but they ain't a chance, and I don't want to hurt you – "

I got no further, because with a bull's beller he heaved hisself offa his bunk and come for me like a wild man. Gosh, what a familiar scene that was – the fierce, hard faces ringing us, the rough bunks along the wall, the dim light of the lantern swinging overhead, and me standing in the middle, barefooted and stripped to the waist, holding my only title against all comers! They ain't a inch of that forecastle floor that I ain't reddened with my blood. They ain't a edge of a upper bunk that I ain't had my head smashed against. And since I been a man grown they ain't a sailor on the Seven Seas that can say he stood up to me in that forecastle and beat me down.

The lurching of the ship and the unsteady footing don't bother me none, nor the close space and foul, smoke-laden air. That's my element, and if I couldst fight in the ring like I can in the forecastle, with nothing barred, I'd be champion of something besides a tramp windjammer.

Well, Sven come at me with his old style – straight up, wide open, with a wild swinging right. I ducked inside it and smashed my left under his heart, following instantly with a blasting right hook to the jaw as he sagged. He started falling and a lurch of the ship throwed him half under a opposite bunk. They's no mercy ast, give, or expected in a forecastle fight; it's always to the finish. I was right after him, and no sooner hadst he got to his feet than I smashed him down again before he could get his hands up.

"Let's call it a day, Sven," I growled. "I don't want to punch you no more."

But he come weaving up, spitting blood and roaring in his own tongue. He tried to clinch and gouge, but another right hook to the jaw sent him down and out. I shook the sweat outa my eyes and glared down at him in some irritation, which was mixed with the satisfaction of knowing that again I hadst proved my right to the title of champion of the toughest ship afloat. Maybe you think that's a mighty small thing, but it's the only title I got and I'm proud of it.

But I couldn't get onto Sven. Me and him was good friends ordinarily, but ever so often he'd get the idee he couldst lick me. So the next day I looked him up between watches and found him sulking and brooding. I looked over his enormous frame and shook my head in wonder to think that I hadst gotten no further in the legitimate ring than I have, when I can lay out such incredible monsters as Sven so easy.

Six feet four he was in his socks, and his 245 pounds was all muscle. I can bend coins between my fingers, tear up decks of cards and twist horse-shoes in two, but Sven's so much stronger'n me they's no comparison. But size and strength ain't everything.

"Sven," said I, "how come you forever got to be fightin' me?"

Well, at first he wouldn't say, but at last it come out.

"Aye bane got girl at Stockholm. She bane like me purty good, but they bane another faller. His name bane Olaf Ericson and he own fishing smack. Always when Aye go out with my girl, he bane yump on me and he always lick me. Aye tank if Aye ever lick you, Aye can lick Olaf."

"So you practice on me, hey?" I said. "Well, Sven, you never will lick me nor Olaf nor any man which can use his hands unless you change your style. Oh, uh course, you're a bear-cat when it comes to fightin' ignorant dock-wallopers and deck-hands which never seen a glove and can't do nothin' but bite and gouge. But you see what happens when you get up against a real fightin' man, Sven," said I on a sudden impulse, like I usually do, "far be it from me to see a deep water seaman get beat up regular by a Baltic fish-grabber. It's a reflection on the profession and on the ship. Sven," said I, "I'm goin' to train you to lick this big cheese."

Well, I hadn't never give much thought to Sven before, only in a general way – you can't pay close attention to every square-head which comes and goes aboard a trading ship – but in the weeks which followed I done my best to make a fighting man of him. I rigged up a punching bag for him and sparred with him between watches. When him or me wasn't doing our trick at the wheel or holystoning the deck, or scraping the cable or hauling on a rope, or trimming sail or exchanging insults with the mates, I tried to teach him all I knowed.

Understand, I didn't try to make no boxing wizard outa him. The big slob couldn't of learned even if I could of taught him. And I didn't know how myself. I ain't a clever boxer. I'm a rough and willing mixer in the ring, but compared to such roughhouse scrappers as Sven, I'm a wonder. The simple ducking, slipping, and blocking, which even the crudest slugger does in the ring, is beyond the ken of the average untrained man, and as for scientific hitting, they never heard of it. They just draw back the right and let it go without any aim, timing, nor nothing. Well, I just taught Sven the fundamentals – to stand with his left foot forward and not get his legs crossed, to lead with his left and to time and aim a little. I got him outa the habit of swinging wild and wide open with his right all the time, and by constant drilling I taught him the knack of hooking and hitting straight. I also give him a lot of training to harden his body muscles, which was his weak spot.

Well, the big Swede took to it like a duck takes to water, and after I'd explained each simple move upwards of a thousand times, he'd understand it and apply it and he wouldn't forget. Like lots of square-heads, he was slow to learn, but once he had learned, he remembered what he'd learned. And his great size and strength was a big asset.

Bill O'Brien says, "Steve, you're trainin' the big sap to take your title away from you." But I merely laughed with great merriment at the idee.

Sven had a wallop like a mule's kick in either hand, and when he learned to use it, he was dangerous to any man. He was pretty tough, too, or got so before I got through with him. He wasn't very fast, and I taught him a kind of deep defensive crouch like Jeffries used. He took to it natural and developed a surprising left for the body.

After six months of hard work on him, I felt sure that he could lick the average alley-fighter easy. And about this time we was cruising Baltic waters and headed for Stockholm.

As we approached his native heath, Sven grew impatient and restless. He had a lot more self-confidence now and he craved another chance at Olaf, the demon rival. Sven wasn't just a big unwieldy slob no more. Constant sparring with me and Bill O'Brien had taught him how to handle hisself and how to use his bulk and strength. A few days outa Stockholm he had a row with Mushy Hansen, which was two hundred pounds of fighting man, and he knocked the Dane so cold it took us a hour and a half to bring him to.

Well, that cheered Sven up considerable and when we docked, he said to me: "Aye go see Segrida, my girl, and find out if Olaf bane in port. He bane hang out at dey Fisherman's Tavern. Aye go past with Segrida and he come out and yump on me, like usual. Only diss time Aye bane lick him."

Well, at the appointed time me and Bill and Mushy was loafing around the Fisherman's Tavern, a kind of bar where a lot of tough Swedish fishermen hung out, and pretty soon, along come Sven.

He had his girl with him, all right, a fine, big blonde girl – one of these tall, slender yet well-built girls which is overflowing with health and vitality. She was so pretty I was plumb astounded as to what she seen in a big boob like Sven. But women is that way. They fall for the dubs and pass up the real prizes – like me, for instance.

Segrida looked kind of worried just now and as they neared the tavern, she cast a apprehensive eye that way. Well, they was abreast of the door when a kind of irritated roar sounded from within and out bulged what could of been nobody but Olaf the Menace, hisself, in person.

There was a man for you! He was fully as tall as Sven, though not as heavy. Tall, lithe, and powerful he was, like a big, blond tiger. He was so handsome I couldst easily see why Segrida hesitated between him and Sven – or rather I couldn't see why she hesitated at all! Olaf looked like one of these here Vikings you read about which rampaged around in old times, licking everybody. But he had a hard, cruel eye, which I reckon goes with that kind of nature.

He had some fellers with him, but they stayed back in the doorway while he swaggered out and stopped square in front of Sven. He had a most contemptuous sneer and he said something which of course I couldn't understand, but as Mushy later translated the conversation to me, I'll give it like Mushy told to me and Bill.

"Well, well," said Olaf, "looking for another licking, eh? Your deep sea boy friend is back in port looking for his usual trouncing, eh, Segrida?"

"Olaf, please," said Segrida, frightened. "Don't fight, please!"

"I warned you what would happen to him," said Olaf, "if you went out with him – "

At this moment Sven, who had said nothing, shocked his bold rival by growling: "Too much talk; put up your hands!"

Olaf, though surprised, immediately done so, and cut Sven's lip with a flashing straight left before the big boy couldst get in position. Segrida screamed but no cops was in sight and the battle was on.

Olaf had learned boxing someplace, and was one of the fastest men for his size I ever seen. For the first few seconds he plastered Sven plenty, but from the way the big fellow hunched his shoulders and surged in, I hadst no doubt about the outcome.

Sven dropped into the deep, defensive crouch I'd taught him, and I seen Olaf was puzzled. He hisself fought in the straight-up English sparring position and this was the first time he'd ever met a man who fought American style, I could see. With Sven's crouch protecting his body and his big right arm curved around his jaw, all Olaf couldst see to hit was his eyes glaring over the arm.

He battered away futilely at Sven's hard head, doing no damage whatever, and then Sven waded in and drove his ponderous left to the wrist in Olaf's midriff. Olaf gasped, went white, swayed and shook like a leaf. He sure couldn't take it there and I yelled for Sven to hit him again in the same place, but the big dumb-bell tried a heavy swing for the jaw, half straightening out of his crouch as he swung and Olaf ducked and staggered him with a sizzling right to the ear. Sven immediately went back into his shell and planted another battering-ram left under Olaf's heart.

Olaf broke ground gasping and his knees trembling, but Sven kept right on top of him in his plodding sort of way. Olaf jarred him with a dying-effort swing to the jaw, but them months of punching hadst toughened Sven and the big fellow shook his head and leaned on a right to the ribs.

That finished Olaf; his knees give way and he started falling, grabbing feebly at Sven as he done so. But Sven, with one of the few laughs I ever heard him give, pushed him away and crashed a tremendous right-hander to his jaw. Olaf straightened out on the boardwalk and he didn't even quiver.

A low rumble of fury warned us and we turned to see Olaf's amazed but wrathful cronies surging towards the victor. But me and Bill and Mushy and Mike kind of drifted in between and at the sight of three hard-eyed American seamen and a harder-eyed Irish bulldog, they stopped short and signified their intention of merely taking Olaf into the tavern and bringing him to.

At this Sven grinning placidly and turning to Segrida with open arms, got the shock of his life. Instead of falling on to his manly bosom, Segrida, who hadst stood there like she was froze, woke up all at once and bust into a perfect torrent of speech. I would of give a lot to understand it. Sven stood gaping with his mouth wide open and even the rescue party which had picked up Olaf stood listening. Then with one grand burst of oratory, she handed Sven a full-armed, open-handed slap that cracked like a bull-whip, and busting into tears, she run forward to help with Olaf. They vanished inside the tavern.

"What'd she say? What's the idee?" I asked, burnt up with curiosity.

"She say she bane through with me," Sven answered dazedly. "She say Aye bane a brute. She say she ain't bane want to see me no more."

"Well, keel-haul me," said I profanely. "Can ya beat that? First she wouldn't choose Sven because he got licked by Olaf all the time; now she won't have him because he licked Olaf. Women are all crazy."

"Never mind, old timer," said Bill, slapping the dejected Sven on the back. "Anyway, you licked Olaf to a fare-you-well. Come along, and we'll buy you a drink."

But Sven just shook his head sullen-like and moped off by hisself; so after arguing with him unsuccessfully, me and Bill and Mushy betook ourselves to a place where we couldst get some real whiskey and not the stuff they make in them Scandinavian countries. The barkeep kicked at first because I give my white bulldog, Mike, a pan-full of beer on the floor, but we overcome that objection and fell to talking about Sven.

"I don't savvy dames," I said. "If she gives Sven the bounce for beatin' up Olaf, whyn't she give Olaf the bounce long ago for beatin' up Sven so much?"

"It's Olaf she really loves," said Mushy.

"Maybe," said Bill. "And maybe he's just persistent. But women is kindhearted. They pities a poor boob which has just got punched in the nose, and as long as Sven was gettin' licked all the time, he got all her pity. But now her pity and affections is transferred to Olaf, naturally."

Well, we didn't see no more of Sven till kind of late that night, when in come one of our square-head ship-mates named Fritz to the bar where me and Bill and Mushy was, and said he: "Steve, Sven he say maybeso you bane come down to a place on Hjolmer Street; he bane got something to show you."

"Now what could that Swede want now?" said Bill testily, but I said, "Oh well, we got nothin' else to do." So we went to Hjolmer Street, a kind of narrow street just out of the waterfront section. It wasn't no particularly genteel place – kind of dirty and dingy for a Swedish street, with little crumby shops along the way, all closed up and deserted that time of night. The square-head, Fritz, led us to a place which was lighted up, though the shutters was closed. He knocked on the door and a short fat Swede opened it and closed it behind us.

To my surprise I seen the place was a kind of third-rate gymnasium. They was a decrepit punching bag, a horizontal bar and a lot of bar-bells, dumb-bells, kettle bells – in fact, all the lifting weights you couldst imagine. They was also a rastling mat and, in the middle of the floor, a canvas covered space about the size of a small ring. And in the middle of this stood Sven, in fighting togs and with his hands taped.

"Who you goin' to fight, Sven?" I asked curiously.

He scowled slightly, flexed his mighty arms kind of embarrassed-like, swelled out his barrel chest, and said: "You!"

You could of bowled me over with a jib boom.

"Me?" I said in amazement. "What kind of joke is this?"

"It bane no yoke," he answered stolidly. "Mine friend Knut bane own diss gym and teach rastlin' and weight liftin'. He bane let us fight here."

Knut, a stocky Swede with the massive arms and pot belly of a retired weight lifter, give me a kind of apologetic look, but I glared at him.

"But what you want to fight me for?" I snarled in perplexity. "Ain't I taught you all you know? Didn't I teach you to lick Olaf? You ungrateful – "

"Aye ain't got no grudge for you, Steve," the big cheese answered placidly. "But Aye tank Aye like be champion of dass *Sea Girl*. Aye got to lick you to be it, ain't it? Sure!"

Bill and Mushy was looking at me expectantly, but I was all at sea. After you've worked six months teaching a man your trade and built him up and made something outa him, you don't want to undo it all by rocking him to sleep.

"Why're you so set on bein' champ of the *Sea Girl*?" I asked irritably.

"Well," said the overgrown heathen, "Aye tank Aye lick you and then Aye can lick Olaf, and Segrida she like me. But Aye lick Olaf, and Segrida she give me dass gate. Dass bane your fault, for teach me to lick Olaf. But Aye ain't blame you. Aye like you fine, Steve, but now Aye tank Aye be champ of dass *Sea Girl*. Aye ain't got no girl no more, so Aye got to be something. Aye lick Olaf so Aye can lick you. Aye lick you and be champ and we be good friends, ya?"

"But I don't want to fight you, you big mutton-head!" I snarled in wrathful perplexity.

"Then Aye fight you on the street or the fo'c's'le or wherever Aye meet you," he said cheerfully.

At that my small stock of temper was plumb exhausted. With a bloodthirsty howl I ripped off my shirt. "Bring on the gloves, you square-headed ape!" I roared. "If I got to batter some sense into your solid ivory skull I might as well start now!"

A few minutes later I was clad in a dingy pair of trunks which Knut dragged out of somewhere for me, and we was donning the gloves a set lighter than the standard weight, which Knut hadst probably got as a present from John L. Sullivan or somebody.

We agreed on Bill as referee, but Sven being afraid of Mike, made me agree to have Mushy hold him, though I assured him Mike wouldn't interfere in a glove fight. They was no ropes around the canvas space, no stools nor gong. However, as it happened, they wasn't needed.

As we advanced toward each other I realized more'n ever how much of a man Sven was. Six feet four – 245 pounds – all bone and muscle. He towered over me like a giant, and I musta looked kinda small beside him, though I'm six feet tall and weigh 190 pounds. Under his white skin the great muscles rolled and billowed like flexible iron, and his chest looked more like a gorilla's than a human's.

But size ain't everything. Old Fitz used to flatten men which outweighed him over a hundred pounds, and lookit what Dempsey and Sharkey used to do to such like giants – and I'm as tough as Sharkey and can hit as hard as either of them other palookas, even if I ain't quite as accurate or scientific.

No, I hadst no worries about Sven, but I'd got over being mad at him and I seen his point of view. Sven wasn't sore at me, nor nothing. He just wanted to be champ of his ship, which was a natural wish. Since his girl give him the air, he wanted to more'n ever to kind of soothe his wounded vanity, as they say.

No, I cooled down and kind of sympathized with Sven's point of view which is a bad state of mind to enter into any kind of a scrap. They ain't nothing more helpful than a good righteous anger and a feeling like the other bird is a complete rascal and absolutely in the wrong.

As we come together, Sven said: "No rounds, Steve; we fight to dass finish, yes?"

"All right," I said with very little enthusiasm. "But, Sven, for the last time – have you just got to fight me?"

His reply was a left which he shot for my jaw so sudden like I just barely managed to slip it. I come back with a slashing right which he blocked, clumsy but effective. He then dropped into the deep crouch I'd taught him and rammed his left for my wind. But I knowed the counter to that, having seen pictures of the second Fitzsimmons-Jeffries riot. I stepped around and inside his ramming left, slapping a left uppercut inside the crook of his right arm, to his jaw, cracking his teeth together and rocking his head up and back for a right hook which I opened a gash on his temple with.

He give a deafening roar and immediately abandoned his defensive posture and come for me like a mad bull. I figured, here's where I end this scrap quick, like always. But in half a second I seen my error.

Sven didn't rush wide open, flailing wild, like he used to. He come plunging in, bunched in a compact bulk of iron muscles and fighting fury; he hooked and hit straight, and he kept his chin clamped down on his hairy chest and his shoulders hunched to guard it, half crouching to protect his body. Even the rudiments of boxing science he'd learned, coupled with his enormous size and strength, made him plenty formidable to any man.

I don't know how to tin-can and backpedal. If Jeffries hisself was to rush me, all I'd know to do wouldst be to stand up to him and trade punches until I went out cold. I met Sven with a right smash that was high, but stopped him in his tracks. Blood spattered and he swayed like a big tree about to crash, but before I could follow up, he plunged in again, hitting with both hands. He hit and he hit – and – he – hit!

He throwed both hands as fast as he could drive one after the other and every blow had all his weight behind it. Outa the depths of his fighting fit he'd conjured up amazing speed. It happens sometime. I never seen a man his size hit that fast before or since. It was just like being in a rain of sledgehammers that never quit coming. All I couldst see was his glaring eyes, his big shoulders hunched and rocking as he hit – and a perfect whirlwind of big glove-covered clubs.

He wasn't timing or aiming much – hitting too fast for that. But even when he landed glancing-like, he shook me, with that advantage of fifty-five pounds. And he landed solid too often to suit me.

Try as I would, I couldn't get in a solid smash under the heart, or on the jaw. He kept his head down, and my vicious uppercuts merely glanced off his face, too high to do much good. Black and blue bruises showed on his ribs and shoulders, but his awkward half crouch kept his vitals protected.

It's mighty hard to hammer a giant like him out of position – especially when you're trying to keep him from tearing off your head at the same time. I bored in close, letting Sven's blows go around my neck while I blasted away with both hands. No – they was little science used on either side. It was mostly a wild exchange of sledgehammer wallops.

In one of our rare clinches, Sven lifted me off my feet and throwed me the full width of the room where I hit the wall – wham! like I was going on through. This made Bill, as referee, very mad at Sven and he cussed him and kicked him heartily in the pants, but the big cheese never paid no attention.

I was landing the most blows and they rocked Sven from stem to stern, but they wasn't vital ones. Already his face was beef. One eye was closed, his lips were pulped and his nose was bleeding; his left side was raw, but, if anything, he seemed to be getting stronger. My training hadst toughened him a lot more than I'd realized!

Blim! A glancing slam on my jaw made me see plenty stars. Wham! His right met the side of my head and I shot back half-way across the room to crash into the wall. Long ago we'd got off the canvas; we was fighting all over the joint.

Sven was after me like a mad bull, and I braced myself and stopped him in his tracks with a left hook that ripped his ear loose and made his knees sag for a second. But the Swede had worked hisself into one of them berserk rages where you got to mighty near kill a man to stop him. His right, curving up from his hip, banged solid on my temple and I thought for a second my skull was caved in like an egg-shell.

Blood gushed down my neck when he drawed his glove back, and, desperate, I hooked my right to his body with everything I had behind it. I reckon that was when I cracked his rib, because I heard something snap and he kind of grunted.

Both of us was terrible looking by this time and kind of in a dream like, I saw Knut wringing his hands and begging Bill and Mushy and Fritz to stop it – I reckon he'd never saw a real glove battle before and it was so different from lifting weights! Naturally, they, who was clean goggle-eyed and yelling theirselves deaf and dumb, paid no attention to him at all, and so in a second Knut turned and run out into the street like he was going for the cops.

But I paid no heed. For the first time in many a day I was fighting with my back to the wall against one of my own crew. Sven was inhuman – it was like fighting a bull or an elephant. He was landing solid now, and even if them blows was clumsy, with 245 pounds of crazy Swede behind them, they was like the blows of a pile-driver.

He knowed only one kind of footwork – going forward. And he kept plunging and hitting, plunging and hitting till the world was blind and red. I shook my head and the blood flew like spray. The sheer weight of his plunges hurtled me back in spite of myself.

Once more I tried to rock his head up for a solid shot to the jaw. My left uppercut split his lips and rattled his teeth, but his bowed neck was like iron. In desperation I banged him square on the side of the head where his skull was hardest.

Blood spurted like I'd hit him with a hand spike, and he swayed drunkenly – then he dropped into a deep crouch and shot his left to my midriff with all his weight behind it. Judas! It was so unexpected I couldn't get away from it. I was standing nearly upright and that huge fist sank into my solar-plexus till I felt it banged against my spine. I dropped like a sack and writhed on the floor like a snake with a busted back, fighting for air. Bill said later I was purple in the face.

Like I was looking through a thick fog, I seen Bill, dazed and white-faced, counting over me. I dunno how I got up again. I was sick – I thought I was dying. But Sven was standing right over me, and looking up at him, a lot of thoughts surged through my numbed and battered brain in a kind of flash.

The new champion of the *Sea Girl*, I thought, after all these years I've held my title against all comers. After all the men I've fought and licked to hold the only title I got. All the cruel punishment I've took, all the blood I've spilt, now I lose my only title to this square-head that I've licked half a dozen times. Like a dream it all come back – the dim-lighted, smelly, dingy forecastle, the yelling, cursing seamen – and me in the middle of it all – the bully of the forecastle. And now – never no more to defend my title – never to hear folks along the docks say: "That's Steve Costigan, champ of the toughest ship afloat!"

With a kind of gasping sob, I grabbed Sven's legs and climbed up, up, till I was on my feet, leaning against him chest to chest, till he shook me off and smashed me down like he was driving a nail into the floor. I reeled up just as Bill began to count, and this time I ducked Sven's swing and clinched him with a grip even he couldn't break.

And as I held on and drew in air in great racking gasps, I looked over his straining shoulder and seen Knut come rushing in through the door with a white-faced girl behind him – Segrida. But I was too near out to even realize that Sven's ex-girl was there.

Sven pushed me away finally and dropped me once more with a punch that was more a push than anything else. This time I took the count of nine, resting, as my incredible vitality, the wonder of manys the sporting scribe, began to assert itself.

I rose suddenly and beat Sven to the punch with a wild right that smashed his nose. Like most sluggers, I never lose my punch, no matter how badly beaten I am. I'm dangerous right to the last second, as better men than Sven Larson has found out.

Sven wasn't going so strong hisself as he had been. He moved stiff and mechanical and swung his arms awkwardly, like they was dead. He walked in stolidly and smashed a club-like right to my face. Blood spattered and I went back on my heels, but surged in and ripped my right under the heart, landing square there for the first time.

Another right smashed full on Sven's already battered mouth, and, spitting out the fragments of a tooth, he crashed a flailing left to my body, which I distinctly felt bend my ribs to the breaking point.

I ripped a left to his temple, and he flattened my ear with a swinging right, rocking drunkenly like a tall ship in the Trades with all sails set. Another right glanced offa the top of my head as I ducked and for the first time I seen his unguarded jaw as he loomed above me where I crouched.

I straightened, crashing my right from the hip, with every ounce of my weight behind it, and all the drive they was in leg, waist, shoulder, and arm. I landed solid on the button with a jolt that burst my glove and numbed my whole arm – I heard a scream – I seen Sven's eyes go blank – I seen him sway like a falling mast – I seen him pitching forward – *bang!* The lights went out.

I was propped up in a chair and Bill was sloshing me with water. I looked around at the dingy gym; then I remember. A queer, sad, cold feeling come over me.

I felt old and worn out. After all, I wasn't a boy no more. All the hard, bitter years of fighting the sea and fighting men come over me and settled like a cold cloud on my shoulders. All the life kind of went out of me.

"Believe me, Steve," said Bill, slapping at me with his towel, "that fight sure set Sven solid with Segrida. Right now she's weepin' over his busted nose and black eye and the like, and huggin' him and kissin' him and vowin' everlastin' love. I knowed I was right all the time. Knut run after her to get her to stop the bout. Gosh, the Marines couldn'ta stopped it! Mushy clean chawed Mike's collar in two, he was that excited! Say, would you uh thought a slob like Sven coulda made the fightin' man he has in six months?"

"Yeah," I said listlessly, scratching Mike's ear as he licked my hand. "Well, he had it comin'. He worked hard enough. And he was lucky havin' somebody to teach him. All I know, I learned for myself in cruel hard battles. But, Bill, I can't stay on the *Sea Girl* now; I just can't get used to bein' just a contender on a ship where I was champion."

Bill dropped his towel and glared at me: "What you talkin' about?"

"Why, Sven's the new champ of the *Sea Girl*, lickin' me this way. Strange, what a come-back he made just as I thought he was goin' down."

"You're clean crazy!" snorted Bill. "By golly, a rap on the dome has a funny effect on some skates. Sven's just now comin' to. Mushy and Fritz and Knut has been sloshin' him with water for ten minutes. You knocked him stiff as a wedge with that last right hook."

I come erect with a bound! "What? Then I licked Sven? I'm still champion? But if he didn't knock me out, who did?"

Bill grinned. "Don't you know no man can hit you hard enough with his fist to knock you out? Swedish girls is impulsive. Segrida done that – with a iron dumbbell!"

Waterfront Law

The first thing that happened in Cape Town, my white bulldog Mike bit a policeman and I had to come across with a fine of ten dollars, to pay for the cop's britches. That left me busted, not an hour after the *Sea Girl* docked.

The next thing who should I come on to but Shifty Kerren, manager of Kid Delrano, and the crookedest leather-pilot which ever swiped the gate receipts. I favored this worthy with a hearty scowl, but he had the everlasting nerve to smile welcomingly and hold out the glad hand.

"Well, well! If it ain't Steve Costigan! Howdy, Steve!" said the infamous hypocrite. "Glad to see you. Boy, you're lookin' fine! Got good old Mike with you, I see. Nice dawg!"

He leaned over to pat him.

"Grrrrr!" said good old Mike, fixing for to chaw his hand. I pushed Mike away with my foot and said to Shifty, I said: "A big nerve you got, tryin' to fraternize with me, after the way you squawked and whooped the last time I seen you, and called me a dub and all."

"Now, now, Steve!" said Shifty. "Don't be foolish and go holdin' no grudge. It's all in the way of business, you know. I allus did like you, Steve."

"Gaaahh!" I responded ungraciously. I didn't have no wish to hobnob none with him, though I figgered I was safe enough, being as I was broke anyway.

I've fought that palooka of his twice. The first time he out-pointed me in a ten-round bout in Seattle, but didn't hurt me none, him being a classy boxer but kinda shy on the punch.

Next time we met in a Frisco ring, scheduled for fifteen frames. Kid Delrano give me a proper shellacking for ten rounds, then punched hisself out in a vain attempt to stop me, and blowed up. I had him on the canvas in the eleventh and again in the twelfth and with the fourteenth a minute to go, I rammed a right to the wrist in his solar plexus that put him down again. He had sense enough left to grab his groin and writhe around.

And Shifty jumped up and down and yelled: "Foul!" so loud the referee got scared and rattled and disqualified me. I swear it wasn't no foul. I landed solid above the belt line. But I officially lost the decision and it kinda rankled.

So now I glowered at Shifty and said: "What you want of me?"

"Steve," said Shifty, patting his hand on my shoulder in the old comradely way his kind has when they figger on putting the skids under you. "I know you got a heart of gold! You wouldn't leave no feller countryman in the toils, would you? Naw! Of course you wouldn't! Not good old Steve. Well, listen, me and the Kid is in a jam. We're broke – and the Kid's in jail.

"We got a raw deal when we come here. These Britishers went and disqualified the Kid for merely bitin' one of their ham and eggers. The Kid didn't mean nothin' by it. He's just kinda excitable thataway."

"Yeah, I know," I growled. "I got a scar on my neck now from that rat's fangs. He got excitable with me, too."

"Well," said Shifty hurriedly, "they won't let us fight here now, and we figgered into movin' up country into Johannesburg. Young Hilan is tourin' South Africa and we can get a fight with him there. His manager – er, I mean a promoter there – sent us tickets, but the Kid's in jail. They won't let him out unless we pay a fine of six pounds. That's thirty dollars, you know. And we're broke.

"Steve," went on Shifty, waxing eloquent, "I appeals to your national pride! Here's the Kid, a American like yourself, pent up in durance vile, and for no more reason than for just takin' up for his country – "

"Huh!" I perked up my ears. "How's that?"

"Well, he blows into a pub where three British sailors makes slanderous remarks about American ships and seamen. Well, you know the Kid – just a big, free-hearted, impulsive boy, and terrible proud of his country, like a man should be. He ain't no sailor, of course, but them remarks was a insult to his countrymen and he wades in. He gives them limeys a proper drubbin' but here comes a host of cops which hauls him before the local magistrate which hands him a fine we can't pay.

"Think, Steve!" orated Shifty. "There's the Kid, with thousands of admirin' fans back in the States waitin' and watchin' for his triumphal return to the land of the free and the home of the brave. And here's him, wastin' his young manhood in a stone dungeon, bein' fed on bread and water and maybe beat up by the jailers, merely for standin' up for his own flag and nation. For defendin' the honor of American sailors, mind you, of which you is one. I'm askin' you, Steve, be you goin' to stand by and let a feller countryman languish in the 'thrallin' chains of British tyranny?"

"Not by a long ways!" said I, all my patriotism roused and roaring. "Let bygones be bygones!" I said.

It's a kind of unwritten law among sailors ashore that they should stand by their own kind. A kind of waterfront law, I might say.

"I ain't fought limeys all over the world to let an American be given the works by 'em now," I said. "I ain't got a cent, Shifty, but I'm goin' to get some dough.

"Meet me at the American Seamen's Bar in three hours. I'll have the dough for the Kid's fine or I'll know the reason why.

"You understand, I ain't doin' this altogether for the Kid. I still intends to punch his block off some day. But he's an American and so am I, and I reckon I ain't so small that I'll let personal grudges stand in the way of helpin' a countryman in a foreign land."

"Spoken like a man, Steve!" applauded Shifty, and me and Mike hustled away.

A short, fast walk brung us to a building on the waterfront which had a sign saying: "The South African Sports Arena." This was all lit up and yells was coming forth by which I knowed fights was going on inside.

The ticket shark told me the main bout had just begun. I told him to send me the promoter, "Bulawayo" Hurley, which I'd fought for of yore, and he told me that Bulawayo was in his office, which was a small room next to the ticket booth. So I went in and seen Bulawayo talking to a tall, lean gent the sight of which made my hair bristle.

"Hey, Bulawayo," said I, ignoring the other mutt and coming directly to the point. "I want a fight. I want to fight tonight – right now. Have you got anybody you'll throw in with me, or if not willya let me get up in your ring and challenge the house for a purse to be made up by the crowd?"

"By a strange coincidence," said Bulawayo, pulling his big mustache, "here's Bucko Brent askin' me for the same blightin' thing."

Me and Bucko gazed at each other with hearty disapproval. I'd had deal-

51

ings with this thug before. In fact, I built a good part of my reputation as a bucko-breaker on his lanky frame. A bucko, as you likely know, is a hard case mate, who punches his crew around. Brent was all that and more. Ashore he was a prize-fighter, same as me.

Quite a few years ago I was fool enough to ship as A.B. on the *Elinor*, which he was mate of then. He's an Australian and the *Elinor* was an Australian ship. Australian ships is usually good crafts to sign up with, but this here *Elinor* was a exception. Her cap'n was a relic of the old hellship days, and her mates was natural born bullies. Brent especially, as his nickname of "Bucko" shows. But I was broke and wanted to get to Makassar to meet the *Sea Girl* there, so I shipped aboard the *Elinor* at Bristol.

Brent started ragging me before we weighed anchor.

Well, I stood his hazing for a few days and then I got plenty and we went together. We fought the biggest part of one watch, all over the ship from the mizzen cross trees to the bowsprit. Yet it wasn't what I wouldst call a square test of manhood because marlin spikes and belaying pins was used free and generous on both sides and the entire tactics smacked of rough house.

In fact, I finally won the fight by throwing him bodily offa the poop. He hit his head on the after deck and wasn't much good the rest of the cruise, what with a broken arm, three cracked ribs and a busted nose. And the cap'n wouldn't even order me to scrape the anchor chain less'n he had a gun in each hand, though I wasn't figgering on socking the old rum-soaked antique.

Well, in Bulawayo's office me and Bucko now set and glared at each other, and what we was thinking probably wasn't printable.

"Tell you what, boys," said Bulawayo, "I'll let you fight ten rounds as soon as the main event's over with. I'll put up five pounds and the winner gets it all."

"Good enough for me," growled Bucko.

"Make it six pounds and it's a go," said I.

"Done!" said Bulawayo, who realized what a break he was getting, having me fight for him for thirty dollars.

Bucko give me a nasty grin.

"At last, you blasted Yank," said he, "I got you where I want you. They'll be no poop deck for me to slip and fall off this time. And you can't hit me with no hand spike."

"A fine bird you are, talkin' about hand spikes," I snarled, "after tryin' to tear off a section of the mainrail to sock me with."

"Belay!" hastily interrupted Bulawayo. "Preserve your ire for the ring."

"Is they any *Sea Girl* men out front?" I asked. "I want a handler to see that some of this thug's henchmen don't dope my water bottle."

"Strangely enough, Steve," said Bulawayo, "I ain't seen a *Sea Girl* bloke tonight. But I'll get a handler for you."

Well, the main event went the limit. It seemed like it never would get over with and I cussed to myself at the idea of a couple of dubs like them was, delaying the performance of a man like me. At last, however, the referee called it a draw and kicked them both outa the ring.

Bulawayo hopped through the ropes and stopped the folks who'd started to go, by telling them he was offering a free and added attraction – Sailor Costigan and Bucko Brent in a impromptu grudge bout. This was good business for Bulawayo. It tickled the crowd who'd seen both of us fight, though not ag'in each other, of course. They cheered Bulawayo to the echo and settled back with whoops of delight.

Bulawayo was right – not a *Sea Girl* man in the house. All drunk or in jail or something, I suppose. They was quite a number of thugs there from the *Nagpur* – Brent's present ship – and they all rose as one and gimme the razz. Sailors is funny. I know that Brent hazed the liver outa them, yet they was rooting for him like he was their brother or something.

I made no reply to their jeers, maintaining a dignified and aloof silence only except to tell them that I was going to tear their pet mate apart and strew the fragments to the four winds, and also to warn them not to try no monkeyshines behind my back, otherwise I wouldst let Mike chaw their legs off. They greeted my brief observations with loud, raucous bellerings, but looked at Mike with considerable awe.

The referee was an Englishman whose name I forget, but he hadn't been outa the old country very long, and had evidently got his experience in the polite athletic clubs of London. He says: "Now understand this, you blighters, w'en H'I says break, H'I wants no bally nonsense. Remember as long as H'I'm in 'ere this is a blinkin' gentleman's gyme."

But he got in the ring with us, American style.

Bucko is one of these long, rangy, lean fellers, kinda pale and raw-boned. He's got a thin, hatchet face and mean light eyes. He's a bad actor, and that's no lie. I'm six feet and weigh 190.

He's a inch and three quarters taller'n me, and he weighed then, maybe a pound less'n me.

Bucko come out stabbing with his left, but I was watching his right. I knowed he packed his TNT there and he was pretty classy with it.

In about ten seconds he nailed me with that right and I seen stars. I went back on my heels and he was on top of me in a second, hammering hard with both hands, wild for a knockout. He battered me back across the ring. I wasn't really hurt, though he thought I was. Friends of his which had seen me perform before was yelling for him to be careful, but he paid no heed.

With my back against the ropes I failed to block his right to the body and he rocked my head back with a hard left hook.

"You're not so tough, you lousy mick – " he sneered shooting for my jaw. Wham! I ripped a slungshot right uppercut up inside his left and tagged him flush on the button. It lifted him clean offa his feet and dropped him on the seat of his trunks, where he set looking up at the referee with a goofy and glassy-eyed stare, whilst his friends jumped up and down and cussed and howled: "We told you to be careful with that gorilla, you conceited jassack!"

But Bucko was tough. He kind of assembled hisself and was up at the count of "Nine," groggy but full of fight and plenty mad. I come in wide open to finish him, and run square into that deadly right. I thought for an instant the top of my head was tore off, but rallied and shook Bucko from stem to stern with a left hook under the heart. He tin-canned in a hurry, covering his retreat with his sharp-shooting left. The gong found me vainly follering him around the ring.

The next round started with the fans which was betting on Bucko urging him to keep away from me and box me. Them that had put money on me was yelling for him to take a chance and mix it with me.

But he was plenty cagey. He kept his right bent across his midriff, his chin tucked behind his shoulder and his left out to fend me off. He landed repeatedly with that left and brung a trickle of blood from my lips, but I paid no attention. The left ain't made that can keep me off forever. Toward the end of the round he suddenly let go with that right again, and I took it square in the face to get in a right to his ribs.

Blood splattered when his right landed. The crowd leaped up, yelling, not noticing the short-armed smash I ripped in under his heart. But he noticed it, you bet, and broke ground in a hurry, gasping, much to the astonishment of the crowd, which yelled for him to go in and finish the blawsted Yankee.

Crowds don't see much of what's going on in the ring before their very eyes, after all. They see the wild swings and the haymakers but they miss most of the real punishing blows – the short, quick smashes landed in close.

Well, I went right after Brent, concentrating on his body. He was too kind of long and rangy to take much there. I hunched my shoulders, sunk my head on my hairy chest and bulled in, letting him pound my ears and the top of my head, while I slugged away with both hands for his heart and belly.

A left hook square under the liver made him gasp and sway like a mast in a high wind, but he desperately ripped in a right uppercut that caught me on the chin and kinda dizzied me for an instant. The gong found us fighting out of a clinch along the ropes.

My handler was highly enthusiastic, having bet a pound on me to win by a knockout. He nearly flattened a innocent ringsider showing me how to put over what he called "The Fitzsimmons Smoker." I never heered of the punch.

Well, Bucko was good and mad and musta decided he couldn't keep me away anyhow, so he come out of his corner like a bounding kangaroo, and swarmed all over me before I realized he'd changed his tactics. In a wild mix-up a fast, clever boxer can make a slugger look bad at his own game for a few seconds, being as the cleverer man can land quicker and oftener, but the catch is, he can't keep up the pace. And the smashes the slugger lands are the ones which really counts.

The crowd went clean crazy when Bucko tore into me, ripping both hands to head and body as fast as he couldst heave one after the other. It looked like I was clean swamped, but them that knowed me tripled their bets.

Brent wasn't hurting me none – cutting me up a little, but he was hitting too fast to be putting much weight behind his smacks.

Purty soon I drove a glove through the flurry of his punches. His grunt was plainly heered all over the house. He shot both hands to my head and I come back with a looping left to the body which sunk in nearly up to the wrist.

It was kinda like a bull fighting a tiger, I reckon. He swarmed all over me, hitting fast as a cat claws, whilst I kept my head down and gored him in the belly occasionally. Them body punches was rapidly taking the steam outa him, together with the pace he was setting for hisself. His punches was getting more like slaps and when I seen his knees suddenly tremble, I shifted and crashed my right to his jaw with everything I had behind it. It was a bit high or he'd have been out till yet.

Anyway, he done a nose dive and hadn't scarcely quivered at "Nine," when the gong sounded. Most of the crowd was howling lunatics. It looked to them like a chance blow, swung by a desperate, losing man, hadst dropped Bucko just when he was winning in a walk.

But the old timers knowed better. I couldst see 'em lean back and wink at each other and nod like they was saying: "See that? What did we tell you, huh?"

Bucko's merry men worked over him and brought him up in time for the fourth round. In fact, they done a lot of work over him. They clustered around him till you couldn't see what they was doing.

Well, he come out fairly fresh. He had good recuperating powers. He come out cautious, with his left hand stuck out. I noticed that they'd evidently spilt a lot of water on his glove; it was wet.

I glided in fast and he pawed at my face with that left. I didn't pay no attention to it. Then when it was a inch from my eyes I smelt a peculiar, pungent kind of smell! I ducked wildly, but not quick enough. The next instant my eyes felt like somebody'd throwed fire into 'em. Turpentine! His left glove was soaked with it!

I'd caught at his wrist when I ducked. And now with a roar of rage, whilst I could still see a little, I grabbed his elbow with the other hand and, ignoring the smash he gimme on the ear with his right, I bent his arm back and rubbed his own glove in his own face.

He give a most ear-splitting shriek. The crowd bellered with bewilderment and astonishment and the referee rushed in to find out what was happening.

"I say!" he squawked, grabbing hold of us as we was all tangled up by then. "Wot's going on 'ere? I say, it's disgryceful – ow!"

By some mischance or other, Bucko, thinking it was me, or swinging blind, hit the referee right smack between the eyes with that turpentine soaked glove.

Losing touch with my enemy, I got scared that he'd creep up on me and sock me from behind. I was clean blind by now and I didn't know whether he was or not. So I put my head down and started swinging wild and reckless with both hands, on a chance I'd connect.

Meanwhile, as I heered afterward, Bucko, being as blind as I was, was doing the same identical thing. And the referee was going around the ring like a racehorse, yelling for the cops, the Army, the navy or what have you!

The crowd was clean off its nut, having no idee as to what it all meant.

"That blawsted blighter Brent!" howled the cavorting referee, in response to the inquiring screams of the maniacal crowd. "'E threw vitriol in me blawsted h'eyes!"

"Cheer up, cull!" bawled some thug. "Both of 'em's blind, too!"

"'Ow can H'I h'officiate in this condition," howled the referee, jumping up and down. "Wot's tyking plyce in the bally ring?"

"Bucko's just flattened one of his handlers which was climbin' into the ring, with a blind swing!" the crowd whooped hilariously. "The Sailor's gone into a clinch with a ring post!"

Hearing this, I released what I thought was Brent, with some annoyance. Some object bumping into me at this instant, I took it to be Bucko and knocked it head over heels. The delirious howls of the multitude informed me of my mistake. Maddened, I plunged forward, swinging, and felt my left hook around a human neck. As the referee was on the canvas this must be Bucko, I thought, dragging him toward me, and he proved it by sinking a glove to the wrist in my belly.

I ignored this discourteous gesture, and maintaining my grip on his neck, I hooked over a right with all I had. Having hold of his neck, I knowed about where his jaw oughta be, and I figgered right. I knocked Bucko clean outa my grasp and from the noise he made hitting the canvas I knowed that in the ordinary course of events, he was through for the night.

I groped into a corner and clawed some of the turpentine outa my eyes. The referee had staggered up and was yelling: "'Ow in the blinkin' 'Ades can a man referee in such a mad-'ouse? Wot's 'ere, wot's 'ere?"

"Bucko's down!" the crowd screamed. "Count him out!"

"W'ere is 'e?" bawled the referee, blundering around the ring.

"Three p'ints off yer port bow!" they yelled and he tacked and fell over the vaguely writhing figger of Bucko. He scrambled up with a howl of triumph and begun to count with the most vindictive voice I ever heered. With each count he'd kick Bucko in the ribs.

" – H'eight! Nine! Ten! H'and you're h'out, you blawsted, blinkin', blightin', bally h'assassinatin' pirate!" whooped the referee, with one last tremendjous kick.

I climb over the ropes and my handler showed me which way was my dressing room. Ever have turpentine rubbed in your eyes? Jerusha! I don't know nothing more painful. You can easy go blind for good.

But after my handler hadst washed my eyes out good, I was all right. Collecting my earnings from Bulawayo, I set sail for the American Seamen's Bar, where I was to meet Shifty Kerren and give him the money to pay Delrano's fine with.

It was quite a bit past the time I'd set to meet Shifty, and he wasn't nowhere to be seen. I asked the barkeep if he'd been there and the barkeep, who knowed Shifty, said he'd waited about half an hour and then hoisted anchor. I ast the barkeep if he knowed where he lived and he said he did and told me. So I ast him would he keep Mike till I got back and he said he would. Mike despises Delrano so utterly I was afraid I couldn't keep him away from the Kid's throat, if we saw him, and I figgered on going down to the jail with Shifty.

Well, I went to the place the bartender told me and went upstairs to the room the landlady said Shifty had, and started to knock when I heard men talking inside. Sounded like the Kid's voice, but I couldn't tell what he was saying so I knocked and somebody said: "Come in."

I opened the door. Three men was sitting there playing pinochle. They was Shifty, Bill Slane, the Kid's sparring partner, and the Kid hisself.

"Howdy, Steve," said Shifty with a smirk, kinda furtive-eyed, "whatcha doin' away up here?"

"Why," said I, kinda took aback, "I brung the dough for the Kid's fine, but I see he don't need it, bein' as he's out."

Delrano hadst been craning his neck to see if Mike was with me, and now he says, with a nasty sneer: "What's the matter with your face, Costigan? Some street kid poke you on the nose?"

"If you wanta know," I growled, "I got these marks on your account. Shifty told me you was in stir, and I was broke, so I fought down at The South African to get the fine money."

At that the Kid and Slane bust out into loud and jeering laughter – not the kind you like to hear. Shifty joined in, kinda nervous-like.

"Whatcha laughin' at?" I snarled. "Think I'm lyin'?"

"Naw, you ain't lyin'," mocked the Kid. "You ain't got sense enough to. You're just the kind of dub that would do somethin' like that."

"You see, Steve," said Shifty, "the Kid – "

"Aw, shut up, Shifty!" snapped Delrano. "Let the big sap know he's been took for a ride. I'm goin' to tell him what a sucker he's been. He ain't got his blasted bulldog with him. He can't do nothing to the three of us."

Delrano got up and stuck his sneering, pasty white face up close to mine.

"Of all the dumb, soft, boneheaded boobs I ever knew," said he, and his tone cut like a whip lash, "you're the limit. Get this, Costigan, I ain't broke and I ain't been in jail! You want to know why Shifty spilt you that line? Because I bet him ten dollars that much as you hate me and him, we could hand you a hard-luck tale and gyp you outa your last cent.

"Well, it worked! And to think that you been fightin' for the dough to give me! Ha-ha-ha-ha-ha! You big chump! You're a natural born sucker! You fall for anything anybody tells you. You'll never get nowheres. Look at me – I wouldn't give a blind man a penny if he was starvin' and my brother besides. But you – oh, what a sap!"

"If Shifty hadn't been so anxious to win that ten bucks that he wouldn't wait down at the bar, we'd had your dough, too. But this is good enough. I'm plenty satisfied just to know how hard you fell for our graft, and to see how you got beat up gettin' money to pay *my* fine! Ha-ha-ha!"

By this time I was seeing them through a red mist. My huge fists was clenched till the knuckles was white, and when I spoke it didn't hardly sound like my voice at all, it was so strangled with rage.

"They's rats in every country," I ground out. "If you'd of picked my pockets or slugged me for my dough, I coulda understood it. If you'd worked a cold deck or crooked dice on me, I wouldn'ta kicked. But you appealed to my better nature, 'stead of my worst.

"You brung up a plea of patriotism and natural fellership which no decent man woulda refused. You appealed to my natural pride of blood and nationality. It wasn't for you I done it – it wasn't for you I spilt my blood and risked my eyesight. It was for the principles and ideals you've mocked and tromped into the muck – the honor of our country and the fellership of Americans the world over.

"You dirty swine! You ain't fit to be called Americans. Thank gosh, for every one like you, they's ten thousand decent men like me. And if it's bein' a sucker to help out a countryman when he's in a jam in a foreign land, then I thanks the Lord I'm a sucker. But I ain't all softness and mush – feel this here for a change!"

And I closed the Kid's eye with a smashing left-hander. He give a howl of surprise and rage and come back with a left to the jaw. But he didn't have a chance. He'd licked me in the ring, but he couldn't lick me bare-handed, in a small room where he couldn't keep away from my hooks, not even with two men to help him. I was blind mad and I just kind of gored and tossed him like a charging bull.

If he hit at all after that first punch I don't remember it. I know I crashed him clean across the room with a regular whirlwind of smashes, and left him sprawled out in the ruins of three or four chairs with both eyes punched shut and his arm broke. I then turned on his cohorts and hit Bill Slane on the jaw, knocking him stiff as a wedge. Shifty broke for the door, but I pounded on him and spilled him on his neck in a corner with a open-handed slap.

I then stalked forth in silent majesty and gained the street. As I went I was filled with bitterness. Of all the dirty, contemptible tricks I ever heered of, that took the cake. And I got to thinking maybe they was right when they said I was a sucker. Looking back, it seemed to me like I'd fell for every slick trick under the sun. I got mad. I got mighty mad.

I shook my fist at the world in general, much to the astonishment and apprehension of the innocent bypassers.

"From now on," I raged, "I'm harder'n the plate of a battleship! I ain't goin' to fall for *nothin*'! Nobody's goin' to get a blasted cent outa me, not for no reason what-the-some-ever – "

At that moment I heered a commotion going on nearby. I looked. Spite of the fact that it was late, a pretty good-sized crowd hadst gathered in front of a kinda third-class boarding-house. A mighty purty blonde-headed girl was standing there, tears running down her cheeks as she pleaded with a tough looking old sister who stood with her hands on her hips, grim and stern.

"Oh, please don't turn me out!" wailed the girl. "I have no place to go! No job – oh, please. Please!"

I can't stand to hear a hurt animal cry out or a woman beg. I shouldered through the crowd and said: "What's goin' on here?"

"This hussy owes me ten pounds," snarled the woman. "I got to have the money or her room. I'm turnin' her out."

"Where's her baggage?" I asked.

"I'm keepin' it for the rent she owes," she snapped. "Any of your business?"

The girl kind of slumped down in the street. I thought if she's turned out on the street tonight they'll be hauling another carcass outa the bay tomorrer. I said to the landlady. "Take six pounds and call it even."

"Ain't you got no more?" said she.

"Naw, I ain't," I said truthfully.

"All right, it's a go," she snarled, and grabbed the dough like a seagull grabs a fish.

"All right," she said very harshly to the girl, "you can stay another week. Maybe you'll find a job by that time – or some other sap of a Yank sailor will come along and pay your board."

She went into the house and the crowd give a kind of cheer which inflated my chest about half a foot. Then the girl come up close to me and said shyly, "Thank you. I-I-I can't begin to tell you how much I appreciate what you've done for me."

Then all to a sudden she throwed her arms around my neck and kissed me and then run up the steps into the boarding-house. The crowd cheered some more like British crowds does and I felt plenty uplifted as I swaggered down the street. Things like that, I reflected, is worthy causes. A worthy cause can have my dough any time, but I reckon I'm too blame smart to get fooled by no shysters.

I come into the American Seamen's Bar where Mike was getting anxious about me. He wagged his stump of a tail and grinned all over his big wide face and I found two American nickels in my pocket which I had. I give one of 'em to the barkeep to buy a pan of beer for Mike. And whilst he was lapping it, the barkeep, he said: "I see Boardin' house Kate is in town."

"Whatcha mean?" I ast him.

"Well," said he, combing his mustache, "Kate's worked her racket all over Australia and the West Coast of America, but this is the first time I ever seen her in South Africa. She lets some landlady of a cheap boardin'-house in on the scheme and this dame pretends to throw her out. Kate puts up a wail and somebody – usually some free-hearted sailor about like you – happens along and pays the landlady the money Kate's supposed to owe for rent so she won't kick the girl out onto the street. Then they split the dough."

"Uh-huh!" said I, grinding my teeth slightly. "Does this here Boardin'-house Kate happen to be a blonde?"

"Sure thing," said the barkeep. "And purty as hell. What did you say?"

"Nothin'," I said. "Here. Give me a schooner of beer and take this nickel, quick, before somebody comes along and gets it away from me."

Texas Fists

The *Sea Girl* hadn't been docked in Tampico more'n a few hours when I got into a argument with a big square-head off a tramp steamer, I forget what the row was about – sailing vessels versus steam, I think. Anyway, the discussion got so heated he took a swing at me. He musta weighed nearly three hundred pounds, but he was meat for me. I socked him just once and he went to sleep under the ruins of a table.

As I turned back to my beer mug in high disgust, I noticed that a gang of fellers which had just come in was gawping at me in wonder. They was cow-punchers, in from the ranges, all white men, tall, hard and rangy, with broad-brimmed hats, leather chaps, big Mexican spurs, guns, an' everything; about ten of them, altogether.

"By the gizzard uh Sam Bass," said the tallest one, "I plumb believe we've found our man, hombres. Hey, pardner, have a drink! Come on – set down at this here table. I wanta talk to you."

So we all set down and, while we was drinking some beer, the tall cow-puncher glanced admiringly at the square-head which was just coming to from the barkeep pouring water on him, and the cow-puncher said:

"Lemme introduce us: we're the hands of the Diamond J – old Bill Darnley's ranch, way back up in the hills. I'm Slim, and these is Red, Tex, Joe, Yuma, Buck, Jim, Shorty, Pete and the Kid. We're in town for a purpose, pardner, which is soon stated.

"Back up in the hills, not far from the Diamond J, is a minin' company, and them miners has got the fightin'est buckaroo in these parts. They're backin' him agin all comers, and I hates to say what he's did to such Diamond J boys as has locked horns with him. Them miners has got a ring rigged up in the hills where this gent takes on such as is wishful to mingle with him, but he ain't particular. He knocked out Joe here in that ring, but he plumb mopped up a mesquite flat with Red, which challenged him to a rough-and-tumble brawl with bare fists. He's a bear-cat, and the way them miners is puttin' on airs around us boys is somethin' fierce.

"We've found we ain't got no man on the ranch which can stand up to that grizzly, and so we come into town to find some feller which could use his fists. Us boys is more used to slingin' guns than knuckles. Well, the minute I seen you layin' down that big Swede, I says to myself, I says, "Slim, there's your man!"

"How about it, amigo? Will you mosey back up in the hills with us and flatten this big false alarm? We aim to bet heavy, and we'll make it worth yore while."

"And how far is this here ranch?" I asked.

" 'Bout a day's ride, hossback – maybe a little better'n that."

"That's out," I decided. "I can't navigate them four-legged craft. I ain't never been on a horse more'n three or four times, and I ain't figgerin' on repeatin' the experiment."

"Well," said Slim, "we'll get hold of a auteymobeel and take you out in style."

"No," I said, "I don't believe I'll take you up; I wanta rest whilst I'm in port. I've had a hard voyage; we run into nasty weather and had one squall after another. Then the Old Man picked up a substitute second mate in place of our regular mate which is in jail in Melbourne, and this new mate and me has fought clean across the Pacific, from Melbourne to Panama, where he give it up and quit the ship."

The cow-punchers all started arguing at the same time, but Slim said:

"Aw, that's all right, boys; I reckon the gent knows what he wants to do. We can find somebody else, I reckon. No hard feelin's. Have another drink."

I kinda imagined he had a mysterious gleam in his eye, and it looked like to me that when he motioned to the bartender, he made some sort of a signal; but I didn't think nothing about it. The bar-keep brought a bottle of hard licker, and Slim poured it, saying: "What did you say yore name was, amigo?"

"Steve Costigan, A.B. on the sailing vessel *Sea Girl*," I answered. "I want you fellers to hang around and meet Bill O'Brien and Mushy Hansen, my shipmates, they'll be around purty soon with my bulldog, Mike. I'm waitin' for 'em. Say, this stuff tastes funny."

"That's just high-grade tequila," said Slim. "Costigan, I shore wish you'd change yore mind about goin' out to the ranch and fightin' for us."

"No chance," said I. "I crave peace and quiet. . . . Say, what the heck . . . ?"

I hadn't took but one nip of that funny-tasting stuff, but the bar-room had begun to shimmy and dance. I shook my head to clear it and saw the cowboys, kinda misty and dim, they had their heads together, whispering, and one of 'em said, kinda low-like: "He's fixin' to pass out. Grab him!"

At that, I give a roar of rage and heaved up, upsetting the table and a couple of cow-hands.

"You low-down land-sharks," I roared. "You doped my grog!"

"Grab him, boys!" yelled Slim, and three or four nabbed me. But I throwed 'em off like chaff and caught Slim on the chin with a clout that sprawled him on the back of his neck. I socked Red on the nose and it spattered like a busted tomater, and at this instant Pete belted me over the head with a gun-barrel.

With a maddened howl, I turned on him, and he gasped, turned pale and dropped the gun for some reason or other. I sunk my left mauler to the wrist in his midriff, and about that time six or seven of them cow-punchers jumped on my neck and throwed me by sheer weight of manpower.

I got Yuma's thumb in my mouth and nearly chawed it off, but they managed to sling some ropes around me, and the drug, from which I was already weak and groggy, took full effect about this time and I passed clean out.

I musta been out a long time. I kinda dimly remember a sensation of bumping and jouncing along, like I was in a car going over a rough road, and I remember being laid on a bunk and the ropes took off, but that's all.

I was woke up by voices. I set up and cussed. I had a headache and a nasty taste in my mouth, and, feeling the back of my head, I found a bandage, which I tore off with irritation. Keel haul me! As if a scalp cut like that gun-barrel had give me needed dressing!

I was sitting on a rough bunk in a kinda small shack which was built of heavy planks. Outside I heered Slim talking:

"No, Miss Joan, I don't dast let you in too look at him. He ain't come to, I don't reckon 'cause they ain't no walls kicked outa the shack, yet; but he might come to hisself whilst you was in there, and they' no tellin' what he might do, even to you. The critter ain't human, I'm tellin' you, Miss Joan."

Well," said a feminine voice, "I think it was just horrid of you boys to kidnap a poor ignorant sailor and bring him away off up here just to whip that miner."

"Golly, Miss Joan," said Slim, kinda like he was hurt, "if you got any sympathy to spend, don't go wastin' it on that gorilla. Us boys needs yore sympathy. I winked at the bar-keep for the dope when I ordered the drinks, and, when I poured the sailor's, I put enough of it in his licker to knock out three or four men. It hit him quick, but he was wise to it and started sluggin'. With all them knockout drops in him, he near wrecked the joint! Lookit this welt on my chin – when he socked me I looked right down my own spine for a second. He busted Red's nose flat, and you oughta see it this mornin'. Pete lammed him over the bean so hard he bent the barrel of his forty-five, but all it done was make Costigan mad. Pete's still sick at his stummick from the sock the sailor give him. I tell you, Miss Joan, us boys oughta have medals pinned on us; we took our lives in our hands, though we didn't know it at the start, and, if it hadn't been for the dope, Costigan would have destroyed us all. If yore dad ever fires me, I'm goin' to git a job with a circus, capturin' tigers and things. After that ruckus, it oughta be a cinch."

At this point, I decided to let folks know I was awake and fighting mad about the way I'd been treated, so I give a roar, tore the bunk loose from the wall and throwed it through the door. I heard the girl give a kind of scream, and then Slim pulled open what was left of the door and come through. Over his shoulder I seen a slim, nice-looking girl legging it for the ranch house.

"What you mean scarin' Miss Joan?" snarled Slim, tenderly fingering a big blue welt on his jaw.

"I didn't go to scare no lady," I growled. "But in about a minute I'm goin' to scatter your remnants all over the landscape. You think you can shanghai me and get away with it? I want a big breakfast and a way back to port."

"You'll git all the grub you want if you'll agree to do like we says," said Slim; "but you ain't goin' to git a bite till you does."

"You'd keep a man from mess, as well as shanghai him, hey?" I roared.

"Well, lemme tell you, you long-sparred, leather-rigged son of a sea-cook, I'm goin' to – "

"You ain't goin' to do nothin'," snarled Slim, whipping out a long-barrelled gun and poking it in my face. "You're goin' to do just what I says or get the daylight let through you – "

Having a gun shoved in my face always did enrage me. I knocked it out of his hand with one mitt, and him flat on his back with the other, and, jumping on his prostrate frame with a blood-thirsty yell of joy, I hammered him into a pulp.

His wild yells for help brought the rest of the crew on the jump, and they all piled on me for to haul me off. Well, I was the center of a whirlwind of fists, boots, and blood-curdling howls of pain and rage for some minutes, but they was just too many of them and they was too handy with them lassoes. When they finally had me hawg-tied again, the side wall was knocked clean out of the shack, the roof was sagging down and Joe, Shorty, Jim and Buck was out cold.

Slim, looking a lee-sore wreck, limped over and glared down at me with his one good eye whilst the other boys felt theirselves for broken bones and throwed water over the fallen gladiators.

"You snortin' buffalo," Slim snarled. "How I hones to kick yore ribs in! What do you say? Do you fight or stay tied up?"

The cook-shack was near and I could smell the bacon and eggs sizzling. I hadn't eat nothing since dinner the day before and I was hungry enough to eat a raw sealion.

"Lemme loose," I growled. "I gotta have food. I'll lick this miner for you, and when I've did that, I'm going to kick down your bunkhouse and knock the block offa every man, cook, and steer on this fool ranch."

"Boy," said Slim with a grin, spitting out a loose tooth, "does you lick that miner, us boys will each give you a free swing at us. Come on – you're loose now – let's go get it."

"Let's send somebody over to the Bueno Oro Mine and tell them mavericks 'bout us gittin' a slugger," suggested Pete, trying to work back a thumb he'd knocked outa place on my jaw.

"Good idee," said Slim. "Hey, Kid, ride over and tell 'em we got a man as can make hash outa their longhorn. Guess we can stage the scrap in about five days, hey, Sailor?"

"Five days my eye," I grunted. "The *Sea Girl* sails day after tomorrow and I gotta be on her. Tell 'em to get set for the go this evenin'."

"But, gee whiz!" expostulated Slim. "Don't you want a few days to train?"

"If I was outa trainin', five days wouldn't help me none," I said. "But I'm allus in shape. Lead on the mess table. I crave nutriment."

Well, them boys didn't hold no grudge at all account of me knocking 'em around. The Kid got on a broom-tailed bronc and cruised off across the hills, and the rest of us went for the cook-shack. Joe yelled after the Kid: "Look out for Lopez the Terrible!" And they all laughed.

Well, we set down at the table and the cook brung aigs and bacon and fried steak and sour-dough bread and coffee and canned corn and milk till you never seen such a spread. I lay to and ate till they looked at me kinda bewildered.

"Hey!" said Slim, "ain't you eatin' too much for a tough scrap this evenin'?"

"What you cow-pilots know about trainin'?" I said, "I gotta keep up my strength. Gimme some more of them beans, and tell the cook to scramble me five or six more aigs and bring me in another stack of buckwheats. And say," I added as another thought struck me, "who's this here Lopez you-all was jokin' about?"

"By golly," said Tex, "I thought you cussed a lot like a Texan. 'You-all,' huh? Where was you born?"

"Galveston," I said.

"Zowie!" yelled Tex. "Put 'er there, pard; I aims for to triple my bets on you! Lopez? Oh, he's just a Mex bandit – handsome cuss, I'll admit, and purty mean. He ranges around in them hills up there and he's stole some of our stock and made a raid or so on the Bueno Oro. He's allus braggin' about how he aims for to raid the Diamond J some day and ride off with Joan – that's old Bill Dornley's gal. But heck, he ain't got the guts for that."

"Not much he ain't," said Jim. "Say, I wish old Bill was at the ranch now, 'steada him and Miz Dornley visitin' their son at Zacatlan. They'd shore enjoy the scrap this evenin'. But Miss Joan'll be there, you bet."

"Is she the dame I scared when I called you?" I asked Slim.

"Called me? Was you callin' me?" said he. "Golly, I'd of thought a bull was in the old shack, only a bull couldn't beller like that. Yeah, that was her."

"Well," said I, "tell her I didn't go for to scare her. I just naturally got a deep voice from makin' myself heard in gales at sea."

Well, we finished breakfast and Slim says: "Now what you goin' to do, Costigan? Us boys wants to help you train all we can."

"Good," I said. "Fix me up a bunk; nothing like a good long nap when trainin' for a tough scrap."

"All right," said they. "We reckons you knows what you wants; while you git yore rest, we'll ride over and lay some bets with the Bueno Oro mavericks."

So they showed me where I couldst take a nap in their bunkhouse and I was soon snoozing. Maybe I should of kinda described the ranch. They was a nice big house, Spanish style, but made of stone, not 'dobe, and down to one side was the corrals, the cook-shack, the long bunkhouse where the cowboys stayed, and a few Mexican huts. But they wasn't many Mexes working on the Diamond J. They's quite a few ranches in Old Mexico owned and run altogether by white men. All around was big rolling country, rough ranges of sagebrush, mesquite, cactus, and chaparral, sloping in the west to hills which further on became right good-sized mountains.

Well, I was woke up by the scent of victuals; the cook was fixing dinner. I sat up on the bunk and – lo, and behold – there was the frail they called Miss Joan in the door of the bunkhouse, staring at me wide-eyed like I was a sea horse or something.

I started to tell her I was sorry I scared her that morning, but when she seen I was awake she give a gasp and steered for the ranch-house under full sail.

I was bewildered and slightly irritated. I could see that she got a erroneous idee about me from listening to Slim's hokum, and, having probably never seen a sailor at close range before, she thought I was some kind of a varmint.

Well, I realized I was purty hungry, having ate nothing since breakfast, so I started for the cook-shack, and about that time the cow-punchers rode up, plumb happy and hilarious.

"Hot dawg!" yelled Slim! "Oh, baby, did the miners bite! They grabbed everything in sight and we has done sunk every cent we had, as well bettin' our hosses, saddles, bridles and shirts."

"And believe me," snarled Red, tenderly fingering what I'd made outa his nose, and kinda hitching his gun prominently, "*you better win!*"

"Don't go makin' no grandstand plays at me." I snorted. "If I can't lick a man on my own inisheyative, no gun-business can make me do it. But don't worry; I can flatten anything in these hills, includin' you and all your relatives. Let's get into that mess gallery before I clean starve."

While we ate, Slim said all was arranged; the miners had knocked off work to get ready and the scrap would take place about the middle of the evening. Then the punchers started talking and telling me things they hadst did and seen, and of all the triple-decked, full-rigged liars I ever listened to, them was the beatenest. The Kid said onst he come onto a mountain lion and didn't have no rope nor gun, so he caught rattlesnakes with his bare hands and tied 'em together and made a lariat and roped the lion and branded it, and he said how they was a whole breed of mountain lions in the hills with the Diamond J brand on 'em and the next time I seen one, if I would catch it and look on its flank, I would see it was so.

So I told them that once when I was cruising in the Persian Gulf, the wind blowed so hard it picked the ship right outa the water and carried it clean across Arabia and dropped it in the Mediterranean Sea; all the riggings was blown off, I said, and the masts outa her, so we caught sharks and hitched them to the bows and made 'em tow us into port.

Well, they looked kinda weak and dizzy then, and Slim said: "Don't you want to work out a little to kinda loosen up your muscles?"

Well, I was still sore at them cow-wranglers for shanghaing me the way they done, so I grinned wickedly and said: "Yeah, I reckon I better; my muscles is purty stiff, so you boys will just naturally have to spar some with me."

Well they looked kinda sick, but they was game. They brung out a battered old pair of gloves and first Joe sparred with me. Whilst they was pouring water on Joe they argued some about who was to spar with me next and they drawed straws and Slim was it.

"By golly, " said Slim looking at his watch, "I'd shore admire to box with you, Costigan, but it's gettin' about time for us to start dustin' the trail for the Bueno Oro."

"Heck, we got plenty uh time," said Buck.

Slim glowered at him. "I reckon the foreman – which is me – knows what time uh day it is," said Slim. "I says we starts for the mine. Miss Joan has done said she'd drive Costigan over in her car, and me and Shorty will ride with 'em. I kinda like to be close around Miss Joan when she's out in the hills. You can't tell; Lopez might git it into his haid to make a bad play. You boys will foller on your broncs."

Well, that's the way it was. Joan was a mighty nice-looking girl and she was very nice to me when Slim interjuced me to her, but I couldst see she was nervous being that close to me, and it offended me very much, though I didn't show it none.

Slim set on the front seat with her, and me and Shorty on the back seat, and we drove over the roughest country I ever seen. Mostly they wasn't no road at all, but Joan knowed the channel and didn't need no chart to navigate it, and eventually we come to the mine.

The mine and some houses was up in the hills, and about half a mile from it, on a kind of a broad flat, the ring was pitched. Right near where the ring stood was a narrow canyon leading up through the hills. We had to leave the car close to the mine and walk the rest of the way, the edge of the flat being too rough to drive on.

They was quite a crowd at the ring, which was set up in the open. I noticed that the Bueno Oro was run by white men, same as the ranch. The miners was all big, tough-looking men in heavy boots, bearded and wearing guns, and they was a considerable crew of 'em. They was still more cow-punchers from all the ranches in the vicinity, a lean, hard-bit gang, with even more guns on them than the miners had. By golly, I never seen so many guns in one place in my life!

They was quite a few Mexicans watching, men and women, but Joan was the only white woman I seen. All the men took their hats off to her, and I seen she was quite a favorite among them rough fellers, some of which looked more like pirates than miners or cowboys.

Well the crowd set up a wild roar when they seen me, and Slim yelled:

"Well, you mine-rasslin' mavericks, here he is! I shudders to think what he's goin' to do to yore man!"

All the cow-punchers yipped jubilantly and all the miners yelled mockingly, and up come the skipper of the mine – the guy that done the managing of it – a fellow named Menly.

"Our man is in his tent getting on his togs, Slim," said he. "Get your fighter ready – and we'd best be on the lookout. I've had a tip that Lopez is in the hills close by. The mine's unguarded. Everybody's here. And while there's no ore or money for him to swipe – we sent out the ore yesterday and the payroll hasn't arrived yet – he could do a good deal to the buildings and machinery if he wanted to."

"We'll watch out, you bet," assured Slim, and steered me for what was to serve as my dressing room. They was two tents pitched one on each side of the ring, and they was our dressing rooms. Slim had bought a pair of trunks and ring shoes in Tampico, he said, and so I was rigged out shipshape.

As it happened, I was the first man in the ring. A most thunderous yell went up, mainly from the cow-punchers, and, at the sight of my manly physique, many began to pull out their watches and guns and bet them. The way them miners snapped up the wagers showed they had perfect faith in their man. And when he clumb in the ring a minute later they just about shook the hills with their bellerings. I glared and gasped.

"Snoots Leary or I'm a Dutchman!" I exclaimed.

"Biff Leary they call him," said Slim which, with Tex and Shorty and the Kid, was my handler. "Does you know him?"

"Know him?" said I. "Say, for the first fourteen years of my life I spent most of my time tradin' punches with him. They ain't a back-alley in Galveston that we ain't bloodied each other's noses in. I ain't seen him since we was just kids – I went to sea, and he went the other way. I heard he was mixin' minin' with fightin'. By golly, hadst I knowed this you wouldn't of had to shanghai me."

Well, Menly called us to the center of the ring for instructions and Leary gawped at me: "Steve Costigan, or I'm a liar! What you doin' fightin' for cow-wranglers? I thought you was a sailor."

"I am, Snoots," I said, "and I'm mighty glad for to see you here. You know, we ain't never settled the question as to which of us is the best man. You'll recollect in all the fights we had, neither of us ever really won; we'd generally fight till we was so give out we couldn't lift our mitts, or else till somebody fetched a cop. Now we'll have it out, once and for all!"

"Good!" said he, grinning like a ogre. "You're purty much of a man, Steve, but I figger I'm more. I ain't been swingin' a sledge all this time for nothin'. And I reckon the nickname of 'Biff' is plenty descriptive."

"You always was conceited, Biff," I scowled. "Different from me. Do I go around tellin' people how good I am? Not me; I don't have to. They can tell by lookin' at me that I'm about the best two-fisted man that ever walked a forecastle. Shake now and let's come out fightin'."

Well, the referee had been trying to give us instructions, but we hadn't paid no attention to him, so now he muttered a few mutters under his breath and told us to get ready for the gong. Meanwhile the crowd was developing hydrophobia wanting us to get going. They'd got a camp chair for Miss Joan, but the men all stood up, banked solid around the ring so close their noses was nearly through the ropes, and all yelling like wolves.

"For cat's sake, Steve," said Slim as he crawled out of the ring, "don't fail us. Leary looks even meaner than he done when he licked Red and Joe."

I'll admit Biff was a hard-looking mug. He was five feet ten to my six feet, and he weighed 195 to my 190. He had shoulders as wide as a door, a deep barrel chest, huge fists and arms like a gorilla's. He was hairy and his muscles swelled like iron all over him, miner's style, and his naturally hard face hadst not been beautified by a broken nose and a cauliflower ear. Altogether, Biff looked like what he was – a rough and ready fighting man.

At the tap of the gong he come out of his corner like a typhoon, and I met him in the center of the ring. By sheer luck he got in the first punch – a smashing left hook to the head that nearly snapped my neck. The crowd went howling crazy, but I come back with a sledgehammer right hook that banged on his cauliflower ear like a gunshot. Then we went at it hammer and tongs, neither willing to take a back step, just like we fought when we was kids.

He had a trick of snapping a left uppercut inside the crook of my arm and beating my right hook. He'd had that trick when we fought in the Galveston alleys, and he hadn't forgot it. I never couldst get away from that peculiar smack. Again and again he snapped my head back with it – and I got a neck like iron, too; ain't everybody can rock my head back on it.

He wasn't neglecting his right either. In fact he was mighty fond of banging me on the ear with that hand. Meanwhile, I was ripping both hands to his liver, belly and heart, every now and then bringing up a left or right to his head. We slugged that round out without much advantage on either side, but just before the gong, one of them left uppercuts caught me square in the mouth and the claret started in streams.

"First blood, Steve," grinned Biff as he turned to his corner.

Slim wiped off the red stuff and looked kinda worried.

"He's hit you some mighty hard smacks, Steve," said he.

I snorted. "Think I been pattin' him? He'll begin to feel them body smashes in a round or so. Don't worry; I been waitin' for this chance for years."

At the tap of the gong for the second round we started right in where we left off. Biff come in like he aimed for to take me apart, but I caught him coming in with a blazing left hook to the chin. His eyes rolled, but he gritted his teeth and come driving in so hard he battered me back in spite of all I couldst do. His head was down, both arms flying, legs driving like a charging bull. He caught me in the belly with a right hook that shook me some, but I braced myself and stopped him in his tracks with a right uppercut to the head.

He grunted and heaved over a right swing that started at his knees, and I didn't duck quick enough. It caught me solid but high, knocking me back into the ropes.

The miners roared with joy and the cow-punchers screamed in dismay, but I wasn't hurt. With a supercilious sneer, I met Leary's rush with a straight left which snapped his head right back between his shoulders and somehow missed a slungshot right uppercut which had all my beef behind it.

Biff hooked both hands hard to my head and shot his right under my heart, and I paid him back with a left to the midriff which brung a grunt outa him. I crashed an overhand right for his jaw but he blocked it and was short with a hard right swing. I went inside his left to blast away at his body with both hands in close, and he throwed both arms around me and smothered my punches.

We broke of ourselves before Menly couldst separate us, and I hooked both hands to Leary's head, taking a hard drive between the eyes which made me see stars. We then stood head to head in the center of the ring and traded smashes till we was both dizzy. We didn't hear the gong and Menly had to jump in and haul us apart and shove us toward our corners.

The crowd was plum cuckoo by this time; the cowboys was all yelling that I won that round and the miners was swearing that it was Biff's by a mile. I snickered at this argument, and I noticed Biff snort in disgust. I never go into no scrap figgering to win it on points. If I can't knock the other sap stiff, he's welcome to the decision. And I knowed Biff felt the same way.

Leary was in my corner for the next round before I was offa my stool, and he missed me with a most murderous right. I was likewise wild with a right, and Biff recovered his balance and tagged me on the chin with a left uppercut. Feeling kinda hemmed in, I went for him with a roar and drove him out into the center of the ring with a series of short, vicious rushes he couldn't altogether stop.

I shook him to his heels with a left hook to the body and started a right hook for his head. Up flashed his left for that trick uppercut, and I checked my punch and dropped my right elbow to block. He checked his punch too and crashed a most tremendous right to my unguarded chin. Blood splattered and I went back on my heels, floundering and groggy, and Biff, wild for the kill and flustered by the yells, lost his head and plunged in wide open, flailing with both arms.

I caught him with a smashing left hook to the jaw and he rolled like a clipper in rough weather. I ripped a right under his heart and cracked a hard left to his ear, and he grabbed me like a grizzly and hung on, shaking his head to get rid of the dizziness. He was tough – plenty tough. By the time the referee had broke us, his head had plumb cleared and he proved it by giving a roar of rage and smacking me square on the nose with a punch that made the blood fly.

Again the gong found us slugging head-to-head. Slim and the boys was so weak and wilted from excitement they couldn't hardly see straight enough to mop off the blood and give me a piece of lemon to suck.

Well, this scrap was to be a finish and it looked like to me it wouldst probably last fifteen or twenty more rounds. I wasn't tired or weakened any, and I knowed Biff was like a granite boulder – nearly as tough as me. I figgered on wearing him down with body punishment, but even I couldn't wear down Biff Leary in a few shakes. Just like me, he won most of his fights by simply outlasting the other fellow.

Still, with a punch like both of us carried in each hand, anything might happen – and did, as it come about.

We opened the fourth like we had the others, and slugged our way through it, on even terms. Same way with the fifth, only in this I opened a gash on Biff's temple and he split my ear. As we come up for the sixth, we both showed some wear and tear. One of my eyes was partly closed, I was bleeding at the mouth and nose, and from my cut ear; Biff had lost a tooth, had a deep cut on his temple, and his ribs on the left side was raw from my body punches.

But neither of us was weakening. We come together fast and Biff ripped my lip open with a savage left hook. His right glanced offa my head and again he tagged me with his left uppercut. I sunk my right deep in his ribs and we both shot our lefts. His started a fraction of a second before mine, and he beat me to the punch; his mitt biffed square in my already closing eye, and for a second the punch blinded me.

His right was coming behind his left, swinging from the floor with every ounce of his beef behind it. *Wham!* Square on the chin that swinging mauler tagged me, and it was like the slam of a sledgehammer. I felt my feet fly out from under me, and the back of my head hit the canvas with a jolt that kinda knocked the cobwebs outa my brain.

I shook my head and looked around to locate Biff. He hadn't gone to no corner but was standing grinning down at me, just back of the referee a ways. The referee was counting, the crowd was clean crazy, and Biff was grinning and waving his gloves at 'em, as much as to say what had he told 'em.

The miners was dancing and capering and mighty near kissing each other in their joy, and the cowboys was white-faced, screaming at me to get up, and reaching for their guns. I believe if I hadn't of got up, they'd of started slaughtering the miners. But I got up. For the first time I was good and mad at Biff, not because he knocked me down, but because he had such a smug look on his ugly map. I knowed I was the best man, and I was seeing red.

I come up with a roar, and Biff wiped the smirk offa his map quick and met me with a straight left. But I wasn't to be stopped. I bored into close quarters where I had the advantage, and started ripping away with both hands.

Quickly seeing he couldn't match me at infighting, Biff grabbed my shoulders and shoved me away by main strength, instantly swinging hard for my head. I ducked and slashed a left hook to his head. He ripped a left to my body and smashed a right to my ear. I staggered him with a left hook to the temple, took a left on the head, and beat him to the punch with a mallet-like right-hander to the jaw, I caught him wide open and landed a fraction of a second before he did. That smash had all my beef behind it and Biff dropped like a log.

But he was a glutton for punishment. Snorting and grunting, he got to his all fours, glassy-eyed but shaking his head, and, as Menly said "nine," Leary was up. But he was groggy; such a punch as I dropped him with is one you don't often land. He rushed at me and connected with a swinging left to the ribs that shook me some, but I dropped him again with a blasting left hook to the chin.

This time I seen he'd never beat the count, so I retired to the furtherest corner and grinned at Slim and the other cowboys, who was doing a Indian scalp-dance while the miners was shrieking for Biff to get up.

Menly was counting over him, and, just as he said "seven," a sudden rattle of shots sounded. Menly stopped short and glared at the mine, half a mile away. All of us looked. A gang of men was riding around the buildings and shooting in them. Menly give a yell and hopped out of the ring.

"Gang up!" he yelled. "It's Lopez and his men! They've come to do all the damage they can while the mine's unguarded! They'll burn the office and ruin the machinery if we don't stop 'em! Come a-runnin'!"

He grabbed a horse and started smoking across the flat, and the crowd followed him, the cowboys on horses, the rest on foot, all with their guns in their hands. Slim jumped down and said to Miss Joan: "You stay here, Miss Joan. You'll be safe here and we'll be back and finish this prize-fight soon's we chase them Greasers over the hill."

Well, I was plumb disgusted to see them mutts all streak off across the flat, leaving me and Biff in the ring, and me with the fight practically won. Biff shook hisself and snorted and come up slugging, but I stepped back and irritably told him to can the comedy.

"What's up?" said he, glaring around. "Why, where's Menly? Where's the crowd? What's them shots?"

"The crowd's gone to chase Lopez and his merry men," I snapped. "Just as I had you out, the fool referee quits countin'."

"Well, I'd of got up anyhow," said Biff. "I see now. It is Lopez's gang, sure enough – "

The cow-punchers and miners had nearly reached the mine by this time, and guns was cracking plenty on both sides. The Mexicans was drawing off, slowly, shooting as they went, but it looked like they was about ready to break and run for it. It seemed like a fool play to me, all the way around.

"Hey, Steve," said Biff, "whatsa use waitin' till them mutts gits back? Let's me and you get our scrap over."

"Please don't start fighting till the boys come back," said Joan, nervously. "There's something funny about this, I don't feel just right. Oh – "

She give a kind of scream and turned pale. Outa the ravine behind the ring rode a Mexican. He was young and good-looking but he had a cruel, mocking face; he rode a fine horse and his clothes musta cost six months' wages. He had on tight pants which the legs flared at the bottoms and was ornamented with silver dollars, fine boots which he wore inside his pants legs, gold-chased spurs, a silk shirt and a jacket with gold lace all over it, and the costliest sombrero I ever seen. Moreover, they was a carbine in a saddle sheath, and he wore a Luger pistol at his hip.

"Murder!" said Biff. "It's Lopez the Terrible!"

"Greetings, señorita!" said he, with a flash of white teeth under his black mustache, swinging off his sombrero and making a low bow in his saddle, "Lopez keeps his word – have I not said I would come for you? Oho, I am clever. I sent my men to make a disturbance and draw the Americanos away. Now you will come with me to my lair in the hills where no gringo will ever find you!"

Joan was trembling and white-faced, but she was game. "You don't dare touch an American woman, you murderer!" she said. "My cowboys would hang you on a cactus."

"I will take the risk," he purred. "Now, señorita, come – "

"Get up here in the ring, Miss Joan," I said, leaning down to give her a hand. "That's it – right up with me and Biff. We won't let no harm come to you. Now, Mr. Lopez, if that's your name, I'm givin' you your sailin' orders – weigh anchor and steer for some other port before I bend one on your jaw."

"I echoes them sentiments," said Biff, spitting on his gloves and hitching at his trunks.

Lopez's white teeth flashed in a snarl like a wolf's. His Luger snaked into his hand.

"So," he purred, "these men of beef, these bruisers dare defy Lopez!" He reined up alongside the ring and, placing one hand on a post, vaulted over the ropes, his pistol still menacing me and Biff. Joan, at my motion, hadst retreated back to the other side of the ring. Lopez began to walk towards us, like a cat stalking a mouse.

"The girl I take," he said, soft and deadly. "Let neither of you move if you wish to live."

"Well, Biff," I said, tensing myself, "we'll rush him from both sides. He'll get one of us but the other'n 'll git him."

"Oh, don't!" cried Joan. "He'll kill you, I'd rather – "

"*Let's go!*" roared Biff, and we plunged at Lopez simultaneous.

But that Mex was quicker than a cat; he whipped from one to the other of us and his gun cracked twice. I heard Biff swear and saw him stumble, and something that burned hit me in the left shoulder.

Before Lopez couldst fire again, I was on him, and I ripped the gun outa his hand and belted him over the head with it just as Biff smashed him on the jaw. Lopez the Terrible stretched out limp as a sail-rope, and he didn't even twitch.

"Oh, you're shot, both of you!" wailed Joan, running across the ring toward us. "Oh, I feel like a murderer! I shouldn't have let you do it. Let me see your wounds."

Biff's left arm was hanging limp and blood was oozing from a neat round hole above the elbow. My own left was getting so stiff I couldn't lift it, and blood was trickling down my chest.

"Heck, Miss Joan," I said, "don't worry 'bout us. Lucky for us Lopez was usin' them steel-jacket bullets that make a clean wound and don't tear. But I hate about me and Biff not gettin' to finish our scrap – "

"Hey, Steve," said Biff hurriedly, "the boys has chased off the bandits and heered the shots, and here they come across the flat on the run! Let's us finish our go before they git here. They won't let us go on if we don't do it now. And we may never git another chance. You'll go off to your ship tomorrer and we may never see each other again. Come on. I'm shot through the left arm and you got a bullet through your left shoulder, but our rights is okay. Let's toss this mutt outa the ring and give each other one more good slam!"

"Fair enough, Biff," said I. "Come on, before we gets weak from losin' blood."

Joan started crying and wringing her hands.

"Oh, please, please, boys, don't fight each other any more! You'll bleed to death. Let me bandage your wounds – "

"Shucks, Miss Joan," said I, patting her slim shoulder soothingly, "me and Biff ain't hurt, but we gotta settle our argument. Don't you fret your purty head none."

We unceremoniously tossed the limp and senseless bandit outa the ring and we squared off, with our rights cocked and our lefts hanging at our sides, just as the foremost of the cow-punchers came riding up.

We heard the astounded yells of Menly, Slim and the rest, and Miss Joan begging 'em to stop us, and then we braced our legs, took a deep breath and let go.

We both crashed our rights at exactly the same instant, and we both landed – square on the button. And we both went down. I was up almost in a instant, groggy and dizzy and only partly aware of what was going on, but Biff didn't twitch.

The next minute Menly and Steve and Tex and all the rest was swarming over the ropes, yelling and hollering and demanding to know what it was all about, and Miss Joan was crying and trying to tell 'em and tend to Biff's wound.

"Hey!" yelled Yuma, outside the ring. "That *was* Lopez I seen ride up to the ring a while ago – here he is with a three-inch gash in his scalp and a fractured jawbone!"

"Ain't that what Miss Joan's been tellin' you?" I snapped. "Help her with Biff before he bleeds to death – naw, tend to him first – I'm all right."

Biff come to about that time and nearly knocked Menly's head off before he knowed where he was, and later, while they was bandaging us, Biff said; "I wanta tell you, Steve, I still don't consider you has licked me, and I'm figgerin' on lookin' you up soon's as my arm's healed up."

"Okay with me, Snoots," I grinned. "I gets more enjoyment outa fightin' you than anybody. Reckon there's fightin' Texas feud betwixt me and you."

"Well, Steve," said Slim, "we said we'd make it worth your while – what'll it be?"

"I wouldn't accept no pay for fightin' a old friend like Biff," said I. "All I wantcha to do is get me back in port in time to sail with the *Sea Girl*. And, Miss Joan, I hope you don't feel scared of me no more."

Her answer made both me and Biff blush like school-kids. She kissed us.

The Fightin'est Pair

Me and my white bulldog Mike was peaceably taking our beer in a joint on the waterfront when Porkey Straus come piling in, plumb puffing with excitement.

"Hey, Steve!" he yelped. "What you think? Joe Ritchie's in port with Terror."

"Well?" I said.

"Well, gee whiz," he said, "you mean to set there and let on like you don't know nothin' about Terror, Ritchie's fightin' brindle bull? Why, he's the pit champeen of the Asiatics. He's killed more fightin' dogs than – "

"Yeah, yeah," I said impatiently. "I know all about him. I been listenin' to what a bear-cat he is for the last year, in every Asiatic port I've touched."

"Well," said Porkey, "I'm afraid we ain't goin' to git to see him perform."

"Why not?" asked Johnnie Blinn, a shifty-eyed bar-keep.

"Well," said Porkey, "they ain't a dog in Singapore to match ag'in' him. Fritz Steinmann, which owns the pit and runs the dog fights, has scoured the port and they just ain't no canine which their owners'll risk ag'in' Terror. Just my luck. The chance of a lifetime to see the fightin'est dog of 'em all perform. And they's no first-class mutt to toss in with him. Say, Steve, why don't you let Mike fight him?"

"Not a chance," I growled. "Mike gets plenty of scrappin' on the streets. Besides, I'll tell you straight, I think dog fightin' for money is a dirty low-down game. Take a couple of fine, upstandin' dogs, full of ginger and fightin' heart, and throw 'em in a concrete pit to tear each other's throats out, just so a bunch of four-flushin' tin-horns like you, which couldn't take a punch or give one either, can make a few lousy dollars bettin' on 'em."

"But they likes to fight," argued Porkey. "It's their nature."

"It's the nature of any red-blooded critter to fight. Man or dog," I said. "Let 'em fight on the streets, for bones or for fun, or just to see which is the best dog. But pit-fightin' to the death is just too dirty for me to fool with, and I ain't goin' to get Mike into no such mess."

"Aw, let him alone, Porkey," sneered Johnnie Blinn nastily. "He's too chicken-hearted to mix in them rough games. Ain't you, Sailor?"

"Belay that," I roared. "You keep a civil tongue in your head, you wharf-side rat. I never did like you nohow, and one more crack like that gets you this." I brandished my huge fist at him and he turned pale and started scrubbing the bar like he was trying for a record.

"I wantcha to know that Mike can lick this Terror mutt," I said, glaring at Porkey. "I'm fed up hearin' fellers braggin' on that brindle murderer. Mike can lick him. He can lick any dog in this lousy port, just like I can lick any man here. If Terror meets Mike on the street and gets fresh, he'll get his belly-full. But Mike ain't goin' to get mixed up in no dirty racket like Fritz Steinmann runs and you can lay to that." I made the last statement in a voice like a irritated bull, and smashed my fist down on the table so hard I splintered the wood and made the decanters bounce on the bar.

"Sure, sure, Steve," soothed Porkey, pouring hisself a drink with a shaky hand. "No offense. No offense. Well, I gotta be goin'."

"So long," I growled, and Porkey cruised off.

Up strolled a man which had been standing by the bar. I knowed him – Philip D'Arcy, a man whose name is well known in all parts of the world. He was a tall, slim, athletic fellow, well dressed, with cold gray eyes and a steel-trap jaw. He was one of them gentleman adventurers, as they call 'em, and he'd did everything from running a revolution in South America and flying a war plane in a Balkan brawl to exploring in the Congo. He was deadly with a six-gun, and as dangerous as a rattler when somebody crossed him.

"That's a fine dog you have, Costigan," he said. "Clean white. Not a speck of any other color about him. That means good luck for his owner."

I knowed that D'Arcy had some pet superstitions of his own, like lots of men which live by their hands and wits like him.

"Well," I said, "anyway, he's about the fightin'est dog you ever seen."

"I can tell that," he said, stooping and eyeing Mike close. "Powerful jaws – not too undershot – good teeth – broad between the eyes – deep chest –

legs that brace like iron. Costigan, I'll give you a hundred dollars for him, just as he stands."

"You mean you want me to sell you Mike?" I asked kinda incredulous.

"Sure. Why not?"

"Why not!" I repeatedly indignantly. "Well, gee whiz, why not ask a man to sell his brother for a hundred dollars? Mike wouldn't stand for it. Anyway, I wouldn't do it."

"I need him," persisted D'Arcy. "A white dog with a dark man – it means luck. White dogs have always been lucky for me. And my luck's been running against me lately. I'll give you a hundred and fifty."

"D'Arcy," I said, "you couldst stand there and offer me money all day long and raise the ante every hand, but it wouldn't be no good. Mike ain't for sale. Him and me has knocked around the world together too long. They ain't no use talkin'."

His eyes flashed for a second. He didn't like to be crossed in any way. Then he shrugged his shoulders.

"All right. We'll forget it. I don't blame you for thinking a lot of him. Let's have a drink."

So we did and he left.

I went and got me a shave, because I was matched to fight some tramp at Ace Larnigan's Arena and I wanted to be in shape for the brawl. Well, afterwards I was walking down along the docks when I heard somebody go: "Hissst!"

I looked around and saw a yellow hand beckon me from behind a stack of crates. I sauntered over, wondering what it was all about, and there was a Chinese boy hiding there. He put his finger to his lips. Then quick he handed me a folded piece of paper and beat it, before I couldst ask him anything.

I opened the paper and it was a note in a woman's handwriting which read: "Dear Steve, I have admired you for a long time at a distance, but have been too timid to make myself known to you. Would it be too much to ask you to give me an opportunity to tell you my emotions by word of mouth? If you care at all, I will meet you by the old Manchu House on the Tungen Road, just after dark. An affectionate admirer. P.S. Please, oh please be there! You have stole my heart away!"

84

"Mike," I said pensively, "ain't it plumb peculiar the strange power I got over wimmen, even them I ain't never seen? Here is a girl I don't even know the name of, even, and she has been eatin' her poor little heart out in solitude because of me. Well – " I hove a gentle sigh – "it's a fatal gift, I'm afeared."

Mike yawned. Sometimes it looks like he ain't got no romance at all about him. I went back to the barber shop and had the barber to put some ile on my hair and douse me with perfume. I always like to look genteel when I meet a feminine admirer.

Then, as the evening was waxing away, as the poets say, I set forth for the narrow winding back street just off the waterfront proper. The natives call it the Tungen Road, for no particular reason as I can see. The lamps there is few and far between and generally dirty and dim. The street's lined on both sides by lousy-looking native shops and hovels. You'll come to stretches which looks clean deserted and falling to ruins.

Well, me and Mike was passing through just such a district when I heard sounds of some kind of a fracas in a dark alley-way we was passing. Feet scruffed. They was the sound of a blow and a voice yelled in English: "Halp! Halp! These Chinese is killin' me!"

"Hold everything," I roared, jerking up my sleeves and plunging for the alley, with Mike at my heels. "Steve Costigan is on the job."

It was as dark as a stack of black cats in that alley. Plunging blind, I bumped into somebody and sunk a fist to the wrist in him. He gasped and fell away. I heard Mike roar suddenly and somebody howled bloody murder. Then wham! A blackjack or something like it smashed on my skull and I went to my knees.

"That's done yer, yer blawsted Yank," said a nasty voice in the dark.

"You're a liar," I gasped, coming up blind and groggy but hitting out wild and ferocious. One of my blind licks musta connected because I heard somebody cuss bitterly. And then wham, again come that blackjack on my dome. What little light they was, was behind me, and whoever it was slugging me, couldst see me better'n I could see him. That last smash put me down for the count, and he musta hit me again as I fell.

I couldn't of been out but a few minutes. I come to myself lying in the darkness and filth of the alley and I had a most splitting headache and dried blood was clotted on a cut in my scalp. I groped around and found a match in my pocket and struck it.

The alley was empty. The ground was all tore up and they was some blood scattered around, but neither the thugs nor Mike was nowhere to be seen. I run down the alley, but it ended in a blank stone wall. So I come back onto the Tungen Road and looked up and down but seen nobody. I went mad.

"Philip D'Arcy!" I yelled all of a sudden. "He done it. He stole Mike. He writ me that note. Unknown admirer, my eye. I been played for a sucker again. He thinks Mike'll bring him luck. I'll bring him luck, the double-crossin' son-of-a-seacook. I'll sock him so hard he'll bite hisself in the ankle. I'll bust him into so many places he'll go through a sieve – "

With these meditations, I was running down the street at full speed, and when I busted into a crowded thoroughfare, folks turned and looked at me in amazement. But I didn't pay no heed. I was steering my course for the European Club, a kind of ritzy place where D'Arcy generally hung out. I was still going at top speed when I run up the broad stone steps and was stopped by a pompous-looking doorman which sniffed scornfully at my appearance, with my clothes torn and dirty from laying in the alley, and my hair all tousled and dried blood on my hair and face.

"Lemme by," I gritted, "I gotta see a mutt."

"Gorblime," said the doorman. "You cawn't go in there. This is a very exclusive club, don't you know. Only gentlemen are allowed here. Cawn't have a blawsted gorilla like you bursting in on the gentlemen. My word! Get along now before I call the police."

There wasn't time to argue.

With a howl of irritation I grabbed him by the neck and heaved him into a nearby goldfish pond. Leaving him floundering and howling, I kicked the door open and rushed in. I dashed through a wide hallway and found myself in a wide room with big French winders. That seemed to be the main club room, because it was very scrumptiously furnished and had all kinds of animal heads on the walls, alongside of crossed swords and rifles in racks.

They was a number of Americans and Europeans setting around drinking whiskey and sodas, and playing cards. I seen Philip D'Arcy setting amongst a bunch of his club members, evidently spinning yarns about his adventures. And I seen red.

"D'Arcy!" I yelled, striding toward him regardless of the card tables I upset. "Where's my dog?"

Philip D'Arcy sprang up with a kind of gasp and all the club men jumped up too, looked amazed.

"My word!" said a Englishman in a army officer's uniform. "Who let this boundah in? Come, come, my man, you'll have to get out of this."

"You keep your nose clear of this or I'll bend it clean outa shape." I howled, shaking my right mauler under the aforesaid nose. "This ain't none of your business. D'Arcy, what you done with my dog?"

"You're drunk, Costigan," he snapped. "I don't know what you're talking about."

"That's a lie," I screamed, crazy with rage. "You tried to buy Mike and then you had me slugged and him stole. I'm on to you, D'Arcy. You think because you're a big shot and I'm just a common sailorman, you can take what you want. But you ain't gettin' away with it. You got Mike and you're goin' to give him back or I'll tear your guts out. Where is he? Tell me before I choke it outa you."

"Costigan, you're mad," snarled D'Arcy, kind of white. "Do you know whom you're threatening? I've killed men for less than that."

"You stole my dog!" I howled, so wild I hardly knowed what I was doing.

"You're a liar," he rasped. Blind mad, I roared and crashed my right to his jaw before he could move. He went down like a slaughtered ox and laid still, blood trickling from the corner of his mouth. I went for him to strangle him with my bare hands, but all the club men closed in between us.

"Grab him," they yelled. "He's killed D'Arcy. He's drunk or crazy. Hold him until we can get the police."

"Belay there," I roared, backing away with both fists cocked. "Lemme see the man that'll grab me. I'll knock his brains down his throat. When that rat comes to, tell him I ain't through with him, not by a dam' sight. I'll get him if it's the last thing I do."

And I stepped through one of them French winders and strode away cursing between my teeth. I walked for some time in a kind of red mist, forgetting all about the fight at Ace's Arena, where I was already due. Then I got a idee. I was fully intending to get ahold of D'Arcy and choke the truth outa him, but they was no use trying that now. I'd catch him outside his club sometime that night. Meanwhile, I thought of something else. I went into a saloon and got a big piece of white paper and a pencil, and with much labor, I printed out what I wanted to say. Then I went out and stuck it up on a wooden lamppost where folks couldst read it. It said:

I WILL PAY ANY MAN FIFTY DOLLARS ($50) THAT CAN FIND MY BULDOG MIKE WHICH WAS STOLE BY A LO-DOWN SCUNK. — STEVE COSTIGAN.

I was standing there reading it to see that the words was spelled right when a loafer said: "Mike stole? Too bad, Sailor. But where you goin' to git the fifty to pay the reeward? Everybody knows you ain't got no money."

"That's right," I said. So I wrote down underneath the rest:

P.S. I AM GOING TO GET FIFTY DOLLARS FOR LICKING SOME MUTT AT ACE'S AREENER THAT IS WHERE THE REWARD MONEY IS COMING FROM. — S. C.

I then went morosely along the street wondering where Mike was and if he was being mistreated or anything. I moped into the Arena and found Ace walking the floor and pulling hair.

"Where you been?" he howled. "You realize you been keepin' the crowd waitin' a hour? Get into them ring togs."

"Let 'em wait," I said sourly, setting down and pulling off my shoes. "Ace, a yellow-livered son-of-a-skunk stole my dog."

"Yeah?" said Ace, pulling out his watch and looking at it. "That's tough, Steve. Hustle up and get into the ring, willya? The crowd's about ready to tear the joint down."

I climbed into my trunks and bathrobe and mosied up the aisle, paying very little attention either to the hisses or cheers which greeted my appearance. I clumb into the ring and looked around for my opponent.

"Where's Grieson?" asked Ace.

"'E 'asn't showed up yet," said the referee.

"Ye gods and little fishes!" howled Ace, tearing his hair. "These bone-headed leather-pushers will drive me to a early doom. Do they think a pummoter's got nothin' else to do but set around all night and pacify a ragin' mob whilst they play around? These thugs is goin' to lynch us all if we don't start some action right away."

"Here he comes," said the referee as a bathrobed figger come hurrying down the aisle. Ace scowled bitterly and held up his hands to the frothing crowd.

"The long-delayed main event," he said sourly. "Over in that corner, Sailor Costigan of the *Sea Girl*, weight 190 pounds. The mutt crawlin' through the ropes is 'Limey' Grieson, weight 189. Get goin' – and I hope you both get knocked loop-legged."

The referee called us to the center of the ring for instructions and Grieson glared at me, trying to scare me before the scrap started – the conceited jassack. But I had other things on my mind. I merely mechanically noted that he was about my height-six feet-had a nasty sneering mouth and mean black eyes, and had been in a street fight recent. He had a bruise under one ear.

We went back to our corners and I said to the second Ace had give me: "Bonehead, you ain't seen nothin' of nobody with my bulldog, have you?"

"Naw, I ain't," he said, crawling through the ropes. "And beside . . . Hey, look out."

I hadn't noticed the gong sounding and Grieson was in my corner before I knowed what was happening. I ducked a slungshot right as I turned and clinched, pushing him outa the corner before I broke. He nailed me with a hard left hook to the head and I retaliated with a left to the body, but it didn't have much enthusiasm behind it. I had something else on my mind and my heart wasn't in the fight. I kept unconsciously glancing over to my corner where Mike always set, and when he wasn't there, I felt kinda lost and sick and empty.

Limey soon seen I wasn't up to par and began forcing the fight, shooting both hands to my head. I blocked and countered very slouchily and the crowd, missing my rip-roaring attack, began to murmur. Limey got too cocky and missed a looping right that had everything he had behind it. He was wide open for a instant and I mechanically ripped a left hook under his heart that made his knees buckle, and he covered up and walked away from me in a hurry, with me following in a sluggish kind of manner.

After that he was careful, not taking many chances. He jabbed me plenty, but kept his right guard high and close in. I ignores left jabs at all times, so though he was outpointing me plenty, he wasn't hurting me none. But he finally let go his right again and started the claret from my nose. That irritated me and I woke up and doubled him over with a left hook to the guts which wowed the crowd. But they yelled with rage and amazement when I failed to foller up. To tell the truth, I was fighting very absent-mindedly.

As I walked back to my corner at the end of the first round, the crowd was growling and muttering restlessly, and the referee said: "Fight, you blasted Yank, or I'll throw you h'out of the ring." That was the first time I ever got a warning like that.

"What's the matter with you, Sailor?" said Bonehead, waving the towel industriously. "I ain't never seen you fight this way before."

"I'm worried about Mike," I said, "Bonehead, where-all does Philip D'Arcy hang out besides the European Club?"

"How should I know?" he said. "Why?"

"I wanta catch him alone some place," I growled. "I betcha – "

"There's the gong, you mutt," yelled Bonehead, pushing me out of my corner. "For cat's sake, get in there and FIGHT. I got five bucks bet on you."

I wandered out into the middle of the ring and absent-mindedly wiped Limey's chin with a right that dropped him on his all fours. He bounced up without a count, clearly addled, but just as I was fixing to polish him off, I heard a racket at the door.

"Lemme in," somebody was squalling. "I gotta see Meest Costigan. I got one fellow dog belong along him."

"Wait a minute," I growled to Limey, and run over to the ropes, to the astounded fury of the fans, who rose and roared.

"Let him in, Bat," I yelled and the feller at the door hollered back: "Alright, Steve, here he comes."

And a Chinese kid come running up the aisle grinning like all get-out, holding up a scrawny brindle bull-pup.

"Here that one fellow dog, Mees Costigan," he yelled.

"Aw heck," I said. "That ain't Mike. Mike's white. I thought everybody in Singapore knowed Mike – "

At this moment I realized that the still groggy Grieson was harassing me from the rear, so I turned around and give him my full attention for a minute. I had him backed up ag'in' the ropes, bombarding him with lefts and rights to the head and body, when I heard Bat yell: "Here comes another'n, Steve."

"Pardon me a minute," I snapped to the reeling Limey, and run over to the ropes just as a grinning coolie come running up the aisle with a white dog which might of had three or four drops of bulldog blood in him.

"Me catchum, boss," he chortled.

"Heap fine white dawg. Me catchum fifty dolla?"

"You catchum a kick in the pants," I roared with irritation. "Blame it all, that ain't Mike."

At this moment Grieson, which had snuck up behind me, banged me behind the ear with a right-hander that made me see about a million stars. This infuriated me so I turned and hit him in the belly so hard I bent his back-bone. He curled up like a worm somebody'd stepped on and while the referee was counting over him, the gong ended the round.

They dragged Limey to his corner and started working on him. Bone-head, he said to me: "What kind of a game is this, Sailor? Gee whiz, that mutt can't stand up to you a minute if you was tryin'. You shoulda stopped him in the first round. Hey, lookit there."

I glanced absent-mindedly over at the opposite corner and seen that Limey's seconds had found it necessary to take off his right glove in the process of reviving him. They was fumbling over his bare hand.

"They're up to somethin' crooked," howled Bonehead. "I'm goin' to appeal to the referee."

"Here comes some more mutts, Steve," bawled Bat and down the aisle come a Chinese coolie, a Jap sailor, and a Hindoo, each with a barking dog. The crowd had been seething with bewildered rage, but this seemed to somehow hit 'em in the funny bone and they begunst to whoop and yell and laugh like a passel of hyenas. The referee was roaming around the ring cussing to hisself and Ace was jumping up and down and tearing his hair.

"Is this a prize-fight or a dog-show," he howled. "You've rooint my business. I'll be the laughin' stock of the town. I'll sue you, Costigan."

"Catchum fine dawg, Meest' Costigan," shouted the Chinese, holding up a squirming, yowling mutt which done its best to bite me.

"You deluded heathen," I roared, "that ain't even a bull dog. That's a chow."

"You clazee," he hollered. "Him fine blull dawg."

"Don't listen," said the Jap. "Him bull dog." And he held up one of them pint-sized Boston bull-terriers.

"Not so," squalled the Hindoo. "Here is thee dog for you, sahib. A pure blood Rampur hound. No dog can overtake him in thee race – "

"Ye gods!" I howled. "Is everybody crazy? I oughta knowed these heathens couldn't understand my reward poster, but I thought – "

"*Look out, sailor,*" roared the crowd.

I hadn't heard the gong. Grieson had slipped up on me from behind again, and I turned just in time to get nailed on the jaw by a sweeping right-hander he started from the canvas. *Wham!* The lights went out and I hit the canvas so hard it jolted some of my senses back into me again.

I knowed, even then, that no ordinary gloved fist had slammed me down that way. Limey's men hadst slipped a iron knuckle-duster on his hand when they had his glove off. The referee sprung forward with a gratified yelp and begun counting over me. I writhed around, trying to get up and kill Limey, but I felt like I was done. My head was swimming, my jaw felt dead, and all the starch was gone outa my legs. They felt like they was made outa taller.

My head reeled. And I could see stars over the horizon of dogs.

" . . . Four . . ." said the referee above the yells of the crowd and the despairing howls of Bonehead, who seen his five dollars fading away. " . . . Five . . . Six . . . Seven . . ."

"There," said Limey, stepping back with a leer. "That's done yer, yer blawsted Yank."

Snap! went something in my head. That voice. Them same words. Where'd I heard 'em before? In the black alley offa the Tungen Road. A wave of red fury washed all the grogginess outa me.

I forgot all about my taller legs. I come off the floor with a roar which made the ring lights dance and lunged at the horrified Limey like a mad bull. He caught me with a straight left coming in, but I didn't even check a instant. His arm bent and I was on top of him and sunk my right mauler so deep into his ribs I felt his heart throb under my fist. He turned green all over and crumbled to the canvas like all his bones hadst turned to butter. The dazed referee started to count, but I ripped off my gloves and pouncing on the gasping warrior, I sunk my iron fingers into his throat.

"Where's Mike, you gutter rat?" I roared. "What'd you do with him? Tell me, or I'll tear your windpipe out."

" 'Ere, 'ere," squawked the referee. "You cawn't do that. Let go of him, I say. Let go, you fiend."

He got me by the shoulders and tried to pull me off. Then, seeing I wasn't even noticing his efforts, he started kicking me in the ribs. With a wrathful beller, I rose up and caught him by the nape of the neck and the seat of the britches and throwed him clean through the ropes. Then I turned back on Limey.

"You Limehouse spawn," I bellered. "I'll choke the life outa you."

"Easy, mate, easy," he gasped, green-tinted and sick. "I'll tell yer. We stole the mutt – Fritz Steinmann wanted him – "

"Steinmann?" I howled in amazement.

"He warnted a dorg to fight Ritchie's Terror," gasped Limey. "Johnnie Blinn suggested he should 'ook your Mike. Johnnie hired me and some strong-arms to turn the trick – Johnnie's gel wrote you that note – but how'd you know I was into it – "

"I oughta thought about Blinn," I raged. "The dirty rat. He heard me and Porkey talkin' and got the idee. Where is Blinn?"

"Somewheres gettin' sewed up," gasped Grieson. "The dorg like to tore him to ribbons afore we could get the brute into the bamboo cage we had fixed."

"Where is Mike?" I roared, shaking him till his teeth rattled.

"At Steinmann's, fightin' Terror," groaned Limey. "Ow, lor' – I'm sick. I'm dyin'."

I riz up with a maddened beller and made for my corner. The referee rose up outa the tangle of busted seats and cussing fans and shook his fist at me with fire in his eye.

"Steve Costigan," he yelled. "You lose the blawsted fight on a foul."

"So's your old man," I roared, grabbing my bathrobe from the limp and gibbering Bonehead. And just at that instant a regular bedlam bust loose at the ticket – door and Bat come down the aisle like the devil was chasing him. And in behind him come a mob of natives – coolies, 'ricksha boys, beggars, shopkeepers, boatmen and I don't know what all – and every one of 'em had at least one dog and some had as many as three or four. Such a horde of chows, Pekineses, terriers, hounds, and mongrels I never seen, and they was all barking and howling and fighting.

"Meest' Costigan," the heathens howled, charging down the aisles. "You payum flifty dolla for dogs. We catchum."

The crowd rose and stampeded, trompling each other in their flight and I jumped outa the ring and raced down the aisle to the back exit with the whole mob about a jump behind me. I slammed the door in their faces and rushed out onto the sidewalk, where the passers-by screeched and scattered at the sight of what I reckon they thought was a huge and much battered maniac running at large in a red bathrobe. I paid no heed to 'em.

Somebody yelled at me in a familiar voice, but I rushed out into the street and made a flying leap onto the running board of a passing taxi. I ripped the door open and yelled to the horrified driver: "Fritz Steinmann's place on Kang Street – and if you ain't there within three minutes I'll break your neck."

We went careening through the streets and purty soon the driver said: "Say, are you an escaped criminal? There's a car followin' us."

"You drive," I yelled. "I don't care if they's a thousand cars follerin' us. Likely it's a Chinaman with a pink Pomeranian he wants to sell me for a white bull dog."

The driver stepped on it and when we pulled up in front of the innocent-looking building which was Steinmann's secret arena, we'd left the mysterious pursuer clean outa sight. I jumped out and raced down a short flight of stairs which led from the street down to a side entrance, clearing my decks for action by shedding my bathrobe as I went. The door was shut and a burly black-jowled thug was lounging outside. His eyes narrowed with surprise as he noted my costume, but he bulged in front of me and growled: "Wait a minute, you. Where do you think you're goin'?"

"In!" I gritted, ripping a terrible right to his unshaven jaw.

Over his prostrate carcass I launched myself bodily against the door, being in too much of a hurry to stop and see if it was unlocked. It crashed in and through its ruins I catapulted into the room.

It was a big basement. A crowd of men – the scrapings of the waterfront – was ganged about a deep pit sunk in the concrete floor from which come a low terrible, worrying sound like dogs growling through a mask of torn flesh and bloody hair – like fighting dogs growl when they have their fangs sunk deep.

The fat Dutchman which owned the dive was just inside the door, and he whirled and went white as I crashed through. He threw up his hands and screamed, just as I caught him with a clout that smashed his nose and knocked six front teeth down his throat. Somebody yelled: "Look out, boys! Here comes Costigan! He's on the kill!"

The crowd yelled and scattered like chaff before a high wind as I come ploughing through 'em like a typhoon, slugging right and left and dropping a man at each blow. I was so crazy mad I didn't care if I killed all of 'em. In a instant the brink of the pit was deserted as the crowd stormed through the exits, and I jumped down into the pit. Two dogs was there, a white one and a big brindle one, though they was both so bloody you couldn't hardly tell their original color. Both had been savagely punished, but Mike's jaws had locked in the death-hold on Terror's throat and the brindle dog's eyes was glazing.

Joe Ritchie was down on his knees working hard over them and his face was the color of paste. They's only two ways you can break a bull dog's death-grip; one is by deluging him with water till he's half drowned and opens his mouth to breathe. The other'n is by choking him off. Ritchie was trying that, but Mike had such a bull's neck, Joe was only hurting his fingers.

"For gosh sake, Costigan," he gasped. "Get this white devil off. He's killin' Terror."

"Sure I will," I grunted, stooping over the dogs. "Not for your sake, but for the sake of a good game dog." And I slapped Mike on the back and said: "Belay there, Mike; haul in your grapplin' irons."

Mike let go and grinned up at me with his bloody mouth, wagging his stump of a tail like all get-out and pricking up one ear. Terror had clawed the other'n to rags. Ritchie picked up the brindle bull and clumb outa the pit and I follered him with Mike.

"You take that dog to where he can get medical attention and you do it pronto," I growled. "He's a better man than you, any day in the week, and more fittin' to live. Get outa my sight."

He slunk off and Steinmann come to on the floor and seen me and crawled to the door on his all fours before he dast to get up and run, bleeding like a stuck hawg. I was looking over Mike's cuts and gashes when I realized that a man was standing nearby, watching me.

I wheeled. It was Philip D'Arcy, with a blue bruise on his jaw where I'd socked him, and his right hand inside his coat.

"D'arcy," I said, walking up to him. "I reckon I done made a mess of things. I just ain't got no sense when I lose my temper, and I honestly thought you'd stole Mike. I ain't much on fancy words and apologizin' won't do no good. But I always try to do what seems right in my blunderin' blame-fool way, and if you wanta, you can knock my head off and I won't raise a hand ag'in' you." And I stuck out my jaw for him to sock.

He took his hand outa his coat and in it was a cocked six-shooter.

"Costigan," he said, "no man ever struck me before and got away with it. I came to Larnigan's Arena tonight to kill you. I was waiting for you outside and when I saw you run out of the place and jump into a taxi, I followed you to do the job wherever I caught up with you. But I like you. You're a square-shooter. And a man who thinks as much of his dog as you do is my idea of the right sort. I'm putting this gun back where it belongs – and I'm willing to shake hands and call it quits, if you are."

"More'n willin'," I said heartily. "You're a real gent." And we shook. Then all at once he started laughing.

"I saw your poster," he said. "When I passed by, an Indian babu was translating it to a crowd of natives and he was certainly making a weird mess of it. The best he got out of it was that Steve Costigan was buying dogs at fifty dollars apiece. You'll be hounded by canine-peddlers as long as you're in port."

"The *Sea Girl's* due tomorrer, thank gosh," I replied. "But right now I got to sew up some cuts on Mike."

"My car's outside," said D'Arcy. "Let's take him up to my rooms. I've had quite a bit of practice at such things and we'll fix him up ship-shape."

"It's a dirty deal he's had," I growled. "And when I catch Johnnie Blinn I'm goin' kick his ears off. But," I added, swelling out my chest seven or eight inches, "I don't reckon I'll have to lick no more saps for sayin' that Ritchie's Terror is the champeen of all fightin' dogs in the Asiatics. Mike and me is the fightin'est pair of scrappers in the world."

Vikings of the Gloves

No sooner had the *Sea Girl* docked in Yokohama than Mushy Hansen beat it down the waterfront to see if he couldst match me at some good fight club. Purty soon he come back and said: "No chance, Steve. You'd have to be a Scandinavian to get a scrap right now."

"What you mean by them remarks?" I asked, suspiciously.

"Well," said Mushy, "the sealin' fleet's in, and so likewise is the whalers, and the port's swarmin' with square-heads."

"Well, what's that got to do – ?"

"They ain't but one fight club on the waterfront," said Mushy, "and it's run by a Dutchman named Neimann. He's been puttin' on a series of elimination contests, and, from what I hear, he's been cleanin' up. He matches Swedes against Danes, see? Well, they's hundreds of square-heads in port, and naturally each race turns out to support its countryman. So far, the Danes is ahead. You ever hear of Hakon Torkilsen?"

"You bet," I said. "I ain't never seen him perform, but they say he's the real goods. Sails on the *Viking*, outa Copenhagen, don't he?"

"Yeah. And the *Viking*'s in port. Night before last, Hakon flattened Sven Tortvigssen, the Terrible Swede, in three rounds, and tonight he takes on Dirck Jacobsen, the Gotland Giant. The Swedes and the Danes is fightin' all over the waterfront," said Mushy, "and they're bettin' their socks. I sunk a few bucks on Hakon myself. But that's the way she stands, Steve. Nobody but Scandinavians need apply."

"Well, heck," I complained, "how come I got to be the victim of race prejerdice? I need dough. I'm flat broke. Wouldn't this mug Neimann gimme a preliminary scrap? For ten dollars I'll fight any three square-heads in port – all in the same ring."

"Naw," said Mushy, "they ain't goin' to be no preliminaries. Neimann says the crowd'll be too impatient to set through 'em. Boy, oh boy, will they be excitement! Whichever way it goes, they's bound to be a rough-house."

"A purty lookout," I said bitterly, "when the *Sea Girl*, the fightin'est ship on the Seven Seas, ain't represented in the mélée. I gotta good mind to blow in and bust up the whole show – "

At this moment Bill O'Brien hove in sight, looking excited.

"Hot dawg!" he yelled. "Here's a chance for us to clean up some dough!"

"Stand by to come about," I advised, "and give us the lay."

"Well," Bill said, "I just been down along the waterfront listening to them square-heads argy – and, boy, is the money changin' hands! I seen six fights already. Well, just now they come word that Dirck Jacobsen had broke his wrist, swinging for a sparrin' partner and hittin' the wall instead. So I run down to Neimann's arena to find out if it was so, and the Dutchman was walkin' the floor and tearin' his hair. He said he'd pay a hundred bucks extra, win or lose, to a man good enough to go in with Torkilsen. He says if he calls the show off, these square-heads will hang him. So I see where we can run a *Sea Girl* man in and cop the jack!"

"And who you think we can use?" I asked skeptically.

"Well, there's Mushy," began Bill. "He was raised in America, of course, but – "

"Yeah, there's Mushy!" snapped Mushy, bitterly. "You know as well as I do that I ain't no Swede. I'm a Dane myself. Far from wantin' to fight Hakon, I hope he knocks the block offa whatever fool Swede they finds to go against him."

"That's gratitude," said Bill, scathingly. "How can a brainy man like me work up anything big when I gets opposition from all quarters? I lays awake nights studyin' up plans for the betterment of my mates, and what do I get? Argyments! Wisecracks! Opposition! I tellya – "

"Aw, pipe down," I said. "There's Sven Larson – he's a Swede."

"That big ox would last about fifteen seconds against Hakon," said Mushy, with gloomy satisfaction. "Besides, Sven's in jail. He hadn't been in port more'n a half hour when he got jugged for beatin' up a cop."

Bill fixed a gloomy gaze on me, and his eyes lighted.

"Hot dawg!" he whooped. "I got it! Steve, you're a Swede!"

"Listen here, you flat-headed dogfish," I began, in ire, "me and you ain't had a fight in years, but by golly – "

"Aw, try to have some sense," said Bill. "This is the idee: You ain't never fought in Yokohama before. Neimann don't know you, nor anybody else. We'll pass you off for Swede – "

"Pass *him* off for a Swede!" gawped Mushy.

"Well," said Bill, "I'll admit he don't look much like a Swede – "

"*Much* like a Swede!" I gnashed, my indignation mounting. "Why, you son of a – "

"Well, you don't look *nothin'* like a Swede then!" snapped Bill, disgustedly, "but we can pass you off for one. I reckon if we tell 'em you're a Swede, they can't prove you ain't. If they dispute it, we'll knock the daylights outa 'em."

I thought it over.

"Not so bad," I finally decided, "We'll get that hundred extra – and, for a chance to fight somebody, I'd pertend I was a Eskimo. We'll do it."

"Good!" said Bill. "Can you talk Swedish?"

"Sure," I said. "Listen: Yimmy Yackson yumped off the Yacob-ladder with his monkey-yacket on. Yimminy, what a yump!"

"Purty good," said Bill. "Come on, we'll go down to Neimann's and sign up. Hey, ain't you goin', Mushy?"

"No, I ain't," said Mushy sourly. "I see right now I ain't goin' to enjoy this scrap none. Steve's my shipmate but Hakon's my countryman. Whichever loses, I won't rejoice none. I hope it's a draw. I ain't even goin' to see it."

Well, he went off by hisself, and I said to Bill, "I gotta good mind not to go on with this, since Mushy feels that way about it."

"Aw, he'll get over it," said Bill. "My gosh, Steve, this here's a matter of business. Ain't we all busted? Mushy'll feel all right after we split your purse three ways and he has a few shots of hard licker."

"Well, all right," I said. "Let's get down to Neimann's."

So me and Bill and my white bulldog, Mike, went down to Neimann's, and, as we walked in, Bill hissed, "Don't forget to talk Swedish."

A short, fat man, which I reckoned was Neimann, was setting and looking over a list of names, and now and then he'd take a long pull out of a bottle, and then he'd cuss fit to curl your toes and pull his hair.

"Well, Neimann," said Bill, cheerfully, "what you doin'?"

"I got a list of all the Swedes in port which think they can fight," said

Neimann, bitterly. "They ain't one of 'em would last five seconds against Torkilsen. I'll have to call it off."

"No you won't," said Bill. "Right here I got the fightin'est Swede in the Asiatics!"

Neimann faced around quick to look at me, and his eyes flared, and he jumped up like he'd been stung.

"Get outa here!" he yelped. "You should come around here and mock me in my misery! A sweet time for practical jokes – "

"Aw, cool off," said Bill. "I tell you this Swede can lick Hakon Torkilsen with his right thumb in his mouth."

"Swede!" snorted Neimann. "You must think I'm a prize sucker, bringin' this black-headed mick around here and tellin' me – "

"Mick, baloney!" said Bill. "Lookit them blue eyes – "

"I'm lookin' at 'em," snarled Neimann, "and thinkin' of the lakes of Killarney all the time. Swede? Ha! Then so was Jawn L. Sullivan. So you're a Swede, are you?"

"Sure," I said. "Aye bane Swedish, mister."

"What part of Sweden?" he barked.

"Gotland," I said, and simultaneous Bill said, "Stockholm," and we glared at each other in mutual irritation.

"Cork, you'd better say," sneered Neimann.

"Aye am a Swede," I said, annoyed. "Aye want dass fight."

"Get outa here and quit wastin' my valuable time," snarled Neimann. "If you're a Swede, then I'm a Hindoo Princess!"

At this insulting insinuation I lost my temper. I despises a man that's so suspicious he don't trust his feller men. Grabbing Neimann by the neck with a vise-like grip, and waggling a huge fist under his nose, I roared, "You insultin' monkey! Am I a Swede or ain't I?"

He turned pale and shook like an aspirin-leaf.

"You're a Swede," he agreed, weakly.

"And I get the fight?" I rumbled.

"You get it," he agreed, wiping his brow with a bandanner. "The square-heads may stretch my neck for this, but maybe, if you keep your mouth shut, we'll get by. What's your name?"

"Steve – " I began, thoughtlessly, when Bill kicked me on the shin and said, "Lars Ivarson."

"All right," said Neimann, pessimistically, "I'll announce it that I got a man to fight Torkilsen."

"How much do I – how much Aye bane get?" I asked.

"I guaranteed a thousand bucks to the fighters," he said, "to be split seven-hundred to the winner and three hundred to the loser."

"Give me loser's end now," I demanded. "Aye bane go out and bet him, you betcha life."

So he did, and said, "You better keep offa the street; some of your countrymen might ask you about the folks back home in dear old Stockholm." And with that, he give a bitter screech of raucous and irritating laughter, and slammed the door, and as we left, we heered him moaning like he had the bellyache.

"I don't believe he thinks I'm a Swede," I said, resentfully.

"Who cares?" said Bill. "We got the match. But he's right. I'll go place the bets. You keep outa sight. Long's you don't say much, we're safe. But if you go wanderin' around, some square-head'll start talkin' Swedish to you and we'll be sunk."

"All right," I said. "I'll get me a room at the sailor's boardin' house we seen down Manchu Road. I'll stay there till it's time for the scrap."

So Bill went off to lay the bets, and me and Mike went down the back alleys toward the place I mentioned. As we turned out of a side street into Manchu Road, somebody come around the corner moving fast, and fell over Mike, who didn't have time to get outa the way.

The feller scrambled up with a wrathful roar. A big blond bezark he was, and he didn't look like a sailor. He drawed back his foot to kick Mike, as if it was the dog's fault. But I circumvented him by the simple process of kicking him severely on the shin.

"Drop it, cull," I growled, as he begun hopping around, howling wordlessly and holding his shin. "It wasn't Mike's fault, and you hadn't no cause to kick him. Anyhow, he'd of ripped yore laig off if you'd landed – "

Instead of being pacified, he gave a bloodthirsty yell and socked me on the jaw. Seeing he was one of them bull-headed mugs you can't reason with, I banged him once with my right, and left him setting dizzily in the gutter picking imaginary violets.

Proceeding on my way to the seamen's boardin's house, I forgot all about the incident. Such trifles is too common for me to spend much time thinking about. But, as it come out, I had cause to remember it.

I got me a room and stayed there with the door shut till Bill come in, jubilant, and said the crew of the *Sea Girl* hadst sunk all the money it could borrow at heavy odds.

"If you lose," said he, "most of us will go back to the ship wearin' barrels."

"Me lose?" I snorted disgustedly. "Don't be aberge. Where's the Old Man?"

"Aw, I seen him down at that dive of antiquity, the Purple Cat Bar, a while ago," said Bill. "He was purty well lit and havin' some kind of a argyment with old Cap'n Gid Jessup. He'll be at the fight all right. I didn't say nothin' to him; but he'll be there."

"He'll more likely land in jail for fightin' old Gid," I ruminated. "They hate each other like snakes. Well, that's his own lookout. But I'd like him to see me lick Torkilsen. I heered him braggin' about the square-head the other day. Seems like he seen him fight once someplace."

"Well," said Bill, "it's nearly time for the fight. Let's get goin'. We'll go down back alleys and sneak into the arena from the rear, so none of them admirin' Swedes can get ahold of you and find out you're really a American mick. Come on!"

So we done so, accompanied by three Swedes of the *Sea Girl*'s crew who was loyal to their ship and their shipmates. We snuck along alleys and slunk into the back rooms of the arena, where Neimann come into us, perspiring freely, and told us he was having a heck of a time keeping Swedes outa the dressing-room. He said numbers of 'em wanted to come in and shake hands with Lars Ivarson before he went out to uphold the fair name of Sweden. He said Hakon was getting in the ring, and for us to hustle.

So we went up the aisle hurriedly, and the crowd was so busy cheering for Hakon that they didn't notice us till we was in the ring. I looked out over the house, which was packed, setting and standing, and square-heads fighting to get in when they wasn't room for no more. I never knowed they was that many Scandinavians in Eastern waters. It looked like every man in the house was a Dane, a Norwegian, or a Swede – big, blond fellers, all roaring like bulls in their excitement. It looked like a stormy night.

Neimann was walking around the ring, bowing and grinning, and every now and then his gaze wouldst fall on me as I set in my corner and he wouldst shudder viserbly and wipe his forehead with his bandanner.

Meanwhile, a big Swedish sea captain was acting the part of the announcer, and was making quite a ceremony out of it. He wouldst boom out jovially, and the crowd wouldst roar in various alien tongues, and I told one of the Swedes from the *Sea Girl* to translate for me, which he done so in a whisper, while pertending to tie on my gloves.

This is what the announcer was saying: "Tonight all Scandinavia is represented here in this glorious forthcoming struggle for supremacy. In my mind it brings back days of the Vikings. This is a Scandinavian spectacle for Scandinavian sailors. Every man involved in this contest is Scandinavian. You all know Hakon Torkilsen, the pride of Denmark!" Whereupon, all the Danes in the crowd bellered. "I haven't met Lars Ivarson, but the very fact that he is a son of Sweden assures us that he will prove no mean opponent for Denmark's favored son." It was the Swedes' turn to roar. "I now present the referee, Jon Yarssen, of Norway! This is a family affair. Remember, whichever way the fight goes, it will lend glory to Scandinavia!"

Then he turned and pointed toward the opposite corner and roared, "Hakon Torkilsen, of Denmark!"

Again the Danes thundered to the skies, and Bill O'Brien hissed in my ear. "Don't forget when you're interjuiced say 'Dis bane happiest moment of my life!' The accent will convince 'em you're a Swede."

The announcer turned toward me and, as his eyes fell on me for the first time, he started violently and blinked. Then he kind of mechanically pulled hisself together and stammered, "Lars Ivarson-of-of-Sweden!"

I riz, shedding my bathrobe, and a gasp went up from the crowd like they was thunderstruck or something. For a moment a sickening silence reigned, and them my Swedish shipmates started applauding, and some of the Swedes and Norwegians took it up, and, like people always do, got louder and louder till they was lifting the roof.

Three times I started to make my speech, and three times they drowned me out, till I run outa my short stock of patience.

"*Shut up, you lubbers!*" I roared, and they lapsed into sudden silence, gaping at me in amazement. With a menacing scowl, I said, "Dis bane happiest moment of my life, by thunder!"

They clapped kind of feebly and dazedly, and the referee motioned us to the center of the ring. And, as we faced each other, I gaped, and he barked, "Aha!" like a hyena which sees some critter caught in a trap. The referee was the big cheese I'd socked in the alley!

I didn't pay much attention to Hakon, but stared morbidly at the referee, which reeled off the instructions in some Scandinavian tongue. Hakon nodded and responded in kind, and the referee glared at me and snapped something and I nodded and grunted, "Ja!" just as if I understood him, and turned back toward my corner.

He stepped after me, and caught hold of my gloves. Under cover of examining 'em he hissed, so low my handlers didn't even hear him, "You are no Swede! I know you. You called your dog 'Mike.' There is only one white bulldog in the Asiatics by that name! You are Steve Costigan, of the *Sea Girl*."

"Keep it quiet," I muttered nervously.

"Ha!" he snarled. "I will have my revenge. Go ahead – fight your fight. After the bout is over, I will expose you as the imposter you are. These men will hang you to the rafters."

"Gee whiz," I mumbled, "what you wanta do that for? Keep my secret and I'll slip you fifty bucks after the scrap."

He merely snorted, "Ha!" in disdain, pointing meaningly at the black eye which I had give him, and stalked back to the center of the ring.

"What did that Norwegian say to you?" Bill O'Brien asked.

I didn't reply. I was kinda wool-gathering. Looking out over the mob, I admit I didn't like the prospects. I hadst no doubt that them infuriated square-heads would be maddened at the knowledge that a alien had passed hisself off as one of 'em – and they's a limit to the numbers that even Steve Costigan can vanquish in mortal combat! But about that time the gong sounded, and I forgot everything except the battle before me.

For the first time I noticed Hakon Torkilsen, and I realized why he had such a reputation. He was a regular panther of a man – a tall, rangy, beautifully built young slugger with a mane of yellow hair and cold, steely eyes. He was six feet one to my six feet, and weighed 185 to my 190. He was trained to the ounce, and his long, smooth muscles rippled under his white skin as he moved. My black mane musta contrasted strongly with his golden hair.

He come in fast and ripped a left hook to my head, whilst I come back with a right to the body which brung him up standing. But his body muscles was like iron ridges, and I knowed it wouldst take plenty of pounding to soften him there, even though it was me doing the pounding.

Hakon was a sharpshooter, and he begunst to shoot his left straight and fast. All my opponents does, at first, thinking I'm a sucker for a left jab. But they soon abandons that form of attack. I ignores left jabs. I now walked through a perfect hail of 'em and crashed a thundering right under Hakon's heart which brung a astonished grunt outa him. Discarding his jabbing offensive, he started flailing away with both hands, and I wanta tell you he wasn't throwing no powder puffs!

It was the kind of scrapping I like. He was standing up to me, giving and taking, and I wasn't called on to run him around the ring like I gotta do with so many of my foes. He was belting me plenty, but that's my style, and, with a wide grin, I slugged merrily at his body and head, and the gong found us in the center of the ring, banging away.

The crowd give us a roaring cheer as we went back to our corners, but suddenly my grin was wiped off by the sight of Yarssen, the referee, cryptically indicating his black eye as he glared morbidly at me.

I determined to finish Torkilsen as quick as possible, make a bold break through the crowd, and try to get away before Yarssen had time to tell 'em my fatal secret. Just as I started to tell Bill, I felt a hand jerking at my ankle. I looked down into the bewhiskered, bewildered and bleary-eyed face of the Old Man.

"Steve!" he squawked. "I'm in a terrible jam!"

Bill O'Brien jumped like he was stabbed. "Don't yell 'Steve' thataway!" he hissed. "You wanta get us all mobbed?"

"I'm in a terrible jam!" wailed the Old Man, wringing his hands. "If you don't help me, I'm a rooined man!"

"What's the lay?" I asked in amazement, leaning through the ropes.

"It's Gid Jessup's fault," he moaned. "The serpent got me into a argyment and got me drunk. He knows I ain't got no sense when I'm soused. He hornswoggled me into laying a bet on Torkilsen. I didn't know you was goin' to fight – "

"Well," I said, "that's tough, but you'll just have to lose the bet."

"I can't!" he howled.

BONG! went the gong, and I shot outa my corner as Hakon ripped outa his.

"I can't lose!" the Old Man howled above the crowd. "*I bet the Sea Girl!*"

"What?" I roared, momentarily forgetting where I was, and half-turning toward the ropes. BANG! Hakon nearly tore my head off with a free-swinging right. Bellering angrily, I come back with a smash to the mush that started the claret, and we went into a slug-fest, flailing free and generous with both hands.

That Dane was tough! Smacks that would of staggered most men didn't make him wince. He come ploughing in for more. But, just before the gong, I caught him off balance with a blazing left hook that knocked him into the ropes, and the Swedes arose, whooping like lions.

Back on my stool I peered through the ropes. The Old Man was dancing a hornpipe.

"What's this about bettin' the *Sea Girl!*" I demanded.

"When I come to myself a while ago, I found I'd wagered the ship," he wept, "against Jessup's lousy tub, the *Nigger King*, which I find is been condemned by the shippin' board and wouldn't clear the bay without goin' to the bottom. He took a unfair advantage of me! I wasn't responsible when I made that bet!"

"Don't pay it," I growled, "Jessup's a rat!"

"He showed me a paper I signed while stewed," he groaned. "It's a contrack upholdin' the bet. If it weren't for that, I wouldn't pay. But if I don't, he'll rooin my reputation in every port of the Seven Seas. He'll show that contrack and gimme the name of a welsher. You got to lose!"

"Gee whiz!" I said, badgered beyond endurance. "This is a purty mess – "

BONG! went the gong, and I paced out into the ring, all upset and with my mind elsewhere. Hakon swarmed all over me, and drove me into the ropes where I woke up and beat him off, but, with the Old Man's howls echoing in my ears, I failed to follow up my advantage, and Hakon come back strong.

The Danes raised the roof as he battered me about the ring, but he wasn't hurting me none, because I covered up, and again, just before the gong, I snapped outa my crouch and sent him back on his heels with a wicked left hook to the head.

The referee gimme a gloating look, and pointed at his black eye, and I had to grit my teeth to keep from socking him stiff. I set down on my stool and listened gloomily to the shrieks of the Old Man, which was getting more unbearable every minute.

"You got to lose!" he howled. "If Torkilsen don't win this fight, I'm rooined! If the bet'd been on the level, I'd pay – you know that. But, I been swindled, and now I'm goin' to get robbed! Lookit the rat over there, wavin' that devilish paper at me! It's more'n human flesh and blood can stand! It's enough to drive a man to drink! You got to lose!"

"But the boys has bet their shirts on me," I snarled, fit to be tied with worry and bewilderment. "I can't lay down! I never throwed a fight. I don't know how – "

"That's gratitood!" he screamed, busting into tears. "After all I've did for you! Little did I know I was warmin' a serpent in my bosom! The poorhouse is starin' me in the face, and you – "

"Aw, shut up, you old sea-horse!" said Bill. "Steve – I mean Lars – has got enough to contend with without you howlin' and yellin' like a maneyack. Them square-heads is gonna get suspicious if you and him keep talkin' in English. Don't pay no attention to him, Steve – I mean Lars. Get that Dane!"

Well, the gong sounded, and I went out all tore up in my mind and having just about lost heart in the fight. That's a most dangerous thing to have happen, especially against a man-killing slugger like Hakon Torkilsen. Before I knowed what was goin' on, the Swedes rose with a scream of warning and about a million stars bust in my head. I realized faintly that I was on the canvas, and I listened for the count to know how long I had to rest.

I heered a voice droning above the roar of the fans, but it was plumb meaningless to me. I shook my head, and my sight cleared. Jon Yarssen was standing over me, his arm going up and down, but I didn't understand a word he said! He was counting in Swedish!

Not daring to risk a moment, I heaved up before my head had really quit singing an' Hakon come storming in like a typhoon to finish me.

But I was mad clean through and had plumb forgot about the Old Man and his fool bet. I met Hakon with a left hook which nearly tore his head off, and the Swedes yelped with joy. I bored in, ripping both hands to the wind and heart, and, in a fast mix-up at close quarters, Hakon went down – more from a slip than a punch. But he was wise and took a count, resting on one knee.

I watched the referee's arm so as to familiarize myself with the sound of the numerals – but he wasn't counting in the same langwidge as he had over me! I got it, then; he counted over me in Swedish and over Hakon in Danish. The langwidges is alike in many ways, but different enough to get me all mixed up, which didn't know a word in either tongue, anyhow. I seen then that I was going to have a enjoyable evening.

Hakon was up at nine – I counted the waves of the referee's arm – and he come up at me like a house afire. I fought him off half-heartedly, whilst the Swedes shouted with amazement at the change which had come over me since that blazing first round.

Well, I've said repeatedly that a man can't fight his best when he's got his mind on something else. Here was a nice mess for me to worry about. If I quit, I'd be a yeller dog and despize myself for the rest of my life, and my shipmates would lose their money, and so would all the Swedes which had bet on me and was now yelling and cheering for me just like I was their brother. I couldn't throw 'em down. Yet if I won, the Old Man would lose his ship, which was all he had and like a daughter to him. It wouldst beggar him and break his heart. And, as a minor thought, whether I won or lost, that scut Yarssen was going to tell the crowd I wasn't no Swede, and get me mobbed. Every time I looked at him over Hakon's shoulder in a clinch, Yarssen wouldst touch his black eye meaningly. I was bogged down in gloom, and I wished I could evaporate or something.

Back on my stool, between rounds, the Old Man wept and begged me to lay down, and Bill and my handlers implored me to wake up and kill Torkilsen, and I thought I'd go nuts.

I went out for the fourth round slowly, and Hakon, evidently thinking I'd lost my fighting heart, if any, come with his usual tigerish rush and biffed me three times in the face without a return.

I dragged him into a grizzly-like clinch which he couldn't break, and as we rassled and strained, he spat something at me which I couldn't understand, but I understood the tone of it. Me, Steve Costigan, the terror of the high seas!

With a maddened roar, I jerked away from him and crashed a murderous right to his jaw that nearly floored him. Before he couldst recover his balance, I tore into him like a wild man, forgetting everything except that I was Steve Costigan, the bully of the toughest ship afloat.

Slugging right and left, I rushed him into the ropes, where I pinned him, while the crowd went crazy. He crouched and covered up, taking most of my punches on the gloves and elbows, but I reckoned it looked to the mob like I was beating him to death. All at once, above the roar, I heered the Old Man screaming, "Steve, for cat's sake, let up! I'll go on the beach, and it'll be your fault!"

That unnerved me. I involuntarily dropped my hands and recoiled, and Hakon, with fire in his eyes, lunged outa his crouch like a tiger and crashed his right to my jaw.

BANG! I was on the canvas again, and the referee was droning Swedish numerals over me. Not daring to take a count, and maybe get counted out unknowingly, I staggered up, and Hakon come lashing in. I throwed my arms around him in a grizzly hug, and it took him and the referee both to break my hold.

Hakon drove me staggering into the ropes with a wild-man attack, but I'm always dangerous on the ropes, as many a good man has found out on coming to in his dressing room. As I felt the rough strands against my back, I caught him with a slingshot right uppercut which snapped his head right back betwixt his shoulders, and this time it was him which fell into a clinch and hung on.

Looking over his shoulder at that sea of bristling blond heads and yelling faces, I seen various familiar figgers. On one side of the ring – near my corner – the Old Man was dancing around like he was on a red-hot hatch, shedding maudlin tears and pulling his whiskers; and, on the other side, a skinny, shifty-eyed old seaman was whooping with glee and waving a folded paper. Cap'n Gid Jessup, the old cuss! He knowed the Old Man would bet anything when he was drunk – even bet the *Sea Girl*, as sweet a ship as ever rounded the Horn, against that rotten old hulk of a *Nigger King*, which wasn't worth a cent a ton. And, near at hand, the referee,

Yarssen, was whispering tenderly in my ear, as he broke our clinch. "Better let Hakon knock you stiff – then you won't feel so much what the crowd does to you when I tell them who you are!"

Back on my stool again, I put my face on Mike's neck and refused to listen either to the pleas of the Old Man or to the profane shrieks of Bill O'Brien. By golly, that fight was like a nightmare! I almost hoped Hakon would knock my brains out and end all my troubles.

I went out for the fifth like a man going to his own hanging. Hakon was evidently puzzled. Who wouldn't of been? Here was a fighter – me – who was performing in spurts, exploding in bursts of ferocious battling just when he appeared nearly out, and sagging halfheartedly when he looked like a winner.

He come in, lashed a vicious left to my midsection, and dashed me to the canvas with a thundering overhand right. Maddened, I arose and dropped him with a wild round-house swing he wasn't expecting. Again the crowd surged to its feet, and the referee got flustered and started counting over Hakon in what sounded like Swedish.

Hakon bounded up and slugged me into the ropes, offa which I floundered, only to slip in a smear of my own blood on the canvas, and again, to the disgust of the Swedes, I found myself among the rosin.

I looked about, heard the Old Man yelling for me to stay down, and saw Old Cap'n Jessup waving his blame-fool contrack. I arose, only half aware of what I was doing, and BANG! Hakon caught me on the ear with a hurricane swing, and I sprawled on the floor, half under the ropes.

Goggling dizzily at the crowd from this position, I found myself staring into the distended eyes of Cap'n Gid Jessup, which was standing up, almost touching the ring. Evidently froze at the thought of losing his bet – with me on the canvas – he was standing there gaping, his arm still lifted with the contrack which he'd been waving at the Old Man.

With me, thinking is acting. One swoop of my gloved paw swept that contrack outa his hand. He yawped with surprise and come lunging half through the ropes. I rolled away from him, sticking the contrack in my mouth and chawing as fast as I could. Cap'n Jessup grabbed me by the hair with one hand and tried to jerk the contrack outa my jaws with the other'n, but all he got was a severely bit finger.

At this, he let go of me and begun to scream and yell. "Gimme back that paper, you cannibal! He's eatin' my contrack! I'll sue you – "

Meanwhile, the dumbfounded referee, overcome with amazement, had stopped counting, and the crowd, not understanding this by-play, was roaring with astonishment. Jessup begun to crawl through the ropes, and Yarssen yelled something and shoved him back with his foot. He started through again, yelling blue murder, and a big Swede, evidently thinking he was trying to attack me, swung once with a fist the size of a caulking mallet, and Cap'n Jessup bit the dust.

I arose with my mouth full of paper, and Hakon promptly banged me on the chin with a right he started from his heels. Ow, Jerusha! Wait'll somebody hits you on the jaw when you're chewing something! I thought for a second every tooth in my head was shattered, along with my jaw-bone. But I reeled groggily back into the ropes and begun to swaller hurriedly.

BANG! Hakon whanged me on the ear. "Gulp!" I said, WHAM! He socked me in the eye. "Gullup!" I said. BLOP! He pasted me in the stummuck, "Oof! glup!" I said, WHANG! He took me on the side of the head. "GULP!" I swallered the last of the contrack, and went for that Dane with fire in my eyes.

I banged Hakon with a left that sunk outa sight in his belly, and nearly tore his head off with a paralyzing right before he realized that, instead of being ready for the cleaners, I was stronger'n ever and ra'ring for action.

Nothing loath, he rallied, and we went into a whirlwind of hooks and swings till the world spun like a merry-go-round. Neither of us heered the gong, and our seconds had to drag us apart and lead us to our corners.

"Steve," the Old Man was jerking at my leg and weeping with gratitude, "I seen it all! That old pole-cat's got no hold on me now. He can't prove I ever made that fool bet. You're a scholar and a gent – one of nature's own noblemen! You've saved the *Sea Girl!*"

"Let that be a lesson to you," I said, spitting out a fragment of the contrack along with a mouthful of blood. "Gamblin' is sinful. Bill, I got a watch in my pants pocket. Get it and bet it that I lay this square-head within three more rounds."

And I come out for the sixth like a typhoon. "I'm going to get mobbed by the fans as soon as the fight's over and Yarssen spills the beans," I thought, "but I'll have my fun now."

For once I'd met a man which was willing and able to stand up and slug it out with me. Hakon was as lithe as a panther and as tough as spring-steel. He was quicker'n me, and hit nearly as hard. We crashed together in the center of the ring, throwing all we had into the storm of battle.

Through a red mist I seen Hakon's eyes blazing with a unearthly light. He was plumb berserk, like them old Vikings which was his ancestors. And all the Irish fighting madness took hold of me, and we ripped and tore like tigers.

We was the center of a frenzied whirlwind of gloves, ripping smashes to each other's bodies which you could hear all over the house, and socks to each other's heads that spattered blood all over the ring. Every blow packed dynamite and had the killer's lust behind it. It was a test of endurance.

At the gong, we had to be tore apart and dragged to our corners by force, and, at the beginning of the next round, we started in where we'd left off. We reeled in a blinding hurricane of gloves. We slipped in smears of blood, or was knocked to the canvas by each other's thundering blows.

The crowd was limp and idiotic, drooling wordless screeches. And the referee was bewildered and muddled. He counted over us in Swedish, Danish, and Norwegian alike. Then I was on the canvas, and Hakon was staggering on the ropes, gasping, and the befuddled Yarssen was counting over me. And, in the dizzy maze, I recognized the langwidge. He was counting in Spanish!

"You ain't no Norwegian!" I said, glaring groggily up at him.

"Four!" he said, shifting into English. "As much as you're a Swede! Five! A man's got to eat. Six! They wouldn't have given me this job – seven! – if I hadn't pretended to be a Norwegian. Eight! I'm John Jones, a vaudeville linguist from Frisco. Nine! Keep my secret and I'll keep yours."

The gong! Our handlers dragged us off to our corners and worked over us. I looked over at Hakon. I was marked plenty – a split ear, smashed lips, both eyes half closed, nose broken – but them's my usual adornments. Hakon wasn't marked up so much in the face – outside of a closed eye and a few gashes – but his body was raw beef from my continuous body hammering. I drawed a deep breath and grinned gargoylishly. With the

Old Man and that fake referee offa my mind, I couldst give all my thoughts to the battle.

The gong banged again, and I charged like a enraged bull. Hakon met me as usual, and rocked me with thundering lefts and rights. But I bored in, driving him steadily before me with ripping, bone-shattering hooks to the body and head. I felt him slowing up. The man don't live which can slug with me!

Like a tiger scenting the kill, I redoubled the fury of my onslaught, and the crowd arose, roaring, as they foresaw the end. Nearly on the ropes, Hakon rallied with a dying burst of ferocity, and momentarily had me reeling under a fusillade of desperate swings. But I shook my head doggedly and plowed in under his barrage, ripping my terrible right under his heart again and again, and tearing at his head with mallet-like left hooks.

Flesh and blood couldn't stand it. Hakon crumpled in a neutral corner under a blasting fire of left and right hooks. He tried to get his legs under him, but a child couldst see he was done.

The referee hesitated, then raised my right glove, and the Swedes and Norwegians came roaring into the ring and swept me offa my feet. A glance showed Hakon's Danes carrying him to his corner, and I tried to get to him to shake his hand, and tell him he was as brave and fine a fighter as I ever met – which was the truth and nothing nelse – but my delirious followers hadst boosted both me and Mike on their shoulders and were carrying us toward the dressing room like a king or something.

A tall form come surging through the crowd, and Mushy Hansen grabbed my gloved hand and yelled, "Boy, you done us proud! I'm sorry the Danes had to lose, but, after a battle like that, I can't hold no grudge. I couldn't stay away from the scrap. Hooray for the old *Sea Girl*, the fightin'est ship on the Seven Seas!"

And the Swedish captain, which had acted as announcer, barged in front of me and yelled in English, "You may be a Swede, but if you are, you're the most unusual looking Swede I ever saw. But I don't give a whoop! I've just seen the greatest battle since Gustavus Adolphus licked the Dutch! Skoal, Lars Ivarson!"

And all the Swedes and Norwegians thundered, "Skoal, Lars Ivarson!"

"They want you to make a speech," said Mushy.

"All right," I said. "Dis bane happiest moment of my life."

"Louder," said Mushy. "They're makin' so much noise they can't understand you, anyhow. Say somethin' in a foreign langwidge."

"All right," I said, and yelled the only foreign words I couldst think of. "Parleyvoo Francais! Vive le Stockholm! Erin go bragh!"

And they bellered louder'n ever. A fighting man is a fighting man in any langwidge!

Cultured Cauliflowers

I been unpopular at the Waterfront Arena in Frisco ever since the night the announcer clumb into the ring and bellered: "Ladeez and gents! The management regrets to announce that the semi-windup between Sailor Costigan and Jim Ash can't come off. Costigan just knocked Ash so cold in his dressin' room they're workin' on him with a pulmoter."

"Well, let Costigan fight somebody else!" the crowd hollered.

"He can't," said the announcer. "Somebody squirted tabasco sass in his eyes."

Them was the general facks of the case, only it wasn't tabasco sauce. I was laying on a table in my dressing room, getting a rub down, when in come a learned-looking gent with colored spectacles and a long white beard.

"I'm Dr. Stauf," he said. "The Commission has sent me in to examine you to see if you're in fit condition to fight."

"Well, hustle," said my handler Joe Kerney. "He's due in the ring in about five minutes."

Dr. Stauf tapped my huge chest, looked at my teeth, and give me the general once over.

"Ah," he said. "Ah ha!" he said. "Your peepers is on the blink. But I'll fix that." He took out a bottle and a glass dropper, and pulling back my lids, dropped a lot of stuff in my eyes, saying, "If that don't fix you, my name ain't Barl-Stauf."

"What is that stuff?" I demanded, setting up and shaking my head. "Seems like my eye balls is kinda expandin' or somethin'."

"A very benefischal drug," says Stauf. "You got eye strain from shootin' craps under a poor light. That drug will make 'em as good as – yow!" Without warning my white bulldog Mike had grabbed him by the spectacles and the white whiskers come off, revealing the convulsed features of Foxy Barlow, Jim Ash's manager.

"What kind of a game is this?" I roared, leaping offa the table. Joe Kerney snatched up the bottle and smelt it.

"Belladonna!" he yelled. "In three minutes you'll be stone blind!"

I give a horrible yell of rage and plunged at Barlow, who with a desperate convulsion tore his mangled leg outa Mike's bear-trap jaws and rushed out, howling bloody murder.

"Why didn't we rekernize him?" squalled Joe. "We mighta knowed them rats would try to rooin you before we got into the ring. But even Mike didn't know him till he smelt of him – "

I shoved him aside and charged blunderingly out into the hall, where I seen a bathrobed figger I knowed was Ash emerging from his dressing-room. My eyes was dilating so fast he was just a kind of blur.

"You dirty double-crossin' son of a half-breed pole-cat!" I roared as I rushed and threw my right mauler at his jaw like a man throwing a hammer. By sheer luck I caught him flat-footed, and when Joe had helped me dress, and led me outa the Arener, they was still trying to bring him to.

Joe took me to his room, and for twenty-four hours I was blind as a bat; then when I got so I could see at all, everything was so blurry and dim I couldn't get around by myself.

"What gets me," I said bitterly, "is how come them dumbbells ever thought up a trick like that. Ash ain't got no sense, and neither has Barlow."

"I understand Ash's cousin from the East put him up to it," said Joe. "I ain't seen him, but he's a fighter, they say, and smart as they come. Red Stalz was tellin' me Ash told this cousin he was goin' to fight a man he was afeard he couldn't lick, and the cousin told him to slip you the blindin' drops. But that bonehead Barlow put so much dope in your eyes you'd of gone blind before you could get in the ring, even if we hadn't discovered the fake. The cousin intended you should lose your sight after the fight started, of course. But Barlow muffed it."

"Well, what am I goin' to do whilst I wait for my eyes to get normal?" I complained.

"Buy you some glasses," advised Joe, so he guided me down to a eye specialist where I spent most of my scanty roll on a pair of spectacles with big wide horn rims. Joe gawped at me.

"By golly," he said, "I didn't have no idee glasses would change a man's looks like that. Why, you look plumb mild and retirin'. Look in the mirror."

I done so and was disgusted. If it hadn't been for my cauliflowers, I'd of looked like a perfessor or something.

"How long I got to wear these blinders?" I asked the specialist.

"Oh, maybe a week, maybe longer," he said. "You've had a terrific overdose of belladonna. I can't say just when your pupils will regain their normal state."

I went back to Los Angeles, and after I paid my fare I was broke and no chance for a fight with them eyes. To add to my troubles, whilst I was setting broodingly in my room at the Waterfront Hotel, the landlord come in and told me if I didn't pay my back rent he was going to throw me out. I evaded the question by throwing him out, and then wandered morosely down to the pool halls to see if I couldn't borrow a few bucks from somebody.

"Steve," said Jack Tanner, which I struck up first, "I'll swear I ain't got a dime – but listen, you could box a exhibition, couldn't you? Reason I ask, I seen a gent over to Varella's gym while ago tryin' to get some heavyweight for some kinda society exhibition. Le's go over and see can we catch him."

So we went over to the gym, and Jack said: "There he is, talkin' with Varella." With the aid of my glasses I seen a elderly gent in a high silk hat with a gold-headed cane. Varella seen me, and said: "Hi, Steve, I'm glad to see you. Maybe you do so beeznizz with deez gentleman, yes, no? Deez is Steve Costigan, Meester. Maybe you use heem, eh, so?"

"I didn't catch the name," I said.

"I am Horace J. J. Vander Swiller III," said the gent, looking at me through one of them there monercals. "My word, what a peculiar-looking individual! With the clothing and general appearance of wharfside hoodlum, yet with the facial aspect of a man with scholarly inclinations."

"Aw, it's these dern glasses," I said. "Without 'em I'm a man among men. Lookit." I took 'em off and Horace III gasped.

"My word!" he said, "what an incredible difference it makes! Put them back on, please! Thank you. I think you'll do – now. As I have told Mr. Varella, I am looking for a pugilist to appear in an exhibition match at my club – the Athenian. He must be a heavyweight and should be fairly well known."

"I've busted snoots from Galveston to Singapore," I said.

"Indeed? Well, I understand you have some reputation, at least. I have secured Mr. Johnny McGoorty for your opponent – "

"The mugg which has just come to the Coast from Chicago?" I asked. "Well, what's the general purpose of the go, and what's my cut, if it's any of my business?"

"You and Mr. McGoorty will each receive five hundred dollars," said Horace. "The exhibition is in the nature of a fete for Mr. Jack Belding, who is being entertained by our set."

"You mean Gentleman Jack Belding which claims the heavyweight title?" I said.

"I understand the New York Boxing Commission has recognized his claim," said Horace. "Mr. Belding is a most delightful gentleman, not at all like the accepted idea of pugilists."

"So I hear," I growled. "He was a college star and a amateur athlete before he turned perfessional; been playin' the sercierty racket strong back East, I hear."

"Mr. Belding is as much at home in a drawing-room as in the ring," frowned Horace. "A highly cultured young man, with good connections, and a credit to any social set. This fete tonight is the climax of the club's program of entertainment for our honored guest. He has agreed to act as referee – in fact, he himself suggested the exhibition, in order to give the ladies of the club an opportunity to witness a typical ring match, without the painful brutality and bloodshed attendant upon a real fight."

"Then it's to be a very tame affair?" I asked.

"Certainly. Of course, we shall expect you to instill a good deal of harmless action into it, and go through the maneuvers of feinting, guarding and countering as realistically as possible, but without striking any damaging blows or descending to any of the brutal strategies so common in actual combat."

"Alright," I said. "For five hundred bucks I'd rassle a Bengal tiger. I reckon I can see good enough to cake walk through a exhibition."

"Wait," he said. "Your garments will never do. You will be forced to mix somewhat with the guests before you don the habiliments of your profession, and possibly after the bout."

"What's wrong with these duds?" I asked impatiently. "I bought 'em at the best slop-shop on the Barbary Coast."

"They may do for the waterfront," said Horace, "but even you must see that they are impossible for the exclusive Athenian Club."

"Well, they're all I got," I growled. "If you don't like 'em, why don't you buy me some other kind?"

"So I will," he said. "Come – let's away to a haberdashery."

"Aw, a gents' furnishin' store'll do," I said. "I ain't particular."

Well, he hauled me into a ritzy joint and they done their worst.

"Something a bit sporty, I should say," said Horace. "An apparel which will suggest the collegiate – the virile yet scholarly playboy of the upper class."

Them clerks went for me, and before I knowed it, I was fitted out in a checkered golf knickers, a silk sport shirt as they called it, with a fool little bow tie, a jacket with a belt in the back, fancy golf socks, low quarter canvas shoes, and a Panerma hat with a turned-down brim. Then Horace had my tousled hair slicked back with some kind of muck that smelt like a – well, never mind.

"Look at yourself in the mirror," they said proudly. I done so and then set down on a goods box and put my head in my hands.

"I'll never live this down," I groaned. "Get me some false whiskers so I won't have to kill any of my acquaintances which might rekernize me in these riggin's."

"The metamorphosis is remarkable," said Horace. "Those garments, coupled with your spectacles, have transformed a wharfside ruffian into a refined-appearing person who might well pass for an athletic student in some large university – wait! One thing more – a pair of mauve-tinted kid gloves to conceal, as much as possible, those huge hairy hands. Now! I flatter myself I have prepared you rather well for the gaze of my club members and guests. The costume is unique – original – suggesting the casual invasion of the field of physical action by a studious and introspective individual of the better classes. You might have just stepped off the golf links of some fraternity."

"And I mighta just stepped out of a circus," I snapped. "I look like any pansy couldst slap me on the wrist and break my neck."

Mike just set down with his back to me and looked into space and wouldn't pay no attention to me at all.

"Don't ack that way, Mike," I said irritably. "I know you're ashamed of me, and I'm ashamed of myself; but we gotta have some dough."

"You'll have to leave that brutal-looking dog somewhere," said Horace. "Yet, no, on second thought, you may bring him along. He will add atmosphere to the occasion."

"Second thoughts or first," I said bitterly, "Mike comes along or I don't go. You done got me into these monkey-clothes, Double J III, but you ain't goin' to give Mike the air."

So we got into his auto and the shawffeur drove us out to the club. It was a scrumptious place. The members was all rich as mud and the clubhouse looked like a castle or something. We drove into the grounds which was surrounded by a high stone wall, and I seen they had a ring pitched on the lawn out to one side of the club house, with chairs all around and lights strung over the ring and amongst the trees.

"Some of the ladies are in the tea room," said Horace. "I am to bring you in and introduce you to them. They are greatly interested in psychology, and since Mr. Belding has proved such a fascinating gentleman, the club ladies are taking a keen interest in persons connected with the ring. You will be a new and interesting type to them. As soon as Mr. McGoorty arrives I will bring him in, also. Try to act as gentlemanly as possible, and reply courteously to the ladies. Remember, they represent the very heights of culture and sensitive refinement."

"I'm always a gent," I growled. "I never socked a lady in my life."

He shook his head like he had his doubts, and we went into the mansion where a butler met us and took Horace's hat and cane. He tried to take my Panerma too, and Mike clamped onto his leg, and you oughta heard him holler. I pulled Mike off, and Horace frowned. "A most vicious beast."

"Naw, he ain't," I said. "He just thought that egg was tryin' to steal my hat."

"Will he not, then," said Horace, "attack Mr. McGoorty in the ring."

"Naw," I answered. "He knows his business, and mine too; but if somebody in street clothes was to sock me, he'd sure go for 'em."

Horace acted kinda nervous, but he led me into a locker room and showed me some silk togs he'd laid out. I hanged my straw hat on a chair and I seen Mike looking at it very mysterious.

Then Horace steered me in another room where half a dozen ladies in evening gowns was sipping tea, and he said: "Ladies, this is Mr. Costigan, one of the participants in the exhibition match."

They all lifted their large-nets and looked at me like I was a jelly-fish or something.

"Indeed!" one said. "So you are a professional pugilist, Mr. Costigan?"

"Yes'm," I said.

"Somehow you do not seem the type at all," said another'n. "Don't you find the profession rather strenuous for one of your evident studious nature?"

"Yes'm," I mumbled, having only a vague idee of what she was talking about.

"Do sit down and have some tea," they said. "You're a college man, of course, Mr. Dorgan – to what fraternities do you belong?"

"Well," I said vaguely. "I'm an A.B. mariner."

They all giggled.

"What a delightfully original sense of humor, Mr. Costigan," one of 'em said. "Tell me – how does a man of your apparent scholarly tastes come to be in such a brutal profession? Do you not find it hard to hold your own against the more primitive types?"

"Well," I said, "I just walk in and start firin' away with both maulers for the head and belly till the other thug drops."

They looked kinda nonplused, and one said: "How many lumps of sugar in your tea, Mr. Costigan?"

"Nary," I said, "I takes my pizen straight." I picked up the cup, smelt the stuff suspiciously, waved the cup at 'em gallantly, and saying jovially, "Well, here's mud in your eye!" I tossed it up with one gulp. I never forgets my etiket.

A kind of dumb silence reigned and one of the ladies said: "Mr. Dorgan, what is your estimate of Einstein?"

"You mean Abie Einstine of San Diego?" I said. "Ah, he's clever enough, but he couldn't punch a dent in a pound of butter, and he ain't got no guts."

At this moment Mike riz up disgustedly and stalked off towards the dressing-room with a mysterious gleam in his eye. The dames was looking at me kinda bewildered, and to my relief up come Horace with a young fellow, and said: "Here is Mr. Dolan of the *Tribune*, who is going to write up the exhibition for his paper."

"Hello, Billy," I greeted, getting up and holding out my hand, mighty glad to meet one of my own kind again.

"This is Mr. Costigan, Mr. Dolan," said Horace, as Billy held out his hand with a blank stare.

"Mr. Costi – holy mackerel! It's Steve!" he gasped.

"Yeah, who else?" I growled embarrassedly, and Billy stared at me like he couldn't believe hisself.

"Ye gods!" he said. "You look like a mildly insane college professor on a drunk! Steve Costigan, in gold panties. Well, I'll da – "

"Perhaps you and Mr. Costigan can talk more freely in the smoking-room," suggested Horace with a nervous glance at the ladies, which was beginning to glare. I was glad to go, and Horace followed us.

"Stay out of sight until the bout starts," he snapped, "and don't try to mix with the guests in the dance afterwards. I should have known you couldn't fit into polite society. Stay here till the bout is ready to begin."

"OK with me, pal," I said, pouring me a drink out of a bottle I found on a table. "Billy, did you bring your camera?"

"No," he said. "Why?"

"I just wanted to warn you not to take no pitchers of me in these duds," I said. "Who's that?"

Horace had just entered with a tall, hard-looking young thug.

"Mr. McGoorty, Mr. Dorgan and Mr. Dolan," said Horace. I stuck out my hand but McGoorty just gaped, and then started laughing like a hyener.

"Sailor Costigan?" he whooped. "The man-eatin' bear-cat of the West Coast? The iron-fisted, granite-jawed terror that was born in a Texas cactus bed and cut his teeth on a Gila monster? Oh boy, this is too much! How come they let you outa the kindergarten for this mill, Costigan?"

"Listen here, you lantern-jawed son of a – " I begun blood thirstily, but Horace said, "Gentlemen, I beg of you! Come, Mr. McGoorty, I will introduce you to the ladies."

They went out and I ground my teeth to hear McGoorty snickering as he looked back at my golf britches.

"Billy," I asked, "where at have I saw that mutt before?"

"I don't know," said Billy, "he just recently arrived from Chicago. Look out this window, Steve, the shebang's getting under way."

Big cars was discharging their cargoes on the lawn, and the seats was filling up with a colorful array, as they say. The cream of Los Angeles sercierty was there, and by squinting my eyes, I made out a tall figger surrounded by a fluttering group of admirers.

"Gentleman Jack, and isn't he putting on the dog?" said Billy sardonically. "He's certainly made the society racket pay. 'College Star Wins Ring Laurels'; 'Favorite Son of the Four Hundred Reaches Heights'; 'Young Society Leader Cops Title.' I've read and written such headers as those till I'm sick of it. I hope he gets his head knocked off in his next fight. Come on, I'll help you into your togs."

"Oughtn't you to be minglin' with the crowd and gettin' interviews and things?" I ast.

"Apfelstrudel," he sneered. "These society exhibitions are all alike. I could write them up asleep."

At this moment Horace appeared. "Come, come!" he said sharply. "The affair is about to begin. What is delaying you?"

"I thought maybe Gentleman Jack wanted to get acquainted with me and McGoorty before the brawl," I said with mild sarcasm.

"Tush, tush," frowned Horace. "A man of his position can hardly be expected to hobnob with the inferiors of his profession."

We went into the dressing-room and I got into my trunks and bathrobe and called Mike. He come out of a adjoining shower room with a satisfied look on his face like a job well done.

"Are you going to wear your glasses into the ring?" Billy asked.

"Yeah," I said. "I couldn't see to get there without 'em. I'll take 'em off before we start sparrin', of course."

Billy laughed. "I'll swear," he said, "I had no idea glasses could change a man's looks so. Even in fighting-togs you look like a book-worm."

Just then Horace come back in to tell us it was time to go on. Me and Billy and Spike followed Horace out onto the lawn between the chairs full of men in dress suits and women in low-cut gowns, and I heered a dame say: "Tee hee! Fawncy a poogilist wearing glawses! What an odd-looking person!" And some bird said back at her, "Odd is no name for it, my deah.

I fawncy he will find it rawtha difficult to hold his own, even in a friendly exhibition."

I clumb into the ring gnashing my teeth slightly. McGoorty was already there, with some gent in a dress suit acting as his second.

"Club members, ladies and gentlemen," said Horace, "this is the feature event of the series of entertainments we have offered in honor of our distinguished guest, Mr. Jack Belding."

Everybody applauded, and Horace said: "These gentlemen, Mr. Costigan and Mr. McGoorty, are about to engage in a friendly exhibition, in the course of which they will demonstrate the science of the profession, thus giving this select audience an opportunity to observe the finer points of the game without being shocked by the display of brutality so characteristic of the ordinary pugilistic affair. Mr. Jack Belding will act as referee."

Belding clumb into the ring and bowed, and the crowd applauded wildly, especially the dames. He was the main show; me and McGoorty was just there to give him a background to show off with.

He called us to the center of the ring and give us instructions, like in a regular go, with a great show of being realistic and all, and I heered the skirts murmuring to each other: "Isn't he splendid?"

But I was glaring at McGoorty, which was snickering in his sleeve, till I jerked off my glasses and threw aside my bathrobe. McGoorty gasped at the sight of my huge body and ferocious features, unmasked, and I heered a sudden murmur sweep around the ringside.

"Heavens!" exclaimed one dame. "It's a gorilla!"

We retired to our corners, and I give my glasses to Billy, impatiently ruffling up my slick hair. Without the spectacles McGoorty looked just like a white blob setting in his corner.

The gong sounded and Gentleman Jack leaped lightly to the center of the ring, snapping his fingers and saying so the dames could hear: "Snap into it, boys! No stalling, now!"

At close range I found I could see fairly well. So we went to work, exhibition style, with lots of showy feinting and blocking and foot-work – well, I gotta admit most of it was McGoorty's. A slugger never shows up well in a exhibition. And then I was handicapped by my short-sightedness. I ain't slow, but I ain't clever, neither.

McGoorty flitted around me, working his left jab fast and purty to my face, and every now and then crossing his right. But when he done that I generally nailed him with a right to the ribs, so he begun to use long-range tactics more and more.

I clinched him and growled wrathfully: "Hey you! These folks didn't come here just to watch you make a fool outa me. They come to see a scientific exhibition. How'm I goin' to do my part if'n you keep so far away all the time I can't even see you?"

"That's for you to figger out," he sneered, which so irritated me that I ripped in a thoughtless left hook that rattled his teeth. I followed it with a smoking right to the belly, and he grabbed my arms with a grunt.

"This here's a exhibition!" he hissed fiercely. "You go easy, dern your hide!"

Gentleman Jack tapped our shoulders, saying: "Come, come, my men, break!"

With heroic self-control I overcome the impulse to bust him in the snoot, and the rest of the round went along polite-like, with us tapping and dancing and jabbing.

We started the second round the same way, and I found that the exertion was making my eyes worse. I blundered around more than ever.

"Costigan," snapped Belding, "you're lousy! Get in there and show some class, if any, before I pitch you out of the ring."

I heered a dame say, "Isn't Mr. Belding masterful?" and I was so irritated I walked in and hit McGoorty harder'n I intended to. He grunted and shellacked me with a left to the chin, I retaliated with a staggering right to the head, and the next minute we was at it hot and heavy. What with the sweat and heat and all, I couldn't hardly see well enough to tell McGoorty from Belding, but as long as he stood up and traded punches with me, I could locate him. I heered a vague murmur from the ringside and Belding hauled us apart.

"Stop it, you boneheads!" he hissed. "This isn't a fight! Go easy, or I'll toss you both out, and you won't get a cent."

"Go roll your hoop, you toe-dancin' four-flusher," snarled McGoorty, but we eased down and coasted through that round and the next.

As we come up for the fourth, I went into a clinch and said: "I just now remember who you remind me of. Are you any kin to Jim Ash of Frisco?"

"First cousin," said he. "And what about it?"

"So!" I bellered, breaking away. "You was the smart gazabo that put him up to blindin' me, hey? I'll show you!"

And with that I smacked him in the mush with a left hook that cracked like a bull whip. He spat out a mouthful of blood and teeth and come back fighting like a wildcat. The ladies screamed, and Horace J. J. give a despairing howl, but I give no heed. I was seeing red and McGoorty was frothing.

We was in the midst of a whirlwind of leather, from which sweat and blood spattered like rain, and the impact of our smashing gloves could of been heard for blocks. Having stopped a slungshot uppercut that nearly tore his head off, McGoorty dived into a clinch, got my ear betwixt his teeth and begun to masticate it like he was eating cabbage, whilst I voiced my annoyance in langwidge which brung more screams from the sercierty folks.

I shook him off, caressing him with a left hook that broke his nose and started the claret in streams, and he begun to give ground. Belding was yelling and cussing us under his breath, but we give him no heed.

By this time McGoorty was just a white blur, but I kept sinking my maulers into the blur and I felt it buckling. Blood was streaming from my nose and smashed lips and crushed ears. Every now and then when I landed solid something splashed into my face which I knowed was Mc-Goorty's gore. The ringside was a bedlam, where the sercierty folks was getting a first-hand glimpse of the polite science of pugilism.

My eye-sight was getting worse all the time, and if McGoorty had kept tin-canning, he could of licked me, but he tried to stand up and trade with me. Feeling his blows getting weaker under my murderous flailing, I put all my beef behind a right hook, and landed solid. I felt McGoorty fall away from me, but the next instant a blob bobbed up in front of me, and I socked it violently. Instantly a most shocking medley of screams busted loose! Sensing that something was wrong, I shook my head violently to get the sweat and blood out my eyes, blinked 'em industriously and bent down towards the blur which was now writhing on the canvas. My straining sight cleared a little, and to my dismay I seen two figgers on the canvas! That last blob had been Gentleman Jack Belding!

I started to help him up, beginning a explanation, but with fire in his eye he leaped up and swung a terrific right to my jaw. I hit the canvas on the seat of my trunks, and I heered Mike roar. The next instant a white streak shot across the ring and Gentleman Jack yelled bloody murder. With my blurry gaze I seen him whirling like a dancing dervish, trying to dislodge Mike which had a death grip on the seat of his britches. Rrrrp! – went something and there was the champeen of the East Coast with no more pants on him than a Hottentot!

All over the place the sercierty belles was screaming hysterically or laughing like she-hyenas, and things was just about like a madhouse. Gentleman Jack give a howl like a lost soul and sprinted for the ropes, and I heered Horace yelling: "Call the police! I'll have them arrested! I'll have them sent to prison for life!"

At that McGoorty bounced offa the canvas and went through the ropes like a jackrabbit. I grabbed Mike under one arm and went through the other side. It was like taking a jump in the dark, everything outside the ring was like a deep fog. I stepped on something, and from the way it squeaked, I believe it was Horace. I mighta tromped others in my blundering dash for liberty, I dunno. My one idee was to get back to the dressing-room, grab my clothes and beat it before the cops come.

The big club house loomed up dimly before me, and I made out what looked like a open door. I blundered through it, continuing my headlong flight – crash! I felt myself falling through space, and Mike flew outa my grasp. Wham! I hit on my neck hard enough to bust a anvil. I reeled up, wondering if they was a unbroken bone in my body. I'd fell on solid concrete, and somewhere near Mike was whining and scratching on wood. I tore off my gloves, and begun to blink and squint around. I made out where I was. My blame near-sightedness hadst made me step into a trapdoor that led into the basement. I was in the basement. Next to me was a big coal bin and Mike had fell into it.

I was fixing to help him out, when I heard somebody else enter the basement in a more regular manner than I had – somebody which panted and cussed in a familiar voice. I peeked around the corner of the coal bin, squinting closely. It was Belding which had sought refuge in his pantsless condition. He was cussing like a mule skinner and trying to arrange such clothes as Mike had left on to him. And I descended on him like a wolf on the fold.

"Sock me just because I made a honest mistake, would you?" I roared, and we went to the floor together.

I wouldn't had much chance with him in a regular ring bout, but in a rough-and-tumble brawl I had the advantage, even with my bad sight. He done his best and tried to gouge out my eye, but I butted the wind outa him, and whilst he was trying to get his breath, I socked him on the chin so hard it curled his hair. I then throwed him and fell on him, and was pummeling him heartily when I was aware that we was not alone. In a modern clubhouse they is no such thing as privacy.

A number of hands sought to drag me off my prey, and I shook 'em off and rose, glaring and blinking around like a owl. I dimly made out Horace – considerably mussed up – Billy Dolan, and a bunch of raging club members.

"You ruffian! You gangster! You pirate!" screeched Horace hysterically. "The Athenian will never live down this scandal! See to Mr. Belding – the brute has nearly murdered him. And grab this scoundrel and hold him until the police arrive!"

Then come a clawing noise and what looked like a black goblin come scrambling over the edge of the coal bin. It was Mike, covered with coal dust. Seeing me surrounded he charged with a roar, and the Athenians scattered like a flock of quails. Gentleman Jack run up a stair that musta led into the front part of the house, because a chorus of feminine screams and laughter, and a despairing howl seemed to indicate that he'd run into a flock of dames again. In a second the basement was empty except for me, Mike, and Billy Dolan. Billy took my hand and led me across the basement and up a short flight of stairs into a big closet.

"Wait here in this linen pantry till I bring your clothes," he said.

So I waited there, and shivered and cussed, whilst sounds of pursuit stormed all over the house, which I later learned was the club members chasing McGoorty, and purty soon Billy come back with them fool golf clothes. I put 'em on in a hurry, and he led me outa the house and across the grounds and out through a small back gate. We walked down the road and didn't stop till we was some distance from the Athenian. Then Billy started to laugh.

"What a scoop!" he said. "I said all society exhibitions were alike – I might have known that with you mixed up in this one, it would be different. If I don't scarehead this! Those snooty sissies of the Athenian – and Gentleman Jack! This is a chance I've sometimes dreamed of. Wasn't he a scream running around before those snobby dames in his B.V.D.'s? Ha ha ha ha!"

"Lend me ten bucks, Billy," I said. "I'll pay you back as soon as I can see good enough to fight. I don't believe it'd be wise to try to collect that five yards from the club."

"I wouldn't advise it," he said, going down into his pocket after the ten. "By the way, the reason I didn't bring your hat was that your dog seems to have chewed it up in the shower room before the fight."

"And as soon as I can get into my regular clothes I'm goin' to give him these monkey-riggin's to play with," I growled. "Gimme them specs, Billy."

"Sure, I'd forgotten about them," said he, handing them to me.

I throwed 'em down on the sidewalk and ground 'em to dust under my heel.

"Gee whiz, Steve," protested Billy, "you can't get around without them."

"I'll let Mike lead me till my sight gets better," I grunted. "If it hadn't been for them I wouldn't of got into this mess. From now on I sails under my right colors, which nobody can mistake me for a college professor or somethin'."

A New Game for Costigan

As I come into the back room of the Ocean Wave bar, Bill O'Brien, Mushy Hansen, Jim Rogers, and Sven Larson looked up from their beer and sneered loudly. And Bill O'Brien said: "There he is, the big business maggot!"

"Lookit that Panerma hat and cane," snorted Jim Rogers. "And a fancy collar on Mike."

Mushy sighed mournfully. "To think that I should ever live to see Steve Costigan blossom out into a dern dude!"

"Look here, you barnacle-bellied sea-rats," I said in some wrath, "just because I'm tired bein' a roughneck and tries to dress like a gent ain't no reason I should swaller all them insults. The bar man told me to come back here. What you want?"

"If you can take time off from your big executive deals," said Bill scathingly, " 'Hard-cash' Clemants here is got a proposition for you."

The aforesaid gent was setting there smoking a big cigar, as hard-boiled and pot-bellied as ever.

"No use," I said. "I ain't fightin' for nobody. I been tradin' punches with cabbage-eared gorillas ever since I was big enough to lift my mitts, and – "

"Just because he had the dumb luck to bet on the right horse down at Tia Juana, he thinks he's too good to fight any more," sneered Rogers. "Takin' the bread right outa his mess-mates' mouths, he is – "

"You shut up!" I roared, brandishing a large sun-burnt fist under his nose. "How'd I get the dough I bet on that nag? By goin' fifteen rounds with the heavyweight champeen of the Navy, under a sun that melted the rosin on the canvas. You set up in the shade and sucked a soda pop and fanned yourself, and then collected the dough you'd won by bettin' on me. I had the luck to put my end of the purse on a fifty-to-one shot which come in first. Bread outa your mouths! You've already won enough dough bettin' on me – well, anyway, I'm through with fightin', and Clemants nee'n to try to – "

"He ain't tryin' to sign you up for no fight," said Bill impatiently. "If you'd shut up a second, he'll explain."

"Yes," snapped Hard-cash, chewing down vicious on his cigar. "It's a personal matter. I came to you, because I have to have a man I can trust. What you lack in sense, you make up in honesty."

"Do you fellows know my son, Horace?"

"Naw," we said.

"YOU wouldn't," he snarled. "He's a sissy. Mizzes Clemants has kept him in fashionable schools most of his life, and he's turned out to be an effeminate sap. Wants to be a musician. A musician! Ha! "

"Well, what about it?" I demanded.

His veins swelled and his eyes flamed, and he chawed his cigar with a noise like a horse chawing cactus.

"What about it?" he roared. "A son of Hard-cash Clemants making his living playing on a *harp*? Not even a jazz band, mindja. A derned harp! I want him to be a credit to me. I want to make a man out of him. I want – "

"Well, well," I said impatiently, "what can I do about it?"

"Just what I'm fixing to tell you," he said, and the others leaned across the table expectantly. "He won't play football, or pool, or box, or drink whiskey, or do anything a normal youngster ought to do. He won't have nothing to do with the fight-promoting business at all.

"He's been brought up too soft. He ought to had to fight his way like I did. Ought to been raised tough like I was!

"Not long ago he wanted to marry the daughter of a bookkeeper who was as poor as a Piute Injun – well, I busted that up, and got him to going with Gloria Sweet."

"That was a hell of an improvement," I remarked.

"Well, there's no danger of Gloria trying to marry him," said Hard-cash. "But that ain't the point. The point is, I want you and your pals here to take Horace on a cruise down in the Gulf of California, and make a man out of him."

"Maybe Horace won't want to go," I remarked.

"He won't," said Hard-cash grimly. "You'll have to persuade him."

"Shanghai him?" I demanded.

"To put it bluntly," said Hard-cash, "yes. I'll pay you a thousand dollars, and the expenses of the cruise, and furnish a yacht. It's tied up now down by Hogan's Flat. I want you to sweat some of his romantic ideas out of him. Make a deck-hand out of him. Put callouses on his hands and hair on his chest. Make him forget such junk as books and music. Make a man out of him like his father was at his age."

"Aw, tripe," I said. "You make me sick. You've blowed about yourself till you got a reputation for hard livin' and hell raisin' that you're beginnin' to believe yourself. I know you. You never done a day's work with your hands in your life. Your callouses ain't nowheres near your hands. You got your start as a kid, promotin' fights between newsboys in your old man's stable. Fight your way! You gypped your way. Raised rough! You're too derned crooked to been raised rough."

He got purple and his eyes bugged, but I continued: "Now because this kid don't measure up to what you think you was at his age, you want him kidnapped and beat into somethin' you think'll look somethin' like you. You're goin' to bust into the kid's life and get him all messed up, tryin' to change his idees and ambitions, just because you think he ain't worthy of the hardboiled, two-fisted reputation you've lied yourself into. Nothin' doin'."

"Steve!" begged my mates, "think of the dough!"

"Think of the devil," I replied with a touch of old world gallantry. "He's got to get somebody else to do his dirty work. I ain't."

"But, Costigan!" expostulated Clemants, mashing his cigar in his fingers.

"Nothin' doin'," I said firmly. "Anyway, I'm too busy. I'm a man of affairs now. Billy Ash, of the *Tribune*, give me a assignment to visit the trainin' camps of Bull Clanton and Flash Reynolds yesterday, and write up my impressions of 'em. I heard him give instructions that what I wrote was to be printed just like I writ it. And here it is in the paper."

I proudly drawed forth a copy of the *Tribune*, unfolded it, and waved it before their wondering sight. "Right on the sport pages, with my name to it," I said. "Billy said bein' I was so well known on the West Coast people would be interested in my opinion. This article ought to sell a whole block of ringside seats. So long. I'm goin' over to Reynolds' camp and see how he likes what I writ about him."

And tilting my new Panerma to them, I stalked, swishing my cane like I seen Billy Ash do, and follered by Mike in his new gold-plated collar.

I thought to myself as I hailed a taxi, I bet Billy admired my work, and maybe I'd get a steady job as a sports' writer. Clemants was promoting the Clanton-Reynolds brawl, which was a couple of weeks off, and he was pushing the ballyhoo hard, trying to ruin the advance sales for Shifty Steinmann's show, which was to take place a week later, a non-title brawl between Terry Hoolihan, the middleweight champion, and Panther Gomez. It was war to the knife between Clemants and Steinmann, each one trying to get control of the boxing business in Frisco. I hoped Billy would let me interview Hoolihan, who was training over in Oakland. I'd never seen him, as he'd just recently come to the West Coast from Chicago.

I dropped Mike off at my hotel, on account of him always fighting dogs that hang around training quarters, and then I went on to Flash Reynolds' hangout. As I entered his quarters, no great distance from the waterfront, I was busting with modest pride. I knew he'd have saw my article by then, and I wondered what he'd say. What he did say smit me with dumfoundment.

Loud voices emerged from the gym, and as I opened the door, I seen Flash and his manager and handlers and sparring partners bending over a paper spread on the table, and they was cussing in a way to curl a Hottentot's wool. They wheeled, and Reynolds give a blood-thirsty yell.

"There he is, the dirty double-crossin' so forth!" he hollered, shaking his fist at me with the paper in it.

"What's the matter?" I demanded.

His manager held his head in his hands and moaned, and Reynolds done a war-dance and squalled like a cougar.

"Matter? " he howled. "Matter? Did you write this?"

He brandished the paper at me, and I said modestly: "Sure I did. Don't you see my name at the top?"

"Listen at this!" he howled. " 'Today I seen Reynolds and Clanton go through their paces at their training camps. Reynolds is a classy boxer, and would be better if he could punch hard enough to dent a hunk of butter.' "

Reynolds was here so overcome by emotion that he paused in his reading long enough for a few more fantastic dance steps.

" 'Reynolds is fast and clever,' " he presently read on. " 'It's a pity he has got a glass jaw. But I do not think he is quite as yellow as some folks think, though only time will tell. I would pick Clanton to win by a k.o. in the first round, only Bull is slow as a ox and ain't got very much sense. Bull is got a very powerful punch and it's a pity he is as dumb as he is. It will probably be a fairly good fight and I won't try to pick the winner at this time, but it is my honest opinion that I could lick both of them in the same ring.' "

Here Reynolds was overcome again and could only howl wordlessly so the goose-flesh riz up on his handlers.

"Well, what's the matter?" I demanded. "I said you was a classy boxer, didn't I?" How much flattery you got to have? You want me to lie about you?"

At that he give a most awful scream.

"I'm on to you!" he squalled. "Clanton's manager hired you to write this to upset me, and make me nervous. But it won't work. I was never cooler in my life!"

And to prove it he ripped the paper to pieces, throwed 'em on the floor and jumped on 'em, throwed back his head and howled like a panther, and impulsively rushed across the room and throwed his right at my jaw with everything he had behind it.

I crashed into the wall and rebounding from it, caught him smack on the button with a right hook, and he went to sleep. Ignoring the frenzied shrieks of his manager, I turned and stalked out, and run full into Bull Clanton, who evidently thought my remarks had been inspired by the Reynolds crowd, and was coming over to clean out his enemy's camp.

By mutual understanding we clinched and rolled hither and yon, to the great damage of the artificial shrubbery, and presently breaking free, we riz and traded punches with great energy and violence, until finally I hung my famous Iron Mike on his jaw, and he crashed down amongst the ruins of a potted palm, and remained motionless.

Shaking the sweat out of my eyes, I glared about, and perceived that a familiar figger had arriv on the scene of carnage and was staring at me with open mouth. It was Billy Ash. He started towards me, calling me. My previous experiences hadst embittered me, and disillusioned me. I dimly realized that my innercent remarks was causing trouble, and I supposed that Billy meant to hop all over me about 'em, verbally. I wasn't in no mood to be criticized further, and at the same time, I didn't want to slug Billy. So I turned and hurried away, ignoring his shouts.

I made a flying leap and landed on the running-board of a speeding taxi, the driver of which yelled loudly in startlement, and cussed.

"You shut up," I admonished, twisting a bony knuckle in his ear. "You take me somewheres quick!"

"Where?" he quavered, turning pale.

"To the lonesomest and most uninhabited place you know of," I said. "I craves solitude."

Well, he said nothing but stepped on it, and I was so engrossed in my gloomy meditations I took little notice of which way he was going, till he pulled up near a dim old street lamp, and said: "This is the lonesomest place I know."

I was still so bewildered at all which had took place, I paid him off like a man in a transom and he hurried away like he thought I might cut his throat.

I then looked about, and presently rekernized where I was. I'd been so busy trying to figger out why Reynolds and Clanton had got mad at me, that I hadn't paid much attention to anything. But now loud and blood-curdling shrieks brung me out of my daze.

I was on a strip of lonely waterfront called Hogan's Flat, a desolate stretch which the only inhabitants was fishermen's shanties. They wasn't even any of them near by, and the only sign of life was a yacht moored a short distance away from a busted old wharf, kinda ghostly-looking in the darkness. From this yacht come sounds of vi'lence and a voice hollered, "Help! Murder! Perlice!"

Thinking I rekernized the voice, I hurried towards the wharf, just as a man clumb down the yacht's gangway into a boat, and begun pulling frantically for shore. As he drawed near I could hear him panting and puffing, and leaning over the wharf, I rekernized Bill O'Brien.

"What the blank dash blank?" I demanded picturesquely.

His face was a white oval in the semi-dark as he looked up and gasped: "Is that you, Costigan?"

"Who else, dope?" I asked impatiently. "What's up?"

He clumb shakily up alongside of me, and he was a rooin. His clothes was tore, he had a peach of a black eye and a lump on his head as big as a egg.

"Lemme get my breath," he puffed "It's that hyener of old Hard – cash's.

"What?" I started convulsively. "You mean to tell me – "

"Me and the boys ain't got dough like you has," he defended. "After you left, we talked it over, and we told Hard-cash *we'd* do the job, without you. He tried to get the boy on the phone, so as to lure him to the yacht, but the servants said Horace had went out, leavin' word that he was goin' to a night club with Gloria Sweet. So Clemants loaned us his car, and we went to that night club, and sent word in that the young man with Gloria Sweet was wanted outside-everybody knows her, even if they don't know Horace. Well, he come out, and we got him out into some shrubbery, and whilst I got his attention by askin' for a match, Mushy hit him over the head with a belayin' pin, and we dumped him into the car and brought him here.

"He come to just after we got him on the yacht, and Steve, I dunno what the old man wants him to be made into, less'n it's a ring-tailed tiger. That dern boy is hell on wheels. I tried to explain the matter to him, but he was like a buzz-saw crossed with a spotted hyener. Old man Clemants said he was too mild-mannered, but in all my sailin' of the Seven Seas, I never heard such cussin' as Horace done. First we tried to be gentle with him, and then we fit for our lives, and he knocked Mushy and Sven and Jim stiffer'n a jib boom. He was killin' me when I got hold of a hand-spike and managed to daze him for a second. I got him locked up in the cabin now. Listen!"

Across the waters I heard a dull reverberation like somebody beating on a steel drum with a maul.

"That's him poundin' on the door with his fists," said Bill with a slight shudder. "He'd rooint it already, only it's made outa bullet proof steel. Everything on that yacht is bullet-proof, it bein' the one old man Clemants used to run rum in.

"After I got him locked up, I seen he was too big a job for me and the rest to handle, and I was afeard to let him out. So I started out to find you – "

"Every time I leaves you saps alone you gets into a jam," I said bitterly. "This reminds me of the time on the African coast when I had to jump overboard and swim ashore to help you let go of a wild cat you'd tried to capture. Come on."

We got in the boat and paddled out to the yacht. The pounding had ceased, and Bill got nervouser than ever, and said he bet Horace was trying to figger out some way to sink the yacht with all hands on board. When we clumb the gangway I seen three recumbent figgers stretched out on deck. Sven and Jim was motionless, but Mushy Hansen was muttering something about saving the women and children first.

"What are you goin' to do?" asked Bill, shivering like he had the aggers. Horace sure had him buffaloed.

"I'm goin' in and talk to Horace," I said. "You stay out here."

"It's suicide," said Bill, whereupon I give a scornful snort, and unlocking the cabin door, I went in. I halted in amazement. I hadn't never seen Horace, but I sure had formed a mental pitcher of him different from the snarling, square-jawed, cold-eyed young pirate which now faced me. I dunno when I ever seen a more formidable physique. He was of only medium height and weight, but his thick neck, square shoulders, deep chest and lean waist was such as ain't often seen, even in the ring. His face was remarkable hard, and his eyes glittered in a most amazing fashion. I was froze with astonishment.

Our guest give vent to a noise which sounded like something in a zoo when he seen me, and begun to move towards me with a sort of supple glide, clenching his square fists. "Another, eh?" he snarled, in a bloodthirsty voice.

"Wait, Horace," I told him. "This has been a mistake all around – "

"Ha!" He laughed like a rasp scraping on a hunk of iron. "I'll say it has – for you. The gamblers put you up to this, didn't they?"

"I dunno what you mean," I said, in some irritation. "If you want to know, the name of the bird which plotted all this is Hard-cash Clemants."

The mention of his old man's name seemed to make Horace madder than ever. He foamed slightly at the mouth, to my horror.

"Oh, he did, did he? I might have known it!" he gritted. "Well, when I get through with him, the old – "

"Now, now, Horace," I reproved. "That ain't no way to talk about your – "

He turned on me like a hungry leopard.

"How much did the old crook pay you?" he asked viciously. "Well, you'll need it for a lawyer. I'll see that you thugs get ten years apiece for this business."

"Now, you wait," I said sternly. "I had nothin' to do with this, and I ain't goin' to have my mates jugged. I'm goin' to let you loose, but you got to promise to keep your mouth shut."

"Sure," he sneered – "till I get to the nearest police station."

"I see they's no arguin' with you," I said, annoyed by his stubbornness. "I repeat I'm goin' to let you go, but I'm goin' to fix it so you can't lead the cops back here. I'm goin' to put a sack over your head so you can't see where at you are, row you ashore and turn you loose some distance from here."

"The hell you are!" he bristled, cocking his fists.

"Be reasonable," I urged. "You think we want to go to jail? Now here's a sack, and if you'll hold still a second – "

With a hair-raising screech he lept at me and caught me on the jaw with a tornado right swing. I was knocked backwards onto a table, and he was right on top of me, ripping rights and lefts to my body and head. I was bigger'n heavier'n him, but he was all steel and whale-bone. One of his smashes closed my eye, another'n tore my ear, and yet another'n started blood from my nose in streams. Rallying myself, I knocked him clean across the cabin with a left hook under the heart, but he come back fighting, and in self defense I crashed my right to his jaw with all my beef behind it. He hit the floor, out cold.

I grabbed the sack and pulled it down over his head, calling for Bill O'Brien, who come in pale and shaky and stared at the recumbent warrior like he couldn't believe it. But he helped me tie him up, and then we lowered him into the row boat and took him ashore.

We had some trouble getting him up on the wharf, because he was coming to, and beginning to twist and writhe in his sack like a eel with the belly ache, but finally we did, and just as we dumped him down, to rest a second, we heard a auto tearing across the Flat. Bill yelped: "The cops!" but before we could run, it swirled up to the wharf and stopped with a screech of brakes, and out boiled a familiar and pot-bellied figger. It was Hardcash Clemants and he was foaming at the mouth. His face looked kinda green by the dim street lamp which was the only illumination on the Flat.

"You jackasses! " he bellered. "You blunderers! Where's my son?"

"Don't get sourcastic," snarled Bill, wiping some blood off his scalp. "We're givin' him back. A thousand bucks ain't enough for us to risk our lives. This cannibal don't need no yacht-tour. He needs a cage in a zoo."

"What are you babbling about?" squalled old man Clemants. "While I thought you half-wits were grabbing Horace, he eloped with that bookkeeper's daughter! They've married and beat it to Los Angeles! Her old man just phoned me."

"Then who's this?" hollered Bill. I jerked the sack offa our captive's head, releasing the choicest flow of profanity I ever heard. Hard-cash screamed and recoiled.

"My God!" he yelled. "That's Terry Hoolihan, the middleweight champion!"

"And when I get through prosecutin' you in the courts," Hoolihan promised blood-thirstily, "you'll all be breakin' rocks the rest of your lives."

"But he was the one that was with Gloria Sweet – " begun Bill dazedly.

"Horace wasn't with her! " hollered Hard-cash, doing a wardance on the wharf he was that crazy. "He just left word to that effect, to fool me! He's been using Gloria as a blind all the time! He's been out with that girl Joan, nearly every time I thought he was with Gloria. I tell you, he's married her! Joan, I mean. A bookkeeper's daughter! My God!"

"Well, what's the difference between an honest bookkeeper and a crooked fight promoter?" asked a harsh voice, and we all whirled – except Hoolihan which was still tied and couldst only twist his head around, which he done. It was Billy Ash, and he was madder'n I ever seen him. He walked up to Hard-cash.

"You say one word against that girl and I'll knock your fat head into the bay," he said between his teeth. "The kid happens to be my sister. I don't know what she saw in that sap son of yours, but they're married now, and you're going to kick in and help them."

"I'll see you in hell first! " roared Hard-cash. Billy laughed harshly.

"You know what happened tonight?" he said. "Steve here tangled up with your two prize stumblebums and knocked them both stiff in Reynolds' training quarters."

Hard-cash jumped convulsively.

"What? Oh my God! Is it in the papers?" he squalled like a stricken elk.

"Not yet," said Billy. "I was the only newspaper man there. But you open your yap about Horace and Joan, and I'll scarehead it in the morning paper. You've been building up these bums till the public thinks they're championship material. You've spent plenty on the ballyhoo. It would look nice, wouldn't it, a big headline how old Steve here cooled both your prize pets? How many tickets you think you'd sell?"

Hard-cash began to shake all over and mop his brow with a palsied hand.

"Don't do it, Billy," he begged. "I've got too much money tied up in this fight. If I don't clear some dough on it, I'm sunk."

"Well," said Billy, "your scrap with Shifty Steinmann is none of my business. But if you don't kick in with some dough for those kids, I'll spill the beans all over the place."

"Sure, Billy, sure!" soothed Hard-cash hurriedly. "I'll mail them a big check the first thing in the morning."

"Ain't nobody ever goin' to turn me loose?" wrathfully demanded Hoolihan. "Wait till I get my lawyer! I don't know what you thugs have been talkin' about but I know Clemants hired me shanghaied to try to interfere with my fight with Gomez. I'll see somebody behind the bars for this!"

Billy turned on him. "Yeah?" he sneered. "How'd you like for your wife back in Chicago to know you're playing around with Gloria Sweet?"

"Hold on," begged Hoolihan. "Don't let that get out. You never saw such a jealous woman in your life. She'd shoot me! Let's just all forget about it, pals."

Whilst Bill O'Brien untied Hoolihan, Billy Ash turned to me.

"Steve," he said, "why did you run away from me for? I've been chasing you all over the city. That article of yours was a knockout. I'd like to have you do a series of them. A laugh in every line! People wouldn't need the comic strips, with them in the paper."

"I dunno what you're talkin' about," I answered, nettled. "That there article represented my best efforts, to say nothin' of a dozen lead pencils and a stack of paper. Anyway, I'm through!

"Hard-cash, I want you to get me a fight in the prelims of the Reynolds-Clanton match."

"You mean you're goin' back to fightin'?" exclaimed Bill O'Brien with joy. "And me and the boys can win dough on you some more?"

"I mean I've found the only way I can get along with my feller man is to bust him on the jaw," I answered, "and I might as well be gettin' paid for it."

Hard-Fisted Sentiment

I was feeling so good when I come into the American Bar that I essayed a handspring in the middle of the floor, to the astonishment of the onlookers and my white bulldog, Mike. I wasn't drunk nor nothing. The *Sea Girl* hadst just been docked in Port Arthur a few hours and I was so blame glad to be on shore leave again. But I reckon I ain't quite as spry as I was in the days when I used to turn handsprings in the ring at the end of my fights to show the customers how little I minded taking a fifteen-round beating.

I kind of piled up on a reef, so to speak, or in other words, I catapulted into a table knocking it over with a feller under it that hadst been setting there with his head in his hands. As I kicked the ruins off of us, I looked with amazement into the wrathful face of the *Sea Girl*'s cap'n.

Before I couldst say a word, the Old Man, which had been more crabby than ever for the past week, give a roar of rage and got up, kicking the table and chairs in all directions.

"You drunken fool!" he roared. "Can't a man set down and brood peacefully nowhere? Ain't a man safe from you no place, you Irish baboon? What do you mean crashin' into my table like that, you brainless, bone-headed, infantile fool?"

Well, I don't much blame him for being mad, but his manner got on my nerves. I got a wild temper myself, and it ain't in me to stand up and take a cussing from any man. I flared up myself.

"Stow that guff, you old sea-goat!" I roared. "You can't abuse me, even if I have been sailin' under you for more years'n I like to remember! Save your cussin's for the square-heads you shanghai. I'm a free-born American citizen and no slave-drivin' old pirate can crack a whip at me! I been takin' orders from you on board so many years you think you can chart my course ashore. Well, you can take some more soundin's. I'm fed up with you, and I'm fed up with that lousy tub you call the *Sea Girl*!"

"Alright!" he roared. "You're fed up with the *Sea Girl*, eh? Well, you've sailed your last cruise aboard her. Her new owners won't be the soft-hearted fools I've always been, to ship such a thick-skulled gorilla as you."

"Huh!" I stopped short in the middle of a roar and glared at him kind of blank. "What you mean, new owners?"

"What I say!" he snarled, and I noticed how old and worn he looked. "I'll never steer the *Sea Girl* again, and when I think of the crew with such apes as you, I'm almost glad of it."

"But I don't understand – " I began.

"When did you ever understand anything?" he yelled, jerking at his chin whiskers. "I owe a company here a lot of money. They hold my note. I can't even pay the interest. If I could get a few weeks more time, I could pay. But they have to have at least a thousand dollars by tomorrow morning before they'll give me any more time, and I haven't a blasted half penny. Even you know what a rotten cruise we've had. I'm losin' the *Sea Girl*, that's what. They're goin' to attach her tomorrow if I can't scrape up a thousand dollars. I'm goin' to lose my ship, that's the very blood and heart of my soul. I'd rather lose a leg, an eye, an arm. The snap of her sails is the sweetest music I know; the creak of her timbers is like old friends a-talkin'. Lettin' her go is like rippin' the heart outa my ribs. But what do you know or care about it, you thick-skulled mick? You got about as much sentiment as that bulldog. I'm a old man and my ship's goin' to be took away from me, and I'll be on the beach in my old age. Now you can cheer all you want to. I guess you're glad to hear it. But get out of here and leave me alone!"

Well, I just turned around and walked out without saying a word. I was kinda dazed, I reckon, I'd knowed the Old Man was deep in debt and hadn't had a good voyage, but I hadn't knowed how it was. I wouldn't have spoke to him like I had, hadst I of knowed. I couldn't hardly realize the *Sea Girl* was going to be took away from him. I got kind of cold and sweaty. Mike sensed what was in my mind and he snuggled up against me and licked my hand.

Well, I racked my brain how to get some money, and turned to the only way I knowed – fighting. And a sudden idee took me so quick I give a yell. The first part of the idee had to do with Shifty Strozza, foremost middleweight contender, who in the middle of a world tour, was in Port Arthur that day. Right in front of me they was a big poster announcing that Strozza and Benny Goldstein was going to fight ten rounds to a decision that night in Jim Barlow's Wharfside Arena.

I beat it up the street, trying to figger out just what to do, when all at once I seen a form ahead of me – a broad-shouldered man of medium height – Shifty Strozza hisself! What luck! He was passing a cheap dive that was run by a Chinaman I knowed – one of these joints where you go down several flights of steps from the street. I met him.

"Hello, Shifty," I greeted him. "Glad to see you agin!"

He gimme the once-over kinda scornful – a dark, handsome fellow he was, and cold and cruel as a panther in the ring.

"Oh, yes," he said, "I remember you – the old Sailor. You ain't risen much in the world since I fought a preliminary to one of your scraps on the West Coast three years ago."

"Naw," I admitted. "But you have – you was just a kid then, with a natural gift uh slippin' and side-steppin'. But now they say the middleweight champ is side-steppin' you."

"He can't duck me much longer," he snarled. "I'm fightin' my way around the world, just to show the fans I'm the best middleweight in the business. When I get back to America I'll make that cheese champ meet me – and the belt's as good as mine. What do you want? A handout? I'm not givin' out no dough to punch-drunk ring tramps."

"And I'm not askin' it," I growled, keeping my temper, but feeling red sparks dancing in my eyes. "I'm askin' you to have a drink with me and talk over a deal I got in mind."

"Well, make it snappy," he snarled. "I'm due at the Arena in an hour and if I'm a minute late that lousy manager of mine will be havin' conniption fits, thinkin' I'm kidnapped or somethin'."

I led the way down into the joint, nodded at Yat Yao, the old Chinee which owned the place, and he showed us a back room – a lousy, moldy place, more like a cellar than a room. He put drinks on the ramshackle table and left, closing the door.

"Well, what do you want?" snapped Strozza. "This is the lousiest dump I ever seen."

"What I want is soon said," said I. "Shifty, this fight tonight don't mean nothin' to you. The only reason you're doin' it is because your manager saw a chance to grab some easy money. This ain't no fight town and you know it. Fifteen hundred dollars Jim Barlow guaranteed you – that's chicken feed to you. You must be worth a hundred thousand, easy. Benny Goldstein's your sparrin' pardner. I know that, if the rest of the town don't. It won't be no fight, it'll be a dancin' match and the crowd will git gypped."

"What's that to you?" busted in Shifty. "They'll see me perform, won't they? Ain't that worth the price of admission?"

"Maybe," I admitted. "But that ain't the idee. That fifteen hundred you won't need would help me a lot. I know better'n to ask you to lend it to me. But three years ago when you was just a unknown prelim fighter in Frisco, you come to me and begged me to git you a fight, as a semi-windup to one of my scraps. I done it, and you know blame well, Shifty, that it was that fight that started you on the right road. All the sportswriters in Frisco featured your showin' that night. Well, I ain't one ask favors for favors I've did, but you could help me a lot tonight if you would.

"All I ask is – don't show up at the Arena! Give me a chance. My cap'n's a old man and they're about to take his ship away from him. It'll break his heart. Fifteen hundred ain't nothin' to you – "

Shifty was setting there with a sneer on his dark handsome face and I knowed my breath was being wasted. White flashes of fury began to zip through my brain and I held onto the table edge to control myself.

"And you want me to pass up a grand and a half," he sneered, "just to help some dodderin' old fool of a sailor! What do you think I am, a charity fund? Fifteen hundred ain't nothin' to me, no. But by the same token I ain't passin' it over to the first tramp that comes along. If anybody asks you, Shifty Strozza is out for himself and nobody else. Now get out."

I was on my feet shaking with rage.

"Yes, you wop rat!" I roared. "You was never for anybody but yourself! You ain't got the heart of a snake in your slimy carcass! Thank the Lord they ain't many fighters like you! Three years ago you come whinin' to me for a chance – now you won't pass up what ain't cigarette money to you to keep a old man off the beach! But get this, you dirty fourflushin' alley-rat, you ain't goin' to get a smell of that fifteen hundred bucks!"

He leaped up with a screech of rage, plumb red-eyed, and I smashed him square on the jaw with a right that had *every* ounce of my beef and about ten tons of red fury behind it. He splintered the table as he went down and he laid among the ruins without twitching. I called for Yat Yao and he come in, without changing expression on his yellow, parchment-like map.

I laid hold of Strozza and dragged him through a door which Yat Yao opened for me, into a small dungeon-like room.

"He won't be out but only for a few minutes," I told the old Chinee. "You lock the door and don't let him out for a couple of hours, anyhow. Better have several strong-arm men on hand when you let him out – he's liable to get rough."

Old Yat Yao nodded and grinned and me and Mike hurried down the waterfront till we come to the Wharfside Arena. They was quite a crowd going in and I went up to the ticket booth.

"How's the gate, Red?" I asked and the fellow grinned.

"Howdy, Sailor," said he. "Boy, I didn't know they was so many fight fans in Port Arthur! They've all turned out tonight – Americans, English, French, Dutch, Japs, and a lot of rich Chinees. Lemme tell you, Shifty Strozza is sure an attraction! It ain't often us fans exiled in the Orient gets to see a first class fighter perform. At five bucks a throw, we got close onto a three thousand dollar gate – maybe more. If Shifty'd knowed they'd turn out like that, he'd demanded a percentage instead of a guarantee."

I got kind of cold and shaky inside. All these fans hadst come to see the great Strozza. Maybe they wouldn't be satisfied with anything I could give 'em. It ain't often that the realization is brung home to me that after all I'm nothing but a ham-and-egger, but it come to me hard then, and the taste was dust in my mouth.

"Lemme go in, Red," I said. "I ain't got a dime, but I wanta see Jim Barlow."

"Sure, Sailor," said Red. "Go right in – I wish you was fightin' a prelim tonight – the fans still remember how you licked Black John Scanlan here six months ago."

I went on in, me and Mike, and I looked over the crowd; they was a big crowd for a Port Arthur fight show and I felt my heart kinda sink. They'd come to see a first-string fighter perform – how could I hold 'em, me with no kind of a scheme?

They was already getting restless, and suddenly, in the back rows, which was the cheapest, I seen three men and a idee flashed into my mind. I made my way down the aisle, and to my delighted surprise the crowd give me quite a hand. They hadn't forgot the old Sailor, after all. I made my way in the dressing rooms; Benny Goldstein was already in ring togs, waiting to go on, but naturally Strozza hadn't showed up. His manager was running in circles and Jim Barlow was cussing. I got hold of Barlow and got him into a small side room he used as a kind of office.

"Jim," I said, "the crowd's gettin' impatient."

"Yes," he growled, "I know it, but what can I do? Where do you suppose that blame Strozza is?"

"Never mind," said I. "He ain't goin' to turn up."

Barlow jumped clean out of his chair. "What!" he hollered. "How do you know? I'm ruint! I'll have to give that crowd their money back – "

"Wait a bit," said I. "I think I can save the day without Strozza."

"You?" sneered Barlow. "They came to see a near champion – not a ring tramp. You're good enough drawing card in your way, Sailor, but you ain't Shifty Strozza."

"Alright," I snapped, "go out and tell them muggs that the show is off and they can get their money back at the box office."

Jim Barlow cussed like he'd have apoplexy.

"Listen to me," said I. "I don't blame you for feelin' put out. You put one over on Strozza and his manager – they figgered you'd lose money by givin' 'em a straight fifteen hundred dollar guarantee. But you was smart; chargin' three, five and ten bucks a seat you've got over a four thousand dollar house. Your expenses ain't nothin' scarcely, you ain't even put on no preliminary shows. You stand to make a clean two thousand dollar profit as it stands. But if you have to give the crowd back their money, you make nothin'. Listen to me, and I'll put you in the clear yet. The crowd won't see Strozza perform, but they will see a real fight, where they wouldn't if they'd seen Shifty and Benny Goldstein cakewalk."

"Lay your cards on the table," said Jim Barlow. Already we could hear the crowd yelling for action and Strozza's manager and handlers and seconds had run out to look for him.

"I seen three men in the crowd we got to use," I said. "They're Frenchy Ladeau, Peter Nogaya, and Bill Brand. Get 'em in here."

Barlow sent a boy for 'em and purty soon they filed into the office. Ladeau and Nogaya was dark and dangerous looking; Brand was a rough, hard-faced blond. All three was tough and hard, fighting men from the word go. They looked on me with little favor.

"Here's the ticket," I said. "First we'll put it up to the crowd – if they want their money back, why of course they ain't nothin' we can do. But I believe they'll agree to what I suggest. If they do, why, I'll fight these three jailbirds, one after another. If I lay all three of 'em, which I probably will, I get a thousand dollars and they gets nothin'. If even one of 'em licks me, they split the thousand between the three of 'em. How's that?"

They licked their chops, being broke, as usual – they was all seamen.

"This is the way it goes," I went on. "Without Strozza showin' up, we got to give the crowd somethin' very unusual to keep 'em contented. Ladeau is a boxer and a savate fighter – he can use his hands and his feet too. Pete is a jujitsu expert – he'll wrestle and hit with his bare hands if he wants to. Brand is a boxer – he'll fight me his way. I'll wear gloves and straight boxing rules for all three fights."

"But what if the first man flattens you?" said Barlow. "The crowd will feel gypped."

"I ain't never been flattened yet," I growled. "But if it should happen, you can bring me to and I'll go on. Don't worry; I'll give the crowd a run for their money."

"Well," said Barlow, "how about it?"

"We'll do it," said the three muggs all together.

So we got into ring togs and climbed into the ring, where Barlow held up his hands for quiet. The crowd quieted down and Barlow said: "Gentlemen, I have a few words to say to you, and I'll ask you to keep quiet till I finish. First, I regret to say that Shifty Strozza is nowhere to be found and we have reason to believe that he will not show up tonight – "

His words was drowned by a roar of rage from the fans who rose up and bellered: "We're gypped! Give us our money back!"

Barlow waved his arms till they kind of quieted down and he said: "Gents, wait till I finish, then if you still feel you want your money back, why you can get it at the box office. Here are four fighting men whom you have seen perform here before. These boys are all hard scrappers and always give the fans the best they have. You know them – Ladeau, Nogaya, Bill Brand, and Sailor Steve Costigan. The Sailor has agreed to fight all three of the others, one at a time, one right after the other. Each man will fight in his own style; you will have an opportunity of seeing straight boxing tactics pitted against the savate science of France and the mysterious jujitsu art of Japan. The Sailor has agreed, in the event of his being knocked out by either or both of his first two opponents, that he will go on with the schedule, just the same. Now, gents, if you wish, your money awaits you at the ticket window. If you want to see these mixed bouts, kindly make it known."

They hesitated a minute, then started yelling: "Go on with the fights, we'll stick!" And not a man left the arena.

Barlow turned to me: "I've done my part. Now it's up to you. Who will you fight first?"

"I'll take Frenchy," I said and Barlow turned to the crowd again.

"The first bout of the evenin'," he bellered, "will be between Sailor Steve Costigan, American, of the trader *Sea Girl*, 190 pounds, and Frenchy Ladeau, of the French S. S. *de Comte*, 180 pounds. Costigan will fight straight ring rules, with regulation gloves. Ladeau will likewise wear gloves, but he will be allowed to kick with his feet in any and all occasions, above the belt or below. Let's go! They will fight ten rounds."

Me and Ladeau approached each other warily. He was lean and rangy, six feet one to my six feet, all steel springs and whalebone. I knowed what a vicious and disabling art this savate was, and I wasn't figgering on taking no chances. I feinted with my left, but he went away from it. I swung hard and vicious with the same hand, but he ducked and cracked a hard left to my ear. I went for him and hooked savagely for his jaw, but he sprang back like a leaping cat and wham! Swaying far back he shot his foot from the floor in a wide curving arc that took me smack on the jaw. Jerusha, it plumb felt like my neck was snapped! My feet went straight up in the air and I hit the canvas on my neck and shoulders. Barlow sprang forward and started counting, but I bounced up before he'd got past "Three!"

Ladeau bounded in and let go a sweeping kick from the floor again, but I was watching. By sheer luck I made a grab and caught his ankle in my left glove and at the same instant I crashed over a right hook to the jaw. Ladeau crumpled and he hadn't moved a muscle at "Ten!" The crowd whooped with hilarious joy.

They hauled him out and Barlow bellered: "The next event, Sailor Steve Costigan and Peter Nogaya of the Anglo-Chinese ship, *The Mongol*, weight

200 pounds. As before, Costigan will use only straight boxing, hitting only above the belt. Nogaya will be allowed to wrestle and strike with his bare fists."

Nogaya was a stocky, squarely built man, a half-caste he was, with Malay, French, and Japanese in him. A tough customer. He was big and smooth, like a big seal. His muscles didn't bulge, they rippled under his glossy skin and he moved as quick and easy as a cat.

I knowed better'n to rush in wide open. I come in fast but wary and he backed away, half crouching, his big long arms swinging wide and low. I sprang in, hooking hard for his head; he side-stepped and I plunged past him, whirling in a big hurry. He was already leaping for me, but he checked hisself almost in mid-air and threw up his arm to block the savage right hook I shot at his jaw. I whipped the left after it as quick as I couldst hit, and he moved his bullet head to let it slide past. Just a second my left was extended its full length, and in that second he grabbed my left wrist with both hands, wheeled and throwed me clean over his head. I seen the ring turning somersaults as I pinwheeled in the air and come down on my back so hard it shook the whole house. The wind was just about knocked outa me, but I seen Nogaya bounding across the ring towards me like a big dusky cat and I sprang up just as he rushed in.

I feinted with my left and again he grabbed it. As he grabbed he twisted with some kind of leverage hold, something snapped in my elbow and a agonizing pain shot up my arm, but at the same instant I ripped a slung-shot uppercut up between Nogaya's arms. It crashed square under his jaw and his head snapped back like it was on hinges and he went to his knees. At "Nine!" he weaved up again, but a right hook to the ear dropped him again, where he lay till his handlers carried him outa the ring.

I walked back into my corner. My left arm was numb and getting stiff, but I said nothing. The crowd was yelling and cheering and I grinned; they might not knowed it, but they was getting a sight more action than they'd of got hadst Shifty Strozza and Benny Goldstein been prancing and tapping in that ring.

"Say," said the handler Barlow had gimme – by some strange whim they wasn't a *Sea Girl* man in the house – "didn't I hear something crack when Pete grabbed your arm the last time?"

"His jaw, I reckon," I growled.

"The third and concludin' event," bellered Jim Barlow, "is between Sailor Costigan and Bill Brand of the English liner, *King William*, 190 pounds."

Brand was a wandering, sea-going fighter like me. They wasn't a inch or a pound of difference betwixt us. He was a rough, square-faced blond, with hard, light eyes. He didn't fight in the orthodox English style. He was a slugger with a wicked sock in each hand.

We come together fast in the middle of the ring and I shot a straight left to his head. And a flash of pure agony leapt up my arm, so that I went blind for a second and the strength oozed from my limbs. I knowed – Nogaya had broke a bone in my elbow and I was up against one of the most dangerous hitters on the Seven Seas, with a useless left hand!

In the second that I sagged, limp from the pain of my broken arm, Brand leaped forward and crashed a terrible right hook to my head. I swayed and floundered like a man of straw, and he ripped left and right! – left and right! – to my head so I staggered into the ropes. The crowed was on its feet, yelling with amazement. But with my back to the ropes I started slugging wild and desperate with my one good hand and I fought Brand off and backed him into the middle of the ring where he made a stand and we stood head to head, trading smashes. But it couldn't last – my left was hanging helpless and I couldn't even raise it to block or feint. Brand split my ear, half closed an eye and cut my lips. Reeling under a regular hail of blows, I hooked a desperate right to his midsection which bent him double and made him back away, and the gong found him sparring to keep me away.

Back on my stool Mike shoved his nose into my right glove and rumbled deep in his throat. He knowed something was wrong.

"Why don't you use your left, you bloody fool?" snarled my handler, as he mopped blood offa my countenance.

"I can't," I muttered, somewhat thickly through my smashed lips. "Nogaya broke it."

He near dropped the sponger. "What? You been fightin' with a broken arm? I'm goin' to throw in the sponge! Brand'll kill you."

"I'll kill you if you throw in the sponge," I snarled. "I'll lick Brand with one hand."

When we come up for the second round Bill Brand had realized that my left was useless, and he come in to make a quick finish. Taking no chances with my terrible right, he bored in, keeping his left guard high and rolling it down quick and clever to block my body blows. He kept weaving to the right, away from my right hand, while he ripped both maulers to my body and head. I fought back fiercely and he couldn't altogether keep away from my good hand. The round wasn't ten seconds old before I staggered him with a smashing swat to the temple, and again I went under his looping left and ripped the skin offa his ribs with a short right hook.

But I was taking more'n two to one. He rained blows on me like a man hammering a barrel. He battered me into the ropes and offa 'em and in the middle of the ring, he ripped three terrific right hooks to my chin. I come back with a savage right under the heart that made him grunt, but he shot a left and a right to my body and a left to my eye that closed it tight shut. A swinging right landed square on my hanging left arm and the pain of it sickened me. I faltered for a second in my stride and Brand, sensing my condition, was on me like a wildcat. He drove me across the ring with a perfect storm of blows and floored me near the ropes. I rose without a count and sent him back on his heels with a desperate right to the head, but he smashed my nose with a hooking left, gashed my jaw with a short jarring right, and tore my already crimson ear with a wicked left chop.

I was short with a swinging right for the jaw and he caught me flush on the button with a right uppercut that snapped my head back. A right hook to the jaw flung me into the ropes and lurching offa them I run right into a flurry of leather that beat me to my knees. I reeled up, blind and bloody, at the count of nine, but a left and right sent me down again. The crowd was yelling for Jim to stop it, as I couldst vaguely hear, but I shook my head, sending drops of blood flying in all directions, and groped up again. I didn't hardly feel the blow that sent me down again, but I felt my shoulders strike the canvas and I went clean out. As they told me later, I lay without a twitch, and the gong sounded just as Barlow said "Nine!"

I come to with my second holding me on my stool and Barlow standing over me. "I'm stoppin' the fight, Steve," said he. "You ain't in no condition to go on."

"Gimme a whiffa smellin' salts," I gasped. "I ain't licked. Don't you dast stop this fight, Jim Barlow."

I sniffed the smelling salts and my head cleared. I looked over at Brand and saw he was bleeding plenty from a gash in the temple where one of my wild right hooks hadst landed. He was tough, but not tough enough to take my blows without wilting – if I could only land them. Oh, for two good hands! I knew – *I knew* – I could stop him if I could only land on him. Was I going through all this for nothing? Hadst I licked Nogaya and Ladeau, only to be turned back by this Englishman? Was the Old Man going to lose the *Sea Girl* after all? I went crazy. I give a kind of wild animal cry and swept my handler aside with a blind sweep of my arm, and lurched offa my stool. The gong sounded and Brand come across the ring.

I charged headlong to meet him. I was frenzied – swept clean offa my feet by the old wild Irish fighting fury. Brand met me with a straight left and I felt his arm bend as I crashed in on it and hooked my right to the wrist in his belly. He grunted and staggered. I was right on top of him, driving in my right as hard and fast as a trip-hammer. I bet that crowd, which was clean hysterical, never seen such a comeback as I give 'em! Brand was fighting back with all he had, but it wasn't enough. His blows rocked me to my heels and spattered the ring with blood, but they didn't stop me. I kept plunging in without a instant's pause, hitting-hitting-hitting! Men that seen that fight said that I was like a man fighting in a nightmare, plunging and hitting, plunging and hitting. I was fighting for the old Man and the *Sea Girl*, and I couldn't be stopped.

I drove Bill Brand before me like a chip on the crest of a high tide. Every body blow I landed sunk wrist-deep and every head blow I landed sprayed blood. His face was bloody as mine now and he was gasping and reeling. He'd give up trying to box out of danger. He was hitting with both hands and all his power to keep me off. But I wasn't to be kept off. I was practically out on my feet; the ring swum red and dim; I was like a man in a scarlet dream. All I seen was Bill Brand's face, white and desperate where it wasn't bloody, floating in the red mist. All I knowed, all I felt, was the instinct to keep plunging into close quarters, and hit-hit-hit!

I couldn't even hear the yelling of the crowd, but I felt the power going from Bill Brand's blows – I felt him floundering – I felt him reeling – crumpling. I felt him going. And I drew on my waning powers for one last ferocious burst of slugging and felt him go limp – felt the jar of my last pile-driving smash to his jaw – saw him drop like a sack of sawdust. And I fell into the ropes and held myself erect while Jim Barlow counted him out.

They say I climbed outa the ring by myself. I dunno how I did it, nor I don't remember doing it. I just remember a wild whooping and yelling and a lot of men slapping me on the shoulder and shaking my hand and telling me over and over what a grand fight it was. Next thing I remember, I was setting on a table in the dressing room and they was setting my arm, setting up my ear and the gash in my temple and putting collodion on my various cuts.

"What a battle, what a battle!" Barlow was saying. "You fought that fight with a broken arm – "

"Where's the dough?" I broke in, mumbling through my smashed lips. "The grand I was to get? I want it now."

Barlow put a wad of bills in my hand and I tried to count it.

"By golly, Steve," said he, "I never seen you so anxious for money before – not that you ain't fought bitter hard for it."

"This ain't my money," I said, still kinda dizzy. "It belongs to a friend. I gotta go – they may take the ship tonight."

They looked at each other like they thought I was punch-drunk, but they helped me dress and I went out into the streets with Mike. The cool night air cleared my mind, but I guess I was a sight, with an arm in a sling, one eye closed and the other partly so, and sticking plaster all over me.

I figgered to find the Old Man in Terence Murphy's little grog shop, playing pinochle with old Terence, so I steered my course there. Sure enough, there the Old Man was, playing cards with old Terence. Just them two. It was purty late. I noticed how the Old Man was showing his years.

"Yes," he was saying to Terence, "tomorrow they take my ship. I'm a old man, Terence, though I didn't realize it till now. I'm all washed up. That ship's been wife and daughter to me – "

He looked around and seen me and his eyes grew bitter.

"Well, Steve Costigan," he said harshly, "what sort of a disgraceful street brawl you been into now? Didn't I tell you to leave me in peace? Will you get out of here – "

I just held out the wad of bills to him without saying anything. I ain't much on fancy words.

"What's that?" he looked startled.

"The thousand dollars you owe," I said. "You can pay 'em and they can't take the *Sea Girl* away from you."

"But I can't take it – " he spluttered.

"You'll take it!" I roared. "I didn't lick three of the toughest eggs in the Asiatics just to have you stand on etiquette. Take it!" And I crammed it into his hand.

The Old Man stood there holding the money and he turned every color they is. For the first time in my life, I seen him plumb speechless. At last he said: "Steve-I-I-I dunno what to say – I feel like a lowdown skunk. I can't tell you how much this here means to me, but I'll pay you back, every cent of it. I said a lotta hard things to you, Steve, but you know I didn't really mean 'em – they's a lotta sentiment under that rough hide of yours and a heap of man – "

"Aw," I said, plumb embarrassed, "that's all right. Don't thank me. I couldn't see you lose the *Sea Girl*, 'cause the old tub would sink with a human being' for her cap'n."

"Don't git insultin', you big baboon," snorted the Old Man, but his eyes was young again and his lips was smiling.

When You Were a Set-up
and I Was a Ham

When you were a set-up and I was a ham
In James J. Corbett's day
And toe to toe and blow to blow
We mixed it in a fray
Or skittered with many a roundhouse right
'Mid the ropes of a third-rate ring
My soul was rife with the joy of strife
As I matched you swing for swing.

And happy we swung and happy we slugged
And happy I knocked you out
And shoulders flat you hit the mat
With the force of that swinging clout.
And champions came and champions went
And battled with might and main
Till we grew in might and signed for the fight
And climbed in the ring again.

We were heavyweights, rough and tough
But cautious at first in the fight
We sparred at ease while the crowd yelled "Cheese!"
Or jabbed with a wary right.
Duck and side-step on dancing feet,
(Golly but you looked dumb!)
While the angry crowd in accents loud
Remarked that we were bum.

Then happy we rushed and happy we slugged
And happy I hit the floor
'Twas a peach of a clout and they counted me out
The while the crowd did roar.
And that was a dozen years ago
In a ring that no man knows
Yet here tonight in a title fight
We are matching swats and blows.

Your right is as strong as a battering ram,
Your left is a peach, you bet,
Your swings are few, your gloves are new,
Your footwork great, and yet,
Your jaw is red from my rights to the head,
Your nose from my lefts is flat
Though my jaw's a sight from your lunging right,
Five times you've hit the mat.
Then as we linger at battle here,
With many a roundhouse slam,
Let us swing anew as in times when you
Were a set-up and I was a ham.

The Spirit of Tom Molyneaux

Readers of this magazine will probably remember Ace Jessel, the big Negro boxer whom I managed a few years ago. He was an ebony giant, four inches over six feet tall, with a fighting weight of 230 pounds. He moved with the smooth ease of a gigantic leopard and his pliant steel muscles rippled under his shiny skin. A clever boxer for so large a man, he carried the smashing jolt of a trip-hammer in each huge fist.

It was my belief that he was the equal of any man in the ring at that time – except for one fatal defect. He lacked the killer instinct. He had courage in plenty, as he proved on more than one occasion – but he was content to box mostly, outpointing his opponents and piling up just enough lead to keep from losing.

Every so often the crowds booed him, but their taunts only broadened his good-natured grin. However, his fights continued to draw a big gate, because, on the rare occasions when he was stung out of a defensive role or when he was matched with a clever man whom he had to knock out in order to win, the fans saw a real fight that thrilled their blood. Even so, time and again he stepped away from a sagging foe, giving the beaten man time to recover and return to the attack – while the crowd raved and I tore my hair. The one abiding loyalty in Ace's happy-go-lucky life was a fanatical worship of Tom Molyneaux, first champion of America and a sturdy fighting man of color; according to some authorities, the greatest black ringman that ever lived.

Tom Molyneaux died in Ireland a hundred years ago but the memory of his valiant deeds in America and Europe was Ace Jessel's direct incentive to action. As a boy, toiling on the wharves, he had heard an account of Tom's life and battles and the story had started him on the fistic trail.

Ace's most highly prized possession was a painted portrait of the old battler. He had discovered this – a rare find indeed, since even woodcuts of

Molyneaux are rare – among the collection of a London sportsman, and had prevailed on the owner to sell it. Paying for it had taken every cent that Ace made in four fights but he counted it cheap at the price. He removed the original frame and replaced it with a frame of solid silver, which, considering that the portrait was full length and life size, was more than extravagant.

But no honor was too great for "Mistah Tom" and Ace merely increased the number of his bouts to meet the cost.

Finally my brains and Ace's mallet fists had cleared us a road to the top of the game. Ace loomed up as a heavyweight menace and the champion's manager was ready to sign with us – when an unexpected obstacle blocked our path.

A form hove into view on the fistic horizon that dwarfed and overshadowed all other contenders, including my man. This was "Man-killer Gomez," and he was all that his name implies. Gomez was his ring name, given him by the Spaniard who discovered him and brought him to America. He was a full-blooded Senegalese from the West Coast of Africa.

Once in a century, ring fans see a man like Gomez in action – a born killer who crashes through the general ruck of fighters as a buffalo crashes through a thicket of dead wood. He was a savage, a tiger. What he lacked in actual skill, he made up by ferocity of attack, by ruggedness of body and smashing power of arm. From the time he landed in New York, with a long list of European victories behind him, it was inevitable that he should batter down all opposition – and at last the white champion looked to see the black savage looming above the broken forms of his victims. The champion saw the writing on the wall, but the public was clamoring for a match and whatever his faults, the title-holder was a fighting champion.

Ace Jessel, who alone of all the foremost challengers had not met Gomez, was shoved into discard, and as early summer dawned on New York, a title was lost and won, and Man-killer Gomez, son of the black jungle, rose up as king of all fighting men.

The sporting world and the public at large hated and feared the new champion. Boxing fans like savagery in the ring, but Gomez did not confine his ferocity to the ring. His soul was abysmal. He was ape-like, primordial – the very spirit of that morass of barbarism from which mankind has so tortuously climbed, and toward which men look with so much suspicion.

There went forth a search for a White Hope, but the result was always the same. Challenger after challenger went down before the terrible onslaught of the Man-killer, and at last only one man remained who had not crossed gloves with Gomez – Ace Jessel.

I hesitated to throw my man in with a battler like Gomez, for my fondness for the great good-natured Negro was more than the friendship of manager for fighter. Ace was something more than a meal ticket to me, for I knew the real nobility underlying Ace's black skin, and I hated to see him battered into a senseless ruin by a man I knew in my heart to be more than Jessel's match. I wanted to wait a while, to let Gomez wear himself out with his terrific battles and the dissipations that were sure to follow the savage's success. These super-sluggers never last long, any more than a jungle native can withstand the temptations of civilization.

But the slump that follows a really great title-holder's gaining the belt was on, and matches were scarce. The public was clamoring for a title fight, sportswriters were raising Cain and accusing Ace of cowardice, promoters were offering alluring purses, and at last I signed for a fifteen-round go between Man-killer Gomez and Ace Jessel.

At the training quarters I turned to Ace.

"Ace, do you think you can whip him?"

"Mistah John," Ace answered, meeting my eye with a straight gaze, "I'll do mah best, but I's mighty afeard I cain't do it. Dat man ain't human."

This was bad; a man is more than half whipped when he goes into the ring in that frame of mind.

Later I went to Ace's room for something and halted in the doorway in amazement. I had heard the battler talking in a low voice as I came up, but had supposed one of the handlers or sparring partners was in the room with him. Now I saw that he was alone. He was standing before his idol – the portrait of Tom Molyneaux.

"Mistah Tom," he was saying humbly, "I ain't nevah met no man yet what could even knock me off mah feet, but I reckon dat niggah can. I's gwine to need help mighty bad, Mistah Tom."

I felt almost as if I had interrupted a religious rite. It was uncanny; had it not been for Ace's evident deep sincerity, I would have felt it to be unholy. But to Ace, Tom Molyneaux was something more than a saint.

I stood in the doorway in silence, watching the strange tableux. The unknown artist had painted the picture of Molyneaux with remarkable skill. The short black figure stood out boldly from the faded canvas. The breath of bygone days, he seemed, clad in the long tights of that other day, the powerful legs braced far apart, the knotted arms held stiff and high – just as Molyneaux had appeared when he fought Tom Cribb of England over a hundred years ago.

Ace Jessel stood before the painted figure, his head sunk upon his mighty chest as if listening to some dim whisper inside his soul. And as I watched, a curious and fantastic idea came to me – the memory of an age-old superstition.

You know it has been said by students of the occult that statues and portraits have power to draw departed souls back from the void of eternity. I wondered if Ace had heard of this superstition and hoped to conjure his idol's spirit out of the realms of the dead, for advice and aid. I shrugged my shoulders at this ridiculous idea and turned away. As I did, I glanced again at the picture before which Ace still stood like a great image of black basalt, and was aware of a peculiar illusion: the canvas seemed to ripple slightly, like the surface of a lake across which a faint breeze is blowing . . .

When the day of the fight arrived, I watched Ace nervously. I was more afraid than ever that I had made a mistake in permitting circumstances to force my man into the ring with Gomez. However, I was backing Ace to the limit – and I was ready to do anything under heaven to help him win that fight.

The great crowd cheered Ace to the echo as he climbed into the ring; cheered again, but not so heartily, as Gomez appeared. They afforded a strange contrast, those two Negroes, alike in color but so different in all other respects!

Ace was tall, clean-limbed and rangy, long and smooth of muscle, clear of eye and broad of forehead.

Gomez seemed stocky by comparison, though he stood a good six feet two. Where Jessel's sinews were long and smooth like great cables, his were knotty and bulging. His calves, thighs, arms, and shoulders stood out in great bunches of muscles. His small bullet head was set squarely between gigantic shoulders, and his forehead was so low that his kinky wool seemed to grow just above his small, bloodshot eyes. On his chest was a thick grizzle of matted black hair.

He grinned insolently, thumped his breast and flexed his mighty arms with the assurance of the savage. Ace, in his corner, grinned at the crowd, but an ashy tint was on his dusky face and his knees were trembling.

The usual formalities were carried out: instructions given by the referee, weights announced – 230 for Ace, 248 for Gomez. Then over the great stadium the lights went off except those over the ring where two black giants faced each other like men alone on the ridge of the world.

At the gong Gomez whirled in his corner and came out with a breathtaking roar of pure ferocity. Ace, frightened though he must have been, rushed to meet him with the courage of a cave man charging a gorilla. They met headlong in the center of the ring.

The first blow was the Man-killer's, a left swing that glanced from Ace's ribs. Ace came back with a long left to the face and a stinging right to the body. Gomez "bulled in," swinging both hands; and Ace, after one futile attempt to mix it with him, gave back. The champion drove him across the ring, sending a savage left to the body as Ace clinched. As they broke, Gomez shot a terrible right to the chin and Ace reeled into the ropes.

A great "Ahhh!" went up from the crowd as the champion plunged after him like a famished wolf, but Ace managed to get between the lashing arms and clinch, shaking his head to clear it. Gomez sent in a left, which Ace's clutching arms partly smothered, and the referee warned the Senegalese.

At the break Ace stepped back, jabbing swiftly and cleverly with his left. The round ended with the champion bellowing like a buffalo, trying to get past that rapier-like arm.

Between rounds I cautioned Ace to keep away from infighting as much as possible, where Gomez' superior strength would count heavily, and to use his footwork to avoid punishment.

The second round started much like the first, Gomez rushing and Ace using all his skill to stave him off and avoid those terrible smashes. It's hard to get a shifty boxer like Ace in a corner, when he is fresh and unweakened, and at long range he had the advantage over Gomez, whose one idea was to get in close and batter down his foes by sheer strength and ferocity. Still, in spite of Ace's speed and skill, just before the gong sounded Gomez got the range and sank a vicious left in Ace's midriff, and the tall Negro weaved slightly as he returned to his corner.

I felt that it was the beginning of the end. The vitality and power of Gomez seemed endless; there was no wearing him down and it would not take many such blows to rob Ace of his speed of foot and accuracy of eye. If forced to stand and trade punches, he was finished.

Gomez came plunging out for the third round with murder in his eye. He ducked a straight left, took a hard right uppercut square in the face and hooked both hands to Ace's body, then straightened with a terrific right to the chin, which Ace robbed of most of its force by swaying with the blow.

While the champion was still off balance, Ace measured him coolly and shot in a fierce right hook, flush on the chin. Gomez' head flew back as if hinged to his shoulders and he was stopped in his tracks! But even as the crowd rose, hands clenched, lips parted, hoping he would go down, the champion shook his bullet head and came in, roaring. The round ended with both men locked in a clinch in the center of the ring.

At the beginning of the fourth round Gomez drove Ace about the ring almost at will. Stung and desperate, Ace made a stand in a neutral corner and sent Gomez back on his heels with a left and right to the body, but he received a savage left in the face in return. Then suddenly the champion crashed through with a deadly left to the solar plexus, and as Ace staggered, shot a killing right to the chin. Ace fell back into the ropes, instinctively raising his hands. Gomez' short, fierce smashes were partly blocked by his shielding gloves – and, suddenly, pinned on the ropes as he was, and still dazed from the Man-killer's attack, Ace went into terrific action and, slugging toe to toe with the champion, beat him off and drove him back across the ring!

The crowd went mad. Ace was fighting as he had never fought before, but I waited miserably for the end. I knew no man could stand the pace the champion was setting.

Battling along the ropes, Ace sent a savage left to the body and a right and left to the face, but was repaid by a right-hand smash to the ribs that made him wince in spite of himself. Just at the gong, Gomez landed another of those deadly left-handers to the body.

Ace's handlers worked over him swiftly, but I saw that the tall black was weakening.

"Ace, can't you keep away from those body smashes?" I asked.

"Mistah John, suh, I'll try," he answered.

The gong!

Ace came in with a rush, his magnificent body vibrating with dynamic energy. Gomez met him, his iron muscles bunching into a compact fighting unit. Crash-crash – and again, crash! A clinch. As they broke, Gomez drew back his great right arm and launched a terrible blow to Ace's mouth. The tall Negro reeled – went down. Then without stopping for the count which I was screaming for him to take, he gathered his long, steely legs under him and was up with a bound, blood gushing down his black chest. Gomez leaped in and Ace, with the fury of desperation, met him with a terrific right, square to the jaw. And Gomez crashed to the canvas on his shoulder blades!

The crowd rose screaming! In the space of ten seconds both men had been floored for the first time in the life of each!

"One! Two! Three! Four!" The referee's arm rose and fell.

Gomez was up, unhurt, wild with fury. Roaring like a wild beast, he plunged in, brushed aside Ace's hammering arms and crashed his right hand with the full weight of his mighty shoulder behind it, full into Ace's midriff. Ace went an ashy color – he swayed like a tall tree, and Gomez beat him to his knees with rights and lefts which sounded like the blows of caulking mallets.

"One! Two! Three! Four – " Ace was writhing on the canvas, trying to get up. The roar of the fans was an ocean of noise which drowned all thought.

" – Five! Six! Seven – "

Ace was up! Gomez came charging across the stained canvas, gibbering his pagan fury. His blows beat upon the staggering challenger like a hail of sledges. A left – a right – another left which Ace had not the strength to duck.

He went down again.

"One! Two! Three! Four! Five! Six! Seven! Eight – "

Again Ace was up, weaving, staring blankly, helpless. A swinging left hurled him back into the ropes and, rebounding from them, he went to his knees – then the gong sounded!

As his handlers and I sprang into the ring Ace groped blindly for his corner and dropped limply upon the stool.

"Ace, he's too much for you," I said.

A weak grin spread over Ace's face and his indomitable spirit shone in his blood-shot eyes.

"Mistah John, please, suh, don't throw in de sponge. If I mus' take it, I takes it standin'. Dat boy cain't last at dis pace all night, suh."

No – but neither could Ace Jessel, in spite of his remarkable vitality and his marvelous recuperative powers, which sent him into the next round with a show of renewed strength and freshness.

The sixth and seventh were comparatively tame. Perhaps Gomez really was fatigued from the terrific pace he had been setting. At any rate, Ace managed to make it more or less of a sparring match at long range and the crowd was treated to an exhibition illustrating how long a brainy boxer can stand off and keep away from a slugger bent solely on his destruction. Even I marveled at the brand of boxing which Ace was showing, though I knew that Gomez was fighting cautiously for him. The champion had sampled the power of Ace's right hand in that frenzied fifth round and perhaps he was wary of a trick. For the first time in his life he had sprawled on the canvas. He was content to rest a couple of rounds, take his time, and gather his energies for a final onslaught.

This began as the gong sounded for the eighth round. Gomez launched his usual sledgehammer attack, drove Ace about in the ring, and floored him in a neutral corner. His style of fighting was such that when he was determined to annihilate a foe, skill, speed, and science could do no more than postpone the inevitable outcome. Ace took the count of nine and rose, back-pedaling.

But Gomez was after him; the champion missed twice with his left and then sank a right under the heart that turned Ace ashy. A left to the jaw made his knees buckle and he clinched desperately.

On the breakaway Ace sent a straight left to the face and a right hook to the chin, but the blows lacked force. Gomez shook them off and sank his left wrist deep in Ace's midsection. Ace again clinched but the champion shoved him away and drove him across the ring with savage hooks to the body. At the gong they were slugging along the ropes.

Ace reeled to the wrong corner and when his handlers led him to his own, he sank down on the stool, his legs trembling and his great dusky chest heaving from his exertions. I glanced across at the champion, who sat glowering at his foe. He too was showing signs of the fray, but he was much fresher than Ace. The referee walked over, looked hesitantly at Ace, then spoke to me.

Through the mists that veiled his muddled brain, Ace realized the significance of these words and struggled to rise, a kind of fear showing in his eyes.

"Mistah John, don' let him stop it, suh! Don' let him do it. I ain't hu't nothin' like dat would hu't me!"

The referee shrugged his shoulders and walked back to the center of the ring.

There was little use giving advice to Ace. He was too battered to understand – in his numbed brain there was room only for one thought – to fight and fight, and keep on fighting – the old primal instinct that is stronger than all things except death.

At the sound of the gong he reeled out to meet his doom with an indomitable courage that brought the crowd to its feet yelling. He struck, a wild aimless left, and then the champion plunged in, hitting with both hands until Ace went down. At "nine" he was up, back-pedaling instinctively until Gomez reached him with a long straight right and sent him down again. Again he took "nine" before he reeled up, and now the crowd was silent. Not one voice was raised in an urge for the kill. This was butchery – primitive slaughter – but the courage of Ace Jessel took their breath as it gripped my heart.

Ace fell blindly into a clinch, and another and another, till the Mankiller, furious, shook him off and sank his right to the body. Ace's ribs gave way like rotten wood, with a dry crack heard distinctly all over the stadium. A strangled cry went up from the crowd and Ace gasped thickly and fell to his knees.

" – Seven! Eight! – " the great black form was still writing on the canvas.

" – Nine!" And then a miracle happened; Ace was on his feet, swaying, jaw sagging, arms hanging limply.

Gomez glared at him as if unable to understand how his foe could have risen again, then came plunging in to finish him. Ace was in dire straits. Blood blinded him. both eyes were nearly closed, and when he breathed through his smashed nose, a red haze surrounded him. Deep cuts gashed cheek and cheek bones and his left side was a maze of torn flesh. He was going on fighting instinct alone now, and never again would any man doubt that Ace Jessel had a fighting heart.

Yet a fighting heart alone is not enough when the body is broken and battered, and mists of unconsciousness veil the brain. Before Gomez' terrific onslaught, Ace went down – broken – and the crowd knew that this time it was final.

When a man has taken the beating the Ace had taken, something more than the body and heart must come into the game to carry him through. Something to inspire and stimulate him – to fire him to heights of super-human effort!

Before leaving the training quarters, I had, unknown to Ace, removed the picture of Tom Molyneaux from the frame, rolled it up carefully, and brought it to the stadium with me. I now took this, and as Ace's dazed eyes instinctively sought his corner, I held the portrait up, just outside the glare of the ring lights, so while illuminated by them it appeared illusive and dim. It may be thought that I acted wrongly and selfishly, to thus seek to bring a broken man to his feet for more punishment – but the outsider cannot fathom the souls of the children of the fight game, to whom winning is greater than life, and losing, worse than death.

All eyes were glued on the prostrate form in the center of the ring, on the exhausted champion sagging against the ropes, on the referee's arm which rose and fell with the regularity of doom. I doubt if four men in the audience saw my action – but Ace Jessel saw!

I caught the gleam that came into his bloodshot eyes. I saw him shake his head violently. I saw him begin sluggishly to gather his long legs under him, while the drone of the referee rose as it reached its climax.

And as I live today, *the picture in my hands shook suddenly and violently!*

A cold wind passed like death across me and I heard the man next to me shiver involuntarily as he drew his coat closer about him. But it was no cold wind that gripped my soul as I looked, wide-eyed and staring, into the ring where the greatest drama of the boxing world was being enacted.

Ace, struggling, got his elbows under him. Bloody mists masked his vision; then, far away but coming nearer, he saw a form looming through the fog. A man – a short, massive black man, barrel-chested and mighty-limbed, clad in the long tights of another day – stood beside him in the ring! It was Tom Molyneaux, stepping down through the dead years to aid his worshipper – Tom Molyneaux, attired and ready as when he fought Tom Cribb so long ago!

And Jessel was up! The crowd went insane and screaming. A supernatural might fired his weary limbs and lit his dazed brain. Let Gomez do his worst now – how could he beat a man for whom the ghost of the greatest of all black fighters was fighting?

For to Ace Jessel, falling on the astounded Man-killer like a blast from the Arctic, Tom Molyneaux's mighty arm was about his waist, Tom's eye guided his blows, Tom's bare fists fell with Ace's on the head and body of the champion.

The Man-killer was dazed by his opponent's sudden comeback – he was bewildered by the uncanny strength of the man who should have been fainting on the canvas. And before he could rally, he was beaten down by the long, straight smashes sent in with the speed and power of a pile-driver. The last blow, a straight right, would have felled and ox – and it felled Gomez for the long count.

As the astonished referee lifted Ace's hand, proclaiming him champion, the tall Negro smiled and collapsed, mumbling the words, "Thanks, Mistah Tom."

Yes, to all concerned Ace's comeback seemed inhuman and unnatural – though no one saw the phantom figure except Tom – and one other. I am not going to claim that I saw the ghost myself – because I didn't, though I did feel the uncanny movement of that picture. If it hadn't been for the strange thing that happened just after the fight, I would say that the whole affair might be naturally explained – that Ace's strength was miraculously renewed by a delusion resulting from his glimpse of the picture. For after all, who knows the strange depths of the human soul and to what apparently superhuman heights the body may be lifted by the mind?

But after the bout the referee, a steely-nerved, cold-eyed sportsman of the old school, said to me:

"Listen here! Am I crazy – or was there a fourth man in that ring when Ace Jessel dropped Gomez? For a minute I thought I saw a broad, squat, funny-looking Negro standing there beside Ace! Don't grin, you bum! It wasn't that picture you were holding up – I saw that, too. It was a real man – and he looked like the one in the picture. He was standing there a moment – and then he was gone! God! That fight must have got on my nerves."

And these are the cold facts, told without any attempt to distort the truth or to mislead the reader. I leave the problem up to you:

Was it Ace's numbed brain that created the hallucination of ghostly aid – or did the phantom of Tom Molyneaux actually stand beside him, as he believes to this day?

As far as I am concerned, the old superstition is justified. I believe firmly today that a portrait is a door through which astral beings may pass back and forth between this world and the next – whatever the next world may be – and that a great, unselfish love is strong enough to summon the spirits of the dead to the aid of the living.

Crowd-Horror

I first spoke to Slade Costigan in his dressing room, where I had hurried immediately after his two-round knockout of Battling Monaghan. The boy was an impressive specimen of manhood, about six feet in height, slim-waisted and tapering of legs, with remarkably broad shoulders and heavy arms. Dark-skinned, with narrow, cold gray eyes, and a shock of black hair falling over a broad forehead, he had the true fighting face – broad across the cheekbones with thin lips and a firm jaw. His face was in a battered condition just now, one eye being partly closed, while his lips were bruised and his cheeks decorated with several small cuts, owing to the last desperate efforts of Battling Monaghan.

I sat down and looked him over.

"My name is Steve Palmer; you've probably heard of me. Now to come to the point; you look fairly intelligent."

He seemed slightly surprised, but grinned.

"With your brains and your body," I said slowly, "you should be fighting in the best rings in the country – not second-rate joints like this. I've followed your career. I've seen you fighting second-raters in small clubs for the last few months, tearing into them, wide-open and reckless. Now, listen, I'm saying this for your own good. As a boxer you're a false alarm. Wait now, don't get sore. I've watched you fight, and you're the toughest, hardest-punching slugger I ever saw, but you don't use your brains. You start your swings from the floor, leave yourself wide open at all times, forget all about footwork, and fall for every trick your opponent tries. You fight almost like a man in a trance. The only reason you've ever whipped anybody is because you're a freak – a regular granite-jawed iron man. But you'll crumble after a while under the steady fire of punches and go around cutting paper dolls. Punch-drunk! Just another Joe Grim."

"I know it," he answered roughly. "But how is it any of your business?"

"Listen, Slade," I said as kindly as I could, "I wouldn't be wasting my time on you if you were of the general run of iron men – a small-brained slugger without intelligence enough to learn. But you have plenty of brains, and probably more education than I have. I don't know how you got into the game, or why you haven't learned some science, but you have the makings of a champion. You've been going along without a manager. I don't say I can make you a ring wizard. But I say this: if you'll throw in with me, try your best to learn and apply what I teach you, I'll make you a champion."

Costigan shrugged his shoulders.

"All right," he answered rather indifferently. "As you say. I've never been knocked out yet, but this incessant battering is beginning to tell on me already."

That was how I came to manage "Iron" Slade Costigan. I liked the boy from the first; and I earnestly set to work to make a scientific slugger out of him. Alone in my training camps I had him study the tactics of Dempsey, McGovern, Ketchel, and Tom Sharkey – men who, lacking real cleverness, adapted themselves to their own particular style of fighting. Costigan learned with an ease which astonished me.

At last I got him Johnny Hilan, a good, clever light-heavyweight, for a sparring partner, absolutely forbidding Costigan to slug him.

I was astounded. To my amazement I watched my iron slugger glide about Johnny for four fast rounds, outstepping and outjabbing him, tying him up in the clinches, and flashing a defense that showed real genius.

"Slade," I said heartily, "I've been all wrong! I've been trying to make a scientific slugger out of you. Now I'm going to make you the classiest boxer the ring has ever seen! You're a queer fellow, Slade. I never heard of a slugger before who concealed such latent cleverness. It's absolutely beyond me how you've been such a tramp in the ring."

He shook his head in a helpless sort of manner and I was vaguely worried to note that he did not seem at all enthusiastic.

"I could always box cleverly in the training quarters," he said, "but the instant I climb into the ring I seem to be transformed into – a tramp," he laughed sardonically.

I imported the cleverest sparring partners I could find and set to work. Slade took naturally to his work and I was wildly enthusiastic. I had stumbled on to the rarest of all finds – a clever heavyweight with a killing punch.

Could I make a cool crafty boxer out of Slade, I knew no man in the world could stand against him. Fast, aggressive, too tough to be worried by the few punches that would slip past his guard, with the power of a projectile in each hand and the speed of light in his feet, he would tower above the general ruck of fighters like a giant above dwarfs. The manager's and fight fans' dream! The superfighter! A Corbett with the ruggedness of a Jeffries and the punch of a Dempsey!

All these things I imparted to Costigan, but he listened silently and his only comment was a despairing, empty, and self-mocking laugh that worried me deeply. But I went on.

At last I deemed my man ready to take the first step in the course I had mapped out for him. Accordingly I matched him with one Joe Handler, a tough fighter, fairly clever, with a wicked hitting ability. His manager was looking for a set-up at the time, and did not object to putting his man in with an unknown.

I impressed upon Costigan that this was his first step on the trail that should lead from second-rater to champion. I instructed him to box Handler, to keep away from him until he saw an opening, then to crash in with the short heavy smashes I had taught him. Slade listened, but said nothing.

The gong sounded. The crowd fell partly silent for a breathless instant, as Handler came to the center of the ring, hands up, and wary. Costigan slid out of his corner in a half-crouch, moving with the smooth cat-like tread that was his. I wondered if this could be the same man who had fought Battling Monaghan.

Handler led with his left, but Costigan was out of reach. Again he led and this time Slade stepped inside it and hooked a short left to the body. Handler grunted and went back on his heels, and instantly Costigan was on him, raining right and left hooks to body and head. Somehow Handler slipped blindly through the hail of gloves and clinched. The referee broke them. Handler, striking out blindly, connected with a hard left. Costigan stepped back from a wild right. The crowd shouted jeeringly, as crowds will, mindlessly, meaninglessly – and then to my horror Costigan went out of his mind and charged in blindly, flailing right and left!

My yells were in vain. He drove Handler about the ring with the force of his onslaught, missing or landing glancingly with most of his wild swings.

The crowd was up, bellowing – they liked this, of course. What do they care about a fighter, or whether he spends his last days maundering about, with a punch-drunk brain?

Handler was so astounded by this metamorphosis that he was unable to work out a plan of defense, and just before the gong Costigan floored him with a wild right swing to the side of the head.

Back in his corner, Slade sat with his head in his hands, paying no attention to my curses and entreaties. For the second round he came out slowly, in a boxing pose, but before the gloves touched, he went to pieces again and reverted to his old style. Handler was so weakened by the punishment he had received in the first round that he was in no shape to withstand Costigan's ferocity, and after missing seven or eight terrific swings, Slade landed a haymaking left to the jaw, and Handler went down and out.

Slade sat in his dressing room in silence, his eyes on the floor. I did not berate him, for I knew he was suffering. I slapped him on the back and said: "Cheer up, kid, better luck next time. After all, this is only the first bout."

"No, Steve," he said with a despairing gesture. "It'll be the same next time and always. I've been this way ever since I can remember. I'll never be anything but a tramp. It was only by chance I won – Handler was so surprised at my change of style that he left himself open. Otherwise he'd have beaten me to a pulp. Oh, I've had this experience before. When I first started fighting it was the same way. I'd come out sparring and dancing, and then the crowd – " He shuddered suddenly and clenched his fists until the nails sank into his palms.

"The crowd! They yell and I go insane! I can hear every shout – 'Fight, you yellow tramp!' 'Get off your bicycle!' 'Stand up and fight, curse you!' The force of those thousands of wills beats on me like a material flood. I've seen psychologists. Mass hypnotism, they say it is. I'm like a man in a trance, as you once said. A part of my brain goes to sleep and all that remains is the wild beast urge to destroy my enemy. The crowd beats down my will power and hypnotizes me."

"I've heard of such things," I said dubiously. "Still, I maintain that it can be overcome. You slug naturally. I believe we can train you until you box naturally, instinctively."

"I doubt it," said Costigan. "When the thunder of the crowd beats on my brain, I'm stunned – dazed, only partly aware of what I'm doing."

I went back to the training camp with one object in mind – to drill Costigan until he boxed as instinctively as he fought. To implant the science of the game so thoroughly in his reflexes that his trained motions would carry him through even if his brain "went to sleep."

The reporters pounced on the sensational knockout of Handler and boosted Costigan's stock sky high. They proclaimed him a second Dempsey, a smashing man-killer of the West, and laughed over his trick of fooling Handler into thinking that he was a defensive boxer – as they said.

I was cautious in getting him his next bout.

I finally selected Tommy Olsen, a clever light-heavyweight, a good boy but not a man-killer. The sportswriters were somewhat surprised at my preference, but the crowd that packed the arena was infinitely more so. As before, Costigan began boxing in a lively manner, but almost instantly blew up and began his wild and futile slugging.

The bout went the full ten rounds. Olsen, boxing cleverly, punished Costigan terrifically, but because of the iron man's incredible stamina, was unable to stop him or even knock him off his feet. At the end of the slaughter, the referee decided that Costigan had gained a draw, owing to his aggressiveness and the fact that his aimless but terrible swings had twice floored Olsen for counts of nine. The crowd booed the decision and even I felt it was unjust to Olsen.

The sportswriters, after recovering from their astonishment, trained their heavy artillery on us, inquiring sarcastically as to what kind of iron man this was, unable to defeat a man fifteen pounds lighter than himself.

As for me, I saw the handwriting on the wall.

"Slade," I said, "our championship hopes have gone glimmering. I hate to quit so quickly, but the crowd has us whipped."

Slade silently grasped my hand. "You're a real friend, Steve, and you're right. It's bitter quitting the game like this, but my face is already more battered than many an old-timer's and my brain will be next. I've seen these punch-drunk wrecks that were once iron men like myself. But I want just one more fight, and then I'll have money enough to go into the kind of business I want, Steve."

I argued against it, but finally gave in. Handler and his manager were clamoring for a return match and as I could get more money for my man there than anywhere else, I agreed with misgivings. Handler was a hard man.

One night, a few days before the fight, Slade came in and after hesitating a while, and making several false starts, he said, blushing like a schoolboy, "Steve, I have a girl."

Following my manager's instinct, I was about to protest; then remembering he was practically through with the game, I congratulated him heartily.

"Her name's Gloria. She dances in some of the higher-class cabarets. Maybe – maybe when I get started good in my business she'll marry me."

He wandered away day-dreaming, and I sighed. It was pathetic to me, for I felt in my heart Slade would fail in his "business" as in everything else.

The night of the fight arrived and I stood in Slade's corner, as I thought for the last time, muttering some words of encouragement to him. Across the ring Joe Handler sat, glowering, grimly intent on wiping out the stain on his record.

"I'm glad Gloria isn't here," muttered Slade just as the gong sounded and I silently echoed his words. If the girl cared for him at all, it would be a terrible sight for her to see the beating I knew he was in for.

At the tap of the gong Costigan leaped from his corner in a vain effort to crush Handler before he could get set. But Handler, while bent on revenge, was taking no chances with the sledges which had knocked him out before. He back-pedaled around the ring with Slade in hot chase, swinging fiercely and futilely. Handler evaded his efforts, frequently beat him to the punch with a stinging left jab, and clinched often. Little damage was done by either that round.

During the minute intermission I thrust my head through the ropes and spoke a few cheering words to Slade, who smiled dazedly at me. The crowd had him. As I was about to climb into the ring to aid his seconds in caring for him, I felt some one tug at my coat. I turned to look into the face of a girl who sat in a front row seat. She was small and slender, not much more than a child, with a winsome face set off by silky blond hair. This hair was cut in a very boyish bob, and a round little hat perched jauntily on top, adding to her appearance of piquant youthfulness.

"You're Mr. Palmer, aren't you?" she asked childishly, her large, violet eyes gazing trustfully up at me. "Slade is going to win, isn't he?"

"How do I know?" I responded irritably, for my nerves were rasped with worry. "What is it to you?"

"I'm Gloria," she answered nervously. "Hasn't Slade told you about me?"

"My God!" I exclaimed. "What are you doing here?"

She shrank back into her seat. "Don't tell him," she cried. "He told me not to come, but I wanted to see him whip Handler."

"You're more likely to see him battered to a bloody pulp," I snarled brutally. "Why can't women stay where they belong? Don't let him see you, whatever you do. He's in for enough suffering as it is."

I instantly regretted my unnecessary roughness. Tears sprang to her soft eyes and she twined her white hands nervously.

"You'd better leave," I said more gently, but she shook her head.

"I'm right behind Slade's corner," she said in a subdued manner. "He can't see me unless he turns right around, and he isn't likely to do that. Mr. Palmer, please let me stay; I won't scream or anything."

"All right." I turned back to my fighter, who was just getting off his stool to answer the gong. Evidently, in the racket the crowd was making, he had heard nothing of our conversation and was unaware of the girl's presence.

I haven't the heart to tell of that fight in detail. Round after round it was the same, Costigan charging and missing, and Handler putting more and more steam behind his jabs and counters as he solved Slade's single style, until he was battering away fiercely at the iron man's crimsoned face and body. The fourth, fifth, sixth, and seventh were alike. The crowd was stunned at two things: Slade's powers of taking punishment, and his senseless manner of fighting. I sighed, thinking of what he might have been.

At the end of the eighth round Costigan went down for the second time beneath a volley of right hooks to the head and had to be helped to his corner. I was on the point of throwing in the sponge, but Costigan, both eyes partly closed, his nose smashed and blood gushing from innumerable cuts on his face, stopped me. Oh, he had courage.

"Take it standing up," he muttered like a man in a dream. "Feeling better now – last out the bout."

It was true that his recuperation was remarkable – more so than in any man I have ever known. He actually charged out for the ninth round with a show of freshness which would have broken some men's hearts – and the slaughter commenced again. Handler, wearying of his efforts, began to take chances in his eagerness.

I heard a sound of sobbing and turned to see the girl, Gloria. She had left her seat and was leaning against the ring at my side. Her pretty little face was streaked with tears, her foolish little hat all awry.

"Oh, why don't they stop it?" she whimpered. "Isn't there some way that Slade can whip that brute?"

"Yes," I said bitterly. "Handler's leaving scores of openings now, but Slade's got only a long roundhouse swing that a blind man could duck. The boy would win if he could box him."

To my amazement her eyes flashed suddenly, she leaped feet first into a seat, and her high shrill voice cut through the din like a knife:

"Box him, Slade, *box him*!"

And before my eyes a miracle happened. At the first sound of that voice, Slade stopped short. His head turned as he sought the author of it, and instantly Handler crashed a sledgehammer right to his jaw. Costigan dropped like a log, but as the referee counted over him, he reeled to his knees and his blood-misted eyes swept the ringside until they rested on the girl; they remained riveted there.

"Slade, oh, Slade!" Her arms were outstretched and all the pleading and love and sacrifice of a thousand centuries of womanhood trembled in her voice: "Box him, kid, *box him*!"

"Nine!" shouted the referee – and Costigan was on his feet. The crowd screamed. I yelled. Handler's manager went white. Handler, rushing in to deliver the finishing blow, had been met with a snaky left jab that set him back on his heels and broke a flow of blood from his lips.

Like a great smooth leopard Costigan was after him, and again and again the left shot to Handler's face, while Costigan easily avoided the boxer's wild and bewildered returns. It was an incredible reversal of form! Now it was Handler who floundered and swung wild, and Costigan who poured a swift fire of jabs and hooks to head and body.

Never before in any ring has such a thing happened. Had Handler had his mind about him, he might have won yet, but just as Costigan had beaten him before by a shift from boxer to slugger, so he beat him now by a shift from slugger to boxer. Handler missed repeatedly, went down, and arose, weakening fast. Back across the ring Slade jabbed his foe and on the ropes sank his right four times to the midriff. Handler sank to his knees and was counted out, crouching and holding dazedly to Costigan's legs.

"For the love of Mike!" exclaimed a dazed reporter to me, as the crowd watched in stunned silence and then broke into bedlam, "what sort of bird are you managing anyhow? You mean to tell me Costigan intentionally took a beating like that to trick Handler, or what?"

"They say that the influence of the mob can be counterbalanced by one person, if you think enough of that one person," I answered, only about half aware of what I was saying. "There's a living proof of that statement!"

And I pointed to the corner of the ring where Costigan had collapsed in the arms of Gloria, who was showering him with tears and kisses absolutely unaware of any one.

"And about this retirement business you hinted at the other day," the reporter plucked at my sleeve. "What about it?"

"I've changed my mind. You can announce for Costigan and me that I'm managing the next world's heavyweight champion!"

That fight marked the beginning of a new era for Slade Costigan. How it came to be I do not know, being no psychologist, but his horror of the crowd was a thing of the past, as long as Gloria was at hand to call to him when the old mists began to steal back over his brain. As he himself expressed it, it was as if her voice woke him from a deep sleep and started his drugged brain cells working again. The crowd roared and thundered as of old, but all my boxer heard now was the beloved voice of Gloria, which outweighed all else.

I always had a seat reserved for the girl just behind his corner, and when the going was roughest, her voice kept him steady and keen. Perhaps it was simply his great love for her which made him instinctively follow her directions under all circumstances. Or perhaps her nature was the stronger, or that like all restless souls, his needed an anchor of some sort and she was his anchor. I do not know; I only know that – with Gloria's war-cry of love quavering through the roar of fans, "Box him, kid, box him!" – Slade Costigan was invincible.

The Unbeatable Triangle the scribes called us, and our onrush for the title will be remembered for a hundred years. With an anchor for Costigan's peculiar mind he developed into what I had visioned him. An irresistible super-fighter.

At last only one man stood between him and the champion – Buffalo Gonzalez, the South American – and then as suddenly as the Unbeatable Triangle had been formed, it was broken.

It was two nights after Costigan had outboxed the Brown Ghost of Atlanta and knocked him out in the seventh. As I came into our training quarters, I met Gloria coming out and saw at a glance that bad weather was brewing. Oh, she had a will of her own, for all her childish gentleness, and was something of a little tigress when roused.

"I hate him!" she exclaimed, stamping her little foot.

"Who, Gloria?" I asked.

"Slade!"

"Slade! Why – " I was struck speechless.

"He was a bully and a brute!" she cried, tears starting to her eyes. "Just because I went to a dance with a fellow he doesn't like, he got rough! Look at this bruise on my arm!"

"But, honey," I soothed, "I know Slade didn't intend to hurt you. He's so strong."

"He had no business grabbing me!" she sobbed, stamping her foot. "I'm through with him forever and a day! I wouldn't come back if he got down on his knees! I'm through-h-h-h!"

And suddenly she threw her arms around my neck like a child, wept briefly on my bosom, jerked away, stamped her foot again – and was gone. And I could see my hopes of a title fading with her. I went on into the training quarters.

Slade sat at a table, head sunk in his arms.

"Slade," said I, "you're a fool. What's come between you and Gloria?"

"Oh, I'm a fool all right," he answered, lifting his head with a sigh. "She went to a dance with this rotter I warned her against, just to show me I wasn't running her affairs, and when they came here afterward I went out of my mind and threw him out. Then we had our first row and she threw my engagement ring at me and swore she was through. And she means it. She won't come back."

I tried to find the girl, but she had left the city. I put a couple of detective agencies on the job, but Slade said, "No use, Steve, she wouldn't come back, even if you found her."

My soul was filled with bitterness. I knew the futility of sending Slade into the ring without her aid. I stopped all other business in my useless efforts to find the girl.

Then one day I came into the training quarters and found my boxer punching the light bag.

"Have you forgotten my match with Gonzalez?" he asked in response to my questions. "Have you forgotten you signed me up four months ago for a fifteen-round bout in Chicago with him?"

"You're not going to fight Gonzalez unless I find that girl."

"Yes, I am. The contract's drawn and you've put up a ten thousand dollar forfeit."

"Do you think I care about the money?" I asked bitterly. "It's yourself I'm thinking about."

"And it's Gloria I'm thinking about," he muttered, hitting the bag mechanically.

"Forget her. She's not worth it. You can't mean you'll fight Gonzalez? Why, man, he's never been whipped! He's a giant, a killer. Boxing him, you have a chance; slugging, he'll kill you. And you know as good as I do, that you'll go to pieces without Gloria to steady you."

"That's true," he muttered. "But I'll fight Gonzalez. I'll close my ring career in a blaze of glory, at least. If you'll have nothing to do with it, I'll fight him anyway. But I'd like to have you in my corner that night, Steve."

Long ago I learned that when a boxer is so determined it is useless to argue. With horrible misgivings I went about my preparations for the bout. There was no need for me to look into the credentials of Buffalo Gonzalez. Once in a hundred years such a man flashes comet-like across the stage. Landing in New York less than fourteen months before, carrying his scanty belongings in a bandanna hankerchief and armed with the high-sounding but empty title of South American Champion, the Buffalo had soon proved his worth by smashing through all opposition, and the record showed a list of twenty straight knockouts to his credit.

I could see but one outcome to the bout. Gonzalez was almost as tough as Slade, and could hit just as hard. He was the greatest natural slugger I have ever seen; he fought with a certain natural science, weaved, circled, feinted, ducked, and fought from a crouch. He knew little of the finer points of the game, but thus far his stamina and punching powers had made him invincible. At his top form, boxing and fighting, I believed Slade would prove even the Buffalo's master. But if he went back to his old way of upright, wide open, useless swinging, it would simply be a slaughter.

Once again the thunder of the crowd tore at us, the ring lights blazed above, and the smell of canvas rosin and sweaty leather filled our nostrils. I helped Costigan through the ropes and watched him as he stood erect and flung off his bath robe.

A fine figure of a man he was: six feet, and one hundred and ninety pounds of lithely muscled young manhood, with the long, smooth sinews rippling along his powerful arms and mighty shoulders. Handsome, too, in a fierce, tigerish way, despite the disfigurations of his many battles, which were, after all, not so bad as one might think. A true iron man, few blows had left their marks on him permanently, and though his nose had been broken many times, it was not altogether shapeless.

I thought as I looked at him how self-confident and efficient he must have seemed to the crowd – but to me he seemed pathetic, a bewildered giant laboring under a handicap he could never overcome, groping blindly through life, and now deserted by his only stay.

He shivered as though from a cold wind when the full blast of the crowd smote him, and into his cold gray eyes stole the blank, unseeing stare as of old. Again and again the crowd thundered his name, a raging ocean of sound on which I knew Slade Costigan's anchorless soul was drifting, against which his numbed brain was vainly struggling. Again and again I asked myself the question – would his trained reflexes carry him through, or would he crack as he had cracked before?

Then the clamor changed, for another form was entering the ring. Gonzalez! A huge hairy giant he was, with the mightiest chest ever seen in an American ring. His shoulders were like iron mountains, his arms like knotted oak limbs. Six feet two he stood, and every ounce of his two-hundred-and-fifteen-pound body was vibrant with savage energy. He was bulky, yet not ponderous. He moved with the ease of a tiger, and from under thick black brows his small eyes gleamed and sparkled with magnetic fierceness.

The men were called to the center of the ring for instructions, and Slade listened with his head bowed on his mighty chest, like a great panther gathering himself for the charge. Then they stepped to their corners, the seconds left the ring, the lights went out everywhere except for the cluster which blazed above the ring, and as I climbed through the ropes, I stopped for a last word.

"Slade, in God's name let me throw in the sponge if it gets too rough!"

His hand grasped mine, and I felt the grip of his iron fingers through the glove.

"No, Steve, let me go out as I lived. The game's not worth the candle. My world has crashed about me, and I guess I've been out of place all my life. Tell Gloria I still loved her to the last. The gong! Now let's see how long the greatest iron man can last against the greatest slugger!"

And like a huge leaping tiger he was out of his corner, leaving me speechless with horror, for I read in his last words a determination to die there in the ring! Oh, don't laugh at the idea of a man dying under a hail of leather gloves. It was happened before, and if there was ever a man built for the destruction of his opponents in the ring, and intent upon their slaughter, it was Buffalo Gonzalez. It was said of him that he had knocked bulls off their feet with his fist, and certainly a squarely landed smash of his right would have caved in the skull of many a man. Consider, then, the prospects of standing up under a blast of such blows – of running full into them, time and again.

No, I knew that unless Costigan should by some miracle be knocked out quickly by one blow, he would be carried senseless from the ring and might never come to.

Over the stadium a hush fell – a breathless silence, as the tiger and the buffalo met in the center of the ring.

Costigan came very close to winning by a knockout in the very first exchange. Charging in like the rush of a whirlwind, he landed first – a trip-hammer left to the jaw and a blasting right that dashed Gonzalez to his knees for his first trip to the canvas. The right was high, else I believe not even the Buffalo could have risen. As it was, he bounced up without a count. Hurt but furious, and roaring like a wounded bull, he staggered Costigan with a crashing left to the jaw. He ducked Slade's return and landed again – hard under the heart with the right.

"My God!" a reporter screamed at me. "Has Costigan gone crazy? What does he mean, trading punches with Gonzalez?"

How could I tell him that my boy was not only following his stunned instinct, but was also bent on his own destruction? How could I tell him of the feelings which prompted Slade's despair – his girl gone, and with her, all his hopes and ambitions? But I understood how the boy felt, crazed with the shattering of his hopes and haunted by the ghosts of all his failures. Life meant nothing to him, and he was willing to lay it down gloriously here in the ring.

Gonzalez was weaving and ducking, and Slade's savage smashes were glancing off his massive shoulders. The South American was confident in the power of his own punches, and he was wild with rage and humiliation. For the first time in his life he had felt the canvas under his knees!

I sighed. That incident showed me that Slade had power enough in his fists to knock out even Gonzalez, could he land often enough. But the man never lived who could flatten the Buffalo with one or two blows, and the infrequent smashes which Slade was likely to land would not turn the trick.

Smash! Smash! Gonzalez's straight rights battered at Costigan's body, and his long, looping left hooks found Slade's temple repeatedly, while the lighter man's swings glanced from the weaving Latin's arms or the top of his skull, or missed him entirely.

A right hook caught Slade off balance and hurled him to the floor. He was up without a count, and as he rose they traded crashing rights to the body. Slade was staggered, but Gonzalez grunted and halted an instant in his rush. Instantly Slade swung blindly and terribly, and by pure luck landed under the heart with his sledgehammer right. Gonzalez gasped and bent double, and another mine-sweeping right straightened him and flung him into the ropes, where he clung, dazed.

Then and there Costigan should have won the fight, but with the South American reeling helplessly before him, Slade missed swing after swing, until, recovering with his usual alacrity, Gonzalez lurched off the ropes and smashed Costigan to the canvas with a long overhand right. The gong sounded, and we lifted Slade to his feet and helped him to his corner.

"Boy," Slade's handler babbled wildly, "he's fightin' wide open! You nearly got 'im that first rush! Duck them slams, an' he's your'n. Whyn't you box 'im a little?"

"Shut up!" I snarled. "The boy doesn't know what you're saying."

Slade sat, lolling back on the ropes as his seconds worked over him. He was able to answer the gong, his body and nerves responding as freshly as ever, but in his eyes still flamed that blank glare that the roaring of the throng induced.

Gonzalez came out more cautiously – feinted – met Slade's rush with a straight left to the face. As the lighter man went back on his heels, the South American, bunching himself into a compact unit of destruction, crashed through and sank his right to the wrist in Costigan's body. Not even an iron man could stand up under such a blow. Costigan dropped as if he had been shot.

"One! Two! Three! Four!"

Costigan was struggling to rise; the blood that trickled from his battered features reddened the canvas. The crowd was chanting in unison to the count of the referee. I reached for the sponge. Then suddenly, at my very elbow, sounded a cry which halted me short.

"Box him, kid, oh, *box him!*"

Gloria! I whirled. She stood at my side, the foolish little hat perched high on her blond head. One hand clutched at a rope, the other reached out in mute appeal toward the battered and gory fighter who was slowly rising in the center of the ring.

"Seven!"

At the first sound of her voice, Costigan's head had whipped about toward his corner. His eyes flared, and he shook his head violently as if to clear his brain. He raked a glove across his eyes to wipe away the blood, and into those eyes, as their gaze fell on the tear-stained face of the girl, came a sudden blaze of light. The blank stare vanished; in its place gleamed a sane and self-confident expression. A sob of grateful relief burst from me.

"Nine!"

Costigan rose with a rather uncertain motion. His trembling legs showed that the punishment he had received had taken its toll. Gonzalez came in warily, expecting the usual savage and aimless charge. But Costigan, with a cat-like movement, ducked between the Buffalo's great arms and clinched, tying up the South American so that he was helpless in spite of his superior strength.

The crowd bellowed; Gonzalez swore. The referee broke them, but before Gonzalez could strike, Slade clinched again. The crowd roared its bloodthirsty disapproval, but Costigan gave no heed. Each moment now was precious to him, for with each passing second the strength was flowing back into his veins.

He stalled, clinched, and held until the referee was weary from tearing them apart, the crowd was frenzied, and Gonzalez was wild. The South American was all at sea. The shift from slugger to boxer bewildered him, just as it had Joe Handler, and the Buffalo knew nothing of the finer arts of the game. Coming out of clinches, Slade kept him off balance with quick jabs, then clinched again. The gong! And I knew, barring accident, Gonzalez's best chance of victory was gone.

Slade did not need to be helped to his corner this time.

"Slade, Slade," the girl sobbed. "I'm a selfish, damn fool! I had to come back to you, Slade, do you still love me?"

A smile curled his battered lips. "Gloria, you know I do."

"I couldn't stay away." She was crying and laughing at the same time, while the crowd looked on, speechless. "I had to come back!"

"Seconds out!"

I gently disengaged the girl's clinging arms and helped her through the ropes, turning to Costigan for a single quick word: "Is it all right, kid?"

"All right, Steve," he grinned. "Watch this for a boxing lesson! I could whip a ring full of buffaloes now!"

The gong! Costigan went out to meet Gonzalez, not with the senseless, wide-open plunge of the slugger, but with the smooth, studied charge of the aggressive boxer.

But Gonzalez was a grim and desperate fighter. Seeing victory fading before the jabs of the rejuvenated boxer facing him, he came out to kill or be killed. His first charge was like the blast of a wind from hell, and Slade, with all his renewed skill, could not wholly evade it. Back across the ring he was hurled in a whirlwind of cannonball smashes, which would have destroyed any but himself.

With his ribs pounded black and blue, and a deep gash opened on his cheekbone, Costigan felt the ropes at his back, and gave up boxing for the moment. As I saw him burst into a ferocious rally of slugging, I thought for an instant he had gone wild again, and so did Gloria.

But Slade knew what he was doing. A human tiger had him pinned on the ropes, where his skill was useless, and he must fight him off as best he could or go down to swift defeat. He went into terrific action, staking all on his toughness and punch. But he was not slugging wildly as of old. Chin low on his chest, body bunched into a defensive crouch, he slashed away with short, terrific hooks and straight jolts. He was taking plenty of punishment, but he was handing it out, too! Already Gonzalez's face was a red mask, and his breath was coming shorter.

Crash! Crash! At close range the mighty blows thundered on each other, and then Gonzalez reeled back from the impetus of a sledgehammer right to the jaw, and Slade bounded away from the ropes. Yet even as he did, Gonzalez reeled back and crashed a terrible overhand right through the air. That return was as sudden and unexpected as the stroke of a cobra.

Costigan ducked, but he was not swift enough. He took it square on the temple, and went down on his face as though the force of the blow would drive him through the boards. The referee sprang forward and began to count, while Gonzalez lurched into a neutral corner, almost in as bad a way as the man he had just floored.

Gloria began to cry, but I had no doubt at all in my mind. I knew Slade would somehow be on his feet before the last count. And he was.

Gonzalez came toward him with dragging steps, and stiffly moving legs. Only his wild beast courage kept him on his feet, but he was still dangerous. He rushed like a great, unwieldy monster, his great fist moving in erratic arcs, his partly closed eyes gleaming furiously. He could not understand this man who stood before him, and who continued to rise after blows that would have killed an ordinary man. After all, this was more a contest of endurance. Both had taken hideous punishment.

They were both on the verge of collapse, but somewhere in him Costigan found the power to carry him through. The Buffalo missed a straight right and attempted to clinch for the first time. Costigan shoved him away and hooked both hands to the head. For the first time Gonzalez was being hit without a return. With a last dying effort he reeled back, and in a semblance of his old ferocity, rushed Slade back across the ring and sank a right to the body that hurt the iron man.

Slade hooked a left to the chin and a terrific right under the heart, and the swart giant's knees buckled. The Buffalo swung – little more than a gesture it was – and a blasting right that carried all of Slade's waning strength, found his chin and dropped him to his knees, whence he slid on his back to the canvas.

Costigan staggered to the farthest corner, and as the referee counted, the Buffalo turned blindly, reeled to his feet, where he stood with his trembling legs braced wide apart, his great, shaggy head bowed upon his mighty chest, unable to lift his hands; out on his feet, but still impelled by that wild beast instinct of battle.

Costigan came slowly out of his corner and approached the South American, uncertainly. A single shove would topple the beaten man, but Slade wished to be spared delivering the final blow. The referee hesitated, then waved Gonzalez to his corner. But the South American did not see the gesture, for as the referee raised Slade's right hand, Gonzalez pitched forward on his face and lay still, completely out.

Costigan collapsed in his corner, unable to climb out of the ring, and Gloria squirmed into his arms and wept and laughed and kissed him.

"Oh, Slade, I never realized how much you need me! Slade, I'll never leave you again!"

Iron Men

CHAPTER I

"Like a Barroom Brawler – "

A cannonball for a left and a thunderbolt for a right! A granite jaw and an iron body that could not be dented! The ferocity of a tiger and the greatest fighting heart that ever beat in a steel-ribbed breast! That was Mike Brennon, heavyweight contender in the year 19 – .

I saw him first in the boxing tent of a traveling carnival, long before any fight fan or sportswriter had ever heard the name of Brennon. This carnival, like many wandering shows of that type, had a retinue of wrestlers and boxers – pork-and-beaners who had passed their prime or hard-eyed kids who were too young for the game. As usual the spieler was offering a prize to any one who could stay so many rounds or minutes with the show-athletes, boxing or wrestling. As a rule there are men planted in the audience who come forward giving fictitious names and claiming to reside in the town in which the carnival is showing.

These men enter the ring, slug or struggle as the case may be with a great show of roughness and anger, while the deluded patrons urge them on, thinking they are encouraging home talent. Then they lose in such a manner as to leave the matter in doubt enough to drive the crowd into a frenzy and assure a "return match" and a crowded house the next night. Occasionally some real native son gets the start on the plant and the carnival fighter is forced to really exert himself. However, as an old timer has said, "There are ways and means," and the native son very seldom stays the limit.

I sat in the "athletic tent" of the carnival which was performing in the small Nevada town through which I happened to be passing, and grinned at the antics of the spieler who was volubly offering fifty dollars to anyone who could stay four rounds with "Young Firpo, the California Assassin, champion of Los Angeles and the East Indies!" Young Firpo, whose real name was doubtless Leary and who was probably fighting in fourth-rate clubs before his illustrious namesake was ever heard of, stood by with a bored but contemptuous expression on his heavy stolid features. This was an old game to him. He was a vast hairy fellow with the bulging muscles of a weight lifter.

"Now, friends," shouted the spieler, "is they any young man here what wants to risk his life in this here ring? We bar no man! Step up, fellers! This is the man that give Johnny Risko his hardest battle, the one man who made the present champeen quit in a private work out! Remember, the management ain't responsible for life or limb! Any man that takes up this offer gits in here at his own risk and-"

At that moment the crowd set up a yell, "Brennon! Mike Brennon! Mike's the boy to fight this bird! Go on, Brennon!"

At last a young fellow rose from his seat and with a rather embarrassed grin on his face, vaulted over the ropes. Young Firpo evinced some interest and from the hawk-like manner in which the spieler eyed the newcomer, and from the ovation given him by the crowd, I knew that he was "on the up and up" – a local boy, in other words.

"You a professional boxer?" asked the spieler.

"I've fought a few times in the club here," answered Brennon, "but you said you barred nobody."

"We don't," grunted the spieler, taking in the difference in size between his man and the local lad.

While the usual rigamarole of argument and instructions was gone through with, I wondered just how the carnival men intended saving that fifty dollars in case the boy should happen to be a match for their man. As a general rule the ring is set close to the back of the tent, with a curtain stretched across the back, behind which are the dressing rooms. A tough local boy is worked up to this curtain in a clinch, his head suddenly pressed against it, and the razor-back lurking behind for that purpose sees the bulge in the curtain and instantly smites it with a blackjack. The carnival boxer, feeling the victim go limp, releases him, striking him on the jaw at the same time. To the crowd it looks like a clean knockout. If they notice the boy crumple before the final punch they think he received a short body blow while infighting.

However, in this case the ring was set in the middle of the tent with no curtain near, the dressing rooms being in another part of the tent. I was sure that something crooked would be tried though I could not figure out just what it would be.

Brennon, after a short trip to the dressing room, climbed into the ring and was given a wild ovation. He was a finely built lad, a good six feet one in height, slim waisted and tapering of legs, with remarkably broad shoulders and heavy arms. He was dark of skin with narrow gray eyes and a shock of black hair falling over a broad forehead, and he had the true fighting face – broad across the cheekbones, with thin lips and a firm jaw. His long, smooth muscles rippled beautifully as he moved with the ease of a huge leopard. Opposed to him Young Firpo looked ponderous and slow; ape-like.

Their weights were announced, Brennon 189, Young Firpo 191. The crowd jeered and hissed at the last; anyone could see that the carnival boxer weighed at least 210.

The battle was short, fierce, and sensational, with a bedlam-like ending. At the first tap of the gong Brennon sprang from his corner and came in wide open, like a barroom brawler. Young Firpo met him with a hard left hook to the chin, stopping him in his tracks. Brennon's hands dropped, he staggered and the carnival boxer swung his right flush to the jaw. This was really a terrific blow but strangely enough it did not seem to worry the young fellow as much as the other had. He shook his head and came plunging in again but as he did so, his foe drew back his deadly left and crashed it once more to the jaw. Brennon dropped face first, like a log. The crowd was frenzied. The referee-the spieler-leaped forward and began counting swiftly; Young Firpo standing directly over the fallen warrior.

At five Brennon had not moved. Not a muscle twitched. At "seven" he stirred and began making aimless motions, the fighter's instinct in his brain seeking to drag him to his feet. At "eight" he reeled to his knees and his reddened dazed eyes, wandering about, seemed suddenly to fix themselves on Young Firpo standing over him. Instantly they blazed with the fury of the killer. As the spieler opened his mouth to say "Ten!" Brennon came reeling up in a blast of breathtaking ferocity that stunned the crowd.

Young Firpo too, seemed stunned. His jaw went slack, his face whitened and he began a hurried retreat. Brennon was after him like a blood-crazed tiger and before Young Firpo could lift his hands, Brennon's wide looping left crashed under his heart, and as the carnival boxer's knees buckled, a sweeping right found his chin and crashed him down on the canvas with a force that shook the whole ring.

The astounded spieler mechanically lifted his hand to begin counting, but Brennon, moving like a man in a daze, or one who is walking in his sleep, pushed him away and stooping, tore the glove from Young Firpo's limp left hand. Removing something therefrom, he held it up to the crowd. It was a heavy iron affair, resembling brass knuckles, and known in the parlance of the ring as a knuckle duster. Seeing this I gasped. No wonder Brennon had gone down as though struck by a trip-hammer. And no wonder Young Firpo had been unnerved when his victim rose! The force with which that iron-laden glove had landed twice on Brennon's jaw should have shattered the bone, and yet he had been able to arise within ten seconds and knock his man out with two blows!

Now all was bedlam. The spieler tried to snatch the knuckle duster from Brennon's hand and one of the wrestlers, acting as Young Firpo's second, rushed across the ring and struck at the winner. The crowd, sensing injustice to their favorite and fired with the unreasoning mob-spirit, surged into the ring with the avowed intention of "wrecking the blank-blank show!" As I made my way to the nearest exit, I saw an infuriated townsman swing up a chair to strike the still unconscious Young Firpo. Brennon sprang forward and caught the blow on his own shoulder, the force of it dashing him to his knees. Then with a breath of relief I was on the outside, and as I walked away, laughing, I heard the shouted commands of the special officers who were seeking to restore peace and order.

Over a year later I sat at the ringside of a small fight club on the California coast, waiting for the main event of the night. One of the habitues of the club was giving me his opinion of the fighters.

"And wait'll ya see this boy. He'll bowl Bat Mulcahy over in a coupla rounds. No boxer, but baby how he can clout! And as for takin' it! Imagine Bat Nelson and Tom Sharkey and Joe Goddard all mixed together, and triple the result! A glutton for punishment, that's him – "

About this time the boxers entered the ring. One was a stocky blond cave-man, the other a tall dark-complexioned youngster. It was Brennon.

He had not improved on his style. As before he came tearing out of his corner, wild and wide open, hitting with both hands. Mulcahy had no skill to speak of, was even more of a dub than Young Firpo had been, yet he managed to last nearly two rounds and to hand out a raft of punishment before one of those sweeping blows landed. It was a left which sank to the wrist in the blond boy's midriff and it was enough.

During the fight my old interest in Brennon was renewed. In spite of his senseless, wide open style, I saw that he had the makings of a champion in him. A perfect build, incredible stamina – Mulcahy's best blows had not even made him wince – as terrific a punch as I have ever seen, it was evident that his one failing was an absolute lack of science. Apparently he had everything but the instinct which makes some fighters do things right in the ring, even lacking proper instruction. He looked like a champion but he had the style of a longshoreman. Still, I did not attach much importance to this, as detracting from his general merit. Many a fighter stumbles through his ring life and never learns anything simply because of an ignorant or negligent manager.

I went to Brennon's dressing room and accosted him.

"My name is Steve Amber. I saw you fight tonight and I saw you knock out a dub by the name of Young Firpo in a carnival in Gantsley, Nevada, about a year ago."

"I've heard of you," answered Brennon without enthusiasm, "What do you want?" Overlooking his abrupt manner, I said: "Who's your manager?"

"I haven't any."

"How would you like for me to manage you?"

"I'd as soon have you as anybody," he answered shortly, "But this was my last fight. I'm through. I'm fed up on knocking out dubs in fourth-rate joints."

"Tie up with me and maybe I'll get you better matches."

"No use. I had my chance twice. Once in Los Angeles against Sailor Slade; once in New York against Johnny Varella. I flopped. I couldn't get a fight at either of the clubs where I fought, now.

"No!" he raised his hand as I started to speak, "no use to argue. I don't want to talk – to you or anybody. I'm through with the game and I want to go to bed."

"Alright," I answered, "Suit yourself. I never was one to coax. But here's my card and if you ever change your mind, look me up. You might do worse for a manager."

The weeks stretched into months; I was busy with my affairs and the memory of Mike Brennon faded. But he was not a man one could forget, having ever seen him. When I dreamed, as all fight fans and fighters' managers dream, of a superfighter, the form of Mike Brennon rose unbidden – a dark, brooding figure, charged with the abysmal fighting fury of the primitive.

And then one day Mike Brennon came to me – not in a daydream but in the flesh. For some reason I could scarcely believe my eyes as I saw him standing before me, in the office of my training camp, his crumpled hat in his hand, an eager grin on his dark face. Something had changed him; he was very different from the morose and moody youth to whom I had talked in the dressing room of the coast fight club.

"Mr. Amber," said he, "if you still want me, I'd like to have you manage me."

"That's fine," I answered, and before I could continue, he broke in:

"Can you get me a fight, right away? I need the money bad."

"Not so fast," I answered, "I can advance you some money if you've got some debts – "

"No," he made a quick gesture, "Its something else – can you get me a fight within a few days?"

"Are you in trim?" I asked, "How long since you've been in the ring?"

"Not since you saw me last. But I always stay in shape."

"I'll see."

I took Brennon to my open-air ring where Spike Ganlon, a clever middleweight, was working out and instructed them to step four fast rounds. Brennon seemed eager to get to business and I was astonished to see him put up a very fair sort of boxing against the shifty Ganlon. True, he was far outstepped and out-boxed, but that was to be expected, Ganlon being a rather prominent figure in the fistic world and Brennon an unknown slugger. Still I did not like the way Mike sent in his punches; he was fairly accurate but his punches lacked the trip-hammer force which had attracted me to him before.

However, when I had him slug the heavy bag he nearly tore it loose from its moorings, and I decided that he had been pulling his punches against

Ganlon. I taught him all the tricks of the trade as I have learned them in my years of experience, and Ganlon, who took a great liking to Mike, added his practical tutelage in the days that followed. But the result was far from satisfying. Brennon was more intelligent than the general run of fighters, but he could not seem to apply what we had taught him. He understood the principle and the theory but it was hard for him to practice the actuality.

Still, I did not expect too much of him at first; I worked with him patiently for a few weeks, and when I sent him against his first opponent in the semi-windup of a fight in the Hopi A.C., San Diego, I felt that I had a man whose terrific hitting, coupled with a fair boxing defense, would carry him to victory.

The opponent I had selected for him was not particularly formidable – one Joe Nogales, a clever but punchless Mexican heavyweight, whose windmill style of milling had prompted sportswriters to dub him an overgrown Harry Greb. I wanted to build self-confidence in my man, also to test his actual ability in the ring before I sent him against a dangerous puncher. You cannot always make a classy fighting man out of a wide-open slugger, especially in the short time I had had Brennon under my wing, and I found – but of that later.

As I climbed through the ropes that night, I repeated my instructions to Mike to feel his foe out and remain on the defensive the first round. I did this to find out how much he remembered of what Ganlon and I had taught him.

The gong sounded and following my instructions, Brennon came out cautiously feinting in a rather awkward manner. Nogales danced around him, jabbed several times, while Brennon shuffled about, apparently growing more clumsy and uncertain every second. I swore amazedly. Mike was certainly no ring leopard now – or rather he looked like a leopard hindered by chains on all his legs.

Nogales continued his dancing tactics, finally decided his foe had nothing, and swarmed all over Brennon. Mike seemed to do everything wrong. He blocked in an ineffective and slouchy manner, his footwork was bad, he missed often, and when he landed there was no kick to his blows. The gong found him pinned in a neutral corner, jabbing vainly at the bobbing, weaving Nogales, while the crowd booed.

"My gosh," marveled Ganlon, who was acting as Mike's handler, "you do everything backwards! What's the matter, kid, you box three times as good in the trainin' camp!"

"You want me to box him this round?" asked Mike.

"Go after him any way you want to," I answered, "You're doing no good this way. I made a mistake, sending you back in the ring before you were seasoned."

The gong sounded. Nogales had decided the man he faced was harmless and he came bouncing out into the center of the ring inclined to make a farce out of the fight. He spread his arms wide, made fantastic gestures and grotesque faces – it was at that moment that the thunderbolt struck him.

At the tap of the gong Brennon had gathered himself like a tiger about to leap upon his prey. The air of repression fell away from him, and as Nogales came dancing toward him, he shot out of his corner as though propelled by a giant steel spring.

Wham! Nogales was entirely off his guard – wide open, and occupied with his comedian tricks. A blind man could have hit him. Brennon's left, starting at the floor, crashed like the crack of doom against the Mexican's chin, and Nogales, lifted clean off his feet, shot back across the ring, rebounded from the ropes and lay sprawled, face down, blasted into senselessness by that terrible swing. The crowd went crazy.

On the way back to our training quarters, I said: "When I'm wrong I'm the first to admit it. I was trying to make a boxer out of you. But you're a natural slugger, though you've never showed any of the natural slugger's aptitude. You hit the widest, wildest swings of any man I ever saw. Looks like you'd have learned something from your actual experience in the ring. Look at Nogales – if it hadn't been for pure luck, likely he'd have outpointed you. But he got to acting the fool. A stevedore could have hit him."

"But not that hard," said Ganlon jubilantly, "oh baby, what a clout!"

"Sure it was hard; but it must have traveled a couple of miles before it landed. And it would never have landed if Nogales had been minding his business. Mike, I'm going to make a slugger out of you – I mean a real slugger, like Dempsey, Sullivan, and McGovern. A scientific slugger. You've got all their instincts; I understand how you feel. You can box in a fair manner in the training camps but when you get into the ring, where its matter of life and death so to speak, you forget everything but your natural style of fighting. Dempsey was a good boxer when he was sparring with his sparring partners, but he never boxed in the ring. He swung too, until De Forest taught him to hit straight. Still, I'll tell you frankly that at his crudest Dempsey showed more aptitude for the game than you do – now, this sounds brutal but I'm saying it for your own good. Dempsey, and Ketchell and McGovern too, for that matter, used instinctive footwork and kept stepping around their men. They ducked and weaved and hit short punches. You never go any way but straight forward – judging from the three fights I've seen. You're as fast as Dempsey was when he was coming up, but you don't seem to know how to use your speed.

"I'm saying all this so you'll realize how important it is for you to master your trade as we teach you. I'm going to make you a second Dempsey."

And for a time it seemed as if my dreams were coming true. In spite of Mike's urging that I get him another fight immediately, I kept him idle for four months. By idle, I mean he was not fighting in the ring. Otherwise he was busy enough. I had him practice hooking the heavy bag with short smashes to straighten his punches and eliminate so much of his wide and useless swinging. He would never learn to put any force behind a straight punch, I saw, but I intended making him a wicked hooker, like Dempsey. It was slow, hard work.

"Mike," said Ganlon one day, "is a queer nut. He's got a fighter's heart, and a fighter's body but he just ain't got a fighter's brain. It don't work right. He understands, but he can't practice what he understands. The simplest trick, he has to work on for hours every day-and then he's liable to forget it. If he was a bonehead, I'd understand it. But he ain't; he's got more brains in other ways than any man I ever saw."

"Maybe it's because he fought so long in second-rate clubs, with his wild style that he formed habits he can't break," I suggested.

"That's partly it; but it goes deeper. I tell ya, Mike Brennon's the hardest hitter, and the toughest fighter I ever saw, but they's a kink in his brain and he ain't cut out for this game."

"What do you mean, a kink?" I asked uneasily.

"I dunno. But its somethin' that breaks down his co-ordination and keeps his mind from workin' with his muscle. When he tries to box clever, he has to stop and think and in the ring you ain't got time – you got to act mechanical. You see a left comin' at you and between the time it starts and the time its to land ain't a split fraction of a second. But in that time you think: here's a jab I can beat with mine, I can't block 'cause that'd leave me open for his right, I'm too close to snap back – I'll slip it, and as it goes over my shoulder I'll sink my right to his ribs. You got to think that in a flash, 'course you don't really study it all out, but you KNOW it, see? That is, if you're a fast boxer; if you're just a wide open Slugger like Mike you don't think nothin'. You just take the jab in the map as a matter uh course, spit out a mouthful uh teeth and keep borin' in."

"But any slugger is that way," I objected.

Ganlon shook his head. "I know. But I tell yuh Mike is different. He ain't cut out for a boxer. If he don't learn a defense, he'll get punched cuckoo in sight of a few years. All the great sluggers had some kind of a defense. Some crouched and weaved like Dempsey and Ketchell and McGovern; some wrapped their arms around their skulls and barged in like Nelson and Paolino. Them that fought wide open didn't last no time especially among the heavies. And when they're through, they're through! The padded cell and the paper-doll cut-outs for the most of 'em. It don't stand to reason a human skull can stand up under the beatin's it gets that way."

"You're a born croacker," I said, slightly worried, "Mike's not a slow-brained gorilla with a ten-inch skull wall. He's rugged but intelligent. He'll learn." "At anything else, yes," was Ganlon's parting shot. "At this game – maybe."

CHAPTER 2

"Bat Nelson True to Life! – "

"Listen, Steve," said Brennon, bearding me in my den so to speak, "I've got to have a fight! You promised to keep me busy and I'm holding you to your contract. I need the money."

"Mike," said I, "It's none of my business, but I don't see where your money goes. Of course, you didn't make such a lot out of that Nogales fight, but it should have been enough to tide you over awhile, for you're at no expense at all here in the camp. You haven't bought any clothes since I began managing you – fact is, you ought to, if I may say so. You look rather seedy. Then, you don't make any whoopee. You're never seen with a girl; you don't drink – you don't gamble – "

"Have I ever tried to borrow money?" he broke in, white about the lips, "have I ever grouched about being broke? Then what business is it of yours – "

"None at all," I hastened to assure him, "you're a model lad as far as training and abstinence go, and I've no kick about anything. Don't get sore; I beg your pardon and I won't intrude on your private affairs again."

The glare faded from his cold eyes.

"I apologize too, Steve," he said abruptly, "I should have known you weren't trying to pry into my business. But I do want another fight, as soon as you can arrange it."

"Alright," I gave in, "Understand, I don't believe you're ready to go in with a first-string man. But since money is the object – Monk Barota is on the coast now, padding his k.o. record. He'll be looking for set-ups and I believe I can match you up with him for a ten rounder at the Hopi A.C. where you fought Nogales. It's your best chance. If you can even hold him even, you'll get plenty of offers. But I expect you to more than hold him even. I expect you to whip him, Mike."

"I do too," grinned Brennon.

I hoped that he was more sincere in his belief than I was. I really felt in my heart that he was not ready for a first-rater, and I had intended building him up more gradually. But there was a fierce, driving intensity about him when he spoke of the money he needed and the matches he wanted, which broke down my resolve. Brennon was, in some ways, a character of terrific magnetic force. Like Sullivan, he dominated all about him, trainers, handlers, and managers. Had he been inclined to shirk his training he would have been ungovernable, for no one could force him into doing anything he did not wish to do. But only in the matter of money-making matches was he unreasonable, and this quirk in his nature amounted to an obsession.

The match maker at the Hopi A.C. greeted my proposal with delight, remembering my man's sensational k.o. of Joe Nogales.

"Sure, I'll get in negotiations with Barota's manager right away. The fans remember Brennon. He stole the show that night from the main event. Several times I've had people ask me why I didn't match him with somebody else. The boys like a puncher. Where have you been keeping him all this time?"

There is little use in stretching the tale out. Barota and Brennon were matched for a ten rounder, and at ringside Barota was a two to one favorite with few takers, even among those fans who had seen Brennon flatten Nogales. The tale of Mike's punching powers had gotten about and the people packed the arena, expecting to see a short but terrific battle, with the unknown slugger succumbing to the superior skill of the Eastern favorite.

My last instructions to Mike were: "Remember! This lad can hit! Don't tear into him wide open. Remember the crouch and weave Ganlon taught you. If you don't use some defense, he'll ruin you!"

The lights went out except those over the ring. The gong sounded. The crowd fell silent – that breathless, momentary silence that marks the beginning of the fight.

The men slid out of their corners and –

"Oh, Hades!" wailed Ganlon at my side, "He's doin' things backwards again!"

Mike wore the uncertain manner which had marked him during the first round of his last fight. He crouched too far over and held his hands awkwardly. Barota led a fast left and Brennon swayed the wrong way and took it squarely in the eye. Again Barota led and again he landed. And again. That flicking left was hard for any man to avoid but Mike was always ducking into it.

Ganlon was cursing at my side. "After all these months of work, he forgets! Just a plain bonehead when it comes to boxin'. You better throw in the sponge now! Look there!"

Barota had attacked, suddenly and fiercely, straightening Brennon with a hard right uppercut and battering his head with a venomous left hook that had Mike's head bobbing on his shoulders.

Mike, stung, tried a left hook of his own. Its force was apparent but Barota ducked it with ease.

"At least," Ganlon said, "we drilled that into him so he remembers to hook instead of swing. But little good it'll do him; he can't even hook without lettin' the whole house know what he's goin' to do. Same as writin' the other bird a letter tellin' him about it."

Barota was taking his time. In spite of the fact that his foe seemed to have nothing but a scowl, no man could look into Mike Brennon's face and take him lightly at the first glance. But a round of clumsy floundering for footwork and ineffectual punching lulled the fear Barota might have entertained and he abandoned his dancing, jabbing tactics.

Ganlon was nearly weeping with rage beside me, as if his pupil's inaptness somehow reflected on him.

"All I know, I taught him, and there's that wop makin' a monkey outa him. Go on, you ham! Let him knock you out and lets get this over with!"

At this moment, with the round about thirty seconds to go, Barota tore in with one of his famous attacks. Mike abandoned all attempts at science and began swinging wildly and fiercely – and futilely. Barota worked between his flailing arms and the Italian's hands, shooting in and out like pistons, beat an incessant barrage against Mike's body and head. The gong stopped the punishment and Barota ran lightly to his corner, raising one glove as an indication that he would finish his man in one more round.

Mike's face was somewhat cut but he was fresh and showed no signs of having just gone through a severe beating.

He broke in on Ganlon's impassioned soliloquy to remark: "This fellow can't hit."

"Can't hit!" Ganlon nearly dropped the sponge, "Why, that boy's got a k.o. record as long as a subway! Ain't he just pounded you all over the ring?"

"I didn't feel his punches, anyway," answered Mike and at that moment the gong sounded.

Barota came out fast; he was in a mood to bring this fight to a sudden termination. He was proud of his skill, preferred to show his wares against a worthy foeman and was rather irritated that he had been pitted against this clumsy aimless slugger.

But Mike was not clumsy, nor was he slow. He only seemed so from his wild and erratic way of battling. Still, he seemed like a sacrifice for the sneering Italian who jabbed his head back cruelly, bringing a flow of blood from his cut lips. Barota launched a sudden attack and began hammering at Mike's body with the left-handed assault which had softened so many of his opponents for a k.o. The crowd went wild as he avoided Mike's returns, but suddenly I felt Ganlon's fingers sink into my arm.

"Bat Nelson true to life!" he whispered, his voice vibrating with excitement, "Look! The crowds thinks, and Barota thinks that them left hooks is hurtin' Mike! But he ain't weakenin'; he ain't even feeling' 'em! That boy's solid iron. Watch now! Mike's got one chance – when Barota shoots the right – !"

At this moment Barota evidently decided that Brennon was "softened" for the kill. He stepped back, feinted swiftly, and then shot his right. Barota was proud of the bone-crushing quality of that right; prouder of it than of all his skill. A clear opening he had and every ounce of his weight went into it. The leather guarded knuckles backed by the spar-like arm and heavy shoulder crashed flush against Mike's jaw. The blow was plainly heard in every part of the house. A gasp went up and nails sank deep into clenching palms. Mike swayed drunkenly but he did not fall. And he returned to the attack on the rebound.

Barota had stopped short for a flashing second. The realization that he had struck his man flush with everything he had, and had even failed to knock him off his feet, stunned him – froze him for a split second. And in that instant Mike swung a wild left and landed for the first time. It was a glancing blow, high on the cheekbone but even so, Barota went down. The crowd rose, screaming.

Dazed, the Italian rose without a count and Mike tore into him with the ferocity of a tiger that scents the kill. Barota, blinded and dizzy from that sudden and fearful blow, was in no condition to defend himself, yet Mike in his eagerness missed with both hands, until a mine-sweeping right-hander caught the Italian flush on the temple and he dropped – not merely out but senseless.

The crowd was screaming, but Ganlon said to me: "He's an iron man, don't yuh see? A natural born freak like Grim and Nelson. He'll never learn anything, not if he trains a hundred years."

CHAPTER 3

"Its Your Brain – A Cog Missin' – "

It was the day after Mike Brennon startled the sports world by his knockout of Monk Barota. Mike, Ganlon, and I sat at the breakfast table, and despite the fact of victory, we were a far from merry gang.

200

"Listen," Ganlon read a morning paper: "The foremost fistic upset of the year occurred last night in San Diego, at the Hopi A.C. when an unknown named Mike Brennon stopped Monk Barota in the second round. This is Barota's first defeat and he wept like a child in his dressing room after he came to, at the thought of losing to a novice. This Brennon, it seems, has been pushing over second-raters on the coast for some time. He is under the management of Steve Amber, known to the sport world as having guided the destinies of two champions. It would seem he has a third title-holder in the making."

Ganlon flung the paper down. "Here's what a local scribe wrote: 'Fans at the Hopi A.C. last night were treated to the surprise of their lives when a local boy, Mike Brennon, stopped the highly touted Monk Barota in two rounds. This boy Brennon looks like the real class. He took Barota's best offerings without wincing and in uncorking his own punch showed a power that Dempsey need not be ashamed of. Fans who saw Brennon flatten Joe Nogales a few months ago will remember the circumstances of that knockout, and will note a startling simularity in the two fights. In each case Brennon shambled and shuffled through the first round, making himself look like the veriest palooka. Then in the next, having lulled his opponent into a feeling of security, he suddenly uncorked the k.o.

" 'That shows class. C-l-a-s-s, with a capital C! Any fighter who can outthink Monk Barota is going some. Old timers are comparing Brennon to Bob Fitzsimmons, who used the same tricks. This boy is the next champion or I miss my guess.' "

"Carried away by his enthusiasm," snorted Ganlon, "Here's a sportswriter who come from Los Angeles to see the fight. This boy's got an eye for the game. Listen: 'San Diego fans are very much worked up over a new wonder which has apparently risen in their midst. I of course refer to Mike Brennon, who put the skids under Monk Barota in the second heat of a scheduled ten frame go at the Hopi A.C. last night.

" 'This was indeed a jolt to the sporting fraternity and I make so bold as to say that it had all the signs of a fluke to me. If I am not mistaken, Brennon is the dub who lost a ten rounder to Sailor Slade last year, in which he got a terrific beating and looked like a deckhand. Slade was not as good then as he is now, and he lost his last fight on points to that same Barota who fell before Brennon's haymakers. They say, Brennon was shamming in the first round. If so, he ought to be on the stage for I never saw a more realistic imitation of a terrible dub. In the second Barota made the mistake of thinking he could drop Brennon with one smash. His failure threw him off his guard. That is a mistake many a man has made. When Brennon failed to go down from that terrific slam, Barota stopped to think what might be holding him up. It is my opinion that the clout which put Barota down for the first time was landed by mere chance – one of those lucky blows which have had such a large part in the annals of the sport. It is significant to note that after Barota rose, stunned, Brennon missed a couple of haymakers before he finally landed.

" 'I do not seek to detract from Brennon's victory. He showed plenty of courage and a ruggedness I never saw excelled. But it is my honest opinion that he is simply a tough, strong second-rater who beat a better man by chance.' "

"A trifle caustic," said Ganlon, "but he just repeats what I been sayin'. As a fighter, Mike, I take pain to say it, but you're a false alarm. It ain't your fault. If it was I wouldn't be urgin' you to step outa the ring. It's your brain; a cog missin' somewhere. Somethin' left out. You got the body and the heart but you ain't got no more natural talent than a ribbon clerk and you can't learn. You got the fighting instinct, but not the fighter's instinct – and they's a flock uh difference!

"You're just a heavyweight Joe Grim. An iron man. Never was a iron man except Jeffries who could learn anything. Every man's got his faults. And each man's got a fault he can't overcome if he fights a hundred years. Look at Johnny Dundee; as brainy, classy a fighter as ever lived but he never learned to hit. Look at Firpo; a natural puncher with a kick like a government mule, but he never could learn to box or use his left. Look at Maher; a game, fast man with a terrible swat, but he had a weak chin. Look at Grim; as tough a man as ever lived but he never learned nothing.

"No, Mike, you're a iron man and as such I'm advisin' you to quit the ring. Your kind don't come to no good end. Specially in the heavies. Its the padded cell and the paper dolls for 'em. Too many punches about the head. They get permanently punch drunk. You don't have to go around countin' your fingers. You got brains enough to succeed somewhere else.

"You got three courses to follow: first, you can go around fightin' set-ups at the small clubs. You can make a livin' that way, and last a long time, 'cause you can beat anybody you can hit. Or, second, you can take advantage of knockin' out Barota and sign up with some of the offers you're bound to get. As a iron man fightin' clever first-raters, you won't win many fights, if any, but you'll be an attraction just like Joe Grim was, and you'll pull down some real money. But you won't last no time. You'll crack under the incessant fire of smashes and wind up in the booby hatch. Last, and best, you can take the money you've got and step out. If you need any more to start in business, why, me and Steve will gladly lend it to you, eh Steve?"

I nodded. Mike shook his head and spread his iron fingers out on the table in front of him. As usual he dominated the scene – a great somber figure of unknown potentialities.

"You're right, Spike, in everything you've said. I could have told you some of that before. I've always known that there was a deficiency somewhere in my mentality – a lack of co-ordination or something. No man could be as impervious to punishment as I am and have a perfectly normal brain. Its not alone in boxing; I've failed at other jobs; I grasped the ideas but it was hard for me to put the theories into effect. Bad co-ordination somewhere.

"As for boxing, the crowd dazes me for one thing. I can't think straight. When I try to remember instructions I get rattled and forget everything. And when I start slugging naturally, as you say, I have none of the true slugger's instinct for the game.

"Nature gave me an unusual constitution and physique but at the cost of my reflexes. Mind and muscle won't act together and all the drilling in the world won't teach me. But – ! I CAN TAKE IT! That's my only hope! That's why I'm not quitting the game. You admit that iron men are drawing cards. I'm an iron man. I've been cut to pieces in the ring but the only man who ever hurt me or knocked me down was Sailor Slade last year in Los Angeles – and he couldn't stop me.

"I've never been knocked out, and I don't believe there's a man in the world who can flatten me for the count. I don't feel the blows. I'm like Battling Nelson – not human when it comes to taking punishment. Eventually, after years of battering, someone will knock me out. When that happens I'll quit the game but before that time, I'll accumulate a fortune, if I'm handled right. I'm going to cash in on my ruggedness! Capitalize on the fact that no man can keep me down for the count!"

"Great heavens, man!" I exclaimed, "do you realize what that means? The frightful punishment, the batterings, the mutilations? You won't be fighting dubs now, you'll be fighting men as fast and strong as you, men who carry terrific punches and who are so clever you won't be able to touch them. They'll hammer you to a red pulp! You have no defense, and you can't learn!"

"My defense is a granite jaw and iron ribs," he answered, "I'll take on everybody who will meet me, and wear them down."

"Maybe you will and maybe not," I said. "A man can wear himself down punching a granite boulder, as I've seen men do with Tom Sharkey and Joe Goddard, but what about the boulder! You've been lucky. Nogales was careless and Barota was astonished and forgot himself. The next man you meet will be watching his step. If he's a boxer, he'll outstep and outpoint you. If he's a slugger, he'll still outstep you and pound you to pieces."

"They can't hurt me. I can beat any man I hit. Win or lose, I'll be a drawing card and that will mean large purses. That's what I'm after. Do you think I'd go through this purgatory for glory, or if the need wasn't great?"

"If it's poverty – " I began.

"What do you know of poverty?" he cried out in a strange passion, "Were you left in a basket on the steps of Saint Joseph's boys' home? Did you spend your childhood mixed in with five hundred others, where the need of all was so great that no one of you got more than the barest necessities of life? Did you pass your early boyhood as a tramp and a hobo worker, riding the rods and starving? Or your early youth as dishwasher, factory hand, and preliminary boy? I did!

"Poverty! I've felt its sting in the soul of me, and its pinch in the brain of me. But that's neither here nor there; nor it isn't my own personal poverty so much that drove me back in the ring – but let it pass. I'm fighting until somebody knocks me out. That will finish me as a drawing card.

"Now then, as my manager, I want you to get busy. Match me with a fellow I can hit. I've been lucky in these last two starts. If I can win another fight it will increase my prestige and draw the fans – with their money. I don't expect to win many. Later I'll pack them in just as Joe Grim did – to see if I can be knocked out. Until the fans find out that I'm an iron man, I'll have to go on my merits. Barota wants a return match. I don't want him now, or any other clever man who'll outpoint me and make me look like a worse dub than I am, even. Get me a man-killer – a puncher who'll come in and try to murder me. Get me Jack Maloney! I want the fans to see me stand up under the blows of a hitter – I want them to see me bloody and staggering, and still carrying on! That's what draws the crowd and the money!"

"It's suicide!" I cried horrified, "Maloney's a slugger but at that I doubt if you can hit him. And he'll kill you! I won't have anything to do with it!"

"Then, by heaven!" Brennon roared, heaving erect and crashing his fist down shatteringly on the table, "I'll get me another manager! I'm in this for the money and if you fail me, our ways part here! But I'd rather have you piloting me than anyone else. You know the ballyhoo. You could help me if you were willing."

"If you're determined," I said huskily, my mind almost numbed by the driving force of his will power, "I'll do all I can. But I warn you, you'll leave this game with a clouded brain."

He gripped my hand with a nervous grasp which nearly crushed my fingers and said shortly, "I knew you'd stand by me. Never mind my brain; its cased in solid iron."

As he strode out, Ganlon, slightly pale, turned to me and said in a low voice: "A twist in his head, sure. Money-money! I never saw an Irishman before who was so crazy about money. This mornin' I says to him, I says: 'Mike, you better get you some new shoes with some of the money you got last night.' He says, 'I can wear these I got for a month yet.' Lord knows I'm no dude but he dresses like a wharfhand. What's he do with his money? He ain't supportin' no aged mother, its a cinch. You heard him say he was left on a doorstep when he was a baby."

I shook my head. Brennon was an enigma beyond my comprehension.

CHAPTER 4

The Rise of the Iron Tiger

The rise of Iron Mike Brennon is now ring history, and of all the vivid pages in the annals of this heart-stirring game, I hold that the story of this greatest of all iron men makes the most lurid, fantastic, and pulse-quickening chapter of all.

Iron Mike Brennon! Look at him, as he was in the year of 19 – when his exploits swept the country. Six foot one from his long, narrow feet to the black tousled shock of his hair; one hundred and ninety pounds of steel springs, whale bone, and iron muscle. With his terrible eyes glaring from under the heavy black brows, his thin, blood-smeared lips writhing in a snarl of battle fury – still in my memory, when I dream of the superfighter, there rises the picture of Mike Brennon – a dream charged with bitterness. Mike Brennon, with his wonderful body and his terrible punch – and the instincts and style of a docks brawler.

Take a man with an incredible stamina; give him a punch that will fell an ox; take from him the ability to even remember one iota of science when in actual combat, and leave out of his makeup the instinct of the natural fighter and you have Iron Mike Brennon. A man who would have been the greatest champion of all time, could he have learned a tenth of what I tried to teach him.

His first fight, after that memorable conversation at the breakfast table, was with Jack Maloney, at San Francisco. Jack Maloney – one hundred and ninety-five pounds of white hot fighting fury, with a right hand that was like a caulking mallet.

I had offers from various promoters, all anxious for the service of the man who had flattened the Italian wonder, Barota – from Chicago came an offer to meet Sailor Slade; from New York, a bid for Johnny Varella. But Mike wanted Maloney.

I set the old ballyhoo to working, with the aid of Spike Ganlon and the various sportswriters who knew me as a friend. The papers were full of the deeds of Mike Brennon. They pointed out that he had over twenty knockouts to his credit, ignoring the fact that these victims were all unknown dubs with the exception of the last two. They glossed over the fact that he had been several times outpointed by second-raters, and twice beaten to a pulp – once by Sailor Slade and once by Johnny Varella. They stressed the fact that Brennon had taken everything Barota could hand out, and angrily refuted the repeated charges made by the old-timers, that the k.o. was a fluke.

The stadium was packed when Mike Brennon met Jack Maloney. The crowd paid their money and they got the worth of it. In his corner before the bell, I was whispering a few instructions which I knew would be useless, when Mike cut in with a sort of fierce eagerness:

"What a sell out! What a purse! Look at that crowd! And if I can win tonight it'll mean more sell-outs! Heavier purses! Oh, God, I've got to win!"

His eyes gleamed with a ferocious avidity – the gong sounded – two giants crashed from their corner.

Maloney came in like the great slugger he was, body crouched to protect his solar plexus, chin tucked beneath his shoulder, hands high. Brennon, forgetting everything before the blast of the crowd and his own fighting fury, rushed like a longshoreman, head lifted, both hands clinched at his hips, straight up and wide open – as iron men have fought since time immemorial – with only one thought, that to get to the foe and crush him.

Maloney landed first, a terrific left hook to the body which brought the crowd to its feet roaring; a short right cut Brennon's lips and spattered him with blood and I heard a note of relief in the shouts of Maloney's manager. This bird was not going to be so hard after all! As for Maloney, like most sluggers when they find a man they can hit easily, he had gone fighting crazy. Left, right, left, right he battered Brennon about the ring without a return while the crowd went roaring wild. He was hitting so hard and fast that Brennon had no time to get set; the few swings he did try, swished harmlessly over the bobbing Maloney's head.

"He's slowin' down," muttered Ganlon to me, as the first round drew to a close, "The old iron man game! Maloney's punchin' hisself out!"

True, Jack's blows were coming, not weaker, but more slowly. No man could keep up the pace he was setting. Brennon seemed strong as ever and just before the gong he staggered Maloney with a sweeping left to the body – the first blow he had landed.

Back in his corner, Ganlon wiped the blood from Mike's battered face and grinned savagely.

"Joe Goddard had nothin' on you. I'm beginnin' to believe you'll actually beat him. You've took terrible punishment but you're fresher than he is. He'll come out strong for this round but each round he'll get weaker and give out quicker."

"I'll beat him," Mike answered grimly, "I can beat any man I can hit; and I can hit him occasionally."

The crowd thundered his acclaim as Jack Maloney rushed out for the second round. But he had sensed something they had not. He had hit this man with everything he had, and had failed to even floor him. Something wrong here! So he tore in like a wild man and again drove Brennon about the ring before a torrent of left and right hooks that sounded like the kicks of a mule and doubtless felt worse. Brennon was badly battered now, his eyes were almost closed, his lips pulped, his nose broken but he showed absolutely no sign of distress, until the latter part of the round when Maloney landed four times to the jaw with his maul-like right. Then Brennon's knees trembled momentarily, but he straightened and opened a cut on his foe's cheekbone with a glancing right.

Now at the gong, the crowd began to sense something. They had been shouting the praises of Maloney, and jeering Brennon for a push-over, but now they realized that Maloney had hit his man again and again with all his power, and yet Brennon's shoulders had not yet touched the canvas. The timbre of their shouts changed slightly. Fans began to inquire at the top of their voices if Maloney was losing his famed punch, or if Brennon was made of solid iron.

Ganlon, wiping Brennon's gory features and giving him the smelling salts to sniff, said swiftly: "His legs trembled as he went back to his corner; he looked back over his shoulder at you like he couldn't believe it, when he saw you walk to your corner straight up without a quiver. He knows he ain't lost his smack! He knows you're the first man that's ever stood up to him, wide open thata way. He knows you been through hell and high water, the last two rounds, and still you ain't even saggin'. You got him buffaloed. Now get him!"

"I'll get him!" muttered Mike almost deliriously, "More fights – more money – "

The gong sounded and Jack Maloney came in like a whirlwind to redeem his slipping fame as a knocker-out. His blows were like a rain of sledge-hammers – left-right-left-right! And before the mallet-like right which crashed again and again against his body and head, Mike Brennon reeled and went down.

The referee began counting. Maloney reeled back against the ropes, his breath coming in great gasps, his legs trembling – completely fought out, finely trained athlete though he was.

"He'll get up," said Ganlon calmly.

Brennon was half crouching on his knees, supporting himself with one arm. He shook his head, looked up at the referee. He was dazed, not hurt. I saw his lips move, and though I could not hear what he said of course, I read their motion – "More fights – more money – "

At "Nine!" he bounded erect. Maloney's whole body sagged; he seemed on the point of collapse. The fact that Brennon was able to arise before the count after the beating he had taken took more morale out of Maloney than any sort of a blow would have done. He lurched forward half-heartedly and Brennon, sensing his mental condition and physical weariness, tore in like a tiger. Left, right he missed, shaking off Maloney's weakening blows as if they had been slaps from a girl. At last he landed – a wide left hook to the head. Maloney tottered, a wild overhand right crashed under his cheekbone, and he went to his knees. At "Nine" he staggered up, but another right, a sweeping haymaker that a blind man in good condition could have ducked, dropped him again. The referee hesitated, then beckoning to Maloney's seconds, lifted Mike Brennon's right hand in token of victory.

As Maloney, aided by his handlers, reeled to his corner on buckling legs, I noted the ironical fact; the winner was a battered and gory wreck as to outward appearance, while the loser had only a single cut on his cheekbone. I thought of the old fights in which the iron men of another day had figured; how Joe Goddard, the old Barrier champion, had outfought the great Joe Choynski, and had finished each of their terrible battles a bloody travesty of a man – but winner. I thought of Tom Sharkey dropping Kid McCoy after a cruel battering – and battling Nelson outlasting Gans – Young Corbett – Herrera. And I sighed. What a champion Mike Brennon would make if he had any defense at all. But he, like all these other great iron men, would eventually crack under the strain and fall, possibly before some second-rater. For of all the men who ever relied on their ruggedness to carry them through, Brennon was the wildest, the most wide open, the most erratic hitter.

As I sponged his cuts in the dressing room, I could not forbear to say: "You see how it is to meet a first-string hitter – you wont be able to answer the gong for a month."

"A month!" he mumbled through battered lips, "you'll sign me up with Johnny Varella for a bout in New York next week!"

Thus was born, figuratively speaking, Iron Mike Brennon. After his fight with Maloney, fans and scribes realized what he was – a fighter with a granite jaw – and as such his fame grew. He became a drawing card just as he had said – one of the greatest of his day. And his inordinate lust for money seemed to grow with his power as an attraction. He haggled over prices with promoters, held out for every cent he could get, but rather than pass a fight up, would always lower his price if he had to. His price, I say, because as a manager I was only a figurehead, for the first and only time in my life. Mike Brennon was the real power behind the curtain.

And he insisted on fighting at least once a month. In vain I argued with him – told him that he should take time to recover fully from one beating before going into another.

"This way," I said, "You'll crack three times as quick. Otherwise you might last for years."

"But why stretch it out?" he asked, "I'm in this game to make all the money I can, as quick as I can. If I can make the money in a few months, fighting every week, that I'd make in that many years, fighting every few months, what's the odds?"

"But consider the strain on you!" I cried.

"I'm not considering anything about myself," he answered roughly. "Get me a match."

The matches came readily. He fought them all – ferocious, rushing sluggers, clever, dancing boxers, crafty, dangerous fighters who combined the qualities of the slugger and boxer. When first-rate opponents were not forthcoming soon enough, he went out into the outlying districts and knocked over second-raters in the small fight clubs. As long as he was fighting and making money, no matter how much or how little, he was satisfied and it mattered not to him whether his opponent were a near champion or a setup dub. What he did with the money thus acquired I did not know. He never made any attempt to swindle me or any of his training staff; he always shot square with his just obligations. But beyond that he was a miser. He stayed at the training camps or at the cheapest hotels in spite of my protests; he bought cheap clothes and allowed himself no luxuries whatever. I could not understand it, but I asked no questions.

At first, he won consistently. The luck of the iron men seemed to be with him, and his style of fighting was new to these modern boxers. His speed, his aggressiveness, his toughness, more than all the strange desperate intensity of his attack brought him many a victory. He was always dangerous because no matter how badly he was outpointed, he always carried TNT in those wild sweeping haymakers, which though easy to avoid, meant destruction if they landed. Many a man sampled this fact on the very crest of victory. Some of his foes, after testing their knuckles on his adamantine skull, retired into their shell and refused to fight. Some punched themselves out on him and went down to defeat.

Two weeks after he fought Maloney, Brennon met Johnny Varella in New York. Mike carried into the ring with him the signs of his battle with Maloney, and before the ferocious appearance he presented, Varella showed his nervousness. He had outpointed this man before but it was easy to see that he was not sure of himself.

Still, he put up a great battle, and made Brennon look bad for eight rounds. Then in the ninth, getting panicky because of his failure to hurt the iron man, the Italian went into a wild frenzy of slugging and broke both his rather brittle hands on Mike's skull. He refused to come up for the tenth, and the referee awarded the fight to Brennon on a technical knockout – yet Mike had scarcely laid a glove on the speedy Italian!

Managers were wary about throwing their men in with Mike. He could make any of them look punchless and he was likely to beat anybody – just as likely to be beaten by the veriest dub. But there was always a crowd out to see him perform and packed houses mean heavy purses. More, the clever boys considered it a cinch to outpoint Brennon and each of the heavy hitters had a secret desire to be the man that should finally drop the iron man for the long count, so we found it easy to get matches.

As I say, Brennon was dangerous to any man in the early part of his career. Coupled with his abnormal endurance was a mental state – a sort of driving savage determination which dragged him off the canvas time and again. This was above and behind his natural fighting fury, and he had somehow acquired it between the time he had first retired and the time I next met him.

Following the Varella fight, he met and knocked out a second-rater whose name I forget, in New York, the next week, then we traveled to Chicago where he met Young Hansen. The powerful Norwegian gave him a terrible hammering but finding himself unable to even floor Brennon, he blew up in the thirteenth round and went all to pieces, going out in the next round from a volley of swings he was too weary and muddled to duck.

The next start was in Los Angeles where Barota outpointed Mike in a return engagement. Barota, taking no chances, boxed cleverly and won the decision with a serpent-like left jab and an occasional very wary right cross; I doubt if Mike landed two solid blows the whole fifteen rounds, but his fame was impaired not at all. His drawing power now rested solidly on his ability to absorb punishment, and no mere decision rendered against him could detract from this fact. The average fan likes blood, action, and courage. They saw plenty in the fights in which Mike Brennon figured, and if he sometimes provoked his admirers by his senseless style and lack of skill, he made up for it by an unflinching gameness that kept him walking stolidly into terrific punishment. Then, there was always the chance that he might land one of his crushers and waft his opponent into dreamland.

At the time he was in his prime, there was a wealth of material in the heavyweight ranks. Not to be compared, perhaps, to the fighters of the Golden Era, that period when Jeffries ruled the greatest assortment of heavyweights the ring has ever seen at one time, Brennon's contemporaries were still good men. Fast, crafty boxers, hard hitters, tough sluggers – good game men all. And Brennon loomed among them as the one man none of them could knock out. That fact alone caused him to stand out and put him on an equal footing with men in every other way his superiors.

Following his second fight with Monk Barota, the public began to clamor for a match between my iron man and Yon Van Heeren, the Durable Dutchman, who up to that time had been considered the toughest heavyweight in the world, and who, like Brennon, had never been knocked out. Like Brennon, his only claim to fame was his durability, and this, as was proven in a most gorily ghastly manner, was inferior to that of Brennon. Matchmakers hesitated, the Commission went into doubtful session, but the public prevailed as it always does, and the match was made. The result aroused a wave of indignation among lovers of boxing science, and a renewal of activities among the foes of the game – the reformers. Even the hard-boiled fans who saw the slaughter were almost nauseated, but one thing is certain – none who saw that horrible affair will ever forget it.

Before they went into the ring, the principals made the referee promise that he would not stop the fight, no matter how badly either or both of them were punished. A rather unusual proceeding, but easily understandable considering that the fame of both rested on their ruggedness, and each considered it a soul-killing humiliation to be forced to quit while still able to stand.

A certain famous sportswriter, referring to this fight as "a brawl between two barroom thugs" said, "This unfortunate affair has set the game back for twenty years. No sensitive person, seeing this slaughter for his or her first fight, could ever be tempted to see another. A few more matches like this will turn public sentiment against the whole game, as people, who do not know the game, are likely to judge the whole boxing fraternity by the two gorillas, who utterly devoid of science, turned the ring into the shambles."

Very true. It was a strange experience to Mike Brennon; most of the punishment was on the other side. Van Heeren, a hulking, burly fellow, six feet two and two hundred and ten pounds in weight, was a terrific hitter but lacked Brennon's dynamic speed. He did not fight quite as wide open as did Mike, but his slowness counterbalanced this advantage. Oh, he hit Mike; hit him hard, time and again. A blind man could hit Mike Brennon. He floored Mike twice, and cut him up, but really hurt him far less than either Maloney or Hansen had done. The fans thought Mike was undergoing terrible punishment before those wide clumsy swings, but those blows lacked the sharp explosive kick of a real hitter. When they landed solidly, they knocked Mike down or hurled him across the ring by their pure force, but there was no great punishment in them for a man like Brennon.

As for Mike, for the only time in his life he had found a man he could hit at will and he sailed in to make a quick job of it. But Van Heeren too was an iron man, and not to be knocked without a hideous beating. And Mike delivered it. Those sweeping haymakers which had missed so many other men, crashed blindingly against the Dutchman's head, or sank agonizingly into his body. At the end of the first round, Van Heeren's face was a gory wreck. At the end of the second, his features had lost all human semblance, and his body was a battered mass of bruised and reddened flesh. Oh, Mike was taking punishment too – punishment that would have wrecked many men, but nothing like the beating Van Heeren was taking. They stood toe to toe, round after round, neither taking a back step, neither making any attempt at defense. They swung and they missed from pure clumsiness, or they landed and spattered each other's blood about the ring. It was evident from the first exchange that Brennon was the harder hitter and the tougher man. But it took time for even a puncher like him to wear the Dutchman down.

The third, fourth, fifth, sixth, and seventh rounds were nightmares in which Mike kissed the canvas twice and Van Heeren went down four times. The end of the eighth found Van Heeren on his knees with the referee counting over him, while Mike held on to the ropes, dizzy and nearly punched out for the only time in his life. All over the stadium, women were fainting or being helped out by their escorts. Fans were shrieking for the referee to stop the fight.

At the beginning of the ninth, Mike launched another desperate attack and dropped the Dutchman with a volley of left and right swings to the head. Van Heeren lurched up, a hideous and inhuman sight, and tried to fight back, but the sting had gone from his weakening punches. A blood- and sweat-soaked glove crashed against his jaw and he dropped face down on the red-stained canvas and lay motionless, four ribs broken and his features permanently ruined. He was still writhing blindly, drunkenly trying to rise when the referee tolled off the "Ten!" that marked his finish as a fighting man.

Mike Brennon stood above his victim, acknowledged king of all iron men. Aye – that fight finished Van Heeren and nearly finished boxing in that state, but it added to Brennon's fame, and his real pity for the broken Dutchman was mingled with a fierce exultation at the knowledge that no one now questioned his strange superiority of ruggedness. More packed houses – more money! To me his greed seemed the one flaw in his nature.

CHAPTER 5

The Trail of the Iron Man

Mike Brennon, the world's greatest iron man! They wrote that after his name, the sportswriters.

Men who fought him called him the toughest piece of human architecture that ever lived, and the fans for whose edification he allowed himself regularly to be butchered proved their appreciation by packing the stadiums in which he appeared.

In the three years he fought under my management, he met them all; all except the champion of his division. He lost about as many as he won, but the only thing that could impair his drawing power was a knockout – and this seemed postponed indefinitely. He won more of his fights against punchers than against light tappers. Sluggers hurt him more, but he preferred to fight them. They battered him to a red ruin but they could not stop him, and many a hard hitter, after bouncing the iron man repeatedly off the canvas, only to see him rise, and after hitting him with everything except the ring posts, lost heart and fell before his aimless but merciless attack. He broke the knuckles and he broke the hearts of the men who tried to stop him.

The light hitters who knew that they could not dent him took no chances and easily outboxed him. They jabbed him and cut him up but did not hurt him. Barota outpointed him, and Tommy Feltz, Jackie Finnegan, Undelo Boriotta, Frankie Grogan, Johnny Thomas, and Flash Sullivan, the clever light-heavy champion. But none of these men was able to put him on the canvas, even for an instant, and he was dangerous even to them, as Flash Sullivan found when one of Mike's wild swings dropped him for the count of nine in the last round of their bout.

With the hard hitters, he found the going rougher and he finished most of his bouts in a dazed condition, terribly battered – but still on his feet. Soldier Handler dropped him five times in four rounds, then got careless and stopped a right-hander that knocked him clean out of the ring and into fistic oblivion. Jose Gonzales, the great hitter from South America, punched himself out on the Iron Tiger and went down and out more from pure weariness than from Brennon's swings.

Gunboat Sloan battered his way to a red decision over him but was unable to stop him; and still believing that he could achieve the impossible, went in to trade punches with him, wide open, in a return engagement and lasted less than a round, thereby proving again Brennon's assertion that he could flatten any man he could hit.

He finished Ricardo Diaz, the Spanish Giant, in a couple of rounds, and pounded down Snake Culberson in eleven, after his ruggedness had broken the Brown Phantom's heart. He won on a foul from Ace Brannigan and lost on a foul to Tom Flynn, on a low blow accidentally delivered, when with both eyes closed tight he could not see his man and did not know where his swings were going. He won a decision from Jacques Descampo when the flashy foreigner, after sampling the power of Mike's right, made a foot race out of their ten-round fight and refused to lead all the way through.

He met Whitey Broad and Kid Allison in no-decision bouts, and he fought a terrible fifteen-round draw with Sailor Steve Costigan, a tough, game man who, though never rated better than a second-class man, yet gave some first-raters terrific battles. He was almost as tough as Brennon and knew only a little more about the game, but Brennon always said that Costigan was the hardest hitter he met in his entire ring life.

The wonder was that Mike could stand up as long as he did, fighting so often. To you readers who are not versed in the game, who do not believe that flesh and blood can endure what Mike Brennon endured, I beg of you to look at the records of the ring's iron men. When they cracked, they cracked suddenly, but until that time they fought often, and in each fight took punishment that would kill an ordinary man.

I point to your attention Tom Sharkey plunging round after round, head-long into the terrible pile drivers that were the fists of Jeffries; of that same Sharkey shooting over the ropes from the blows of Joe Choynski, head-first onto the concrete outside the ring – twice! – and yet finishing the fight a winner. I call your attention to Mike Boden, whose only blow was a roundhouse right, and who had no more defense than Brennon had, staying the limit with Choynski, taking without wincing every blow of that really wonderful puncher – the puncher who knocked out Jack Johnson and once put Bob Fitzsimmons on the canvas – yet Boden was on his feet at the last gong. And consider Joe Grim taking the punches of that master of all punchers, Bob Fitzsimmons – was it fourteen or fifteen times that Fitzsimmons knocked him down? But Grim was still fighting back when the round ended. No; no man can understand the iron men of the ring. Theirs is a long, hard, bloody trail with oftentimes nothing but poverty and a clouded mind at the end, but the red chapter their clan has written across the chronicles of the game will never be effaced.

And so Mike Brennon fought on, taking all his cruel punishment, hoarding his money, saying little – as much a mystery to me as ever. The sportswriters discovered his passion for money and raked him in their papers. They accused him of being miserly and refusing aid to his less-fortunate fellows – of refusing to aid the battered tramps who occasionally will strike up a successful fighter for a hand-out. This was partly true. Brennon did occasionally give money to men who needed it badly, but rarely.

Then Brennon began to crack. Ganlon, his continual companion, first sensed it. Crouching beside me behind Mike's corner, the night Brennon fought his no-decision bout with Kid Allison, Spike whispered to me out of the corner of his mouth.

"He's slippin', Steve! Look-he's slowin' down. And punches that once wouldn't have shook him, stop him in his tracks. Its the beginnin' of the end."

Brennon finished that fight in a blaze of glory, for the rough and rushing Kid grew winded toward the last, and the iron man floored him twice in the last two minutes of the bout.

That night Spike spoke plainly to his friend.

"Mike, you're about through. Its time to step down and out. You're slippin', no use to deny it. Its just barely perceptible now – but you're slower than you was and the punches jar you worse than they used to. You knew you couldn't last at this pace. I'm surprised you've lasted this long. I expected to see you punched cuckoo within a few months. You've lasted three years of terrible hard goin'. You've got plenty of money – or ought to have."

"I said I'd quit when I got knocked out," said Mike said stubbornly. "I haven't taken the count yet."

"But man," cried Ganlon, sharply, "when a man like you takes the count, its somethin' terrible! It means he's a punch-drunk wreck! When the blows begin to hurt you, it means the shock of them is reaching the brain and hurtin' it. Remember Van Heeren, the Dutchman you finished! He's wanderin' around, doin' road work, says he's trainin' to fight Fitzsimmons, that's been dead for years. Clean batty! And so'll you be, too, if you don't stop."

A shadow crossed Mike's dark face at the mention of the Dutchman's name. The batterings he had taken had disfigured him and given him a peculiarly sinister look, which however did not rob his face of that strange dominating quality.

"I'm good for a few more fights," he answered, "I need more money – "

"Money!" I exclaimed, "Always money! You must have half a million dollars, at least. You've saved every cent above expenses – at least I suppose you have. You never spend any. I'm beginning to believe what the sportswriters say – that you're a miser! Why risk your future for more money, when you have enough to set you up in business now?"

"Steve," said Ganlon suddenly, "I found out that cuckoo Van Heeren was around here yesterday."

"What of it?"

"Mike," said Ganlon almost accusingly, "give him a thousand dollars."

I gaped in astonishment.

"What if I did?" cried Brennon in one of his rare, inexplicable passions. "The fellow was broke – and he's in no condition to hold any kind of a job. I finished him in the ring – why shouldn't I help him a little? Whose business is it?"

"Nobody's," I answered, "But it only shows that you're not what I said – a miser. And it deepens the mystery about you. Won't you tell me why you feel that you must have more money?"

He made a quick impatient gesture.

"There's no need. There's no point to the question. You get the matches, I do the fighting, we split the money, and that's all there is to it."

"But Mike," I said as kindly as I could, "there is more to it. I like you. I feel your interest more at heart than just as a manager. You've made me more money than either of the champions I've managed, and if I didn't sincerely wish for your own good, I'd urge you to stay in the ring. Yes, you have a few fights left in you. You can take a few more beatings before you go under. You don't seem to have slipped much. But men like you crack quick and sudden, and the first signs of slipping are danger signals.

"You're on the border line. Quit now and you'll be alright. You can even get your features fixed up so you won't look quite so terrible – plastic face building is a wonderful art. Fight one more time, even, and you may spend the rest of your days in a padded cell."

"I'm still tougher than you think," he answered, "I don't feel the blows, even if you do say I flinch. I'm as good as I ever was, and I can still prove it. Anyway – the press has been raving for a match with Sailor Slade. Sign him on; it'll pack any stadium in the country. I've always ducked him since that first time I met him – you know, before you started managing me. He's the one man I've always figured might have a chance to knock me out. He's got everything, including my goat. He's tough and fast, can hit nearly as hard as Steve Costigan and is ten times as clever as Costigan.

"Get him for me. I'll beat him."

"If he beat you once, how do you figure to stop him now? You're no better than you were then – worse, if anything, and Slade has improved."

"When I met him before, I didn't have the incentive to win that I have now," he answered.

I nodded. What this incentive was, I did not know, but I had seen him rise again and again from what looked like certain defeat – had seen him, writhing on the canvas, turn white, seen his eyes blaze with sudden terror as he dragged his bruised and battered form upright with a determination that overcame the flesh. Terror? Of losing! A terror that kept him going despite himself, when even his iron body was tottering on the verge of collapse, and when the old fighting frenzy had ceased to function in the numbed brain. What prompted this dread? I could no more fathom the reason than I could fathom his strange money-lust.

"You'll get me Slade," he was saying, "I'll beat him, or stay the limit. If I can beat him, my next fight ought to be the greatest sell-out yet. It ought to pack the fans in solid. You'll sign me for four fights – with Sailor Slade, Young Hansen, Jack Slattery, and Mike Costigan."

"Mike Costigan!" I exclaimed sharply, "Mike, you're out of your mind! Its suicide, I tell you! You've picked the four toughest battlers in the world!"

"Sign me up," he answered, "I know you can. Hansen will be easy. I beat him once and I can do it again. Slattery, I don't know. I want to fight him last. He looks like the greatest battler we've had since Dempsey's time. First I've got to hurdle Slade, though. And after him, I'll take on Costigan. He's the least scientific of the four, though the hardest hitter. If I'm slipping like you say, I want to get him before I've gone too far along the line."

I was sweating profusely and Ganlon's eyes were gleaming.

"It's suicide, I tell you," I cried. "If you've got to fight, pass these sluggers up and take on a few set-ups. Even if Slade don't knock you out, he'll soften you up so that Costigan will punch you right into the nut-house. That fellow's a murderer! They call him Iron Mike, too. He's nearly as tough as you are and he can hit as hard – almost. He's a better man than his brother Steve, who held you to a draw when you were better than you are now."

"I'll pack them in," he answered heedlessly, "Slade's nearly the drawing card I am, and as for Costigan – the fans always turn out to see two iron men matched. There's no use talking; you do as I say."

As usual, there was no answer to be made.

CHAPTER 6

"For a $100,000 Purse And – "

It was a few nights before the date of the Brennon-Slade match. I had wandered into Mike's room at the training quarters, and my eye chanced to fall on a partially completed letter on his writing table. Idly and without any intention of violating any rule of manners, my eyes wandered down the written page, noting that it was addressed to a girl named Marjory Walshire, at a very fashionable girl's school in New York state.

I had never known Mike to go with any girl at all. I knew he sometimes received letters addressed in a feminine hand, but I had never asked him, and he had never volunteered any information about it. I wondered what a girl in a society school like that would be doing writing to a prize-fighter. I noted that a letter from this girl lay beside the one Mike had been writing. I admit it was not a sporting thing to do, but I took up the partially completed letter and glanced idly over it. A few phrases caught my eye and the next moment I was reading the letter with a fierce intensity, all scruples forgotten. Having finished it, I took up the other – the letter the girl had written Mike – and ruthlessly tore it open.

I had scarcely completed reading it when Mike entered, with Spike Ganlon. His eyes blazed with fury when he saw the letter in my hand, his mighty fists clenched but before he could say a word, I launched an offensive of my own. For one of the few times in my whole life, I was wild with anger.

"You born fool," I snarled. "So this is why you've been forcing me to get you matches that I knew were ruining you! This is why you've stinted yourself at every turn! This is why you're a battered wreck, ready for the junk heap today! And why you insist on going on, like a fool, until your brain crumbles! Maybe it seems noble to you, but as far as I'm concerned, you're a born fool!"

"What do you mean by getting into my private correspondence?" His voice was husky with fury.

I sneered. "I'm not going to enter into a discussion of manners and etiquette. You can beat me up afterwards, if you want to, but just now I'm going to have my say!

"You've been keeping some frail in a ritzy finishing school back East. Finishing school! Its nearly finished you! What kind of a dame is she, to let you go through hell for her, that way? I'd like for her to see you now, with your battered map! While she's been lolling at her ease in the most expensive school she could find, you've been flattening out the rosin with your shoulders and soaking it down with your blood! Why, she – "

"Shut up!" Brennon roared, white and shaking, "shut up! Or before God, I'll kill you!"

He leaned back against the table, trembling, gripping the table edge so hard that his knuckles whitened – fighting for control. At last he spoke more calmly.

"Yes, that's the incentive that's kept my going – that will keep me going to the end. That girl is the only girl I ever loved. The only thing I ever had to love.

"Listen, do you know how lonely a kid is when he has absolutely nobody in the world to love? The priests in Saint Joseph's home were kind to me, but there were too many children there for any one to get any real affection. I got the beginnings of a good education – that's all.

"Out in the world it was worse. I hobo'd around, working, fighting, starving. I fought for every thing I ever got. I have a better education than most, you say. I worked my way through high school, and read all the books, in my spare time, that I could beg, steal, or borrow. Many a time I went hungry to buy a book.

"I drifted into the ring gradually – from fighting in carnivals and the athletic shows small-town fight clubs put on. You know – I never got anywhere. I told you the night I whipped Battling Mulcahy that I was through. I started drifting again. Then in a little one-horse town out on the Arizona desert, I met Marjory Walshire.

"Poverty? She knew poverty! Supporting herself by working her fingers to the bone in a cafe. Good blood in her too – just as there is in me, some-where. She should have been born to the satins and velvet – instead she was born to the greasy dishes and dirty tables of a second-class cafe.

"I loved her, and she loved me. She told me her dreams, dreams that she never believed would come true – of education – culture – nice clothes – refined companions – everything that any girl wants.

"I swore I'd take her out of the cafe, at least, but where was I to turn? There was nothing I could do; I could only get a job – and introduce her to the household drudgery of a working man's wife. I remembered what you had told me. I looked you up and went back into the ring. You know what happened.

"As soon as I could, I sent her to the school. I've been sending her money enough to live in as much style as any girl there, and I've managed to save some too, so when she gets out of school, and when I have to quit the game, we can be married and start in some kind of business – some business that won't mean drudgery and poverty for us.

"Poverty! It didn't strike home to me what a terrible thing it is, until I saw Marjory working in that infernal cafe. But poverty is the cause of more crimes and cruelty, more hatred and suffering than anything else. Poverty kept me from having a home and people like other kids. You know how it is in the slums of the cities – parents toiling for a living, babies coming too fast; they can't support all of them. Mine left me on the doorstep of Saint Joseph's with a note: 'He's honest born. We love him but we can't keep him. Call him Michael Brennon and please be kind to him.'

"Aye – poverty! And poverty can be as cruel in a small town as in a city. There was Marjory, who'd never been out of the town in which she was born – with her soul pinched and starved for the beautiful and good things of life, and her little white hands already reddened and callused from overwork.

"Its thinking of her that's kept me going. It's the thought of her that's kept me on my feet when the whole world was red and blind and the fists of my opponent were like hammers beating on my shattering brain – that's dragged me off the canvas when the body of me was without feeling and my arms hung like lead to my shoulders. And its the love of her that's sent me crashing through the cruel blows, blind and bloody, to strike down the man I could no longer see.

"And as long as the thought of her waiting for me at the end of the long trail upholds me, there's no man on earth can make me take the count!"

His voice crashed through the room like a clarion peal of victory, that somehow thrilled me to the bone, but my old doubts returned.

"But how can she love you so much," I exclaimed, "when she's willing for you to go through all this for her?"

"What does she know of fighting? She never saw a fight in her life, and besides me, she never saw a fighter. Before I sent her away – or rather before I went away to meet you, I made her promise she'd never see a fight I figured in, or any other fight. I made her promise she'd never listen to an account of my fights over the radio, never go to a movie that showed them, or even read about them in the papers! Oh, I knew what I was in for – and she's kept her word. She's never opened a newspaper that carried an account of my battles.

"I made her believe that boxing was more or less a dancing, tapping affair; she'd heard of Corbett, Tunney, those clever fellows who could go through a twenty round battle without a mark, and she vaguely supposed I was like them. She hasn't seen me for four years – not since I left the town in which she worked. I sent her the money to go to New York on, and arranged things with the school by letter. I've put her off when she's asked to come to see me, or for me to come to see her. When she does see my banged-up face it'll be a terrible shock, but I was never very handsome anyhow – "

"Do you mean to tell me," I broke, "that she'll never tune in on one of your fights, or even read an account of them, when the papers are full of how you look after a fight, how much punishment you've taken, and all that?"

"Sure, I do. Anyway, if she should happen on to my picture in the papers I doubt if she'd recognize it – what with my disfigurations and the faults of these newspaper pictures. And another thing – she don't know me by my real name. After I quit the game the first time, everywhere I went, some two-by-four promoter that I'd fought for was writing me or coming to see me, to get me to fight for him again. When I blew into this town, I was going under the name of Mike Flynn – trying to duck these fellows. The first time I saw Marjory, I began to dally with going back into the ring, and I never told her any different. The money I've sent her has been in cashier's checks. To her, I'm simply Mike Flynn – a name she never sees in the papers, in case she does sneak a look."

"But her letters are addressed to Mike Brennon – " I began.

"No – you didn't notice closely. They are addressed to Michael Flynn, care of Mike Brennon, this camp. She don't know Mike Flynn and Mike Brennon are the same – she thinks Brennon is merely a friend of mine and owner of the training camps.

"No – she's been my only guiding star and will be as long as I live. It's for her I've been stinting myself, acting the part of the miser – refusing to hand out money to every fellow that came along, Steve. Van Heeren – that's different. I'm responsible, largely for his condition. I had to help him.

"These four fights now, one of them may be my last. Maybe I'm slipping, but I'll get by Slade and I may get by Costigan. I've got money, yes. But I want more. I intend that Marjory shall never want again for long as she lives. I'm to get a hundred thousand dollars for this bout with Slade. My third purse of that size, as you know. I've been lucky. Since I knocked out Barota I've gotten heavy purses – have made more than many champions. Luck, good management, thanks to you, and my own attraction. Don't mention quitting to me until I'm counted out, and don't mention this matter of my girl to anyone – not even to me, unless I bring the subject up myself."

CHAPTER 7

The Border Line

I haven't the heart to tell of the Brennon-Slade fight, round by round. Mike had slipped even more than we had thought. The steel spring legs which had carried him through so many whirlwind battles unweakened, had slowed down. They trembled and faltered. His sweeping haymakers crashed over with their old power, but they did not continually wing through the air without a cessation as of old. After the first few rounds he slowed up badly. He hit less often. Blows that should not have jarred him staggered and seemed to daze him. The squat Sailor, with his abnormally long arms and broad shoulders, sensed this weakness and wild with the thought of scoring a knockout, threw caution to the winds and went to kill or be killed. He hammered the reeling slugger about the ring, broken and bleeding before a perfect red torrent of smashing blows, each of which carried the kick of a mule. He floored Brennon again and again – how many times I never dared try to remember.

But Mike Brennon was still Iron Mike, the man with the granite jaw. Blind, bloody, and reeling he carried on. Again and again he rose, barely beating the final count. Four times in as many rounds the gong saved him, and we had to carry him back to the corner. But we dared not throw in the sponge and the referee dared not stop the slaughter.

Toward the last Slade began to weaken. With Brennon helpless before him, he could not keep him down, and his morale began to go to pieces, as many a man had done. More, he had been fighting more or less wide open, and the body blows Mike had landed from time to time were sapping even the Sailor's iron strength. All these factors, coupled with Slade's terrific exertions, eventually caused him to blow up. And blow up at last he did, when he had punched himself out.

But the fight went fourteen hideous rounds before Slade went to pieces and the iron tiger whom he had punched into a red smear tore him to shreds. Somehow Mike found his foe in the red mist that surrounded him and blindly blasted him into unconsciousness.

Brennon collapsed in his corner after Slade was counted out, and both men were carried senseless from the ring; and the punishment Mike took that night nauseates me and takes the stiffening from my knees today when I think of it.

I sat by his side that night while he lay in a semi-conscious state, occasionally muttering brokenly as his bruised brain conjured up red visions. He lay, both eyes closed fast, his oft-broken nose a crushed ruin, cut and gashed all about the head and face, now and then stirring uneasily as the pain of two broken ribs stabbed him.

Now for the first time he spoke the name of the girl he loved, whimpering over and over, "Marjory! Marjory!" – groping out his hands like a lost child. Again he fought over his fearful battles and his mighty fists clenched until the knuckles showed white, and low, bestial snarls tore through his battered lips.

Once in his delirium he muttered a sportswriter's parody of Chesterton's lines, which had once taken his fancy:

"I call the muster of iron men

From ship and ghetto and Barbary den,
To break, and be broken God knows when
"And only God knows why."

Then raising himself painfully on one elbow, his burning, unseeing eyes gleaming like slits of flame between the battered lids, he spoke in a low voice as if answering and listening to the murmur of ghosts:

"Joe Grim! Battling Nelson! Mike Boden! Joe Goddard! Iron Mike Brennon."

I sat listening and my flesh crawled with a sort of ghostly horror. I cannot impart to you the uncanniness of hearing the muster of those iron men of days gone by, muttered in the stillness of night through the pulped and delirious lips of the grimmest of them all.

At least he fell silent and seemed to fall into a natural slumber. I rose stealthily and noiselessly left the room. And as I went into the outer room, two figures entered. One was Spike Ganlon, his savage eyes blazing with a kind of fierce triumph. The other was a girl – the darling of high society, she seemed, with her costly garments and air of culture, but she was perturbed now and her eyes and actions showed it. She exhibited an elemental anxiety such as no pampered and sophisticated debutante would have done. Four years of culture and polish, but now the real woman showed through the veneer. For even before Ganlon spoke, I knew this girl was Marjory Walshire.

"Oh, where is he – where is Mike?" she cried, a kind of desperation in her tone, "Is he badly hurt? You've got to let me see him!"

"He's asleep now," I said shortly, and then added in my cruel bitterness, "leave him alone. You've done enough to him already. He wouldn't want you to see him like he is now."

She cringed as from a blow, but with the thought of all the agony Mike had gone through on her account I could not find it in my heart to pity her. For I still believed in my inmost soul that she had known all the time and was merely callous.

"Oh, let me just look in the door!" she begged, twining her white fingers together – and I thought how often Mike's hand had been bathed in blood so that those white fingers should remain white and unstained by work – "I won't wake him! Oh, you've GOT to let me see him!"

I hesitated, and her eyes flamed like a cat's in the night; her whole body tensed. Now she was the primal woman.

"You'll let me see him or I'll kill you!" she cried sharply, and before I could stop her, she rushed past me and opened the door.

She stopped short on the threshold. Mike muttered restlessly in his sleep and turned his blind face toward the sound of the door opening, but he did not waken. As her eyes fell on that frightfully disfigured face, I saw her sway drunkenly as though from a death blow. Her hands went to her temples and a low whimper like an animal in pain escaped her. Then, her face corpse-white and her eyes set in a deathly stare, she stole to the bedside. A moment she hung above the battered form on the bed and then with a heart-rending sob she sank to her knees, cradling that bruised head in her arms, weeping with great shaking silent gasps that seemed tearing her heart out, while her tears fell in a burning rain on her lover's face.

Mike murmured, but still he did not waken and at last I drew her gently away and lead her into the next room, closing the door behind us. She made no resistance, walking like one asleep or in a trance.

But out of hearing of the sleeping man, she burst into a torrent of weeping that did her good.

"I didn't know!" she kept sobbing over and over. "I didn't know! I didn't know that fighting was like that! I obeyed him – he told me never to go to a fight or listen to one over the radio, and never to read about one, and I didn't. Sometimes I heard men talking about Iron Mike Brennon but I didn't know it was my Mike! I didn't know – until I got Mr. Ganlon's letter.

"Why, how could I know – " she suddenly thrust at me a crumpled letter.

"This is one of the few letters in which he even mentioned his fights. I've kept them all – "

The date was nearly four years ago. I read an extract:

"It looks like I'm getting into the real money now, Marjory darling. Last night I stopped Jack Maloney, a foremost contender, in three rounds. He scarcely laid a glove on me, and I came out of the bout without a scratch. Don't worry about me; this game is a cinch. None of them can hit me."

I laughed bitterly, remembering the wreck Maloney had made of Mike's features before he went out.

"I've been doing you an injustice," I said shortly to hide my emotions, "I've been hating you because I thought you were merely a heartless woman – I see now that you're the true blue. I didn't think a man could keep a girl in such ignorance but I guess it's true. Now that you're here, maybe you can persuade Mike to give up the game – none of the rest of us can do anything with him."

"Surely he can't think of fighting again, if he lives?" she cried.

I laughed. "He isn't going to die. He'll be laid up a while but I don't think he'll have any lasting injury if he don't fight again. It's up to you to persuade him. Now, I'll take you to a hotel – "

"I'm going to stay right here close to Mike," she answered passionately, "I'm never going to let him out of my sight again. Oh, I could kill myself when I think of the easy life I've been leading, the luxury and all – while Mike was going through this agony, all for me. Tomorrow I'm going to marry him and take him away."

There was a spare room in the training quarters. After she was safely ensconced there, I turned to Spike.

"I suppose you're responsible for this," I said angrily. "You might have waited until Mike was out of bed. That was a terrible shock to her."

"I intended it should be," he snarled, "I wrote and told her did she know her boy Mike Flynn that was supportin' her in such style was really Iron Mike Brennon which was swiftly bein' punched into the booby-hatch? I give her some graphic account of his battles, and I told her what I thought of a dame that would let a boy go through such for her.

"I wrote her in time for her to get here for the fight – I wanted her to see the bout herself. But she missed a train, she says. I believe she's lyin'."

I gave an exclamation of protest.

"You're buffaloed," he flamed, "She's made a monkey outa you with her sob stuff. I didn't fall for that! She don't care! All she wants outa Mike is his money."

"I don't believe that – now. If you say she was acting you're a fool."

"Who cares what you believe – or say? Anyway, now if she's got a spark uh real womanhood in her, she'll make Mike quit the ring. I wanted her to see him in all his glory – the marks of his money-makin'."

"I imagine," I said slowly, "I've got an idea that Mike will kill you when he finds out about this."

"Let him," Spike snarled shortly. "Mike Costigan will kill him – if they fight. I know. I've seen these iron men crack before. I was in Tom Berg's corner the night Jose Gonzales knocked him out. It was Berg's first k.o. – and I helped carry his corpse out of the ring. He died while the referee was countin' him out. Some men you got to kill to stop – Mike Brennon's one of 'em. If he lives, he's got to quit the game – NOW."

Morning found the battered iron man conscious and clear of mind, his wonderful recuperative powers already asserting themselves. I brought Marjory to his bedside, and before he could recover from his astonishment enough to speak, I left them alone.

Later she came to me, her eyes red with weeping.

"I've argued and begged," she cried desperately, "and he still says he's going to fight again. Oh, what can I do?"

All of us went to Mike's room and surrounded his bedside.

"Mike," I said caustically, "you're a fool. This punching's gone to your head worse than I thought. You can't mean you'll fight again!"

"I've never been knocked out," he answered. "Of course, Slade beat me up badly but no worse than I thought he would. I'm good for some more hundred-thousand-dollar purses yet."

Marjory cried out as if he had stabbed her.

"Mike, for heaven's sake, for MY sake – ! We have more money now than we'll ever use! Do you think I care for money? If I'd known what you were going through with, do you think I'd have stayed where I was a minute? I'd have rather gone in rags and worked my fingers to the bone in the lowest kind of work imaginable. You haven't been fair to me, Mike."

His face lighted with one of his rare smiles – a wonderful smile in spite of the copious bridge-work it revealed. He reached out a hand amazingly gentle considering its strength and touched the girl's soft hand and the sleeve above it.

"White little hands," he murmured, "soft as God meant them to be, and clad in silks too, as is right and proper. Why, just looking at you now and thinking that you've been living as you should live repays me a thousand times for all I've gone through. And what have I gone through? A few beatings! And think of the old timers who took worse beatings and got little or nothing. But we're wealthy."

"And there's no reason for you're crucifying yourself – and me – any longer."

He shook his head with that strange abnormal stubbornness which was the worst defect in his character.

"I said I'd never quit till I was counted out of the game. Then I won't be a drawing card any longer and there'll be no reason for me staying in it. But as long as I can draw down a hundred thousand dollars a fight, I'd be a fool to quit."

"Then I hope you'll be counted out in your next fight!" the girl cried with passionate intensity.

Ganlon laughed like a jackal snarling, all the bitterness engendered by his friendship and worry for Mike sounding in his voice.

"Yes! He'll be counted out when he meets Iron Mike Costigan! And the referee that counts him out will be the Man with the Hood! And after that they won't be no worryin' about hundred-thousand-dollar purses, or beatins or anything! They'll just be another slugger knockin' at the Golden Gates!"

Marjory blanched and wrung her hands, and Brennon scowled.

"Spike, I'm overlooking the fact that you wrote that letter to Marjory, after the way she begged for you, but you needn't go frightening her. What's the matter with you and Steve? You act like I was ready for the cleaners right now."

"You are." I rapped out, bluntly, "If you take one more beating, it'll either kill you or make an imbecile out of you."

"Nonsense," he answered imperturbably, "I'm tougher than even you fellows think. A hundred thousand dollars!" his eyes gleamed with the old light. "The packed stadium! The crowd roaring! And Iron Mike Brennon taking everything they can hand out, and finishing on his feet! No! No! I'll quit when I'm counted out. Not before."

"Mike!" the girl cried piercingly, "If you fight again, I'll swear I'll give you back your ring and go away! I'll never see you again."

His eyes sought hers and held them. His gaze beat her down and her head sank on her breast from the intensity of his magnetic eyes. I never saw the human – except one – who could stand the stare of Mike Brennon's eyes.

"Marjory," his deep powerful voice vibrated with confidence, "you're bluffing."

"No-no!" she cried desperately, "I mean it."

"You don't! You're mine! You're just trying to force me into doing what you want! If you go away, you'll come back. But you won't go away! You won't desert me no matter what I do! You're mine and you always will be! You don't mean what you're saying – you couldn't, after all I've endured."

"No, no," she whimpered weakly, hiding her tear-blinded face in her hands, "I don't mean it. There's no use trying to bluff you."

"No use in the world," he answered tenderly stroking her bowed head. I moved restlessly. A failure in the ring, perhaps, but Mike Brennon had a power over those with whom he came in contact outside, a power that none seemed able to overcome. There was something almost brutal in the way he had beaten down the girl's weak pretense – though he himself did not realize it.

"Mike!" snarled Spike Ganlon, speaking harshly and bitterly to hide his emotion; for a second the hard-faced middleweight with his hard-lived life and two hundred savage ring battles behind him dominated the scene:

"Mike, you're crazy! Here you've got everything a man could want – things that lots uh men work their whole lives out for and never get! You got money – a fine girl – fame – and you're still young. You're right on the border line, steppin' on the other side, fistically speakin'. You can't win another fight. Even a second-rater'd knock you stiff. And this Costigan ain't no second rater! He's as tough as you ever was, and as hard a hitter. He shoots his punches straight, and he's never been floored. He's whipped men that's outpointed you.

"If I thought he'd flatten you in a punch or two, I'd say, go in once more. But he won't. He can't. He'll knock you out, but it will be after a long hard batterin' that'll ruin you for life. You'll keep gettin' up after your brain's pounded numb. You'll die or you'll spend your life in a cuckoo house. And what good will your money do then? And what about Marjory here – you want to kill her?"

Mike took his time about replying, and again his strange influence was felt like a cloud over the group.

"Costigan's overrated," he answered, "I'll show the dub up. He never saw the day he could take as much as I can, right now. As for hitting, if I can hit him, I'll knock him out. And I can hit him."

Spike let fall his hands in a sort of helpless manner and turned away with one parting shot: "Yes, you can hit him; but you can't keep him down, and what will he be doin' to you?"

Later he said to the girl and me: "No use arguin' with Mike. It's more than money, now. He thinks it's the kale, but it ain't. The game's in his blood. And again he's jealous of Mike Costigan. He don't realize it, but he is. Remember how Van Heeren fought? These iron men is terrible proud of their toughness and terrible jealous of each other. Mike thinks he can take more than Costigan and hit harder and he's goin' to try to prove it, in spite of all we can do. And all we can do is humor him along, help him train, and hope Costigan flattens him with the first punch. Which ain't possible."

"Doesn't Mike have a chance to win?" Marjory asked tremulously.

"A bird like Mike always has a chance to win – but always, its just a chance. And win or lose, ten rounds with Mike Costigan means Mike Brennon's finish. Each too tough for the other to finish quick. Whichever way it goes, it'll be a long, hard fight, with both terribly battered. It don't matter whether Brennon wins or loses, as to that. He'll end that fight punched nutty or dead. It may finish Costigan too, but it'll sure finish Brennon. Costigan's younger; he ain't been fighting as long as Mike has, and he ain't met the men Mike's met – ain't took the punishment. At his best, Brennon would likely have wore him down and knocked him out like he did Van Heeren. But Mike's slippin' and Costigan ain't begun to crack. He's at his prime – which in a iron man is the same as sayin' that you couldn't hurt with him with a pile-driver."

CHAPTER 8

The Fall of a King

Mike Brennon, always a conscientious worker in his training, trained for the Costigan battle as he had never trained before. Which meant, mainly, that he endured just much more punishment from his sparring partners until I called a halt and discharged all of them. I realized that so far back had Mike slipped, that even the blows he received in sparring would take just that much away from his endurance and ability to absorb punishment. The last few weeks I had him punch the light bag for speed and do a great deal of road work in a vain effort to recover some of the former steel spring quality of his weakening legs. But I knew it was vain. It was not a matter of conditioning with Mike – his trouble lay behind him, in the thousands of cruel blows that his frame had absorbed. A clever boxer may get out of condition, lose a number of fights, get knocked out, and still train up and come back; when an iron man slips he is through and there is no come back.

In the four months which proceeded Mike's fight with Costigan, an air of gloom surrounded the camp which affected all but Brennon himself. The girl, after days of passionate pleading, threatening, weeping, and cajoling, gave it up and sank into a sort of apathy – the same helpless resignation which has been womankind's last refuge down all the ages. Mike was as impervious to pleading as he was to punishment in the ring. To all her pleas and tears he had one answer: that he was better than we thought, that he was still too tough to be hurt, that we underrated him and overrated his opponent, and that as long as he was a drawing card he would be a fool and a coward to step out of the game.

That he was being bitterly cruel to the girl who loved him never occurred to Mike, and we could not make him see it. He laughed at her fears and spent hours in pointing out elaborately why he was in no danger – weaving sophistry that none believed but himself. He could not realize his own stubbornness but was rather provoked at what he called our perverseness – insisting that he quit the game when he was practically at his prime – as he said. He scoffed at the results of his fight with Slade – hadn't the Sailor suffered almost as much as had he? As for that fight showing that he had slipped – far from it! It only proved what he had said – that Slade was the best man in the ring, barring only Mike Brennon! As for Costigan – forget him! A crude slugger, Brennon's own counterpart, but slower and less rugged. A few rounds of ferocious slugging and the upstart would crumple and go down and out. Who was this newcomer in the ranks of the iron men to oppose the greatest of them all?

This may seem monstrously and offensively conceited, but to hear Mike Brennon talk in that cool, self-confident way of his was not offensive or blatant. Mike was aware of his own fistic faults. He frankly admitted that any second-rater who could avoid his blows could outpoint him, but he sincerely believed that he was superior in ruggedness to any men who ever lived and that he could beat any man whom he could hit. Nor did he believe that any man could hit hard enough to knock him out. Deep in his heart, I doubt if Mike Brennon really believed he would ever be knocked out.

And so he prepared for his battle. One thing he insisted on: that Marjory should not see the fight.

"It would unnerve me to know that you were watching. I'd know that you'd think I was being terribly hurt. I'll be cut up a good deal, as usual, likely as not, and I'll cut the other fellow up worse. We'll be bloody and battered, and while I won't be feeling the blows, you'll think I'm being killed."

"But I want to see it," protested Marjory, "and I'm going to – "

"You're not," said Mike grimly, "for the simple reason that if you insist, I'll lock you into your room before the fight starts. I'm not going to go into that fight knowing that you're watching me. Oh, I know I'll win, but I also know that this fellow Costigan will give me a tough tussle. And I don't want you there. If it was a light-hitting boxer, it would be different. But you're too gentle and soft-hearted to stand the sight of blood and punishment and I don't want you there."

"Alright," she sighed and I pitied her from the depths of my heart. She was thinking, just as I was, of the battered wreck that would probably be carried out of the ring at the conclusion of the fight.

"Mike!" she cried out desperately, "for the last time, I beg you, don't do this! Don't go through with this insane thing!"

"No use to start all that," he answered calmly, "Think, Marjory! My fourth hundred-thousand-dollar purse! That's a record that few champions have set! A hundred thousand dollars with Flash Sullivan – and with Jose Gonzales – and Sailor Slade – now with Mike Costigan! A sell-out! Thousands of tickets already sold in advance! No, no! Don't ask me! I've got to go on, now, anyhow. And I'm a cinch to win."

This confidence he carried with him into the ring. As if it were yesterday I visualize the scene: the ring bathed in the white glow of the lights above it, Costigan scowling in his corner, Brennon climbing through the ropes; while the great crowd that filled the huge outside bowl, swept away into darkness on each side. A circle of white faces looked up from the nearest ringside seats. Further out only a twinkling army of glowing cigarette ends evidenced the multitude, though the impression was given of a great shadowy throng. This throng was breathlessly silent while the announcer was talking – only a vast rippling undertone of whispers and rustlings came from the soft darkness.

"Iron Mike Brennon, in this corner, 190 pounds; in this corner, Iron Mike Costigan, 195. These boys have come here to decide the question once and for all as to which is the tougher man – "

Mike sat in his corner with his head bowed, a contrast to the nervous feline-like picture he had offered in his dressing room, when he paced the floor, afire with a white hot fighting fury, trembling to get at his opponent. I wondered if he was still seeing the tear-stained face of Marjory, and still hearing her sobs as she kissed him in the dressing room before he came into the ring.

The men were called to the center of the ring for instructions. Costigan came with alacrity. Brennon, to my surprise, seemed apathetic. He walked with dragging feet and slow movements. However, in front of his foe, he came awake with fierce energy and I doubt if the two rivals heeded what the referee was saying, so savagely intent upon each other they were. Iron Mike Costigan was dark, also, with tousled, black hair and heavy brows. Five feet eleven inches in height and heavier than Brennon, he lacked something of Brennon's fierce ranginess of appearance, but he made up for that in power. He gave the impression of oak and iron massiveness, with his mighty arms and shoulders and his barrel chest. The eyes of the two men burned into each other with savage intensity – volcanic blue for Costigan; steel gray for Brennon. Their sun-browned faces were set in unconscious snarls that writhed their thin lips into an appearance of black hatred, but this was involuntary. Neither was aware of the fact that he was scowling; to each of them, the other was merely a symbol of his own fighting fury, a rival to his own peculiar vanity, and though they were ready to tear each other to pieces, they felt no real hatred toward one another.

But as they stood facing each other, Brennon's stare of concentrated cold ferocity waved and fell momentarily before Costigan's savage blue eyes. I realized that this was the first time a man had looked Mike down and I thought of Corbett staring down Sullivan – of McGovern's eyes falling before the glare of Young Corbett.

Then the men were back in their corners again and the seconds and handlers were climbing through the ropes.

"Remember!" I hissed as a parting word to Mike, "I throw the sponge in if the going gets too rough."

He did not reply. He seemed to have sunk into that strange apathy again.

The gong sounded. Costigan hurtled from his corner, a compact bulk of fighting fury, vibrant with energy. Brennon came out more slowly.

At my side Ganlon hissed: "What's the matter with Mike? He acts like he was drunk!"

The two Iron Mikes had met in the center of the ring. Costigan might have been slightly awed by the fame of the man he faced; at any rate, he did not tear in as he usually did. Brennon walked toward his foe, but his legs dragged and he moved with an effort.

Then Costigan suddenly launched an attack and shot a straight left to Brennon's face. As if the blow had suddenly aroused him to his full tigerish fury, Mike went into terrific action. Crash! Crash! The old sweeping haymakers began to thunder with all their ancient power and speed. Costigan had, of course, no defense. A sweeping left crashed under his heart with a sound like a caulking mallet striking a ship's side; a blasting right that whistled as it shot through the air cannonballed against his jaw. Iron Mike Costigan went down as though struck by a thunderbolt.

Then even as the crowd rose, thundering, even as the referee sprang forward to count over him, Costigan reeled to his feet again. An iron man never stays on the canvas a second if he can help it. But I was watching Brennon. It seemed as though that sudden burst of action had taken all the strength out of him. He sagged against the ropes, limp, cloudy-eyed. Now sensing that his foe was again on his feet, his fighting instinct dragged him forward with halting and uncertain motions, like a man drunk or walking in his sleep.

Costigan, still dizzy from that terrific knockdown, was conscious of only one thought – get to his foe and smash him! The old instinct of the iron man – walk into punishment and keep hitting till somebody fell! Now he crashed through Brennon's groping arms and shot a right hook to the chin. Brennon swayed and fell, just as a drunken man falls when a prop against which he has been leaning has been removed.

Over his motionless form the referee was counting – "Eight-Nine-TEN!" And the ring career of Iron Mike Brennon was at an end. A silence reigned, as if the throng were stunned, and Mike Costigan, new king of all iron men, leaned dazedly against the ropes with parted lips and staring eyes, unable to believe his own senses. MIKE BRENNON HAD BEEN KNOCKED OUT!

About the ring the typewriters of the reporters were ticking out the fall of a king: "Evidently Mike Brennon's famous iron jaw has been turned to crockery. Tonight Mike Costigan, his nearest rival in the way of ruggedness, stopped him in less than a round, after being floored himself, for the first time in his life. The only miracle is that Brennon has lasted as long as he has, considering the terrific punishment to which he has been subjected for the last four years. Any jaw will lose its hardness under such punching and – "

We carried Mike to his dressing room, still senseless. Ganlon was muttering under his breath and as soon as we had Mike safely ensconced on a cot, with a physician looking to him, the middleweight vanished. Marjory had been waiting for us, and now she said nothing, standing close by the cot where her lover lay, with white lips and clasped hands.

At last Mike opened his eyes and looked about him. Then he bounded to his feet and starting throwing punches, while the rest of us scurried for cover. No use trying to seize and hold him and all of us had visions of stopping one of his terrible swings. Then he halted, swayed slightly and drew his hand across his eyes.

"Sit down, Mike!" Marjory was at his side and gently forced him back on the cot.

"What happened? Did I win?"

"You were knocked out in the first round, Mike." I answered, feeling it better to answer him directly. Amazement flared in his eyes.

"I? Knocked out? Impossible!?"

"Yes, you were, Mike," I assured him, expecting him to do any of the things I have seen fighters do on learning of their first knockout – burst into a torrent of savage weeping, faint, rave and curse, or rush out looking for the man who beat him.

But being Mike Brennon, and a never to-be-solved enigma, he did none of these things. He rubbed his chin and laughed cynically, but resignedly.

"Guess I'd gone further back than I thought, and underrated Costigan. I don't remember the punch that put me out. Unusual thing – I've come through my last fight without a mark."

"And now you'll quit!" cried Marjory, "This is the best thing that could have happened! Costigan knocked you out with one punch and you weren't punished any. You promised you'd quit when you were knocked out, Mike, you promised!" Her voice was painful in its intensity.

"You'll have to quit now, Mike." I said, "You're no longer a drawing card."

At that moment a knock sounded on the door and the face of Costigan hesitantly appeared. His ferocious features were clouded by both an air of uncertainty and of anxiety.

"Are you after bein' alright, Brennon?" he asked.

"Sure, Costigan, come in."

Still the other hesitated.

"You ain't aimin' to be hittin' me with a chair like Young Hansen did after I knocked him out?"

Brennon laughed. "Come in. I want to shake hands with you."

With an apparent sigh of relief Costigan entered, his face relaxing into a broad Irish grin. He shook hands with sincerity and said:

"Be the saint, Brennons, but that was a slam you gimme! What a polthogue you're after packin' in each mauler. I ain't mesilf yet. The first toime I iver hit the canvas, and this toime I thought I'd be goin' on through to the basement. Its the real regret that's on me, if this k.o. is ruinin' you as a drawin' card."

"That's all right, Costigan," Brennon answered, "I'm quitting the game. And I guess I'm lucky. And Costigan, I'm telling you this, quit it yourself when you feel you're slipping."

Costigan grinned. "There, Brennon, you know yoursilf we never quit till they count 'ten' over us! A great battle that was, and a fine man ye are."

After his conqueror left, Brennon sighed, ruefully, "There goes the new 'greatest of all iron men.' I wonder who'll level him, finally!"

At that moment Ganlon burst in, panting with suppressed excitement. His eyes blazed.

"Mike," he fairly snarled, "Steve! Don't you two boneheads see there's something wrong here? Mike, when did you begin feeling drowsy?"

Brennon started. "That's right! I'd forgotten. As I climbed into the ring I began feeling queer, now that I remember. Costigan's punches seemed to have knocked all recollection of it out of my mind. As I sat in the corner, I got dizzy and things floated in front of my eyes. I felt like a drunken man. Then I sort of woke up and we were in the center of the ring with the referee talking. It all comes back now, but how strange and vague it seems! For a moment I was perfectly normal, and I remember how Costigan's eyes blazed, then when I turned to go to my corner, I got dizzy and drunken again. But I swear I hadn't had anything to drink. Steve said something to me as he climbed out of the ring but I could scarcely hear his voice. It seemed a way off. Then I faintly heard the gong and felt myself moving out in the ring as if my limbs were working independently of my mind.

"Then I saw Costigan through a fog and he hit me a punch under the cheekbone. It was a hummer and it woke me up. I seemed to come to myself with a start; I started swinging and saw Costigan go down. That's the last I remember and it's why I couldn't believe it when they said he knocked me out."

Ganlon laughed bitterly. "Sure. I noticed how you walked and acted. That last burst of fighting was all you had in you, and you wouldn'ta had that much if you wasn't a human tiger. You was out on your feet before Costigan hit you. That right hook was plenty hard but you've kept your feet lotsa times before blows a sight harder. A girl coulda pushed you over and that's all Costigan done!"

"But what – " began Brennon.

"Doped!" I exclaimed.

"Sure, doped! And you oughta kick yourself, Steve, for not seein' it right off the bat. And you with thirty years uh boxin' experience behind you! Great cats, these managers!"

"Costigan's crowd! Or the gambling ring-"

"Naw! You been crossed by a person you wouldn't believe capable of it! I been doin' some detective work. Mike, just before you left your dressin' room, you drunk a small cup uh tea, didn't you? Kinda unusual preparation for a hard fight, eh? But you drunk it to please somebody – "

Marjory was cowering in the corner, white-faced. Mike looked at her, puzzled and troubled.

"But Spike, Marjory made that tea herself-"

"YEAH, AND SHE DOPED IT HERSELF. SHE FRAMED YOU TO LOSE!"

Our eyes turned on the shrinking girl; surprise in mine, I suppose, anger and accusation in Spike's, a deep and puzzled hurt in Mike's.

"She framed you! She slipped you the dope!" snarled Spike, "And – "

"Marjory, why did you do that?" asked Mike in bewilderment, "Why did you want me to lose? I might have won – "

"Yes, you might have won!" she cried in a sudden desperate gust of defiant fury; she was as one who has been pushed past human endurance and who no longer cares what happens. "You might have won – after Costigan had battered you into a red ruin! After your brain had been pounded numb and you had been knocked just another step along the road that leads to the padded cell!

"Yes, I drugged the tea! It's my fault you got knocked out! And you can't go back for you won't draw the crowds! I've saved you in spite of your mad vanity – you're safe now – you're out of the game for good with a sound brain. I've gone through hell since I saw you lying on that cot after you fought Slade. Now that's over at least. I've saved you in spite of yourself! I've saved you, I tell you – from your avarice and your mad cruel pride! And it doesn't matter what you do to me now. You can beat me or kill me – I don't care!"

She stood panting before us, her small fists clenched, her eyes blazing. Then as no one spoke, all the fire went out of her. She visibly wilted and moved forlornly toward the door, her slight shoulders drooping. Her wrap which had enveloped her slender form slid to the floor, revealing her in a cheap gingham dress. As she fumbled at the door Mike seemed to awake from a deep trance. He started forward: "Marjory! What are you going in that rig?"

"It's the dress I was wearing when you found me," she answered listlessly, "I wrote and got my old job back at the cafe – "

"Why, in God's name?" he exclaimed, crossing the room with one stride. He caught her slim shoulder and whirled her about to face him, with unconsciously brutal force. "What's the meaning of all this?"

She collapsed suddenly into a storm of weeping. "Don't you hate me for drugging you?" she sobbed. "I didn't think you'd ever want to see me again!"

He crushed her to him hungrily. "Girl, I swear I didn't realize how it all was hurting you. I've been a blind fool. I couldn't realize how you'd suffered. I'm like a mad man coming back to sanity. I see things in a different light now – thank God you doped me! I must have been insane! You're right – it was pride – vanity. My eyes were blinded to my best interests – and your happiness. And darling, that's all that matters now! We've got our life and love before us, and if it rests with me, you're going to be happy all the rest of your life."

Ganlon beckoned me and I followed him out. For the only time since I had known him, the fierce middleweight's hard face was softened. The sentiment that lies at the base of the Irish nature, however deeply hidden sometimes, made his steely eyes almost tender.

"I had her down all wrong," he said softly, "I take back everything I said about her. She's a regular – and Mike – well, he's the only Iron Man I ever knew that got the right breaks at last."

Kid Galahad

When my manager, Jack Reynolds, says to me, "Kid, the ring game's changing; we've got to make a gentleman out of you," he was plumb surprised when I give a howl and throwed a chair at him.

But he soon found out about my grouch, and so will you.

See this here scar on my scalp? That's a mark of gentility – well, anyway, it's what I got for being a gent.

It started by Jack leaving me in a certain small city on the West Coast while he went east to New York to see if he could get me a bout at the Garden. He wanted to get me matched with Lopez, the Cuban Shadow, knowing that a win over that sensational boy would boost my stock a heap.

But I'd never fought in the East, and promoters was dubious about my ability and drawing power. Lopez was high powered, and they didn't want to feed him no set-up.

Can you feature that? And me the talk of the West Coast!

Well, Jack went to New York, as I said. He left Abe Garfinkle with me, under the hallucination that the presence of this looneytick would aid in keeping me outa trouble.

Jack told me to do as little as possible of anything while he was gone; not to get in no rows of no sort, not to sign no papers, and not to answer no incriminating questions. He departed with the cheerful and flattering remark that he fully expected to find me in jail when he got back.

My manager's inexcusable attitude irritated me; I reckon I can take care of myself. But after seeking in vain to amuse myself in various ways, Abe suggested that I go over to the public library and enlighten myself.

Well, that was all right; I ain't one of these mutts to which books is just so much waste material taking up space. But the catch was that Abe insisted on going with me and picking out the books for me to read.

I wanted a book about pirates and Indians and things, but he got one which he said would help improve my general manners, and just for the sake of peace, I glanced over it.

Well, I got real interested. It was about folks called knights, which flourished many centuries ago, long before the Civil War, even. These birds wore fighting togs made outa battleship steel, with wash pots on their heads, and spent all their time rescuing fainting damozels – whatever them is – and socking dragons and things over the bean with meat cleavers.

They was a knight named Galahad, which was the champion of them all. He barred nobody! He met all contestants, from flyweights to superheavies, and they all took the count. None of 'em went the limit with him. The way that boy could handle his dukes was a caution.

But the main thing that interested me was: he was a amateur – what I mean, he never hedged for the gate receipts. If somebody'd offered him a big purse, with the movie rights, he'd probably felt insulted.

He cared nothing at all about the gelt. He spent all his time chasing hither and yon, looking for some girl which was getting a raw deal. The minute he heard a skirt howling for a cop, he bounced in and took a hand.

Zip! Zim! Zam!

Another one-round kayo for Sir Galahad, and he took the frail back to her folks, made a courtly bow, and galloped away on his milk-white steed in search of more hero business.

Well, I got all steamed up over this jobby, and when I put down the book with a deep sigh and strode forth into the streets, I felt as noble as all get out.

I was a fighting man, too. And, I thought, had I lived in them times, I bet I'd made him step to hold his title.

While ruminating thus, I found myself passing a gym in a sort of rough neighborhood, when out came a girl crying and holding one hand over her eye. Instantly I felt my heroic impulses rising.

Here was a girl which was being abused! This woulda been pie for Galahad, and by golly, Kid Allison wasn't no slouch hisself when it come to the rescue business!

Here, I says to myself, is where I revives the ancient codes of chivalry and proves myself a gent. Jack Reynolds will be proud of this, I says. So I went up to the girl and, removing my hat with a sweeping bow that knocked over a garbage can, I said,

"Miss, can I be of any assistance?"

She glanced at me outa her good eye, and I seen the other one had evidently just stopped a large masculine fist. She sniffed a few sniffs and dabbed her good eye with a tiny handkerchief, and I might mention that this eye was gray. And what with her wavy black hair, she wasn't hard on the eyesight.

"What a break I got!" said she.

"Miss," said I, swelling out my chest unconsciously, "show me the skunk which done this here vile and contemptible deed and I will flail the livin' daylights outa him."

She give a sort of hard, contemptuous laugh, and says, "Be your age, boy; the bozo that just socked me was Bat Brelen."

This burnt me up, but before I could voice my annoyance, she looked at me closer and said, "Say, you're a pretty hard-looking customer yourself – aren't you Kid Allison?"

On my replying the affirmative, her eyes began to sparkle with a kind of dangerous light.

"I've seen you fight," said she. "You're tough and clever – shifty. If anybody around here could lick Bat, you could.

"The big ham! He's got it coming to him – he ankles around with a dizzy blonde at a dance last night, and then, just because I protest about it, he poked me in the eye! I'll show him he can't put nothing over on Katherine Flynn! Hang the old k.o. sign on his chin and I'll make it worth your while!"

"I don't wish no dough," I answered with quiet dignity. "The mere fact that I am pertectin' a helpless female is pay enough for me. Wait here till I go in and fling the dizzy and punch-drunk carcass of this big false-alarm at your feet!"

"No!" she grabbed my arm. "All his handlers and seconds are in there! If you go in and start a fight you'll come out on a shutter!"

"Then wait'll I get my own merry men," said I, but she shook her head.

"No! Getting soaked in a gang fight wouldn't hurt his reputation, and that's what I want. I want him to get it before a crowd! I want him to hear a referee counting over him, and the crowd cheering the man that flattened him!"

By golly, the concentrated venom with which she said this sort of chilled me, but I reflected that she had plenty of cause to be sore.

"Now listen," she said, getting all excited. "Bat's matched to fight One-round Donovan to-night at a local club. Are you on the level, or are you just dishing out a line when you say you want to help me?"

"It's straight goods, Miss Flynn," I swore. "It's a man's duty to help a lady in distress."

"All right!" she snapped. "We'll get Donovan to run out on him, then you'll bob up as a substitute and chop Bat's ears off! Come on!"

She grabbed me by the arm, and hustled me to the curb where a small roadster was parked. We got in, she saying that Donovan was likely to be doing his roadwork about then.

I admit she was moving so fast she had me slightly groggy. When I could get my wits together, I asked her about Brelen.

"Oh," she said carelessly. "Just a big mutt that drifted in from no place in particular last month and won a few fights. He's got a big local rep, and he's a little bigger than you, but that don't mean nothing to a fighter with your record."

"Well," I says, "how are we goin' to persuade this Donovan palooka to run out?"

"Oh," she said, "that's up to you."

While I was racking my brain for ways and means, we got outa the city limits and, as we motored down a road, I seen what looked like a human mountain trotting along ahead of us.

"That's Donovan, and he's alone!" Katherine exclaimed. "We're in luck!"

We swished on past him and I got a swift glance of a set of shoulders more like a ox than a man, a square Irish face with a flat nose, and a wicked mouth.

Around the corner the girl stopped and hissed, "Quick! Go back and talk to him! Be diplomatic!"

Well, I climbed out obediently and went back, meeting Mr. Donovan just as he prepared to round the corner. Another glance at him did not reassure me; the thought of trying to argue this bull elephant into anything turned me slightly cold.

He was just another ham, I seen, with the usual cabbage ears and dumbly ferocious glare, and there ain't no stubborner critter in the world. Well, I took a deep breath and prepared to be diplomatic.

"Hey you!" I says. "Pull up, big boy. I craves to converse with you."

"Well, make it snappy," he growled. "I ain't got time to chin with every yam I meet."

"Well, to come to the point," I says, "I want you to run out of this bout with Bat Brelen tonight –

"How much?" he scowled.

"Well, be reasonable," I says, "I ain't got but fifteen dollars – "

"One side, tramp!" he snarled. "I'm gettin' a hunnerd and fifty for the fray."

"Well, you'll ondoubtedly get the socks knocked offa you," I urged. "And this is to oblige a lady – "

"Har-har-har!" he har-har'd brutally. "Applesauce! Gangway, before I lay you like a rug!"

Seeing diplomacy had no effect on him, and being burnt up by his callous attitude, I lost my temper and socked him heartily in the mush. He give a roar like a maddened elephant and went for me, and the dance was on.

Well, in a regular ring I could of cut him to ribbons without being touched, but he seemed to think that just because they wasn't no referee, it give him the right to use every foul trick he could think of – which is the natural style of such mutts, anyhow.

After missing a horrible haymaker and taking a right hook that split his ear, he dived for me like a halfback making a line plunge, and we went to the earth all in a lump. His fifty-odd pounds of extra weight advantage sure helped him here, and while I was trying to keep him from chewing my ear off, he banged me in the eye with a wham that shook me to my toes.

I uppercut him, and sunk my knee in his belly, but he merely give a pained but bloodthirsty howl, and his huge ham-like hands closed around my throat like a steel vise.

I thought I was a gone goose when-*wham!* Donovan let go and flopped over on his back with his mouth open and his eyes shut.

Katherine had stole up behind us, and seeing I was getting the worst of it, had clouted him over the head with her handbag.

"You got to do better than that tonight," said she.

"I'll have a referee to keep Brelen from gougin' and bitin'," I snarled, smarting with irritation, and booting the fallen warrior heartily in the short ribs. "He's comin' to already, but I betcha he won't be in no shape to fight tonight – Say, what you got in that hand bag?"

"A flatiron," says she. "Come on! I know the matchmaker, and I can get you the match without any trouble now!"

Not long later, I waltzed into my training camp, kicked my handlers awake, and shouted to Abe Garfinkle, "Get my shower ready, Abe, I'm goin' through a fast workout to limber me up – "

"Yeah?" says he. "And, how come? Didn't Reynolds tell you not to train hard whilst he was gone? You're liable to go stale."

"Applesauce!" I said gayly. "I'm fightin' tonight!"

Abe give a howl. "You tow-headed idjit! You been street-fightin' already! Who you goin' to fight?"

"A local ham-and-egger named Brelen," said I absently, socking the bag. "Get out my lucky red trunks – "

"What kind of a dub is this Brelen?" asked Abe.

"How should I know?" I replied with some irritation. "I ain't got time to go around lookin' up the pedigrees of all the hams I'm called on to flatten. I wouldn't be sluggin' this set-up at all, if it wasn't a matter of principle."

Abe gloomed around and muttered things till I had a pretty fair case of the willies just listening to him, but I went ahead and ignored him as much as possible, and fight time found me on the job.

Katherine was waiting for us at the fight arena and she said, "Come, sneak in this back way. I've persuaded the manager to spring you as a last-minute surprise. Bat still thinks he's fighting Donovan, who he knows is a spread for him, the big slob!"

Me and Abe and "Red" Darts and Heinie Steinman and the rest of my stable slipped into the dressing room, and pretty soon in come the manager. He was sweaty and nervous.

"I dunno what Bat'll do to me if he finds out about this," says he.

"Well," said Katherine, "Donovan wasn't in no shape to fight, and you had to have somebody, didn't you?"

"Yeah, but Bat'll think I shoulda told him before he got in the ring."

"Don't worry; when this boy gets through with Bat, Bat won't be thinking about hitting anybody – much less a defenseless girl."

"We'll let him think Donovan ran out at the last minute. Don't be so scared; you're getting a break. Most promoters would jump at the chance of getting Kid Allison to perform for a yard-and-a-half."

"Well, come on," said the manager, mopping his brow. "Bat's in the ring. Come on."

Miss Flynn grabbed my arm and whispered fiercely, "I'll be in the front row, Kid, watching! Beat his ears down! If you win, I'll be waiting for you, after the fight!"

"Katherine," I says, feeling heroism surge through my veins like a flood, "the spirit of Sir Galahad is ridin' me hard tonight, and I can't lose!"

As we followed the promoter, Abe hissed in my ear, "What kind of a game is this? Where does she get that yard-and-a-half business? You mean to tell me you're fightin' this mutt for a measly hundred-and-fifty bucks?"

"Shut up, you low-minded muskrat," I snarled. "It ain't the dough I'm doin' this for – they's higher things than dollars."

Abe give a low moan like a stricken elk and babbled vaguely under his breath.

Whatever he mighta said was drownded out by the roar that greeted me as I went down the aisles. Everybody knowed it wasn't Donovan, and some of them knowed me. These last whopped in amazement.

I climbed through the ropes after the promoter and took a look at the fellow who sat scowling in the opposite corner. I stopped short and my mouth gaped. Abe Garfinkle give a howl and dropped the sponge.

"That ain't no local pug!" he squawked. "Migosh, Kid, what have you let us into?"

"Aw, shut up!" snarled I with a confidence I was far from feeling. "I'll take him, just the same."

The man in the other corner wasn't no Bat Brelen; it was Battling Worley. And he was a first-string heavyweight, the big crook, with a kayo record as long as the Grand Canyon.

He'd been suspended on the East Coast for dirty fighting and I seen his game. He wasn't well enough known in the West for anybody to be likely to spot him as long as he stayed clear of the big fight centers; so while he was waiting for his manager to get him back in favor with the Commission, he was staying in shape and picking up some change by pushing over a bunch of palookas.

Small-time stuff for a first-class heavy? Sure – but it's been done before. It's easy money and no risk.

Bat was fighting under an assumed name because the California Commission was working hand-in-hand with the New York Commission, and he knowed they'd bar him if they knowed who he was.

All this flashed through my mind while I glared at Bat, and then I was aware of Abe jerking at my arm like he was trying to pull it off.

"The fight's off!" he yammered. "I ain't goin' to let you go in there with that man-killer at a minute's notice thisaway! He'll chop your ears off! Where's the reporters? I'll spill the whole story! I'll spoil his party – "

"Shut up!" I snapped, getting back some of my normal senses. "We can't back out now – and this is the chance of a lifetime, anyway! Here Jack's been tryin' for months to lure some of the first-string men of both classes into the ring with me, and this big tramp falls right into my lap.

"After I clean him, we'll tell the papers who he really is, and it'll be a big boost for us!"

"He's been suspended!" howled Abe. "You'll get foul of the Commission for fightin' him."

"I'm fightin' Bat Brelen," I said. "I ain't supposed to know who he really is. They can't do nothin' to me for fightin' a mutt named Brelen. We won't have to spill the story ourselves. This fray will get into the papers, and some of the press boys is bound to recognize him."

"But if he licks you, we're rooint!" wailed Abe, pulling his hair. "The promoters would cancel every bout you got comin' up, if this egg lays you!"

"That's a chance we gotta take," I growled, though I was pretty shaky myself. "Anyway, I ain't fightin' for you or me, of even Jack Reynolds right now – I'm fightin' for a principle, same as Sir Galahad fought for."

Abe give a scream and commenced to gibber aimlessly to hisself, and meantime I heard the scowling Battler growl, "What's this mean? That ain't One-round Donovan – that's Kid Allison. I wasn't matched with him. Watcha tryin' to put over?"

"Donovan snapped his wrist in his trainin' camp at the last minute, Bat," says the promoter, wiping his bald head. "The Kid is trainin' here, you know, and he agreed to substitute at a minute's notice."

Worley swore under his breath, and I kinda wonder if he liked the looks of it, either. Of course, he was sure he could lick me, but he'd been expecting a pushover, and he wasn't getting enough money to justify him meeting a fighter like me.

But with both of us in the ring and the crowd raising merry Cain, he wouldn't back out. He wasn't only tough and stubborn, but vain as all get out, and he couldn't of stood the razzing he'd of got if he'd of stepped out.

So he just nodded, shortlike, and the promoter turned to the crowd and waved his hands and when they quieted down some he yelled:

"Ladies and gentlem'n! The management wishes to regret that One-round Donovan, who was scheduled to step ten rounds with Bat Brelen to night, has been slightly inured in a training bout and will be unable to appear. However, you will not be disappointed; we have found an opponent for our boy – Kid Allison, uncrowned boxing king of the Southwest, and nationally known contender for the light-heavyweight title!"

Well, if they's anything that makes a crowd mad, it's to have a substitute run in on 'em. But they knowed me by reputation, though I'd never fought there, and they give me quite a hand.

It's a funny thing – had everybody knowed who Bat really was, the odds would of been about three to one on him, with no takers. But as it was, I was a heavy favorite in the ringside betting that instantly begun; still and all, the sports rallied valiantly to the defense of their local boy.

Local boy, my pet pig's knuckle! Crowds is funny; let a fellow stay in a place a month and fight two or three out-of-town boxers, and you'd think, from the way folks talk, that he was born and raised there.

Katherine hadn't let herself be seen with us, but I sat her in a ringside seat and give her a secret wink and she nodded and punched her open left hand with her little right fist to show she got me.

The referee give us our instructions, to which we paid no attention to as usual, and all the time Bat tried to give me the eye – but I merely sneered at his ferocious glares. That hypnotic stuff's the bunk with a smart fighter.

"Bat Brelen," roared the announcer. "Weight, 194; and the well-known fighter, Kid Allison, 179." Then he beats it outa the ring.

"Watch this bird's left," says Abe all in a tremor just before the gong.

"He's got three inches of height on you – maybe more. If you try to box him at long range he'll jab you to a pulp."

"Then I'll work in close and mix it," I said to reassure him, though I needed some reassuring myself.

"Oh, gosh, no!" Abe squalled. "He'll rip you apart infightin'!"

Irritated beyond all self-control, I turned and narrowly escaped becoming a murderer only because Abe ducked my bloodthirsty right by a fraction of a inch. This wowed the multitude, and about that time the gong sounded.

We approached each other warily and as I eyed Bat, who came in half crouching with his chin sunk on his broad and hairy chest and his eyes glaring from under his tousled shock of black hair. I knowed I was in for a rough and bruising mill.

Bat was dirty – a fierce, foul fighter. I knowed he'd blind or cripple me for life if he could. Thank gosh they ain't many fighters like him.

We come in close, fiddling and feinting, and Bat went into a clinch.

"What's your game?" he muttered. "Where do you get this small-time racket?"

"The same thing right back at you," I grunted. "How are you gettin' by – did you forge yourself a boxin' license under the name of Brelen?"

"Listen, you rat," he hissed in my ear, at the same time trying to grind his heel into my instep, "I'm going to carry you for three rounds to give the crowd a run for their money. Then when I come up for the fourth, you better flop!"

"Old stuff!" I sneared. "That line was musty in old John L.'s day."

"Get this, you!" he snarled bloodthirstily, trying his best to shove his thumb in my eye. "I'm Bat Brelen, see? If you spill anything about me, you'll go for a long ride, see? You never saw me before, see?"

"And if I never see you again it'll be plenty soon." I grunted. "As for me betrayin' the secret of your real identity," I says, pulling out of the clinch and casually cocking my left, "I won't have to. They's a newspaperman in the first row which knows you."

He started.

"Where?"

His head involuntarily jerked around and I instantly cracked him on the jaw with a trip-hammer left hook that dropped him flat on his back.

The crowd went wild, and Bat's handlers begun to howl like a passel of hyenas. I dropped back quick to the furtherest corner, watching Bat like a hawk. He got to his all fours, shaking his head, and he was red-eyed with fury and cursing steadily.

I cast a quick glance at Katherine and she was whooping gleefully and threw me a kiss.

Bat coulda got up quicker than he did, but he was cagy and took a count of nine. He come up reeling, and the crowd shrieked for me to go in and finish him.

But you don't catch me that easy. Knowing he was playing fox, I refused to mix it and in a instant Bat abandoned his pretense of grogginess, and with a roar of rage, come in to pulverize me.

He come in fast but wary, because he knowed I could punch, and began feinting with his right. Well, knowing that he wouldn't be fool enough to lead with that hand, I give him a supercilious sneer and stuck a straight left against his mouth.

Infuriated, he lost his head for a second and tore in, wild and wide open, trying to smother me by the weight and fury of his onslaught. But that was pie for me. He run right into a blinding flurry of leather that had him floundering and spitting red in a second.

The blood trickling from his lips seemed to cool him and he steadied hisself and begun to bore in, boxing hard.

Taking advantage of his extra size, he forced the fighting, crowding me close and shooting both hands steadily for head and body. But I was fighting cautious, not tin-canning – because that ain't my style – but keeping elbows close and letting go a punch only when I was reasonably sure of landing.

He kept trying to bull me into a corner where he could hem me in and mash me, but I was too shifty. I kept moving, and didn't give him time to get set. He was a wicked puncher, and I wasn't taking no chances.

Toward the end of the round he got in a hard left hook to the head and a right to the body, but I rocked his head back with a wicked right uppercut and we went into a clinch.

We tied each other up and he tried to nail me on the break, though it was against the rules, but I was watching for it, and I was under his arm and sunk both hands to the midriff, bringing up a hard left to his head as he missed a savage right.

However, just before the gong he slipped my left and rocked me to my toes with a sizzling right cross, following this with a hard left to the body just as the gong sounded.

He come out for the second thinking he had me figured out, and intending to finish things quick, but I wasn't figuring on trading swats with him just yet. I side-stepped his rush and hooked him hard on the ear, getting in a good right to the body as he turned.

That second round was full of action.

Bat was clever, I admit. He had a trick of shooting his left straight to the face, dropping it to the ribs, and then jerking it back up to the jaw in a kind of half-uppercut that nearly finished me the first time he worked it. It staggered me, and his right come in behind it like a pile-driver, but I took it on my shoulder and ripped my right under his heart.

The next time he tried that triple-combination, I was watching. I let him lead to the face and then the body, but instantly shot my left straight to his jaw, beat his uppercut, and set him back on his heels.

After I'd done this a few times, he quit this trick altogether and began trying to feint me into position for a right cross.

But the men which can feint me out is few and far between. I kept my jaw low and my left shoulder hunched every time I jabbed, and his smoking right glanced offa my shoulder. He tried again and again for my solar plexus, too, but I kept my elbows well in.

He had a nice one-two also: a straight left to the face and a straight right to the body, but that was meat for me. I paid little attention to the left, knowing they would be no great force behind it; I just pulled my head a little to one side and at the same instant shot my left to his ribs, beating his right.

I'd done this three or four times when *wham!* Instead of driving for my body, he shot that right up under my arm in a uppercut that tagged my chin and staggered me. Instantly a whistling left hook to the temple flung me back into the ropes and Bat was on me like a blood-mad puma, and the crowd went crazy.

But I'm tough, and I wasn't hurt as much as he thought; I ducked and rode the punches he throwed at me and in spite of the furious efforts he couldn't land a solid swat that mighta ended it.

In a minute of this I seen a opening and smacked Bat on the nose with a neat right that drove him back on his heels with a grunt. Then the gong sounded.

"The mutt's got a slight edge this round," grunted Red Darts.

"Never mind about that," I growled. "They ain't neither of us figurin' on this scrap goin' the limit. Let him stack up the points – I'm out to knock him stiff."

I shot a meaningful glance at Miss Flynn, who nodded vigorously, her lips set in a straight hard line.

As we come out for the third round, he started his one-two again. I was on to him; he wanted to work that trick uppercut on me again.

Again he led lightly for my head, and again I pulled my head aside and started my left for his ribs. But it was just a feint; quick as a flash of light I checked it, dropped my elbow in time to block his swishing uppercut, and banged him solid in the mouth with a smoking right-hand counter.

I went for him silent and deadly like a hunting panther and slashed him right and left for a full five seconds before he managed to close and clinch.

He hung on like a grizzly, his eyes glassy. I cussed and struggled, trying to break away and finish him and the referee just stood and gawped.

Bat's mind was clearing. He turned his head and spat out a mouthful of blood and a shattered tooth, and then he went into action, crafty and foul.

His thumb was gouging murderously at my eyeball, when all of a sudden his knee come up, quick and deadly, against my groin.

I went limp with the sick pain of the foul, and as Bat felt my muscles involuntarily relax, he broke away and hit me hard on the jaw as I crumpled.

I heard Abe and Red Darts and Heinie and the rest of my seconds screaming, "Foul!"

And I seen, through a red mist of agony, Abe holding onto Red who was trying to climb into the ring with a razor in his hand. The crowd was whooping it up. Some of 'em had seen the foul, but not many – Bat was too smooth in his dirty tricks.

I dunno whether the referee seen it or not; I dunno whether he wanted to see it. Anyway, he started counting over me. Maybe, like most of the crowd, he thought Bat had simply floored me with a sock on the jaw.

I reckon I oughta say that I looked down in the ringside seats and seen Katherine, which give me the strength to get up. But the fact is, I was so mad and sick and hurt so, I clean forgot all about Katherine and Sir Galahad and everybody except Bat Worley.

All I thought about was – get up and knock that coyote's head off!

I got up – just how I dunno. It brung out beads of cold sweat all over me, and once I fell down again when I was nearly up, but somehow I made it. I was on my two legs just as the referee opened his mouth to say, "Ten!"

My legs felt dead, and I was groggy and sick, but I wasn't through by a long shot. Bat come down on me like a wolf on the fold and smashed in a short savage left hook that crushed by lips and loosened my teeth.

Maddened by the sight of the blood which streamed down my chin, Bat plunged in hitting so hard and so fast that the air seemed like it was full of flying gloves, but I broke through with a staggering plunge and clinched.

The referee broke us and Bat crossed a sledgehammer right to my ear and I hit the canvas again.

I was purty groggy, but not too much so to notice that Bat stepped across me and took up his position right behind me so he could sock me behind the ear as I got up and gawped around for him.

I shifted about while the referee was counting, and got a grip on Bat's legs-he was standing that close to me – and climbed up him. He raged and complained to the referee, and tried to kick me loose, but I hung on.

I couldn't of got to my feet without pulling myself up by something. I was like a man in a transom – everything was dizzy and dreamy. I couldn't hardly hear the crowd, and the lights looked dim.

I hung on till Bat and the referee together shook me loose, and Bat roared and come at me head-on, swinging a maul-like right for my head. I blocked it, but my feet slipped in a smear of my own blood on the canvas and down I went.

But that was a break for me; I needed a count bad. You got no idea how a few seconds rest will help a groggy fighter. I rested, shaking my head to clear it, while the referee counted, and I could feel my strength surging back and the clouds scattering from my brain.

Again I was up at "Nine!" and this time I clinched before Bat could hit, and neither him nor the referee could tear me loose. Bat cussed and raved and hammered at me, and the referee threatened me and the crowd roared and cussed, but I give 'em all a sneer.

To blazes with them! It was me that was taking the punches, not them. I go in to win my fight, and I don't care whether the crowd likes my style or not.

The gong sounded and I was able to give Bat a sneer as I walked rather uncertainly to my corner. My handlers pounced on me and Abe hollered, "I'm goin' to throw in the sponge; he'll kill you this round."

"The round I'll finish him," I answered as Heinie mopped the blood offa me and Red massaged the back of my neck with ice water and pulled the waistband of my trunks out from my body to give my insides free play.

Abe dropped the sponge in amazement. "You're crazy! You can't hardly stand up even!"

"I'm all right," I grunted. "My recuperative powers has amazed all the sportswriters, and my toughness has broke the hearts of better men than Bat Worley. You ought to know by this time that I never lose my punchin' ability, no matter how bad I'm hurt or how groggy I am.

"Ain't the scribes compared me to old Fitz, account of all the men I've dropped just when they thought they had me? Well, you watch!

"Would Sir Galahad of quit just because some knight hit him below the belt with a battle ax? Bah!"

"He's punch-drunk," says Abe despairingly. "He'll be cuttin' out paper dolls next!"

"Outside for you!" I snapped, sitting up. "They're fixin' to jerk the gong – now's my big chance – Bat'll be overconfident – "

The gong!

I come out slow and hesitatinglike. Bat come out just like I knowed he would – wild for the kill and careless.

That always was one of his greatest faults, and the reason he never won a title. When he scented a kayo, he got reckless and over-confident, and left hisself wide open.

I'd found out something about him.

When he feinted with his left, he swayed his shoulders toward the right, kind of setting hisself for the right-hand blow that was to follow the feint. When he was going to really hit with the left, he didn't sway.

We come together just outside my corner, and I was watching him like a hawk. We fiddled and sparred for a second, and he was wide open in his eagerness to shoot over a haymaker. He stepped in and started his left and

I seen him sway toward the right and knowed it was a feint; and quick as a flash I shot my right, beat his punch by a flashing fraction of a instant and landed square on the button.

Bat hit the canvas like he'd been shot. I'd put everything I had behind that punch, and he was coming full into it as he started his right.

He was so addled he hopped up without a count, when his handlers was yelling for him to take one. I was on him like a bloodthirsty wild cat, and when he tried to fall into a clinch I straightened him with a torrid right uppercut and battered him back across the ring with a shower of sizzling left and right hooks to the head and body.

I floored him almost under the ropes, where he took the count of "nine" before he got up, all at sea, bleeding plenty at the nose and mouth, and from a deep gash in his temple.

Here is where many a fighter makes a bad mistake by tossing everything to the head. I shot both hands to the belly, and Bat, being too groggy to keep his body muscles tensed, went to his knees with a gasp. He staggered up at "nine," ripe for the kill, and I measured him coolly and dropped him with a right to the jaw.

He fell face forward, and I knowed he was through.

As he went down the crowd rose as one and bust into a regular cataract of noise that drownded the count of the referee, but I distinctly heard a woman's scream cut through the din, and it sounded like Katherine.

Abe Garfinkle and my handlers had grabbed me in a second, wrapped my bath robe around me, and was fairly carrying me outa the ring, despite my struggles and profanity, and they carried me clean into my dressing room.

"Get the club physician, Red," said Abe. "I wanta find out just what that foul done to him."

"Lemme down, you mutts!" I hollered. "I gotta go and accept the admirin' plaudits of as fair a rose as ever bloomed on the tree of beauty!"

"He's clean off his bat," said Abe. "Beat it, Red; we gotta get him examined. I think that beatin' he got affected his mind."

Then in comes a figure I knowed.

"Billy Ash!" said Abe. "What you doin' here? Did the *Tribune* send you down to cover the fight?"

"How could they know anything about it?" returned Billy. "They sent me down here to see if I could get a story at the Kid's training camp – naturally, I didn't know anything about the fight until I blew in here tonight.

"But I'll say I've got my story! Kid, are you crazy to fight Battling Worley in a third-rate ring like this – and him suspended, too?"

"I didn't know I was goin' to fight Worley when I agreed to the match," I answered impatiently. "You heard 'em announce him as Bat Brelen. Besides, it was a matter of honor."

"Oh-ho," said Billy, giving me a long look. "A lady, eh? What about your girl friend, Franky Jones?"

"Well, gee whiz," I said in a rage. "Can't a man aid a damozel in distress without some yellow scandal sheet makin' a headline out of it? I ain't tryin' to spark Miss Flynn – I was just avengin' her on that big lout she had the misfortune to fall for once.

"If she's stuck on me, can I help that? I got a fatal fascination for women, I reckon. And look here – they ain't no use in scare-headin' all this. I give Bat what was comin' to him tonight. No need in showin' him up to the public."

"Heh-heh-heh!" said Billy sarcastically. "After what I saw, anything's too good for that yellow, foul-fighting skunk. You think I'm goin' to pass up a story like this? It's the duty of a newspaperman to protect the public interests; I'm goin' to expose Bat Worley as the crook he is."

"All right!" I yelled in a passion of irritation. "ALL RIGHT! Write it up! Show Bat up! Show us all up! Tell 'em Brelen's Worley, and Abe Garfinkle is Napoleon, and you're John L. Sullivan!

"Tell 'em I eloped with Katherine Flynn and the whole Ziegfeld Follies! Get me cooked with the Commission and Jack Reynolds and Franky Jones if you want to, but stand away from that door! I'm goin' to receive my thanks from the grateful maiden I just avenged!"

"I seen her goin' into Bat's dressin' room!" yelped a prelim boy.

Wondering what she was doing there, I hastened down the corridor and pushed into the aforesaid dressing room, heedless of the black looks give me by the handlers and seconds who was working over the still recumbent warrior. To my amazement, Katherine was hovering anxiously over him. She turned as I entered and I seen she'd been crying.

"Why, Miss Flynn," I said solicitously, "you should not weep; your champion has safely avenged your wrongs – "

To my dumfounded amazement she give a howl like a hornet-stung, bloodthirsty tigress.

"You conceited chimpanzee!" she raved, stamping her heels till they sounded like a drum on the floor. "I must have been crazy, framing poor Bat into such a deal!

"I thought I was enjoying it at first, but when I saw you – you cold-blooded murderer – cut the poor boy to pieces and knock him out, I realized what a fool I'd been! I'll never, never forgive myself! Treating poor Bat like that, when all he did was to sort of smack me – he was just playing, anyhow! And I knew in my heart, all the time, he didn't care anything about that peroxide blonde!"

"Well, gee whiz – " I began vaguely, plumb scatter-witted, and she interrupted me with a yell.

"Shut up! Get out of here! I ought to shoot you, you brute! Throw him out, boys!"

The boys hesitated, more especially as Abe, Red, and the rest of my gang came ominously through the door, and Miss Flynn gasped in rage.

"You cowards!" she shrieked, looking about – for that iron-loaded handbag, I reckon. "You won't slug him, eh? You'll let a weak, defenseless girl fight her own battles, will you? A-ha!"

This last exclamation was a yell of triumph as she spied a brickbat and snatched it up. Then, while I stood in utter dumfoundment, kinda frozen, she give that brickbat to me with the full swing of both arms.

Wham!

I was too addled to duck. I still got the scar to prove it.

I come to on a bed up at my training camp, with my head all bandaged · up. The first thing I heard was Abe raving.

"Well," said he, sarcastically, "I hope you like it. Of all the dumb, boneheaded – "

"Where is Miss Flynn?" I asked groggily.

"Her and Bat is departed for parts unknown," snapped Abe. "The last seen of them two love birds, they was billin' and cooin' like a couple of turtledoves. I heard, on good authority, that Bat was headin' for Australia, where he ain't so well known.

"When Billy Ash and the *Tribune* gets through pannin' him, the West Coast is goin' to be just as hot for him as the East is. And Miss Flynn ain't nowhere to be found, neither. Yes, Mr. Allison, your rose of beauty has flew the coop!"

"Shut up!" I roared wrathfully. "Ain't I told you I never did care nothin' about her? Franky Jones's little finger is worth a dozen Katherine Flynns. I licked Bat for the principle of the thing."

Well, the sequence is a telegram I got from Jack Reynolds later. It read:

JUST READ THE ASSOCIATED PRESS STORY OF YOUR FIGHT WITH WORLEY IN A THIRD-RATE CLUB FOR HUNDRED AND FIFTY STOP ARE YOU CRAZY STOP HAD JUST ABOUT GOT YOU MATCHED AT THE GARDEN STOP THIS WILL PROBABLY COOK THE WHOLE DEAL STOP

While Abe was still cussing and whooping about that, another wire come from Jack Reynolds which read:

BILLY ASH DID US A GOOD TURN WHEN HE SPRUNG THAT STORY STOP PAPERS ARE FULL OF YOUR SENSATIONAL KAYO STOP YOU HAVE NO SENSE BUT PLENTY OF FOOLS LUCK STOP GARDEN AGREES TO MATCH YOU AGAINST LOPEZ ON STRENGTH OF YOUR SHOWING AGAINST WORLEY STOP THINK YOU WILL PACK THE HOUSE STOP DONT GET IN ANY MORE JAMS TILL I GET BACK OR I WILL HIT YOU WITH A BRICK

I immediately dictated a answer to Abe Garfinkle for Jack, which went as follows:

I HAVE DONE BEEN HIT WITH A BRICK STOP COME BACK HERE AND HELP ME EXPLAIN THINGS TO FRANKY JONES STOP AND IF YOU MEET A DAME BY THE NAME OF KATHERINE FLYNN START RUNNING AND DONT STOP

Fists of the Desert

A small railroad station, its sun-blistered paint cracking in the heat – across the tracks a scattering of adobe huts, a cluster of frame buildings – that was Yucca Junction, baking in the desert that stretched from horizon to distant horizon.

Up and down, in the scanty, breathless shade of the little station, Al Lyman paced restlessly, his patent-leather shoes grinding dryly in the cinders. A small man, Lyman, with narrow, stooped shoulders; cheap, flashy, a product of city slums. Predatory beak of a nose, gimlet eyes – tinhorn was written all over him.

His meal-ticket lumbered beside him – big Spike Sullivan, well known to the habitues of the Barbary Street A.C. Shoulders like an ox, big hands hanging low, half open like an ape's, matted with stiff black hair. A sullen face, jutting jaw, murky black eyes. He was as incongruous in his present setting as Lyman was. His real name sounded nothing like Sullivan.

He glared around him as he shuffled up and down with Lyman – both men walking because moving was more tolerable in that heat than keeping still. Sullivan scowled at the tiny town across the tracks, at the man just visible inside the waiting room, and at the mongrel dog under a bench beside the wall.

The dog mistook the man's glare. He stretched himself and came from under the bench, wagging his tail. Sullivan cursed him away stormily. At the impact of his angry rumble on the stillness, the man in the waiting room came to the door and surveyed the strangers impersonally.

He was as much a part of the scene as they were alien to it. He was as tall as Sullivan, though lacking something of the pugilist's bulk. But he was clean cut, forged in a mold of sun and desert that had bronzed his skin and stripped all surplus weight from his lean-waisted, thick-chested frame. Tranquilly he folded his massive arms and stared off across the

261

wastes to where, in the distance, the train for which all three were waiting was struggling up a long grade.

The dog trailed after the strangers, dejected, but still hopeful of a pat on the head. Sullivan reached the edge of the shade, turned suddenly and fell sprawling over the surprised canine, rasping his hands on the hot cinders. The dog yelped and scurried out of reach just as Sullivan scrambled up, launching a heavy foot after him. The boot grazed the dog's back and the animal darted under his bench and cowered there. Sullivan rushed at him, all the beast roused in him. He was hardly responsible for his actions – merely a slow-witted, evil-tempered brute who reacted unreasoningly to his chance environment.

"Easy, Spike!" whined Lyman anxiously. "Let the mutt be."

Sullivan paid no heed. Deliberately he drew back his foot to crush in the ribs of the shivering animal, when the man in the doorway took a hand in the game. With no appearance of haste he stepped between Sullivan and the bench, and pushed the man backward, not gently.

"Let that dog alone," he said.

"Is that your mutt?" the fighter snarled, balling his huge fists.

"No, it ain't," answered the desert man. "If it was, I'd throw a hunk of lead through you. As it is – "

Just then Sullivan let go with a right that had murder behind it. Sullivan could hit; any man who is a favorite in the Barbary Street A.C. must be a puncher. The desert man was caught flat-footed. Square on the jaw he took the full drive of Sullivan's murderous right. Lyman yelped and jumped back to let the victim fall clear.

But he did not fall. He reeled backward from the impact, with blood starting from the corner of his mouth. But he kept his feet, and Sullivan, instead of following up, gaped and half lowered his hands with the surprise of it. And that was Sullivan's mistake. The desert man's return was like the strike of a big cat.

Cinders spurted from under the balls of his feet as he hurtled in, and his left fist crunched savagely into Sullivan's ribs. He was wide open; Sullivan's fists slugged home. No man had ever stood up and outslugged him in the Barbary, where the toughest ham-and-eggers of the West Coast display their wares.

The stranger knew nothing of boxing. His blows were swings, but each carried behind it the weight of the broad shoulders and the drive of the muscular thighs. He seemed built of granite and steel. Sullivan's fists tore skin and brought blood, but the man shook them off, redoubling his fury. Desperation grew in Sullivan's eyes as his breath began to whistle between his teeth. No human could take what he was handing out – yet this man was taking it.

An agonized grunt burst from Sullivan as his opponent's left, smashing through his weakening guard, sank wrist-deep in his belly. Involuntarily his hands went down. And for the first time the stranger's mallet-like right exploded square in the prize-fighter's face. Sullivan's features vanished in a flood of crimson. With a groan he staggered, groping; and the stranger threw his right again, as a man throws a hammer.

At its impact Sullivan went down sidewise and lay where he fell. The mongrel crawled from under his bench, whimpering. Inside the click-click of the telegraph was the only sound. The station agent had not left his seat. Impassively he stared through the open window.

"W-who are you?" whispered Al Lyman, tugging at his sweat-soaked collar as if it choked him.

"Kirby Karnes," answered the other briefly, turning to glance down at the shaking manager.

"Are you a fighter?" Lyman seemed to have forgotten Sullivan, lying there on the cinders. "What do you do for a living? Did you ever fight – in the ring, I mean?"

Karnes shook his head.

"I've been dressin' tools in the San Pedro oil field, lately, until they shut down. I'm lookin' for a job now."

"Listen!" urged Lyman excitedly, glancing toward the train, which was chugging up the last grade before it hit Yucca Junction. "You're wasting your talents in an oil field. You know what you've just done? You've flattened Spike Sullivan, one of the toughest eggs on the West Coast! You'd be a sensation in the ring."

"I've fought plenty with bare fists," said the other, unconsciously flexing his thick biceps. "I never thought of fightin' in the ring."

"Let me handle you!" urged Lyman. "You'll make more in a month in Frisco than you'll make in a year hammering drill bits. What do you say?"

Karnes glanced out across the aching emptiness of the desert before he replied.

"I've always wanted to see Frisco," he said at last. "I've got no job, and none in sight. Work's awful scarce now."

"Good!" Lyman almost capered in his delight. "Help me pack this egg into the waiting room." A few seconds later the still-senseless Sullivan was stretched on a bench in the sweltering station. Flies buzzed about his bloody head.

"Come on!" Lyman grabbed Karnes' sleeve. "The train's pulling in, and it only stops a few minutes."

"What about him?" Karnes indicated the recumbent figure.

"Let him lay," yelled Lyman, pulling his find toward the door. "I'm through with the big palooka. Let him go back to the mines, where he belongs. Come on!"

The click of the wheels as they whirled westward was like the rattling clink of falling coins to the ears of Al Lyman. Easy money! The phrase beat a refrain to the clash and rumble of the wheels. A cheapskate de luxe, Al Lyman. Already he had worked out his frame for Kirby Karnes, and it was a typical Lyman set-up. And Karnes, unused to judging men, ignorant of Lyman's type, no more recognized the tinhorn brand than he could foresee the role for which Fate had already cast him.

CHAPTER 2

Fall Guy

Lyman had no trouble getting Kirby Karnes a match at the Barbary. The promoter knew that Lyman's fighters always had *something*. Lyman knew how to cater to the mob. He took care that Karnes' first opponent was not dangerous – a fading veteran who never had much to begin with.

Barbary Street interest was roused, however cynically, for Lyman talked loudly of his "desert tiger's" ferocity and ruggedness.

"He don't know nothin', gents," Lyman proclaimed to the boys. "He don't have to know nothing. He's all rawhide and whalebone, see? Joe Grim was a sissy beside of him! You all seen Spike Sullivan fight. Spike was a bum, but you know he could punch. Well, Spike hits this boy on the button with all he's got, and the fellow don't even blink. I tell you, they can't knock him out!"

Not old Joe Harrigan, at least. Karnes plunged out of his corner at the gong like a desert sandstorm, wide open, fighting the only way he knew. He didn't suppose that ring-war was any different from the fights he had had in the bars and wind-blown streets of the desert towns. The lights, the noise of the crowd bothered him at first, but he forgot all that when the bell shot him out into the ring.

At his best Harrigan had never been much. Now his knuckles were knobs of brittle chalk, the muscles in his legs were rotten cords, and the jolt of a glove against his battered jaw sent waves of blackness across his brain.

For a round he evaded the swirling maulers of Kirby Karnes – jabbed at the brown, grim face before him, ducked the sweeping swings and tied up the desert man in the clinches.

But in the second round Karnes' right, swishing up from the floor, sank deep in Harrigan's midriff, and the old-timer went to his knees, green-faced and gagging, just as the bell ended his torment.

Lyman babbled praise in Karnes' ear, bade him hark to the roar of the fans. What the Barbary crowd wanted was always action – gloves smashing, blood, somebody writhing in the resin. Lyman smirked as they yelled; but in the first row, ringside, a slender man with silvered temples shook his head and muttered under his breath, twisting his lips as though he smelled something repugnant.

Harrigan came up for the third with his belly heaving spasmodically. Karnes rushed and threw his right like a hammer. Harrigan was too weary to duck, too sick to care. The weighted glove only grazed his jaw, but it was enough. Harrigan hit the resin, as he had in his last four fights, and the referee raised Kirby Karnes' arm. The crowd jeered and cheered – jeered because they knew old Joe Harrigan was washed up – but cheered because, after all, Karnes had done what it was his job to do.

"Great stuff, Kirby!" babbled Lyman, throwing a bathrobe about his man's shoulders. "I told you! Fight your natural style. Take all they got and wear 'em down. You don't have to box. Nobody can knock you out."

As the crowd moved out through the doors, one fan nudged another and indicated a slender, silver-templed man making his way toward the street.

"See him? That's John Reynolds. Managed a dozen first-raters. Always hanging around these small clubs, looking for material."

The other, impressed, found himself pushed against the slender man in the crowd, and, admiring his own temerity, spoke: "Well, Mr. Reynolds, how did you like the fights?"

"They were rotten, as usual," answered Reynolds. "Lyman has a good man – but he'll ruin him, as he always does his fighters."

The truth of this prophecy was not at first apparent. Karnes became intensely popular at the Barbary. He could hit and he could take it. That was all Barbary Street asked.

Karnes' ignorance of the game was monumental. He followed Lyman's guidance unquestioningly. He never even knew how much Lyman cheated him when his manager gave him his cut of the purse. He lived in a cheap room not far from the arena, trained in a dingy gym that was built in an old stable. Between fights he worked behind the bar of a beer joint.

A broken-down veteran taught the desert man the simplest rudiments of the game. No more. Lyman did not want Karnes to learn anything. He was capitalizing on his ability to soak up punishment. The less he knew, the more punishment he must absorb, the more highly emphasized must appear his unusual stamina.

"Rush 'em and clout 'em," he instructed. "Nobody can hurt you."

Karnes won his first four or five fights by the k.o. route. Green youngsters and worn-out trail horses could not evade his ferocious charges and hurricane swings. Then they matched him with Jim Harper, who was neither a clumsy kid nor a washed-up ruin. He could box and he could hit. He outpointed Karnes in ten furious rounds. Karnes was not discouraged. Lyman assured him that such setbacks were inevitable to any fighter; all boxers lost fights. Loss of a decision hurt nobody. The main thing was that no knockout should be chalked up against him.

In a rematch, Karnes, pitting raw strength and iron jaw against Harper's superior skill, slugged out a draw by pure ferocity. In that fight the customers for the first time realized the desert man's full stamina and toughness. His ribs were like oak, his jaw like iron. Blows that crushed the bones of other men bounced harmlessly from his steely frame.

And so the exploitation of bone and nerve and muscle began in earnest. They matched him with the hardest hitters that could be persuaded to show their wares in the dingy old Barbary. He dropped decision after decision, his roughhouse style futile against clever men. That did not matter – to the promoter and Al Lyman. His drawing power lay in his iron jaw. The fans did not expect him to win; they turned out to see whether he could weather the storm and finish on his feet. Occasionally he did score a k.o. when some opponent wearied and one of the desert man's hammer-like smashes crashed home.

They billed Kirby Karnes as the man who could not be knocked out. Night after night the roof of the Barbary echoed to the roar of the pack – and under the lights, Kirby Karnes, reeling before some hard-faced slugger with dynamite in his forearms, doggedly keeping his feet and fighting back till the last gong ended his torment.

And night after night John Reynolds sat at the ringside, watching with inscrutable eyes.

At last Lyman, watching his man like a hawk, decided that the time had come to gather in the harvest. They matched Karnes against Jack Miller.

Miller was a better fighter than the general run of those who passed through the portals of the Barbary. Not a headliner, nor a man-killer, but a fair hitter, and clever. None doubted that he would win; the only question was whether he could supply the k.o. which Karnes had so far avoided. Plenty of money – for Barbary Street – was in sight; and considering Karnes' record and Miller's lack of real dynamite, the odds were about three to one that Karnes would finish on his feet.

Before the go, one Big John Lynch held conclave with Al Lyman.

"Remember, Lyman," rumbled Lynch in conclusion, "Karnes flops in the ninth or earlier."

"I'll see to it," promised Lyman. "I've got plenty of my own dough up. Karnes is about washed up. He's taken too many on the chin. Back to the desert for him. Miller might do the job without any help. But I'm taking no chances."

Lyman was shrewd enough to sense Karnes' innate honesty, and to say nothing about the set-up. He kept assuring Karnes that his chance would come, that his best bet was to keep on plugging and await the breaks. Karnes knew that in any job in life a man had to keep plugging. He never doubted his manager. But doubts of his own ability assailed him. He could not realize how ruthlessly he was being exploited.

When he sat in his corner that night, waiting for the bell, he stared idly around the ring at the faces that had grown familiar to him. He saw the lean, keen face of the man he knew vaguely as John Reynolds. He saw the swarthy, brutal face of Big John Lynch, flanked by his hard-jawed henchmen – Steinman, McGoorty, and Zorelli. Lynch was a gambler, almost the boss of Barbary Street.

Across the ring, Jack Miller, lean, hard with corded muscles, a merciless face unmarked except for a dented nose. A man who would never reach the top himself, but over whose form an ambitious fighter must climb. By far the best man Karnes had ever faced.

Lyman fumbled with towels and bucket, glancing furtively toward Big John Lynch, chewing his cigar in the first row. Mechanically Karnes shuffled his feet in the resin dust. This was an old story, now. He despaired of beating Miller. But he would stay the limit. The idea was beginning to crystallize in his mind that that was all he had – an iron jaw. Each man has his niche in life; his was the role of the iron man, fighting not so much to win as to stay the limit. To finish on his feet constituted a victory for him. It was strange – but Lyman said it was so.

The life into which he had plunged was too complicated for the desert man. Blindly he had followed Lyman's guidance. He never even knew what his purse was. It seemed consistently small. He wondered dully about that now. Of late he had found it difficult to think straight. At times he seemed to be moving in a fog, and often there was a throbbing at the base of his brain. It was harder to shake off the numbing paralysis of squarely landed blows than it had once been. He passed his gloved hand absently over his thickened ears. Already he was marked like a veteran. A revulsion shook him. A man must start at the bottom in any game – but he seemed fated to remain at the bottom. He shook himself and came erect at Lyman's quick warning.

The gong brought him out of his corner in a rush that carried him straight across the ring. The roar of the throng was a familiar thunder in his battered ears. Karnes! Karnes! Karnes! The man they can't knock out!

Miller smiled coldly. He'd met iron men before. He was more dangerous to them than a man-killer was. Wear him down with an endless stream of jabs and hooks. Make him miss and sweat. Don't kill yourself trying to knock off his block with one haymaker.

Miller backed away, stabbing. Karnes crowded in. Miller didn't make the mistake of trying to prop Karnes off with the left. He drifted before the onslaught, shooting his jab on the run. Karnes' swings looped around his neck; in close he hammered away at the slugger's body. Nobody had ever taught Karnes anything about infighting. He could only grab Miller awkwardly and hold on till the referee broke them. His belly muscles were like rigid steel cords under Miller's knuckles. Miller grunted. This boy would take a lot of wearing down.

Round after round Karnes surged in, his fighting spirit undimmed. When he landed Miller felt those lashing swings clear to the end of his toes. But few licks landed. Miller was fighting a heady fight, pouring a steady hail of lefts and rights to Karnes' head and body. Blood trickled from Karnes' nose; his face lacked some skin. Otherwise he was unmarked and breathing easily. He looked a cinch to finish on his feet, at the end of the seventh.

Big John Lynch took his cigar from his thick lips and nodded ponderously to Lyman. Lyman's hand snaked into his hip pocket, came out with a small flask. Karnes' stupid-faced second held a towel so it masked the fighter from the crowd. Under this cover Lyman fumbled for Karnes' lips.

"Drink this!" he hissed.

Karnes drank without question. It was his manager's orders. The liquid had an aromatic tang that was unpleasant. He grunted, spat, started to speak – the gong banged.

Karnes started up and was almost in Miller's corner before he realized that something was amiss. The lights seemed to waver, and while he blinked, puzzled at this phenomenon, Miller's left hook swished to his jaw.

Karnes reeled back into the ropes – rebounded from them and waded in. He kept shaking his head, feeling as if a glove were still jammed against his jaw. His feet dragged. His arms lacked their spring. His brain was clouded. Dumbly he groped for understanding. That punch had been hard, but no harder than many he had shaken off. There was something the matter with him.

He was wilder than ever. To the crowd this seemed merely the result of Miller's cleverness, but Karnes knew better. Something ailed him – something that tied up his muscles and misted his vision. Miller sensed the change in his foe, but was wary. This might be a trick. He took no chances. He worked his long, sharp-shooting left hand in Karnes' face like a piston, but kept his right cocked. Karnes was on his feet at the bell.

Back in his corner, Lyman glanced toward Big John Lynch, glowering and chewing his cigar savagely. Lyman bent over the fighter.

"How do you feel, Kirby?"

"Queer," muttered Karnes. "What was that you gave me to drink?"

"Just a little brandy and water," lied Lyman. "You looked wilted. Must of been something you ate."

"I'll stay the limit!" Karnes lurched to his feet. "They can't knock me out – "

They can't knock me out – the thought beat in Karnes' numb brain as he reeled and staggered, bloody and battered, before merciless fists. Miller, sensing his condition at last, unleashed his full fury. They can't knock me out. The crowd thundered the refrain to the roof; louder than their roar it cried out in his dizzy brain. He must stay the limit. It was his one bid for glory in a life bitter with failure. He must keep his feet, though those agonizing fists that rained ceaselessly upon him tore his brain loose from his skull, though the very roof crashed down on him – he must finish on his feet.

Back in his corner, limp on his stool, he saw Al Lyman's face, white in the arc-lights.

"Quit, Karnes, quit!" Lyman begged over and over, his voice sounding as if from far away. "For God's sake, take it on the chin and flop!"

It would do no good to throw in the sponge. Bets were laid on a ten-count k.o. The referee would not stop the fight, knowing Karnes' reputation. Lyman was caught in his own trap.

"I'm all right," mumbled Karnes through bloody lips. "I'll stay the limit. They can't knock me out."

Clang of the gong and thunder of the crowd. Crunch of knuckle-loaded leather, sweat in pain-misted eyes. And Kirby Karnes, keeping his feet in spite of hell and high water.

Karnes had but one defense. In his extremity he simply wrapped his arms about his head, crouching. It was pitifully inadequate. Miller knifed uppercuts between his arms, looped smashes over his ears. When he unwound with swiping swings they cut empty air and Miller's leather-guarded knuckles were like knives against his flesh. The gong found him on the floor, fighting frantically for his feet.

His handlers dragged him to his corner, dumped him onto his stool. Lyman was wild with rage and fright. But the second shook his head.

"He can't last half a round," said he. "Nobody could."

"They can't knock me out," mumbled Karnes. The crowd's roar was a distant echo. The light of the ring was a bloody mist. Jack Miller was a white blur, armed with weighted bludgeons. The gong was a faint tinkle, somewhere on the other side of the universe.

Drunkenly he lurched up, rolled out into the ring. Miller was on him like a panther, afire for the kill.

Karnes, bent in a half crouch, fighting back spasmodically, felt Miller's blows only as dull impacts that no longer hurt his frozen nerves. He had reached that dangerous point where a man must be killed to be stopped – and where he wavers perilously close to the deadline. A few more rounds and the career of Kirby Karnes might have ended forever.

But it was only a ten round bout. And when the gong ended it, a disheveled, bloody figure swayed upright in the center of the ring-beaten and yet invincible. Karnes collapsed in his corner as the crowd filed out, cheering him to the last echo, booing the disgusted, exhausted Miller, as crowds will.

Kirby Karnes seemed floating in a gray mist. Faintly he remembered staggering to his dressing room, supported by his seconds. He lay on the rubbing table while somebody looked for the club physician, who was out of the way somewhere, as was usual in the Barbary.

But his incredible vitality was already asserting itself. He wondered dully why Al Lyman shivered as if with an ague. Lyman started convulsively as the door lurched inward under the impact of a heavy boot. Big John Lynch shouldered in, followed by his henchmen, and Big John's face was like a thunder cloud.

"Scram!" he mouthed at the hangers-on, and they scurried out in stumbling haste. Lyman made as if to follow them, but Big John's beam-like arm barred his way.

"You dirty, double-crossin' rat!" he said, and Lyman shriveled. "You'd fix it! Yes, you fixed it! And I lose three grand! You – "

"Don't John!" screamed Lyman. "I tried to make him quit! Honest to God, I did! Didn't I, Karnes? Didn't I keep telling you to quit?"

"Yes, you did," mumbled Karnes, his muddled brain not understanding.

"You see?" chattered Lyman. "I gave him the dope, too. You saw me give it to him. It just wouldn't work on him. He ain't human – "

An open-handed slap sent him staggering across the room. Karnes painfully hauled himself to his feet. He didn't know what this was all about. His head whirled and the lights wavered. But nobody could knock his manager around that way. Nobody –

"So you was the smart boy that crossed us!"

Big John struck out unexpectedly. The blow was clumsy, but heavy. Karnes reeled back against the table, and Zorelli struck him from behind with a blackjack. Karnes sagged, trying to fight back. To his dizzy brain it seemed that he was in the ring again, trying to stave off the rushing tide of blackness. But this time it would not be denied. Blackjacks, fists and gun barrels beat down upon him. Big John's furious voice bellowed orders. A back door crashed back against the wall. Through it a bleeding, senseless form was hurled, to lie motionless in the dust of the alley.

CHAPTER 3

Law of the Desert

John Reynolds sat beside the dingy bed in the drab little room where Kirby Karnes lay. A week had passed since the night of the Miller fight, and Karnes' face was still scarcely recognizable. Only a man of rawhide and steel could have recovered from the double beating he had received.

"Lyman been around to see you?" asked Reynolds casually.

A scornful grunt was his only answer.

"I thought not." Reynolds was silent for awhile, and then he said, abruptly: "I've been watching you for months. It was none of my business, but I hate to see a good man ruined. Lyman's a cheap crook, and a fool. All he could see in you was a chance to make a few dirty dollars."

"And what do you see in me?" asked Karnes cynically.

"Everything. Speed, guts, punch. You could learn. You do everything wrong now. Lyman taught you nothing."

"He taught me one thing," Karnes answered grimly. "He taught me what kind of a game this is."

"You can't judge a whole profession by a few rats hanging around the fringe. You've never met the real men of the ring. Let me handle you! You've got a future before you."

Karnes' laugh was not pleasant to hear.

"That's what Lyman was always tellin' me. Then he doped me and sold me out to Lynch. I was so dizzy after the fight it took me days to dope it out, but I got it at last. I never had anything but an iron jaw. Lyman built me a reputation on that, just so he could make a haul by framin' me for a k.o."

"That sounds like Lyman. But you've got more than an iron jaw. It was Lyman's fault that you never got anywhere."

"It'll be my fault if I stay in this racket," growled Karnes. "I'm goin' back to the desert, where I belong – after I've settled this score."

Reynolds paled at the red glare of Karnes' eyes.

"Don't try that!" he begged. "They're not worth getting into trouble over. Come in with me. I'll make something out of you."

"A bigger sap than Lyman made out of me," answered Karnes roughly. "Get out of here. I don't want to talk to anybody that looks like a fight manager. What I do is my own business."

Reynolds started to speak, then rose and left the room silently. Karnes rose and dressed himself, moving stiffly. From among his scanty belongings he took a blue-barreled .45. This he thrust into the waistband of his pants, under his coat. His battered face was grim as that of a craven image, his eyes bleak.

A few moments later he emerged into the dingy street. He walked hurriedly down it a few blocks, then turned into an alley. The slink of a stalking panther was in his walk now. At the other end of that alley there was the back door of a speakeasy where Big John Lynch and his mob hung out.

But as he stepped into the alley, a figure moved out from the wall and confronted him. It was Reynolds.

"I thought you'd come this way," said Reynolds. "I've seen the killer look in men's eyes before. Give it up, Karnes. You'll only land in the chair. I tell you, it's not worth it."

"Where I come from," said Karnes somberly, "there's only one answer to the deal they gave me. Get out of my way."

Karnes threw out an arm to brush him aside, but Reynolds grabbed it and hung on with surprising strength. Karnes tried to shake him off, unwilling to hurt him. In the scuffle his coat fell back, revealing the ivory stock of the gun. Reynolds caught at it, dragged it from Karnes' belt, tried to throw it over the board fence. Karnes grabbed at it, swearing, twisted it out of Reynolds' clinging fingers. Somebody's thumb slid over the hammer, unavoidably, pulling the fanged head back. There was a crashing report, a burst of smoke, and then Karnes stared stupidly at Reynolds on the ground, white-faced, blood gushing from his leg.

A policeman ran into the alley, shouting. Reynolds reached up and jerked the gun from Karnes' hand before the cop saw.

"What is this?" demanded the officer. "What happened?"

"An accident," panted Reynolds. "I was showing Karnes my gun and I shot myself in the leg."

Karnes opened his mouth – closed it at the look Reynolds gave him. He dropped beside the wounded man and made a tourniquet of his belt, while the cop ran to a phone box.

Days later Karnes sat beside the bed where John Reynolds lay. Karnes fumbled his hat, glancing sidewise at Reynolds' right leg, which ended in a bandaged stump. The heavy bullet, crashing downward through the thigh, had severed arteries, splintered the bone beyond repair. To save John Reynolds' life they had taken off his leg above the knee.

Reynolds stared at the ceiling, his thin face tranquil. There was no tremor in his hands when he moved them on the sheets.

"What are you goin' to do?" Karnes blurted out, his voice like a physical impact on the silence of the little hospital room.

"I've saved a little," answered Reynolds.

"Not very much. I've been findin' out about you. You're square. You ain't like Lyman. I might've known. You've managed a lot of good men, but you ain't got nothin' to show for it. You gave away all your dough. And now – I'm responsible for this. I don't know how to repay."

"If you want to do anything for me, forget Lynch and Lyman," responded Reynolds. "You wouldn't bother hating a rat because it bit you, would you?"

"All right, I won't touch 'em. But that ain't nothin'. If you still want to manage me – well, you don't need a leg to manage a fighter. I'd like to fight for you, if you still want me to. I don't want a cent, except just what it takes to live on. You can have all the rest I make. I'm no boxer, but they can't knock me out – "

A rare smile lit Reynolds' pain-lined face. His hand reached out, closed on bronze fingers.

CHAPTER 4

Rungs of the Ladder

Seven months later John Reynolds, walking a little awkwardly on his artificial leg, came to the matchmaker of the Golden Glove.

"As a favor, Bill," he said, "match my boy Kirby Karnes with Jack Miller."

"Karnes?" scowled Bill Hopkins. "Isn't he that palooka that Lyman used to feed to the lions every week down at the Barbary? Why, John, that fellow is no good."

"He is now," answered Reynolds. "I knew he had the stuff from the start. All he needed was proper coaching. I sat in a wheelchair in my gym and taught him the game from the ground up, with some first-class sparring partners. He never knew there was that much science in boxing, and Lyman had made him believe he couldn't learn anything. Learn? He took to it like a duck to water.

"He was nearly punch-drunk when I got him, but he's sound as a steel bolt now. He's ready for anything. A bit green, yes; but all he needs now is experience. He's fast. He can box. He can hit. He's what I've dreamed of for years. None of my other boys quite made the grade. But at last I've got a champion in the making. As a favor to me, put him on."

"All right, John." Bill's voice was gentle as he reached for a phone. He didn't look toward Reynolds' leg, but it wasn't difficult to guess what he was thinking. Hard lines for a man to just miss his goal, all his life, and then be crippled as old age approached. That fight with Miller would be in the nature of a benefit for John Reynolds.

Miller did not particularly relish the match. His failure to stop Karnes still rankled. This time, he swore, he would walk in from the first bell and trade swats with the punch-drunk tramp. Why John Reynolds, a wise hombre, wanted to pick an also-ran like Karnes out of the ash-heap was more than Miller could understand, and he said so, vindictively.

The Golden Glove, with its clean, modern dressing rooms, was like a dream to Kirby Karnes, used to the dingy, musty-smelling dens of the Barbary. There was a subtle difference about everything. It wasn't merely that the crowd was bigger. It seemed cleaner. Men and women of prominence and prosperity occupied the ringside. Kirby Karnes breathed deeply, feeling like a man coming into his own at last.

Reynolds, leaning against the corner of the ring, patted his glove.

"The first rung on the ladder, boy!" he said. Karnes smiled faintly. It was the first time anyone in Frisco had ever seen him smile. Across the ring Miller scowled and sneered. The gong!

Karnes came swiftly out of his corner, not in a wide-open rush, but sliding smoothly in a half-crouch. Miller came at him like a hornet, then hesitated, backed up. There was a change in Karnes that puzzled him – a dynamic certitude. Memory of that silver-templed man in Karnes' corner roused caution in Miller's wary mind.

Karnes glided in, perfectly poised. Miller poked out a long left. Karnes exploded into breath-taking action. In a blur of speed he was inside that extended arm and his right ripped under Miller's heart. The impact of the blow brought the crowd to its feet. Miller gasped, stiffened. Karnes' left swished up to his jaw, loaded with dynamite. The desert man was not swinging now, his punches were short hooks, blinding in speed, explosive in effect.

Miller swayed forward, his knees buckling, but before he could fall a right hook to the chin pitched him backward to the canvas, out cold. In their clamorous acclaim the crowd hardly noticed the main event that followed.

It was the boxing world's introduction to Kirby Karnes, the new star cast in an old-time mold. Into a dizzy world of jazz, cocktails, and fallen idols had come a breath out of the past, a fighting man who believed his proper business was fighting.

Turn back the years and look at him. Kirby Karnes! A bronze barbarian from the desert, surcharged with the speed of a panther and the devastating fury of a sandstorm.

Kirby Karnes was John Reynolds' masterpiece. Into his making went all the hard-won experience of the old master. Shades of old-time champions stalked with Karnes across the resined ring – shades of the days when boxing was an art, not a burlesque show.

Emerging from obscurity, Karnes blazed like a meteor across the fistic heavens. Sportswriters hailed him as a fighting man who *fought*. While the heavyweight champion was enacting the role of a Broadway butterfly, Kirby Karnes was battling his way up the long, hard trail that leads through the resin dust rings under the blazing white lights.

He was known no longer as an iron man – not that he was less rugged than of old, but because he no longer need depend on his toughness. Under John Reynolds' coaching he had become a boxer. Illusive as a ghost, quick as a cat, with TNT in either hand, Kirby Karnes was the fighter of which managers have dreamed in vain since the days of Jem Figg.

Within a year from the night he knocked out Jack Miller, he had fought his way up through the ranks – eighteen fights, eighteen knockouts, and not a set-up among them! – and only one man stood between him and the champion. Diego Lopez. A caveman, this giant from Honduras. Not clever, but strong as a bull, with a right fist like a lead-weighted club. While Karnes was mowing them down on the West Coast, Lopez was clubbing the best men of the East into senseless pulps.

That the two should meet was inevitable. The cartoon by Ledgren, the dean of sportswriters, presented the situation well: Karnes and Lopez each standing amidst a heap of senseless figures that represented the foremost contenders, glaring at one another across the continent.

The go was looked upon almost as a title fight. The champion must meet the winner, and everybody knew that either man was more than a match for the titleholder, who, since winning the crown, had done his training in night clubs.

The big clubs of Chicago and New York bid for the match, but it went to a smaller one – the Golden Glove, which was John Reynolds' way of repaying Bill Hopkins for a favor.

The papers headlined the match, and down in the dingy alleys that flank Barbary Street, certain tinhorns put their heads together and muttered beneath their breath, like rattlers, coiling and hissing together among the weeds.

CHAPTER 5

Ghosts of the Past

It was the evening of the fight. The boxers had weighed in that afternoon – Karnes 196, Lopez 210. Physicians had pronounced them in perfect shape.

Now, in the lull before the fight, Karnes sat alone in a back room of his training quarters, reading. He and Reynolds had plenty of money now, but their tastes were simple. He still trained in a gym a few blocks from the Golden Glove. And he liked to relax a few hours before the fight. Up in the front part of the building his handlers and seconds and sparring partners were shooting craps or clowning for the reporters. Reynolds was due any minute from the club.

A knock sounded at the back door.

"Come in," Karnes called, frowning slightly. That would not be Reynolds.

A figure entered hesitantly – a slight figure in cheaply flashy garb. Karnes stared in silence, memories of a sordid past oozing over him sickeningly.

"Well?" he demanded harshly. "What do you want?"

Al Lyman licked his lips. A green pallor underlay his pasty skin.

"Big John Lynch sent me," he stammered.

"Well?"

"They've got Reynolds!" blurted Lynch, bringing it all out in a rush. "They snatched him off the street an hour ago!"

"*What?*" Karnes was on his feet.

"Wait, Kirby!" begged Lyman, dodging away. "It wasn't my idea. Lynch had got me in a spot. He's gone clean bad in the last year. If I squawked he'd bump me off. Lynch is sinking all his dough on Lopez, and he's working for a ring of big gamblers, who want to see Lopez go in there against the champion next fall.

"So Lynch says for you to take a dive in the fifth, or they'll bump Reynolds off. They'll do it, too, Kirby. If you spill it to the cops, they'll take it out on Reynolds. If you do like they say, they'll send Reynolds back OK after the mill. They know you won't squeal to the cops then. That'd be to admit that you took a dive."

Karnes stood silent. This was like a foul, evil breath out of the past. He had not forgotten Lynch and the score against him. His memory was that of the desert, which never forgives. But for John Reynolds he had put his smoldering hate aside. Rage surged up in Kirby Karnes so deep and hot that it did not show in his eyes, nor sound in his voice.

"Could I come and talk this over with Lynch?" he asked.

"Sure," Lyman agreed. "Lynch said you could come, alone. He figured you might want to. Don't hold it against me, Kirby. I don't even know where they've got Reynolds. Honest I don't. Come on. My car's outside."

By back streets and alleys they came to that speak where Lynch hung out, in the alley of which a bullet had wrecked John Reynolds' leg. Karnes' big hands clenched into knobby mallets, the skin over the knuckles showing white. He did not speak as he followed Lyman into a back room.

Big John Lynch sat in a chair near a desk, dark, gross as ever, chewing the inevitable cigar. Behind him stood Zorelli, his right hand in his coat pocket. Lyman mopped his forehead with a shaky hand.

"Here he is, John," he offered.

"I can see that, you fool," grunted Lynch. "Shut that door."

"Where's Reynolds?" Karnes demanded.

"You don't see him, do you?" asked Lynch sardonically.

Karnes shook his head, sweeping the room with his eyes. He fumbled his hat, turning it round and round in his hands. His eyes crossed the floor, lingered briefly on the rug upon which stood the legs of Lynch's chair.

"He's where you nor the cops won't never find him," said Lynch, pointing his cigar at Karnes. "Don't try no funny stuff. Zorelli's got a rod trained on you right now. Lyman gave you the lowdown. Are you going to play ball with us?"

"Looks like I'll have to," muttered Karnes. Lynch exhaled gustily in satisfaction and tilted back his chair on its hind legs, feeling in his vest pocket for a cigar. Karnes dropped his hat. It fell on the rug. Karnes bent, reached for it – gripped the edge of the rug and heaved. Lynch went over backward with a bellow, catapulting into Zorelli, bearing him down with him. Karnes was into the heap instantly, with the silent fury of a berserk tiger.

Zorelli heaved up, tugging at the gun which had stuck in the lining of his pocket. He fired once through the cloth as Karnes plunged on him, then threw up his right arm as a guard, and lunged low with a knife in his left hand.

Karnes felt a stinging pain above the groin, and then his mallet fists beat down the Italian's guard, smashed him senseless to the floor.

Lyman had bolted out down the alley. Lynch floundered up, waving a pistol. It had been years since Lynch had done his own fighting. He was slow, awkward. Before his fumbling thumb could find the safety catch of the automatic, Karnes gripped his thick hairy wrist and twisted it savagely, a cold grin of hate writhing his thin lips.

Something snapped like a breaking stick, and Lynch bellowed. The pistol clattered on the floor, Lynch turned green; he retched, sagging in Karnes' merciless grip.

Voices sounded outside the door.

"What's the row, boss? Are you OK?"

"Tell 'em to scram," Karnes muttered. "Tell 'em, before I twist your arm off."

"Beat it!" howled Lynch, his eyes bloodshot with the pain of his broken bone. "Get away from that door, damn it!"

The voices receded, muttering.

"Where's Reynolds?" demanded Karnes.

All the fight had gone out of Big John Lynch.

"McGoorty and Steinman have got him," he groaned.

Karnes dragged Lynch up, slammed him down in a chair by the desk where the phone stood.

"Get McGoorty, quick!"

Sobbing with pain, Lynch dialed a number with a shaky finger.

The voice that came back over the phone was audible to Karnes, stooping close.

"Tell him to bring Reynolds back to the gym," muttered Karnes. "Tell him to put him out at the door, unharmed."

Lynch cringed away from the wrath in Karnes' eyes.

"McGoorty!" he bawled into the mouth-piece. "The snatch is off! Take Reynolds back to his gym and let him go. Yes, I know what I'm talking about. Damn you, don't you argue with me!"

"OK," the voice came plain to Kirby Karnes, puzzled, disgusted but resigned. "I'll do it. Right now."

Karnes dialed the gym. To a surprised sparring partner he spoke briefly: "When Reynolds gets there, all of you go on to the Golden Glove. I'll be there right away. Yes, Reynolds is on his way to the gym now."

He looked down for a moment at the great, gross figure moaning in the chair, and then without a word he turned and went into the alley.

Blood was trickling down his leg. In the light of an arc, inside the alley mouth, he investigated. Zorelli's bullet had missed, but not his knife. Karnes' trousers and underwear were soaked with blood which oozed from a gash just above where the groin meets the belly. It looked deep – felt deep. With each step he took the wound gaped and more blood spilled.

Turning, he walked quickly and with purpose through the alley and into a little, dimly-lighted side street. There he knocked on a certain door. A voice answered him.

"Doc Allister!" he called. "Let me in, quick!"

The physician stared at Karnes, surprised at his presence, not at his wound. Such things were common on Barbary Street.

"Don't waste time," said Karnes hurriedly, throwing off his blood-soaked clothes. "Get busy. I'm due in the ring within the hour."

"Why man, you can't fight with a gash like that in your body!" Allister expostulated.

"I want to borrow some of your clothes, too," said Karnes. "I'd have every reporter in town on his ear if I showed up in these bloody rags."

CHAPTER 6

Showdown

Reynolds was fidgeting with nervousness in the dressing rooms of the Golden Glove when Karnes entered.

"You're all right? They didn't hurt you?"

"No, no!" exclaimed Reynolds, impatiently brushing aside his own experience, which was still a mystery to him. "What about you? Where have you been? What happened? You look pale."

"I was worried about you," answered Karnes, beginning to shuck his shoes. "I'll give you the whole yarn later. Chase everybody out of here till I get dressed. Get out there and chin with the reporters. We don't want a scandal."

With the room to himself, Karnes hurriedly got into his togs, noticing with relief that his trunks hid the neat bandage Doc Allister had strapped over his wound. Donning his bathrobe, he opened the door. Handlers, seconds and newspaper men swarmed in. Karnes hardly heard their babble. He sat like an image, hoping that the time would pass swiftly. He felt Reynolds' gaze on him, with a curious hunger. The old master was nearer to his dream of a title now than he had ever been. He wondered what would prevent it this time. Repeated failure had instilled fatalism in him.

A newspaper man blurted out: "Odds are four to three on Karnes. The boys are banking on his footwork. He'll outstep Lopez."

Reynolds nodded. "His footwork will win the title for us."

Karnes bent his head; under the bandage that none could see the raw wound ached. The door flew open. Somebody yelled: "All right, Karnes! Let's go!"

Karnes moved up the aisle between the yelling human masses, stepping slow and leisurely. He did not bound into the ring as Lopez did. He crawled carefully through the ropes.

Lopez was already in the ring, a giant of bone and muscle. A great hairy chest, heavy brows which overhung small glittering black eyes; a shock of tangled black hair. He looked the caveman, all right. While the referee instructed them in the center of the ring, he glared at Karnes like a wild man. Back in their corners again, and the crowd tense, waiting.

"Box him, boy!" Reynolds' voice was urgent in Karnes' ear. "Keep stepping. Fight as we planned it."

Karnes did not reply, remembering long hours spent in planning this fight, with carefully chosen sparring partners and moving pictures of Lopez' fights.

The gong! Lopez roared across the ring like a hurricane, right hand ready.

The crowd roared in amazement. Karnes did not glide out to meet the attack in his swift, easy illusive stance. He took a few steps forward, crouched – met the hurtling onslaught squarely.

All the experts looked to see him sidestep, spring in again like a panther to rip lefts and rights into a man off-balance. He did nothing of the sort. He ducked under the downward flailing right, edged in close and began to smash away at the Honduran's midsection. This was meat for Lopez. A roaring rumble of gratification rose from his throat. At last, a man who would stand up to him. His ponderous right began to whirl like a flail, crashing and thundering.

Behind his corner, Reynolds stood frozen, unable to believe what his senses told him. He had drilled into Karnes that his footwork was his best bet against the ponderous Honduran. And now Karnes had abandoned any attempt at footwork, was standing still and trading punches with the foremost man-killer of the age.

Not that he was fighting wide open. With superlative skill he was ducking, blocking, riding with the punches. But they showered on him so thickly and terrifically that he could not avoid all of them. Blood trickled from his nose, oozed from cuts on his scalp. At the gong the delirious broadcaster shouted to radio listeners all over the continent that Lopez had taken that round by a wide margin, that Karnes had apparently gone crazy.

In Karnes' corner Reynolds was pleading frantically, a bewildered, grief-stricken man who looked suddenly old.

"Kirby, for God's sake, box him! Fight as we planned!"

Karnes sank his face in his gloves to shut out the pain in Reynolds' stare.

Back in the ring again, he ducked his head, crouched and smashed away at the huge, hairy torso before him. Lopez' matted muscles were like ridges of iron. Karnes' murderous left hooking up from below rocked the Honduran's head back.

But Diego Lopez was not to be felled by one blow from any man. He roared and came lashing back like a typhoon. His right was a constant threat of destruction. He whirled it like a war club, threw it like a hammer. Its thunderous impact against Karnes' head or body resounded all over the house, and John Reynolds winced with each impact. Between rounds he worked over Karnes. His lips moved soundlessly; his face was ashen. Why was this fighter taking punishment he could avoid so easily?

Karnes could not change his tactics. He had fought this far along the ladder according to Reynolds' instructions; this fight he must fight in his own way.

Blood was in his eyes, the salt of blood in his mouth. He staggered to the impact of that thunderous right hand, but all the time he was slashing back, and he could see pain growing in the eyes of the giant. A fierce joy surged in him. Again he was the iron man, fighting his old fight, pitting his toughness against dynamite in loaded gloves. Blood was oozing through his trunks, but there was so much blood on both men that no one noticed.

Before the gong opened the fifth, Reynolds made a late desperate appeal.

"Kirby, for God's sake, snap out of it! Are you throwing me down?"

Karnes lowered his head. The crowd groaned to see him shuffle out and resume his crouching stance. The torturing grind began once more.

That destruction-weighted right had reduced the side of Karnes' face and head to a pulp. He knew he had at least one broken rib, that his left side was raw beef. But he had not been merely taking it; he had been handing it out – savage, slashing hooks that ripped and crushed.

Smash, smash, smash! Four gloves flashing past each other, ripping savagely into quivering flesh. The experts said no man could stand up and trade punches with Diego Lopez. What did the experts know of the Barbary, and the man who served his apprenticeship there? Time rolled back to Kirby Karnes, to a smokier, dingier ring, a fiercer crowd. Again he was the iron man, staking all on his granite jaw, his oaken ribs. They can't knock him out! It seemed the rafters shook with the roar.

And now Karnes saw, through the blood and mist, a look growing in the eyes of Lopez – the same desperate look he had seen so often in the eyes of the men he had fought in the Barbary. Lowering his head, he slugged away with full body-drive behind each punch, iron fists sinking deeper and deeper in the Honduran's flesh. Lopez reeled back, spattering blood and roaring – rallied and flailed back. Karnes straightened from his crouch, hooking for the head, and missed. That clubbing right ripped in, low. Karnes distinctly felt the tearing of his own flesh. Blood cascaded down his thigh and a gasp of amazed horror rose from the crowd. The dumfounded referee sprang forward, but before he could interpose, Karnes sprang like a panther. Caution to the winds now, everything staked on one blasting plunge.

He did not heed the knifing agony in his side. He did not heed the bludgeoning right, falling weaker and weaker upon him. He fought as he fought of old, like a wild man, with fury and destruction behind every smashing blow. Dazed by the whirlwind he had loosed, the giant reeled backward, his eyes glazing, his knees buckling, vainly striving to fight back.

Left to the head, right to the head – left, right – in a constant stream, and each loaded with dynamite – and one last terrible hook ripping up from Karnes' right hip, with every nerve and sinew and muscle behind it – and there was Diego Lopez motionless on the canvas, his shaggy head in a pool of blood.

Time rolled back again to the Barbary and a gory, terrible figure fighting to keep his feet – "Ten!" tolled out the referee, and Kirby Karnes toppled headlong across the body of the man he had conquered.

The first voice he heard was that of Reynolds, and it shook with horror: "Good God, that wound! It's been sewed up, and that body blow Lopez landed tore out the stitches. Kirby! Kirby! Why didn't you tell me?"

The battered lips grinned.

"You wouldn't have let the fight go on. That's why I stood still and slugged; had to crouch to protect that wound, and was afraid if I stepped around too brisk, I'd tear it open again. I'm all right. Don't look so sick. You're goin' to manage a champion yet. They can't knock me out!"

They Always Come Back

"Three years ago you were the foremost heavyweight contender – now you're a whiskey-soaked tramp in a Mexican saloon!"

The voice was hard and rasping, with a bitter contempt that cut like a knife. The man to whom the words were addressed flinched and blinked his liquor-reddened eyes.

"And what business is that of yours?" he demanded roughly.

"Just the fact that I hate to see a man make a hog of himself – just because I hate to see a man with championship material in him lying around in a one-horse border village!"

They made a strange contrast, those two, and the loafers and Mexicans who lounged in the rear end of the 'dobe saloon eyed them curiously. The man who lolled half across the beer-stained table was young, and in spite of his ragged garments his athletic frame was evident. His face was not a bad face, in spite of the lines of wild dissipation. The face was surprisingly finely molded, with a thin-bridged regular nose that spoke of good blood. About the mouth there was a sign of weakness, at first glance. A second glance showed a keen observer that it was a sensitive mouth, rather than a weak one – an index to a certain flaw in the character that was erratic and unstable rather than bad.

The man who stood looking down on the other was a slender, wiry man of more than middle age. His lips were thin and straight, his nose beak-like, his eyes hard and bitter. He was dressed in a manner costly but plain, and seemed out of place in this sordid dive.

"Three years ago," continued his inexorable voice, "you were touted for the next heavyweight champion. Jack Maloney – a classy boxer and a terrible puncher. The man with the mallet right! You slashed through opposition like a second Dempsey. Starting at eighteen, you cleaned up your division and at the age of twenty-one, you were beating at the doors of the title. Twenty-one! An age at which most men are fighting in the preliminaries for ten dollars a round. And you were drawing down the thousands. In three years you came up from nowhere. You were fast as a cat, keen, brainy, and tough. You hit like the blow of a caulking mallet. You were wined, dined, and petted as the favorite of society – the classy pride of the ring!

"Then what happened? You were matched with Iron Mike Brennon, then an unknown. He stopped you in three rounds. You went all to pieces. You lost your guts. You were knocked out in your next start by Soldier Handler, a hard-hitting second-rater. Then you quit the ring; disappeared. You went to the gutter. You'd lost your nerve; turned yellow – "

"That's a lie!" Maloney was stung out of his indifference.

"Alright, I won't say you were yellow. But you'd lost your guts. You took to booze fighting. Went to the gutter. Went broke. Now, in three years you've made a no-stop flight from Broadway to this dump."

Maloney's mighty fists clenched into iron knots on the table. His eyes flamed through the tousled mass of black hair.

"I ought to kill you," he said huskily, inflamed by the stuff he had been drinking. "Just because you've managed a few champions you think you can talk to a man any way. You don't manage me."

"I'm not in the habit of managing whiskey-soaks," sneered the other. "The men I managed may not have been as fast or as hard hitting as you were, but they were men. They didn't go all to pieces just because somebody hung a k.o. sign on their chin."

Suddenly he changed his manner and sat down opposite the ex-fighter.

"You're still young, Maloney," said he slowly. "Why don't you try to come back?"

"Fight again?" Maloney shuddered as from a nightmare memory. "Ugh!"

"You've brooded over that knockout until it's become an obsession with you. Get yourself in shape again – "

"No! No! I couldn't. I don't want to try – to even think about it."

"Then you've no more guts than I thought," the bitter rasp had come back into the voice. "I thought – "

"Listen!" the other cried with a desperate note in his voice. "What do you know of my trouble? You never fought in your life."

"No," the other admitted, "but I know you fighters better than most of you know yourselves. And I know you could come back if you had the guts."

"Sit down," Maloney ordered huskily. "I'll tell you my side of it."

"Alright, I'll listen to your tale of woe – and buy you a drink, too," the older man added with a cutting sneer.

Maloney's eyes momentarily flashed, but he had sunk too low to be over-resentful of anything beyond a direct insult. He motioned to the bartender, gulped down the fiery draught, and said savagely:

"Guts! Bah! What do you know of a man who has the heart knocked out of him? Listen, I was all you said and more. Till I met Brennon. I thought I was invincible. I wore myself out punching him. I ruined myself – "

"And why?" broke in the other. "You mean you were ruined mentally. You came out of that fight with only one mark. A cut on your cheekbone and a few bruises. I've seen fights in which the winner was carried out of the ring. You took that defeat to heart. Just because you couldn't stop Brennon, you lost all your nerve, permanently.

"And why couldn't you stop him? Because he's a freak. An iron-jawed, steel-bellied gorilla that can't be knocked out! No man's ever turned the trick, and won't until he cracks from the continual punishment. Remember Joe Grim, what Gans, Fitzsimmons, and Johnson failed to stop! But you punched yourself out and took the count. And you let it beat you! Bah! Your vanity couldn't stand the shock. You'd gotten to the point where you didn't believe any man could hurt you.

"If you'd had the stuff it takes to make a real man, that beating would have done you good – taken some of the conceit out of you. As it was, it ruined you."

"Listen!" There was fury and agony in Maloney's voice; he was drunk but his mind was lucid. "Listen! I'll try to tell you –

"I'd never met a man like Brennon. I didn't credit much those stories I'd heard of Grim, Goddard, and Boden – those old-time iron men. I didn't believe the man lived who could stand up to my punches.

"Then I met Brennon at the Hopi A.C. in San Francisco. I'd heard he was tough – been knocking over a bunch of second-raters on the coast till Steve Amber took him over and began getting him good matches.

"At the first I was impressed by the ferocity of Brennon's face and the steady glare of his eyes. I half expected him to be awed by my name and k.o. record, but he glared at me as if I were one of the second-raters he had been punching over. Or rather, as if he were a tiger and I a bison he was going to tear limb from limb. I tell you, the fellow isn't human! He's made of solid iron and there's room in his skull for only one thought – the killer instinct!

"At the gong he came out of his corner wide open; no defense at all. And he knew nothing about scientific hitting. He lifted his swings from the floor, in the old rough-house style. I went in to finish him quick. I expected to flatten him with the first rush, but when I landed my first blow, a left hook to the body, I got the surprise of my life. Brennon didn't even flinch; instead of sinking wrist deep into his body, my fist rebounded just as if I had struck a metal boiler instead of a human body!

"I tell you, he was almost as hard as steel. But I didn't stop to worry; I began throwing rights and lefts to the body and head with everything I had. I was the first first-class man Brennon had met, the papers said. That was his introduction into the first-rate ranks, and I gave him a baptism of fire and blood.

"I battered him all over the ring without a return. He didn't even know enough to duck or wrap his arms around his jaw. Blood spattered all over us; I closed one of his eyes nearly shut. But he wouldn't go down. And just before the gong, when I thought he must be weakening, he suddenly landed one of those wide sweeping left-handers under my heart. It felt for a second as if he had caved me in. Took my breath away. But it wasn't the blow that sent me to my corner so discouraged; it was the fact that for three solid minutes he'd taken everything I could hand out, and was apparently as strong as ever.

"Between rounds my manager and handlers urged me to go slow; they were getting afraid that I'd fight myself out. But my pride was stung. I'd trained perfectly, but I was beginning to feel fatigued. None of my fights had been at such a pace as this! Just imagine battering away, with all your power, for three minutes straight! And consider the fact that Brennon had taken every blow I started! I could scarcely believe it, but at the gong here he came with his wild beast eyes glaring in his bloody face.

"I threw caution to the winds. Mike Brennon must have gone through hell in that second round. Near the end of it his nose was smashed flat, both eyes closed to mere slits, his face one red mask of pulped flesh and blood. But through the slits of his eyelids his eyes still blazed with their old light – I tell you, you have to kill a man like Iron Mike Brennon to stop him! He's tougher than Battling Nelson was.

"I felt myself slipping. My blows were coming slower I knew. My arms seemed to be turning to lead; my legs were trembling, my chest heaving. I rallied with one more ferocious attack just before the gong, and crashed my right four times to his jaw. Think of that! And I'd knocked men out with one blow of that right many a time, to the side of the head or face. For the first time Brennon reeled. His knees buckled, but just as I thought 'He's going!' he straightened and glanced a right from my cheekbone. It opened a cut and for a second I was blinded by a flash of white light in my brain. Oh, I'd been hit before. Hit hard; knocked down. But never such blows as those; and what was worse was the knowledge that I couldn't hit Brennon hard enough to weaken him.

"My knees trembled as I walked back to my corner, and I looked over my shoulder to see if Brennon was showing the effects of his beating. I shouldn't have done that. When I saw him walk to his corner without a quiver, something went out of me. I had an all-gone feeling. As I sank onto my stool, I heard the crowd yelling: 'Hey, whatsa matter, Jack? Lost your punch? How come you ain't stopped this tramp? This boy must be made outa iron!'

"I began to wonder if I had lost my punch. My brain reeled. This was a nightmare! I, the hardest puncher since Dempsey's days, had pounded this wide-open dub for two solid rounds without even weakening him! Surely there must be some limit to his endurance! There must be an end even to his incredible vitality!

"My manager was begging me to box him, take my time. Be content to outpoint him. I scarcely heard. I was in a panic. The factor that sent me out to kill or be killed wasn't so much wounded vanity as you think – it was more fear than anything else! Yes, fear! Just like a man penned in with a tiger who must kill or die!

"I gathered my waning powers and tore out for the third round like a wild man. Brennon with his longshoreman's style was easy to hit. He fought straight up and wide open. I fought like a man in a trance. Left, right! My left hand broke on his head, but I didn't notice it. I threw my right again and again, with a wild desperation. Every ounce of weight, power and fighting fury went behind that right hand at every blow. When it landed it sounded like the blows of a caulking mallet. And Brennon reeled, wavered – went down!

"When he fell, all my unnatural fury went out of me; I staggered back against the ropes, completely fought out – an exhausted shell of a man. The referee was counting. Then to my utter horror, Brennon shook his head and began to get his feet under him. I nearly fainted. I thought I'd finished him – I knew I was done. And he was getting up! The ring floated before my eyes.

"Then Brennon was up and coming for me. I tottered away from the ropes on buckling legs and lifted arms that were no stronger than a girl's. I was all gone – out on my feet. Even then he missed-missed-missed. At last he crashed a leaping left-hander to my head. There was a flash of white light again, I reeled and he smashed a terrible swing under my cheekbone. The lights went out. They said I came up again at the count of nine, and he floored me the second time before I was counted out. I don't know. I don't remember anything after that fearful right-hander that first dropped me."

A momentary silence fell. Maloney's blood-shot eyes burned unseeingly and when he continued he seemed to be talking more to himself than to his listener.

"That fight made Iron Mike Brennon," he said huskily, at last. "It broke me. My mind was in a chaotic whirl. I couldn't get down to training. I couldn't settle on anything. I stayed out of the ring for four months, then went back in against Soldier Handler. I was all at sea. I hit with my old force, but I had no timing or accuracy. Every time I started a blow the vision of Iron Mike Brennon's bloody and snarling face rose up before me. I was wild and awkward. Every time I saw a blow coming, the memory of Brennon's terrific knockout smashes made me flinch and back away. The crowd booed me, hissed me, called me yellow. At last, in the fifth round I went down and out from the swings of a man I should have stopped in the first rush. The sportswriters said I quit. Maybe I did. I could hear the referee counting over me; I wasn't unconscious but I couldn't drag myself to my feet."

Grendon moved restlessly. His quick nervous energy made it impossible for him to keep still a long time.

"It's the mind," said he. "Your superiority complex got a jolt. You should have recovered by this time. It wouldn't be impossible for you to get back in shape. I saw the Handler fight. You were like a man dazed or drugged. Even so he staggered every time you landed, and it took him five rounds to beat you down, in the condition you were in. You were not in shape, mentally or physically.

"As for Brennon," the harsh rasping note stole in again, "you said you were in shape for him. You weren't. You thought you'd trained. You'd been going through the motions, but your heart wasn't in your work. You were too sure of yourself. And that same conceit whipped you; you fought yourself out and when Brennon dropped you – as he might have dropped any man that ever lived – you didn't have the stuff to take it and come back.

"Once more I ask you: will you let me take you and put you back in the ring?"

Maloney's sole answer was to turn his back on his interrogator and reach for the bottle of tequila which the bartender had left on the table. He felt the cold eyes of Grendon on him for a few moments, then was vaguely aware that the manager had gone.

Maloney had been drinking hard three years. Today he plunged into his old vice with a sort of desperation, to drown the old ghosts which Grendon had conjured up. In a short time he was too muddled to even wonder why the bartender kept bringing the liquor for which he, Maloney, had no money to pay.

He swiftly passed into the hazy semi-consciousness of extreme intoxication and as he hovered on the borderline of complete oblivion, he was dimly aware of a commotion. There were shouts, a fall of chairs, the crash of broken bottles – something struck him a powerful blow and he struck back. Or at least that was his intention, but he was so far gone in drink that he never knew whether or not he put the thought into action.

Jack Maloney awoke with a thirst and a splitting headache. Neither particularly worried him, since the last few years this had been a common phenomenon on waking. But he at last realized that he was in strange surroundings. A pitcher of water close at hand first occupied his attention, then he looked about him. He was in a small room, walled, floored and roofed of 'dobe. There was one door which was closed; one small heavily barred window.

The ex-fighter lurched and tried the door. It was locked. Slowly the truth dawned on him. He was in jail. A sort of panic struck him. He knew the horrors of these Mexican jails in whose vermin-ridden cells men die forgotten. He pounded on the door and shouted loudly.

Steps sounded outside in the corridor and presently the door swung open. Two heavy-faced Mexican soldiers, heavily armed, stood on either side of a third man.

"Grendon!" Maloney exclaimed. "What's all this mean?"

There was no sympathy in Grendon's cold eyes.

"Don't you remember last night?"

Maloney passed an uncertain hand over his throbbing brow.

"I don't remember anything after our talk."

"No," Grendon rasped, "you were drunk as a swine. Anyway, after I left, a row started in that joint where you were and when the police came in to stop it, one of them bumped into you and you knocked him stiff. It's a serious offense to strike an officer in this part of Mexico. You've been given a heavy fine."

"I haven't any money," said the ex-fighter. "Pay my fine and I'll pay you back."

"Pay out five hundred dollars, American money, for a rum-soaked ruin?" Grendon's voice was more bitter than Maloney had ever heard it.

"Five hundred dollars!" Maloney was dumfounded.

"Sure. And if you can't pay it, you'll lay it out – and not in this cool cell either. These soldiers have come to take you to the bull pen, they tell me. You know what a few months there means."

Maloney shuddered. He had looked into these "bull pens" and had seen the men imprisoned there, the maundering wrecks that milled ceaselessly to and fro beneath the merciless sun. For a Mexican bull pen is simply a jail with high walls and no roof. No breeze can blow upon the men there; only the semitropical sun beats down upon their defenseless bodies all day long. There is no shade; nowhere to sit or lie save on the hard flagstones or the packed dirt floor, in the broiling sunshine. Men go insane there.

"You won't leave a man of your own race for a fate like that?" the fighter cried desperately.

"No?" Grendon sneered. "Watch me!" Then seeing the utter despair on Maloney's face, he said:

"The alcalde happens to be a friend of mine. I'll do this much for you. There's a sort of one-horse fight club here, run by an American gambler, as you probably know. Alright. A Mexican heavyweight by the name of Diaz is in town looking for a match. They'll let you out of jail to fight him. You'll get nothing, of course, but I'll bet five hundred dollars on you *and you'll win!* If you don't, it's the bull pen."

Maloney cried out in horror: "Fight? After three years of idleness and dissipation? Why, I couldn't even spar a round! I've no wind, stamina or punch. A child could push me over."

"Alright," Grendon snapped, "suit yourself; maybe you'll have an easier time in the bull pen, anyhow." He turned away.

"Wait!" Maloney shouted in desperation. "I'll fight! But how can I expect to win?"

"A man can do anything he has to," Grendon answered grimly. "I'll go arrange things. They won't let you out of this cell till Diaz is in the ring. Till then you might while away the time thinking about the sun on the bare walls of the bull pen!"

Maloney lay face down on the dirt floor, his aching head forgotten. How could he even stand up to a fighter, even such a dub as this Mexican most undoubtedly was? Much less, how could he win? Then the vision of the bull pen rose up in his mind. The thought of the fight nauseated him; the thought of the prison crazed him.

Time passed. At last the door opened and two Mexican guards entered. They motioned him to precede them, and they followed close behind, their bayonets barely touching his back.

In the ring in the squalid little sheet-iron fight stadium, Diaz lolled in his corner and awaited the coming of the dub he was to slaughter. Diaz was sure of himself; he had been told that they were taking an American out of the jail to meet him, and surely no fighter of any consequence could be in a jail in this tiny border town which owed its sole existence to the thirst of the white men across the river, and which even Diaz held in contempt. He had not even taken the trouble to learn the name of his opponent.

He glanced up languidly. A black-haired American was climbing unsteadily though the ropes, aided by a wiry man of late middle age whom Diaz, with a start, recognized as the great Grendon himself. Diaz' heart skipped a beat. What was the manager of champions doing here, and why was he seconding a fourth-rater? Something wrong here!

Diaz stole a look at the other fighter with quickened interest. He looked

closer, with unbelief in his eyes. He blanched and spoke swiftly and passionately to his manager.

Jack Maloney felt an involuntary shudder go through him as he looked
about at the old familiar sight – the ropes of the ring, the stained canvas,
the shouting crowd. Again there rose dizzily a bygone vision – a vaster,
more pretentious ring, a huger throng – and a black-haired battler who
writhed broken at the feet of a gory slugger. Then another vision blotted
this out – a vision of a roofless Hades where men went staring crazy.

He glanced at his opponent, a second-rate Mexican he had never heard
of. He saw recognition flare in Diaz' eyes, saw the pallor on the dark face.
A faint pride stirred in him. As low as he had sunk, the very memory of his
name was enough to frighten this second-rater. Bitterness flooded him at
the thought of his past glory and his present degradation.

The referee called the men to the center of the ring and gave them the
usual unheard instructions. Diaz was beginning to get back some of his
confidence. His manager had told him that this man was the same one
who had been lying about the saloons for months, and he himself knew
that Maloney had not fought for three years. The lines of dissipation in
the American's face and the lack of training evident in his whole frame
cheered him; but he must be careful. Must take no chances and be sure that
this man was harmless before risking anything. Diaz had once fought a
preliminary to one of Maloney's fights and the memory was still fresh in his
mind, of the sledge-like smashes that had flattened the man's opponent on
that occasion.

The men went back to their corners and as Grendon climbed through
the ropes he hissed one parting word: "I've sunk five hundred dollars on
you! Win and you're a free man; lose and it's the bull pen!"

The gong sounded. Maloney rose and walked slowly toward the middle
of the ring. Diaz came out even more slowly and carefully. Maloney scarcely
saw him; in his mind he saw a snarling blood-stained demon who rushed
and smote like the very spirit of the primitive.

A moment the men circled each other. At last Diaz led halfheartedly;
his left got home under Maloney's heart and the Mexican, awed by his
own audacity, involuntarily closed his eyes, expecting to be blasted out of
existence instantly. But Maloney made no attempt to return the blow. It
had not been hard, but the feel of it brought back in a nauseating wave

all his old fears; again in that instant he relived his nightmare battle with Brennon, his slaughter by Soldier Handler.

Finding himself still alive, the Mexican repeated his lead. This time Maloney countered with his own left and Diaz, shrinking away from it, was surprised to feel it glance lightly from his shoulder. No force there. Diaz' intelligence told him that the once-great Maloney was only a shell of himself; but his instinctive fears kept him from rushing in to make a quick finish of it.

He attacked warily, jabbing at Maloney's face, then as the American retreated heavily, he followed up his advantage with a right to the body that carried force. Maloney felt as if a keen knife had cut off his breath for a fleeting instant. Already he was beginning to feel the effects of his lack of training. His knees were beginning to tremble, his breath to come in gasps. And the first round had scarcely progressed a minute.

Only Diaz' caution kept him from flattening his opponent in the first round. He kept a steady stream of straight lefts in Maloney's face, blows that cut and hurt but did not stun, and occasionally he drove his right hard to the body, knowing that Maloney was in no shape to take punishment there.

Maloney was already in a bad way. Those right-handers sank deep in his flabby midriff; sweat soaked his body, his gloves and trunks and it seemed his heart would burst with the exertions of his labored breathing. Worse than all, the blows that rained steadily upon him brought up the memories of those last two fights –

Diaz grew in confidence. So far his opponent had not laid a glove on him. The great Maloney was staggering before his blows! As this feeling grew, Diaz increased the savagery of his attack. Just before the gong Maloney went down, partly from the increasing force of the Mexican's blows, partly from his own exhaustion.

He came to himself in his corner. Grendon was working over him with all the skill of an old-time handler, but Maloney gasped: "I'm through. I can't even get up off my stool."

Grendon reached for the sponge to toss it in. His eyes were bitter.

"All right, the bull pen for you. This fourth-rater's punched you right into it."

At that moment the gong sounded. From whence his renewal of strength came, Maloney never knew. He always secretly believed it was a flare of momentary insanity and perhaps he was right. But at Grendon's words, a fearful chaos of hatred flamed up in his brain; hatred for Grendon who was consigning him to a living death, hatred for the Mexican soldiers who stood about to see that he did not escape, hatred for Iron Mike Brennon who was the prime cause of all his trouble. And, naturally, all his hate centered on the man in the ring with him.

Diaz came rushing from his corner like a great tiger. He was wild with the killer instinct, inflamed with the desire to stretch this once-great battler at his feet. But he met a different man. Somehow Maloney heaved up off his stool, knocking the sponge out of Grendon's hand. His legs seemed dead, but he lurched forward and, as Diaz plunged savagely in, Maloney steadied him with a straight left to the face, and crashed his right under the heart with a force which even surprised himself.

Diaz staggered, whitened. For the first time in his life he had run full into the blow of a real hitter and the sensation left him weakened and nauseated. He felt as if he had been caved in; as if his heart had momentarily stopped. No longer did he dally with a desire to see the great Maloney stretched at his feet. He only desired to avoid utter destruction.

He commenced a hasty retreat and Maloney, realizing that his strength was swiftly fading, and with the bull pen before his eyes, lurched desperately after him. Diaz was still unmanned by that blow under the heart and on the ropes Maloney caught him. And there, holding the ropes with his left hand to keep him on his feet, Maloney crashed another right-hander over, this time to the jaw, and Diaz dropped for the full count.

As the referee said "Ten!" Maloney dropped likewise, his fading thought being that he was going to die of fatigue.

He came to himself to see Grendon bending over him, and if the manager felt any satisfaction, his face did not show it.

"Alright, hustle out of it," he rapped harshly. "We're leaving town. I paid your fine."

"You can go to hell," snarled Maloney, sitting up, all his hatred of Grendon blazing in his eyes. "I fought my bout like you said and I'm grateful for what you did – getting me the fight. Otherwise I owe you nothing."

"You owe me five hundred dollars," Grendon retorted. "The stakeholder skipped with the money I bet on you. I paid your fine out of my own pocket. That way I've lost a thousand dollars on you, but we will just call it five hundred. And you're going to work it out for me."

"Work it out?"

"Fight it out, if you like the word better. That fight showed one thing; you're not as far gone as I thought. You still know how to hit and you've got more than a shadow of your old punch. Close, careful training will sweat the booze out of your system and get you back in shape. You'll never be much, maybe, but you can slap down a flock of pushovers and pay back my money."

"I won't do it," Maloney answered shortly. "I went through Hades last night. I won't do it again for anybody."

"Maloney," said Grendon, looking at him piercingly, "you hate me, don't you?"

"As much as one man could hate another," answered Maloney with his characteristic honesty.

Grendon seemed not displeased. In fact he grinned thinly.

"Alright, do you want to go through life knowing you're obligated to a man you hate?"

Maloney's black-crowned head jerked up and his eyes glinted into Grendon's hawk-like gaze.

"I'll do it," he said abruptly. "You ought to make your money back off me in one fight. Then we're through, understand."

Grendon's only answer was a wintry smile.

Thus came Jack Maloney, once a coming champion, now a has-been, to the managerial care of "Iceberg" Grendon. No words of love passed between them, their conversation was limited to short abrupt advice or requests on the part of the manager and shorter replies on the part of the fighter.

After the affair at the border town, they went directly to the coast and took ship for Australia, Grendon's native land. Maloney having no money, Grendon paid all expenses, and the fighter wondered that he should spend so much merely to assure himself of the payment of five hundred dollars. Grendon seemed not at all parsimonious except in this matter, and Maloney decided that the man hated him as much as he hated Grendon and was merely taking this revenge. He remembered that in his early career he had knocked out one of Grendon's proteges, and though the Australian was not a man to harbor grudges, Maloney for lack of a better reason decided that Grendon had never forgiven him. He determined to pay back not only the five hundred that Grendon had spent paying his fine, but the five hundred which the crooked stakeholder had stolen. After that – Maloney's fists slowly clenched as the black tide of his hate surged through his brain.

Grendon had a training camp in the country back of Sydney and there Maloney plunged into the work of conditioning himself.

Grendon proved himself a first-class trainer, whatever else his faults. He made Maloney go easy at first, start very gradually to building up his long-abused body, and Maloney, realizing his manager's wisdom and experience, followed his instructions to the letter.

Months passed; slowly Maloney was rounding into shape. He was training harder now, and his muscles were vibrant with strength and life. He felt no craving for liquor. He had never been a natural sot, had drunk only to drown his dreams. He could do miles of roadwork now without discomfort and when he struck the heavy punching bag, it leaped and tossed like a ship on a windy sea. In the daily bouts with his sparring partners he felt that his timing and speed had come back to a remarkable extent. Speed and punch – the secret of his earlier successes – and now he strove to regain them. The punch that numbed and shocked the toughest fighter, the speed that carried him through the guard of cleverer men. Maloney had never been a really clever boxer in the fullest sense of the word. He had been more of the slugger; but his defense was not to be sniffed at and his shifty footwork would have done credit to many a more crafty boxer. Speed to catch his man and the punch to finish him!

At last when he believed he was ready to face a fairly good opponent, Grendon kept him at light training a month longer. In a way Maloney was eager to fight and get it over. His labor had been one of hatred, not love, and the sooner he could fling the money he owed into Grendon's face with a curse, the better it would suit him. But when he thought of entering the ring again, the old red ghost came back and left him weak and trembling.

Still, he was secretly grateful for one thing: he was no longer a whiskey-soaked hobo, but a man. Like all natural athletes, he reveled in the feel of his new strength and vibrancy – in the smooth flowing muscles and the work of the great clean lungs. He decided that he would never again sink into the gutter; he was still young, scarcely twenty-five years old. He would get some sort of a job and if he could not be a fighter, he would at least be a man.

Then at last Grendon announced that he had gotten Maloney a match.

"An American by the name of Leary," said Grendon. "You ought to draw a good crowd, if the fight fans down under remember you. And they always turn out to see a couple of Americans battle. I don't know what's the matter with Australia; she turns out so few fighters worthy of the name these days. I remember when Young Griffo, Hall, Murphy – "

Maloney gave him no heed. The vanished glories of Australia's fistic past was the one subject on which Grendon was prone to grow garrulous.

The old all-gone feeling came back when Maloney stood in the ring that night in Sydney. The crowd, some of them remembering him, had given him quite a hand, but he was remembering –

With an effort he jerked himself out of his crimson reveries and looked across at his opponent: a rangy red-headed fellow, taller than himself but lighter. The announcer was saying:

" – Jack Maloney, America, weight 195; Red Leary, also of America, weight 180 – "

At the gong, Grendon hissed: "Remember my five hundred – and that you hate me!" And Maloney found time to wonder at the avariciousness of the man.

Leary, like Diaz, knew Maloney of old, and like the Mexican, he had no desire to serve as a stepping stone on the comeback road of a former great one. But differently from Diaz, he attacked instantly, though warily. Grendon had taught Maloney more of the real art of boxing than he had ever known before, and now as he blocked and side-stepped the rangy boxer's leads, Maloney realized that he was a better boxer than ever before. But the knowledge is not all – the heart must be in the game – and with no horror of bull pens before his eyes, not even his hatred of Grendon could keep the old red memories from Maloney.

He retired on the defensive, flinched involuntarily from blows that did not hurt, and could not seem to untrack himself. The first round was slow; toward the end Leary drew first blood with a volley of straight lefts to the face. Maloney scarcely felt them and retaliated with a whistling left hook which Leary cleverly blocked.

"Can't you untrack yourself?" rasped Grendon back in his corner.

"You're in perfect shape; his best blows are not hurting you. You're hitting as hard as you ever did in your life. But you don't hit often enough. You've been on the run since the tap of the gong. This second-rater is going to outpoint you if you don't take a chance." Then as Maloney made no reply, Grendon snarled bitterly, "Bah! Your heart's not in your work. You're going to take a whipping just from pure lack of guts."

Maloney went out brooding over his manager's words and Leary, taking advantage of his abstraction, smashed a wicked left hook to the body and staggered his man with a sweeping right to the body. Stung out of his apathy, Maloney came back with a hard left hook to the ribs, knocking Leary into the ropes and bringing the crowd to its feet yelling. But the burst of action was brief. As Leary rebounded from the ropes, Maloney seemed to see Mike Brennon's shadow wavering between, and the heart went out of him. His reason told him that the blow he had dealt Leary had not landed solidly enough to knock down any trained man, but his blind unreasoning inhibitions clamored that here was the old tale all over again – a man whom his blows could not hurt.

Thus passed the second, third and fourth rounds, and the sixth and seventh rounds. Leary, boxing carefully, taking no chances, piling up an enormous lead, with Maloney defending in his half-hearted manner. Then came the eighth round.

Maloney came up as fresh as he had been at the first gong. He felt no fatigue whatever. But Leary saw only his cut and blood-stained features. He did not know that Maloney, tough and in perfect trim, had scarcely felt the jabs which had marked him. Leary believed that Maloney's lack of aggressiveness was from weakness. "They never come back!" And as he rushed out for the eighth, Leary suddenly discarded his former intention of winning on points and went savagely in for a knockout.

The crowd rose roaring; it was in hopes of this that they had sat so patiently through the fight. Maloney found himself the center of a whirlwind. Leary, though no match in hitting power for his opponent, carried a wicked punch and knew how to use it. Throwing caution to the winds, he battered Maloney all over the ring and floored him in a neutral corner.

Maloney took a count of nine, though he could have risen sooner. He was dizzy, not hurt. As he rose, Leary was on him, wild with the instinct of the kill. Maloney missed a vicious left, landed hard under the heart with the same hand and took a volley of lefts and rights to the head as he backed away, covering up.

Leary gave him no rest. He feinted him out of his position, ducked a venomous right and crashed his own right to Maloney's jaw. Again he landed. Maloney was dizzy; out on his feet. Suddenly it seemed that he was fighting, not Red Leary, but Iron Mike Brennon. Through the blood which veiled his eyes, he seemed to see Brennon's snarling face floating before him.

Suddenly Jack Maloney went crazy. He had suffered enough from this phantom. At last his instinct was fight, not run. He had forgotten all about Leary. Now he bunched himself into a solid cannonball of destruction and shot forward, blasting his terrible right hand full into the ghostly face which mocked him. And that blind smash found Red Leary's jaw.

Maloney, waking as from a nightmare, heard the referee counting and saw at his feet the limp form of his victim.

Grendon came to him in his dressing room.

"Here's your part of the purse; five hundred and fifty-five dollars."

Maloney snatched it from his hand. "Now then, here's your money, you – "

Grendon seemed not to notice him; he drew from his pocket a newspaper cutting. "Read this."

The date of the paper was a month old. The paper itself had been torn and was pasted together in a crude manner. Maloney read it and cried out incredulously: "Mike Brennon knocked out! Why, this can't be true! It says, 'Red Leary knocked out Iron Mike Brennon tonight in the first round of a scheduled fifteen-frame go. It was Leary's last fight before leaving for Australia.' Why – "

He sat down, his brain reeling. He had whipped the man who knocked out the terrible Mike Brennon. A wild feeling of exultation swept over him. He whirled on Grendon, his hatred of the man submerged in his new emotion.

"You'll keep on managing me! You'll get me some more fights! If I whipped the man who whipped Brennon, I can whip any of them! Including Brennon!"

"Handler's in England," said Grendon with a strange eager gleam in his cold eyes. "Do you think you can take him?"

Maloney laughed like a boy. A terrible load seemed lifted from his shoulders and only then did he realize how black and terrible it had been, distorting his entire viewpoint on life.

"I can take a roomful of him! Grendon, you're managing the next champion! First Handler! Then Brennon! Then whoever stands between me and the title! I'll flatten them all!"

"And, say," as Grendon started for the door, "here's your money."

"Keep it!" Grendon rapped. "I never accept money from my fighters. Keep it and pay me back by winning the title!"

Fight fans of London will remember the Maloney-Handler battle as long as they live, after the memories of longer, harder-contested struggles have passed into oblivion. It was short, but it was sensational – the kind of fight which brings fans to their feet holding their breath and which sends them away babbling deliriously.

Before the gong sounded, Maloney sat in his corner, fresh and glowing with health after his long sea-trip, vibrant with fierce energy, which many took for nervousness. Across from him Handler sneered confidently. Had not he stopped this youth three years before? Maloney had been better then, surely. The burly Soldier had heard of his life since then. What if he had pushed over a couple of dubs since he started his comeback? Handler laughed confidently; he himself was at the height of his career.

At the gong Maloney shot from his corner like a thunderbolt. And like a thunderbolt he smote the astounded Soldier. Gone were all the red ghosts that once lurked in Maloney's brain, chaining his limbs. Again he was Jack Maloney, the Virginia Thunderbolt.

Handler had scarcely time to get out of his corner before the whirlwind struck. A sizzling straight left rocked his head back and as his jaw came up from behind the hunched and protecting shoulder, Maloney's fearful right crashed over. Only a born hitter can deliver a blow like that; the whole body working in unison, the mighty shoulder following the drive of the arm, the body pivoting at the waist, the feet thrusting powerfully upward and forward – and all done in the flash of a split second.

Handler dropped face down, nor did he move until he was brought to in his dressing room. His first words have come down the years with other ring classics:

"Baby!" caressing his chin, "That galoot don't hit! He explodes!"

Two more fights followed in England; to Maloney they were mere incidents, stepping-stones on his upward trail. His eventual goal was the title, he felt, but even that was subordinate to his desire to meet Iron Mike Brennon again. For this he lived.

Shortly after he knocked out Soldier Handler, he was matched with Tom Walshire, the champion of England. The clever Briton eluded the wrath to come for nine rounds, but Maloney was not to be denied, and in the tenth he cornered Walshire and smashed him to the canvas for the full count.

Gunboat Sloan followed. The Gunner was past his prime, but he still had his old-time ring craft and a left hand as deadly as a crossbow bolt. Boxing superbly, he kept Maloney at bay for four rounds and in the fifth landed that terrible left flush to the jaw. Maloney's knees buckled, but even while the crowd held their breath expecting his fall, he lurched headlong into the Gunner and brought him down with an inside right under the heart.

It was a few days after this victory when Maloney rushed into Grendon's room. The relations of the two men had changed subtly. Grendon's manner had altered after Maloney's decision to continue in the ring, and Maloney's feeling had changed from hatred to a grudging admiration. He had stayed with Grendon because he realized that the man was one of the cleverest pilots in the game and could aid him in his climb. At last he had come to have a secret liking for the Australian and had often wondered if the man's cold, hard attitude were not a mask to hide his real sensitive nature.

But now as he entered Grendon's room, his brain was in a turmoil.

"Look here!" he waved a newspaper in his manager's face. "Last night in America, Iron Mike Brennon was knocked out by a fellow they call Iron Mike Costigan! In the first round! And the paper says that's the first time Brennon has been flattened!"

Grendon nodded.

"But you told me," stammered the fighter, all at sea, "you told me that Red Leary, whom I whipped in Sydney, had knocked Brennon out! The knowledge that I'd whipped Leary has been what's holding me up!"

Grendon shook his head. "More than that, Jack. You needed something then to brace you. Now you're able to go on your own."

Maloney frowned and cogitated, then suddenly threw back his shoulders and grinned with the pleasant arrogance of youth.

"You're right; I'm over all that stuff. I realize that it was just mental – just an inhibition or complex or something that I'm rid of. I'll go on and fight – "

He halted, suddenly realizing something of which he had not thought before.

"Brennon must be terribly battered, or he couldn't have been knocked out."

"The last time I saw him," said Grendon, "months before I first met you in Mexico, he was a battered wreck. Nearly ready for the padded cell. Anybody could have pushed him over in this last fight. That's the way these iron men go; they seem invincible for years, then they crack suddenly."

Maloney shook his head pityingly. "I've hated him for three years. I don't hate him any longer and I don't want to fight him. Anyway, the paper says he's retiring. If he wasn't, I wouldn't push over a punch-drunk ruin – say, get me Costigan, the fellow that knocked him out!"

"But, Jack, he's an iron man too! Just a counterpart of the Brennon who knocked you out nearly four years ago."

"No matter – and Grendon, I want to say that at last I appreciate everything you've done for me. I was a hog and you made me a man against your will. What your original object was I don't know – "

"Why, Jack," Grendon's hard eyes were strangely soft, "years ago when you were just a hard-slugging kid, I kept my eye on you; wanted to manage you but couldn't buy your contract. I've always liked you as a fighter; of late I've come to like you as a man.

"When I found you wasting your life in that little border town, I wanted to see if you were capable of getting out of the gutter, even with help. I told you that time that the alcalde in the town was my friend. He was and is. I framed the whole thing. You didn't sock an officer; you were too drunk to do anything, or remember anything. I didn't bet any money on you. There wasn't any fine to pay.

"I admit it was cruel sending you in against Diaz in your condition. But I wanted to find out if you had anything left. Even if he flattened you with the first punch, I didn't intend leaving you there to rot in those low-class dives.

"But you showed me in that fight that you still had your superhuman physical ability. I don't believe the man ever lived before who could have knocked out a fighter in good condition after having gone through what you'd been through! And I saw your heart was in the right place, too. Nothing wrong there. The same old fighting heart. But it was your mind. You needed a bracer.

"I was afraid to show you the paper about Leary and Brennon before the fight, and if you'd lost I'd never had used it. But you see the result."

"How'd you frame that?" Maloney asked.

Grendon smiled. "You noticed how the paper was torn? I simply tore out a few words and pasted the torn edges together. The original lines were: 'Red Leary *was knocked out by* Iron Mike Brennon in one round!"

Maloney laughed. "It served the purpose. It made me regain my confidence. Now I'll never lose it again if I live to be a hundred. And now I want a match with Costigan!"

"Jack, you'll gain nothing by fighting this iron man; just now he's at his prime. Dempsey couldn't knock him out, neither could Fitzsimmons. If you beat him you'll gain considerable prestige, but if he beats you, you're ruined. These iron men are the worst opponents in the world for nervous, sensitive fighters like you. Pass him up and take on a fast, clever fellow like yourself!"

Maloney shook his head. "I'm older now. I won't make a fool out of myself again. I won't punch myself out on Costigan as I did on Brennon, but I want to beat the man who beat the man who broke me. Till then I won't have regained my fullest self-respect and self-confidence."

This is an item which appeared in the newspapers a month later: "Jack Maloney, whose sensational rise and fall four years ago was the talk of the sporting world, rose another step on the fistic ladder which he is re-mounting when he outpointed Iron Mike Costigan, the conqueror of Iron Mike Brennon. Maloney seems to have regained all the speed and punch which four years ago caused sportswriters to christen him the Virginia Thunderbolt, and to predict his early accession to the heavyweight crown.

"This was Maloney's first battle in an American ring since he began his comeback campaign. He held the upper hand throughout the bout, taking every round of the fifteen-round go, and in the last frame sent Costigan twice to the canvas for counts of nine. Only Mike's superhuman endurance and vitality saved him from the first knockout of his career, and it seemed that if it had gone a few more rounds, he would have taken the count in spite of his ruggedness, which is of a quality to make Joe Grim jealous. Maloney, though he did not score a knockout, deserves praise for superb work, and seems a cinch for the title."

Kid Lavigne Is Dead

Hang up the battered gloves; Lavigne is dead.
Bold and erect he went into the dark.
The crown is withered and the crowds are fled,
The empty ring stands bare and lone – yet hark:
The ghostly roar of many a phantom throng
Floats down the dusty years, forgotten long.

Hot blazed the lights above the crimson ring
Where there he reigned in his full prime, a king.
The throngs' acclaim roared up beneath their sheen
And whispered down the night: "Lavigne! Lavigne!"
Red splashed the blood and fierce the crashing blows
Men staggered to the mat and reeling rose.
Crowns glittered there in splendor, won or lost,
And bones were shattered as the sledges crossed.

Swift as a leopard, strong and fiercely lean,
Champions knew the prowess of Lavigne.
The giant dwarf Joe Walcott saw him loom
And broken, bloody, reeled before his doom.
Handler and Everhardt and rugged Burge
Saw at the last his snarling face emerge
From bloody mists that veiled their dimming sight
Ere they sank down into unlighted night.

Strong men and bold lay vanquished at his feet
Mighty was he in triumph and defeat.
Far fade the echoes of the ringside cheers
And all is lost in mists of dust-dead years.
Cold breaks the dawn; the East is ghastly red.
Hand up the broken gloves; Lavigne is dead.

NOTE ON THE TEXTS

The texts of the stories and poems in this collection are taken either from their original periodical appearance or from Howard's original typescripts. In some cases, Howard's original titles have been restored for stories that first appeared under other titles, but were otherwise intact.

Howard made substantive changes in two stories in this volume, "Cultured Cauliflowers" and "A New Game for Costigan," to disguise his authorship, so that they could appear under a pseudonym in the same issues of magazines where other stories of his were also to appear. These two stories were originally written as Sailor Steve Costigan tales, but Howard changed "Steve Costigan" to "Dennis Dorgan" and "Mike" to "Spike" (by erasing the names and retyping over the erasures on the typescripts) so that they could be submitted to the magazine *Oriental Stories*, edited by Farnsworth Wright. The two stories were not published in *Oriental Stories* (or any magazine) during Howard's life, and the typescripts remained as altered by Howard and were published in that form in *The Incredible Adventures of Dennis Dorgan* (FAX Collector's Editions, 1974). In fact, Leo Grin and Patrice Louinet have performed much research between them showing that the Dennis Dorgan character was never intended to be anything other than an expedient disguise for Sailor Steve Costigan, invented solely as a publishing necessity; see also Glenn Lord, *The Last Celt: A Bio-Bibliography of Robert Ervin Howard* (West Kingston, Rhode Island: Donald M. Grant, 1976). For these reasons, the texts of these two stories in this volume restore the original names of the characters, as they were originally written and intended by Howard.

The following is a list of the sources of the texts that are used in this edition:

"In the Ring" appeared in REH *Fight Magazine* #4, Necronomicon Press, October 1996.

"The Pit of the Serpent" appeared in *Fight Stories*, July 1929.

"Vikings of the Gloves" appeared in *Fight Stories*, February 1932.

"Waterfront Law" appeared in *Action Stories*, January 1931, under the title "The TNT Punch."

"The Bull Dog Breed" appeared in *Fight Stories*, February 1930.

"Cultured Cauliflowers" first appeared in *The Incredible Adventures of Dennis Dorgan* (FAX Collector's Editions, 1974), under the title "In High Society." The version in this volume is based on the author's typescript in the collection of the Cross Plains Library, and restores the characters' original names.

"Texas Fists" appeared in *Fight Stories*, May 1931.

"A New Game for Costigan" was sent to *Fiction House* on May 17, 1931, but was rejected by them. It first appeared in *The Incredible Adventures of Dennis Dorgan* (FAX Collector's Editions, 1974), under the title "Playing Journalist."

"The Champion of the Forecastle" appeared in *Fight Stories*, November 1930, under the title "Champ of the Forecastle."

"Hard-Fisted Sentiment" first appeared in *REH Fight Magazine* #4, Necronomicon Press, October 1996.

"The Fightin'est Pair" appeared in *Action Stories*, November 1931, under the title "Breed of Battle."

"Kid Lavigne Is Dead" appeared in *The Ring*, June 1928.

"The Spirit of Tom Molyneaux" appeared in *Ghost Stories*, April 1929, under the title "The Apparition in the Prize Ring," attributed to Howard's pseudonym "John Taverel."

"Crowd-Horror" appeared in *Argosy All Story Weekly*, July 20, 1929.

"Kid Galahad" appeared in *Sport Story Magazine*, December 25, 1931.

"When You Were a Set-Up and I Was a Ham" was written May 24, 1925. It was first published in *REH Fight Magazine* #2, Necronomicon Press, September 1990, with the title suggested by Glenn Lord.

"Iron Men" appeared in *Fight Stories*, June 1930, under the title "The Iron Man." That version was heavily edited by the magazine editors, and over ten thousand words were eliminated. The text in this volume has never before been published, and is based on the unedited typescript submitted to the magazine by Howard.

"Fists of the Desert" appeared in *Dime Sports Magazine*, April 1936, under the title "Iron Jaw."

"They Always Come Back" appeared in *The Iron Man* (Donald M. Grant, 1976).

THE WORKS OF ROBERT E. HOWARD

Boxing Stories
Edited and with an introduction by Chris Gruber

The Black Stranger and Other American Tales
Edited and with an introduction by Steven Tompkins

The End of the Trail: Western Stories
Edited and with an introduction by Rusty Burke

Lord of Samarcand and Other Adventure Tales of the Old Orient
Edited by Rusty Burke
Introduction by Patrice Louinet

The Riot at Bucksnort and Other Western Tales
Edited and with an introduction by David Gentzel